This book is dedicated to all those who feel like an outcast or outsider, excluded because they are "different."

Do not oppress the foreigner, for you yourselves know how it feels to be excluded.

Exodus 23:9

CITY of SORROWS

SORROWS

A Novel

Susan Nadathur

First published in the United States of America
November 2012 by Azahar Books

This is a work of fiction. Names, characters, places, and incidents either are the product of the author's imagination or are used fictitiously, and any resemblance to actual persons, living or dead, businesses, companies, events, or locales is entirely coincidental.

Unless otherwise noted, all Scripture quotations are taken from the King James Version of the Bible (public domain)

Cover design by Lisa Amowitz

Stock photos provided by Dreamstime.com

Author website: www.SusanNadathur.com

ISBN-13: 978-0615604701
ISBN-10: 0615604706

Rajiv Kumaran
Ahmedabad, India

"We shrink from change, yet is there anything
that can come into being without it?"

Mohandas Gandhi

Prologue

From India to Gypsy Spain

From a young age, Rajiv Kumaran had learned to listen to the keys. Frantic keys meant that his father was furious. The angrier Appa was as he climbed the stairs to their flat in the working-class sector of northeastern Ahmedabad, the more violently the keys spun from the ring he twirled around his calloused forefinger.

When the keys swung lightly, Appa was reasonable, open to suggestion. Approachable.

Tonight, the keys were angry.

"Quickly, please." Rajiv's mother shoved her South Indian novel under the sofa, flipped the end of her sari over her shoulder, and edged her arthritic body off the sofa.

Rajiv's stomach jolted, but he continued to read from the torn copy of *Gandhi's Truth* open upon his lap, hoping to find courage in the words of a man who was his model of valor.

We shrink from change, read Gandhi's words, *yet is there anything that can come into being without it?*

His eyes shifted to the blue airmail envelope hidden in the outside pocket of his satchel. He would have to wait for a more opportune moment to show Appa the letter.

"Rajiv, please. Don't upset your father tonight." Amma scurried to switch off the family's new TV.

The screen faded into an insignificant dot of white light as Amma hobbled to the door to receive her husband.

Before unlatching the chain, she looked back over her shoulder.

"Rajiv, *please*, I don't want *any* problems."

Rajiv tensed but did not move, his gaze fixed on the picture of Lord Krishna hanging above the altar beside the front door. He stared at the lilac face of his mother's favorite god, sending up a silent prayer to a deity he was no longer sure he believed in. Slowly, he closed the pages of *Gandhi's Truth,* shoved the book into his satchel, and replaced it with *Biology of the Cell.* His head landed hard against the back of the sofa as he took in a long, deep breath.

Glancing upward, Rajiv stiffened as he watched the ceiling fan wobble precariously on its base, the four white blades churning furiously at its center, their edges grimy. The top page of the calendar flapped against the wall behind him as the fan rotated.

Amma clicked open the deadbolt lock and Appa crossed the threshold. Rajiv inhaled sharply, his eyes glued to the white "U" painted on his father's forehead, divided down the middle by a scarlet line. His father had been to the temple.

Appa always went to the temple when his mood was off.

Rajiv frowned and lowered his eyes to the floor. The servant hadn't swept today. A thin layer of dust dirtied the quarry tiles.

"Come, please, time for dinner," Amma said.

"I'm barely in the door, woman!" Appa kicked off his sandals and left them by the door. A scowl distorted the shape of the sacred mark painted on his forehead. The red line drawn through the middle was no longer straight, but a rippled wave caught on the creases of his angry brow.

Amma made a sharp, clicking sound, but did not speak.

Appa turned to face Rajiv.

"There's a matter of importance we need to discuss," Appa said, in heavily accented English.

Appa always switched to English when asserting control. Thirty years under British supervision had taught him there was power in the language.

Bloody hell. Rajiv responded in the English his father had insisted he learn, but only in his mind. The keys never lied.

"Sit down." Appa pointed to a slat-back wooden chair at the dining-room table.

Rajiv rose from the sofa but hesitated before pulling out the chair. He stared at his reflection in the mirror on the far wall. The crease between his eyes matched his father's and the firm set to his mouth—identical. A brief flash of anger passed over his eyes.

"Sit down, *now!*"

Rajiv saw his eyes flicker in the mirror, and then they were still. Slowly, he lowered his gaze and folded himself onto the chair, proud that until now he had managed to remain silent.

"Please serve our food," Appa said in Tamil, addressing his wife in the kitchen.

Amma appeared at the table, nodded to indicate she had heard, then shuffled back to the kitchen to serve the same food she had prepared every day since her fifteenth birthday, when she became his wife—boiled lentils and vegetable curry. A traditional South Indian meal. His parents had left Madras over thirty years ago, but their home—in the middle of the state of Gujarat in northern India—was a bastion of South Indian culture and tradition.

"I have come from speaking with Mr. Sundaram," Appa said. "He wants to—"

"Sell his daughter?" Rajiv groaned as he heard himself speak.

"Do not mock me! You think it's easy to find an appropriate match for you here in Ahmedabad? There's only one other South Indian family of equivalent social and financial status, and—"

"Appa, please, I don't want to talk about marriage right now." Rajiv spoke carefully. This was not the conversation he had planned for tonight.

"Lakshmi is a good match for you," Appa said. "She just completed her degree in chemical engineering, and is—"

"Intolerable."

Rajiv heard his mother catch her breath and then detected the heavy shuffle of her bare feet against the tiled floor as she fled to the kitchen after serving the food. Mother never got involved in family conflict. She knew her place. The kitchen was her sanctuary, a safe haven where she could hide while Appa sorted out family business.

"She's a devout Hindu," Appa said. The paint on his forehead had mixed with sweat and taken on a wet shine. "She would bring stability and tradition to your erratic lifestyle."

"What erratic lifestyle?" Rajiv carefully unleashed his frustration. "You talk as if I have the freedom to control my life."

Appa's mouth twitched. To an outsider, that twitch could have been interpreted as a reaction against a blow that had hit its mark. To Rajiv, who knew every tremor and flicker that ever crossed his father's face, it was a warning sign. Control would be reasserted.

"As I know you have been . . . resistant to the idea of marriage with Lakshmi," Appa said, his voice chilling in its resumed control. "I have selected two other women for your consideration. One holds a master's degree in commerce, the other a PhD in chemistry." He pulled a creased photograph from his shirt pocket and handed it to Rajiv. "One is fairer-skinned than the other, but both are equal in family assets and stature. They're cousins, nieces to Mr. Sundaram. They're from Chennai, but are currently here, in Ahmedabad."

Appa concentrated on his food, forming a ball out of the rice and vegetable and popping it into his mouth.

"I have arranged for you to meet the girls tomorrow afternoon, and expect your decision within a week. A winter wedding would be most auspicious. The stars are well aligned for either match."

Rajiv did not respond immediately, taking the time to fortify his resolve in silence. He studied the worn photograph in his hand. Two pretty girls looked back at him, smiling.

Gita, his sister-in-law, once smiled like that too. In old photographs. In her marriage portrait. She smiled a lot—before she moved into her father-in-law's house. Now, she was mostly somber.

And his brother Sanjay, once carefree, was now a serious, unpleasant man—not yet thirty but with the burden of ten more years. Rajiv couldn't even remember the last time he saw his brother smile. His lips remained unmoving when Gita informed the household of her pregnancy. They did not tremble when his child was born. He frowned when Appa demanded that after delivery Gita would no longer work outside the house. He scowled when Gita objected, but did not defend her. How could he? He lived in his father's flat. And in Appa's home, there was a hierarchy. Appa was at the top, then came Amma (an extension of him), followed by Sanjay, then Rajiv, and finally came Gita.

That's the way it was. And the way it would always be. For Amma. For Sanjay. For Gita. And for Rajiv, if he remained in India.

His wife would come to live with him, and by the order of the family, would be the seventh member, on the very bottom of the scale of privilege and position. Her loyalty would be to him, her husband, but her duty would be to the household. And Appa, as head of the household, would decide whether she worked, where she worked, and what her duties would be as a member of his family. Rajiv, like his brother, would respect his father's wishes. In the process, he would lose what little was left of himself.

Slowly, Rajiv looked up.

"Appa, please try to understand." Rajiv paused, forcing a careful pace to his words. "I'm not getting married . . . to either one of them." He handed the photograph to his father. "If and when I decide to marry, it will be with the woman I fall in love with. But right now, I can't think about love or marriage. I have other, more important things on my mind."

The room was so quiet that even Amma in the kitchen must have heard the slow exhalation of pent-up air.

"How dare you defy me?" Appa rose from the table. The white "U" that marked his forehead had sunk further into the deep crevice that had formed between his eyes.

Rajiv tensed. How could something as holy as a sacred mark be utterly intimidating?

"You make no decisions outside of me," Appa said, his voice so quiet Rajiv feared he had lost it. "You will choose a wife by the end of the week, as I promised Mr. Sundaram."

"You promised?" Rajiv could hear the shrill note of hysteria rising in his voice as he pushed himself from the table. "How can you make such a promise?"

He stood before his father, and for the first time, Rajiv noticed something interesting.

At five feet eleven inches, he stood taller than his father.

"Don't you *dare* raise your voice to me!"

Appa flung back his chair and with a violent sweep of the hand, hurled his plate of food across the room. Sticky grains of rice and oily vegetable curry flew against the wall.

The stainless steel plate clattered to the floor, a hollow, tinny, reverberating sound.

Appa moved forward. The heavy whack of his hand against Rajiv's face bounced off the cement walls of the apartment.

Rajiv froze. His skin burned where Appa had struck, but he did not move or attempt to strike back. He opened his mouth to speak, knowing he was going to say the very thing he knew he should not say. A wiser man would have waited for a more opportune moment, but he no longer felt himself a wise man.

"I'm leaving." Rajiv hated the way his voice trembled, but it was impossible to defy someone like Appa without fearing him as well.

"I was invited to join a lab in Spain."

Appa opened, and then clenched his fist against his side.

"Are you threatening me?" Appa's knuckles had turned yellow under his dark brown skin. "You wouldn't dare apply for a position without my approval."

Rajiv turned to the sofa, grabbed his satchel off the floor, and pulled out the letter. He handed his father the envelope.

Appa hesitated as he reached for the letter.

Then Rajiv saw something on his father's face, an emotion he didn't recognize right away because he had never seen it before: fear. Appa's fingers trembled as he pulled a pair of reading glasses from his pocket and unfolded the paper.

Rajiv followed the words his father mouthed in silence.

Then slowly, Appa pushed his glasses onto his forehead and spoke, his voice barely above a whisper.

"I have struggled for thirty years to give you and your brother a good education . . . the education that was denied to me. And for what? So that you can use it to *defy* me?"

Rajiv's heart sank as he heard his father's words.

"Appa, I—"

"They told me if I completed my education, they would promote me to middle management. It took me ten years to finish my studies. *Ten years.* At the age of fifty-five, I received my college degree, but not the position of general manager they promised me once I achieved my education. Do you know how that feels?"

"Appa, please, listen to me." A burning weight pressed against Rajiv's chest like a hot iron upon his heart. He knew all too well the sacrifices his father had made for his family.

"They brought in a younger, Oxford-educated Indian to fill the position."

"I know, Appa . . . I know. Please, just listen—"

"On the night I accepted my diploma, I vowed my two sons would never have to struggle to get the education I was denied."

Rajiv stared in silence at the fine line of white paint dripping along the bridge of Appa's nose as his father continued without listening.

"And the only thing I have ever asked, the only thing I've ever expected in return—"

"Is absolute loyalty and total control of our lives." Rajiv lowered his face into his hand and shook his head.

How could he have dared speak those words that before had been so safely guarded in his heart?

"Appa, I'm sorry, I—"

"How dare you!"

Appa rushed forward and Rajiv fell back against the family altar near the door. His hand shot out, sending the soapstone statue of Lord Ganesha crashing to the floor.

"You should be grateful I didn't throw you out on the street," Appa shouted. "Like my father did to me!"

"Yes! I *am* grateful for that."

Rajiv steadied himself, frantically shifting his eyes from his father to the elephant-headed deity shattered on the floor. Ganesha's body lay strewn among the grains of rice.

"But it doesn't give you the right to control my life." Rajiv spoke slowly, allowing the truth to finally emerge. "You told me to study biology, and I did. Even though what I really wanted to study was—"

"What you *want* to do is of no importance to me. My only concern is what is *best* for you."

"Then you should be happy with my decision." Rajiv swallowed against the lump that had formed in his throat. "I accepted the position in Spain."

The sound of a steel cooking vessel clattering to the kitchen floor broke the heavy silence that had overtaken the room.

"What?" Appa's voice trembled.

Rajiv stared at the crack along the window caused by the last monsoon rains. Never had he seen a more forceful storm than the one that pounded the city on July 14th last year, on his twenty-sixth birthday. Appa had gone out that day to buy a box of sweets, though Amma protested. The winds were too strong, she had argued, the rain relentless. Appa went out anyway, determined that his son would enjoy something sweet on his birthday.

"I'm going to talk to your advisor." Appa struggled to speak. "I'll clear up this . . . this . . . misunderstanding." He stumbled toward the door and put on his sandals. "Dr. Gobi promised you a research position at the university after you defend your thesis." Appa staggered forward and then fell back, grasping the arm of the sofa. Rajiv rushed to his side.

"You're defending next week," Appa said, holding onto Rajiv's shoulder. "So you should be able to start your new position by—"

"Appa, I declined Dr. Gobi's offer. I'm going to Spain." Rajiv's heart ached as he heard the finality of his defiance. "The only group in the world close to finding a viable strategy for global eradication of the polio virus is working in Seville. Dr. Matos is a world expert—"

"Oh, now I see." Appa's voice turned cold. "You think you're going to find the cure for polio . . . for that Punjabi friend of yours."

No, that's not it. You don't understand. Rajiv screamed at his father in his head. *I just want to be allowed to take my own decisions, make my own mistakes. For once in my life, I want to be in control of my future.*

"I thought I forbade you from seeing that girl." Appa spoke and Rajiv's heart plunged.

"You did," Rajiv said.

"You will *not* humiliate me in front of our community." Appa's chest swelled. "You will take up the position in Dr. Gobi's lab and get married, or you will no longer be my son."

Appa turned his back on Rajiv and stormed out the door.

His fury left with him, echoing along the corridor and down the dusty stairwell.

"Fine! Then I'm no longer your son!"

Rajiv's belligerence was quickly tempered with remorse. If he left India unmarried, Appa would be shamed. He would lose face in the community where no one respects a man who has lost control of his family.

What have I done? Rajiv raked his hand through his hair. My selfish dream to find my own strength will leave my family weak.

Appa would never forgive him. Rajiv knew that once he walked out the door of his father's home, there was no turning back. His was not a simple rebellion of a son against his family, but of a son against all that his family stood for. Their values. Their dreams. Continuity and tradition.

Should things go badly in Spain, there would be no safe ride home. Not because Appa did not love him enough to take him back, but because if he failed, he would return defeated. And then his weakness would become Appa's even greater strength.

Rajiv's heart tripped and then fell, beating wildly against his chest.

Failure was not an option.

He took a sharp breath, and then knelt to the floor. Methodically, he dug through the dirty rice and picked out shattered pieces of the elephant god, placing them into the palm of his hand.

He was going to Spain, and he was going to succeed. Along with Dr. Matos, he would find the strategy to eradicate polio as a world health threat.

And he would not return to India until the day he could present a research discovery that his father would be proud of.

Slowly, Rajiv raised his eyes. Then he spoke to the empty space between himself and the door that had just been slammed in his face.

"I may no longer be your son," he said quietly. "But you will always be my father." His eyes moistened but he fought back the tears as the impact of his decision hit fully upon his heart.

Amma shuffled back into the living room and joined him on the floor. Shaking her head and clicking her tongue, she pulled Ganesha's delicately carved trunk out of a mound of rice.

"Aren't you going to say anything?" Rajiv gave her what was in his hand and then quickly wiped his eyes.

His mother did not answer him. Having gathered the remaining pieces of her idol, she now worked diligently to remove the rice and curry from the walls and off the floor. The yellow of the turmeric would be hard to get out, but she would keep scrubbing until the last of the oily stain was gone, just as she always did.

"You are a disrespectful son." Amma spoke quietly, then turned her back on him as she limped to the kitchen with her broken shards and her dirty rice.

"Is that all you can say?" Rajiv asked, defeated.

Amma returned from the kitchen, wiping her arthritic hands with the free end of her sari.

"No more will Lord Ganesha bless this home," she said.

Rajiv stared at the empty space on the altar near the door where Ganesha once sat.

And so his journey to Seville began.

Without the blessing of his family or their god.

Diego Vargas
Seville, Spain

"Revenge, at first though sweet,
Bitter ere long back on itself recoils."

John Milton, *Paradise Lost*

1

Diego

Diego Vargas stared out the kitchen window, looking over his neighborhood on the Southside of Seville. He had his back turned to his wife. A painful position. But he had to assume it. If he didn't, her dark black Gypsy eyes would break him down. Catalina could compel him with a simple stare. Bend him with a blink.

Break him with a single tear.

He parted the curtains, eyes fixed firmly on the *barriada*. Row upon row of government housing stretched before him, three thousand units, each looking identical to all the rest. There was no joy in the buildings, but there was color in the bright curtains that flapped in open windows, in the clothes strung on lines hung across dusty balconies, in the angry graffiti painted on the walls. Most of what was written screamed about getting out. Few ever did.

He let the curtain fall back into place.

"I'm going out," he said, turning toward the door.

She blocked his exit.

"Please, Diego. I want to go to the ranch with you."

"No, Catalina." He gripped the doorknob, channeling the tension out of his voice and into his white-knuckled hand. *"Te dije que no."* He hated the macho sternness he heard in his voice, but she was pushing him. How many times did he have to say no?

"Don't talk to me like that." She straightened her shoulders, standing taller before him. "I'm your wife, not your dog."

A knot formed in the pit of his stomach. For the first time in their nine-month marriage, he and Catalina were exchanging angry words.

"Sorry," he said, immediately softening his tone. "But I can't take you with me." He wished he could explain why. But he had nothing more concrete to offer than a vague feeling that Catalina would not be safe. "You're not well," he eventually said.

Flustered, he moved back into the room, snatched his leather jacket off the kitchen chair, and stuffed a pack of cigarettes into his shirt pocket. He rarely smoked. But now he needed nicotine.

"I'll be back." He jerked open the door.

"I'm fine!" she shouted after him. "Why can't you trust me?"

Diego turned, about to answer her. But her face stopped him.

She flinched. Her eyes fluttered. And then grew extra wide. Her hands moved down over her stomach. Then they were still, pressed against the underside of her belly.

Immediately, he dropped his jacket and reached for her stomach. It felt hard under her pajamas.

"Are you all right?" he said, all the anger gone.

A wave of movement floated under his hands.

"I told you, I'm fine." Her eyes were still, unblinking. Shiny black river stones. Wet, but strong. "Pregnant women often feel sick in the morning." She placed her hands over his. "It's *normal*, my love."

Maybe. Maybe not. He didn't know what to think. Just turned nineteen and only six months into being an expectant father, Diego admitted he didn't have much experience with pregnant women. But he did have experience with his wife.

Something was not right.

"Why don't you go lie down." Gently, he rubbed her belly. "I'll go buy some chamomile tea and then—"

"We'll drive out to Huelva, you'll do whatever work your boss has called you to do at the ranch, and then we'll ride out to Emerald Lake." She spoke as if nothing had happened.

As if she had not just said something meant to be provocative.

He looked away, almost weakening. Emerald Lake was their private sanctuary. The place they went to when they wanted to be alone. To be intimate. To be free.

"No, Catalina." He did not allow himself to falter. "We'll go some other day, when you're feeling better."

Again he could not explain the overwhelming need he felt to take care of her. To protect her.

As if something terrible might happen if he did not.

She grabbed his face and looked him directly in the eye.

"Diego, please, don't treat me like an invalid." Her gaze was bright. Intense. And then all of a sudden, her eyes were wet. "I'm pregnant, yes, but I'm not your eighty-eight-year-old great-grandmother." The tear that rolled down her cheek completely undid him. "I know it sounds selfish, but I want to have you completely to myself. To make love to you without worrying that your mother or your little sister might be overhearing."

"*Tranquila,*" he whispered in her ear, desperate to ease her distress.

"I'm sorry." She turned her face from him. "I'm not complaining, it's just that . . ."

He closed his eyes. "I know," he whispered.

When he opened his eyes, she was blinking rapidly.

He could barely speak, but managed to choke out a few words.

"As soon as we've saved up enough money, I promise we'll move into our own place. I know it's not easy living with my family."

"It's not so bad," she said, lying sweetly. "They're good to me."

She smiled and the beauty of it melted him. He took a long, slow breath, clueless as to what he was supposed to do or say next.

"There's nothing I want more right now than to be with you," he said, opting for the truth. "But it's *I* who am selfish if I ignore the fact that you've been nauseous all morning, that—"

She stopped him with a kiss.

"What are you so afraid of?" she said.

"Losing you."

"That's never going to happen." She lay her head on his chest.

"I hope not." He ran his fingers through her hair. "Because I'd die without you."

"Go." She wriggled away from him and opened the door. "Go buy the tea." She pushed him out. "And a loaf of bread, too."

Diego scooped up his jacket, watching her as he put it on.

"Anything else?"

"Manchego cheese would be good. Oh, and a bottle of water."

She reached behind her head and suddenly, a cascade of shiny black hair tumbled down her back.

Diego stiffened. Catalina let her hair down on only two occasions. One: when they were making love, which he wished were the reason now, and two: when she was combing it to go out. Nine months of marriage had made him an expert on reading signs. This one was clear. She was going with him.

And there was nothing he could do to stop her.

Whoever said men were in control of the women they married knew absolutely nothing about women. AT ALL.

He sprinted down the steps and out into the street. Propping his foot against the outside wall, he fumbled for a cigarette.

A restless wind blew, stirring up odors and saturating the Southside of Seville with the raw stench of humanity. Diego turned his face away, but the smell of the ghetto assaulted him. Uncollected garbage. Beer. Urine. The olfactory reality of life in the barrio was never pleasant. But today, it was particularly oppressive.

Digging the pack of Ducados and a small box of matches from his jacket pocket, he tapped out a cigarette and stuck it into the corner of his mouth. With one sharp swipe, he lit a match.

Smoke curled over his fingers as he took a long, deep drag.

"¡Amigo!" His friend Joaquín limped out of the building and came to join him. "What's up?" He drew a cigarette from Diego's pack.

"Lo mismo," Diego said. The same.

"Same is good." Joaquín cupped his hand over Diego's cigarette and lit his own. "How about lending me twenty euros?"

Diego took a drag, and then watched a trail of cigarette ash fall into a crack on the sidewalk.

"What do you need money for this time?"

"You know how it is, brother. I got expenses. I've a wife now."

Diego shook his head. Maribel was not Joaquín's legal wife. But by Gypsy law, the two were married the night he took her virginity. He pulled out his wallet and shoved a few bills into Joaquín's hand. Hopefully, Maribel would get the special soy formula she needed to feed her lactose-intolerant baby.

Diego's mind strayed as he listened to the sounds of the *barrio*. A series of chords strummed on a flamenco guitar floated down from an open window. A donkey brayed.

Maybe it *was* a good idea to take Catalina up to the ranch with him. She said the fresh air would make her feel better.

Maybe it would.

He studied the ground. Took another drag.

Catalina thought he was being overly protective.

Maybe he was.

She wanted him to trust her.

Maybe he should.

Despite the small twist in his gut trying to convince him otherwise.

"Hey." Joaquín knocked him on the shoulder. *"¿Qué te pasa?"*

Diego ignored the question. How could he possibly verbalize what was wrong with him when he hadn't quite figured it out yet?

He watched young Chucho Sánchez offer a handful of grass to El Bobo, the donkey.

Ten years ago, it was Chucho's father who fed the ass.

Life went on but little changed. Everything was, is, and always would be—the same.

"Sorry," he said, slowly refocusing on Joaquín. "I was thinking—"

"You think too much, my friend." Joaquín wrapped his arm around Diego's shoulder. "That can't be good."

Diego's fingers tightened over the half-smoked cigarette he drew up to his mouth.

"Hey, you feel like going over to Rafi's place?" Joaquín shifted his weight over to his crippled leg. "A few of us are getting together this afternoon. Juanjo's bringing his guitar."

"Can't," Diego said, wondering why Joaquín wasn't wearing his raised shoe. "I'm heading up to the ranch. My boss needs help with a new filly."

Joaquín's expression hardened. "That rich *payo* you work for doesn't pay shit for all you do for him."

Diego frowned and looked past his friend.

"Don't start with me, Joaquín."

Joaquín took any opportunity to reinforce his belief that the *payo*, the Spanish, were all racist bigots.

"Just don't forget who you are while you clean the crap out of his stalls." Joaquín dropped his cigarette and crushed it out.

Diego shifted his gaze to Joaquín.

"I know exactly who I am. And for your information, I don't clean stalls. I train horses."

"Está bien." Joaquín ended the conversation with his hand.

An awkward silence fell between them.

Then Joaquín's phone rang and he reached into his pocket.

Diego tossed his cigarette butt into the dumpster. He was going to be one of the few who got out of this wretched place.

"Talk to you later, *primo*." Joaquín ended his call and pocketed the phone. He turned to Diego and said, "You taking Catalina up to the ranch with you?" His tone was no longer hostile.

Diego stared at his friend, wondering why he would ask that.

"Heard you arguing." Joaquín squeezed Diego's shoulder. "Learn from my experience. The best way to get what you want is to give her what she wants first. You know what I mean?"

Diego rubbed his neck, relaxed his stance. Joaquín had an annoying way of turning tension into camaraderie. Even if what he said made absolutely no sense at all.

"I don't know." Diego kicked away a loose stone, easing up a little. "Maybe you're right. She loves being out in the country."

"Well go, then. Have fun in the country. As for me . . ." Joaquín looked up at the window to the bedroom he shared with his wife. "I'm going to a more . . . sensual place."

Diego looked down at the ground, smiling faintly.

"You have obviously never been to the country," he said.

Joaquín laughed off Diego's reply, locked fists with him in their customary gesture of solidarity, limped down the street, and entered the corner store.

Diego watched his friend, wondering how they had grown so far apart. They had once shared everything, every thought, every dream. But one thing Diego would never share with his life-long friend was his attitude of unjustified intolerance. Life was too short to be so angry.

He looked up at the sun. It was already midmorning. Later than he usually liked to leave for Huelva. He quickly bought what he needed at the supermarket and then headed home.

Before going back up to the apartment, he stopped at his father's car, wondering if the old Renault sedan would even start. When he opened the door, a piece of rusted metal fell from the edge of the frame, landing on the street.

He frowned. The car needed to be looked at by a mechanic. But until sales got better at the market, he was the only mechanic his family could afford. He shoved the key into the ignition.

The engine shuddered. And then it died.

He cranked the key again.

Nothing.

He forced the key against the starter. A little more violently than before. Finally, the engine turned over.

But the smile that had started to form faded fast.

He had forced the key.

2

Diego

It was early March, but the warm western wind had already coaxed the orange blossoms into full bloom. The seductive scent of citrus perfumed the country air. Diego inhaled. The sweet scent of spring filled his senses. He was going to make the most of this beautiful day.

Carefully, he entered the round pen, his fingers wrapped around the lariat rope coiled loosely in his right hand.

Fuego was a skittish young horse still nervous around human contact. She sensed his approach and turned away. Diego took two steps back, waited, and then three steps forward. Slowly, he uncoiled the rope. Then he tossed it in the direction of Fuego's hind legs to drive the filly forward into movement around the pen.

Fuego bolted but Diego held onto his position, following the horse's movement with both his body and his eyes.

After a while, he raised his left hand and tipped his head, giving Fuego the signal that he wanted her to turn.

Fuego ignored his directive and continued running.

Diego slapped the ground hard with his rope. Fuego heard the loud snap and initiated an outside turn, showing Diego that she did not trust him. He continued to pressure Fuego into following his lead. Eventually, the mare cocked her inside ear and made smaller circles around the pen. And then finally, she dropped her head.

Immediately, Diego backed off, releasing the pressure. He went limp, turned his shoulder to the horse, and removed eye contact. Fuego slowed down and eventually stopped running. Diego remained with his back turned. And then slowly, he moved out of the pen.

"Well done." Don Enrique strolled out of his office. "*Muchacho*, you were born to train horses." He squeezed Diego's shoulder. "Now go, spend some time with your wife." Don Enrique nodded at Catalina, who sat under the shade of a large oak tree, sewing glass eyes onto a hand-stitched doll.

She looked up at him and smiled.

"I love to watch you work." She rested the doll in her lap. "You're so gentle with the horses."

He sat down beside her, picked up the doll.

"How can anyone not be gentle with something he loves?" He looked up at her, smiled, and then kissed her on the cheek. "Come on, let's take a walk." He stood, pulling her up beside him.

He started to walk, but she stopped him with a kiss.

"Take me to Emerald Lake," she said, moving her mouth from his lips to just outside his ear.

He took in a sharp breath. He knew what she wanted. And desired the same thing. But the lake was an hour's ride on horseback.

He struggled with conflicting emotions. It wasn't a hard ride. And she was feeling better. But, he sensed a change in the air, in the weather. And though his body craved the pleasure it would find at the lake, his mind wondered if it was wise to risk the distance.

"Please," she whispered.

Her warm breath sent shivers down his spine.

He gripped the fence post and scanned the horizon. Rain threatened, but Diego knew he would not be able to keep Catalina away from the forest.

That didn't mean he wouldn't try.

"We shouldn't go riding," he said, trying to follow his instincts while unsuccessfully ignoring the pressure in his crotch.

He studied the horses as a form of forced distraction. They had gathered in a corner of the paddock, heads turned from the wind. He flirted with lying about what the animals' behavior meant, but then forced his brain to wrestle with his body.

"A storm's forming," he said responsibly.

His body revolted. *Are you an idiot? Stop fighting it.*

Catalina joined the protest and argued that the sky was blue.

He counted to twenty.

"The horses always know," he said. His blood pounded as he watched one of the horses stretch out its neck and sniff the air. "It's going to rain."

"So?" Her eyes opened in innocent inquiry.

"So we can't go."

His hormones raged. But somewhere in the back of his brain where his hormones had no access, Diego knew he needed to talk her out of riding.

Something did not feel right.

"You shouldn't get wet," he finally said, for lack of anything better.

"Why?" Catalina laughed. "Don't pregnant women take showers?" She stood with her hands folded over the top of her blossoming belly.

Her laughter made him slightly uncomfortable. Nine months into their marriage, he was still learning how to love her.

"I just want to protect you," he said, lowering his foot from the fence. He framed her face in his hands and kissed her gently.

"You worry too much." She slipped her hands under the back of her hair and lifted it to the wind.

The air filled with the fresh lavender scent of her shampoo.

"And you not enough." He caressed her belly as he breathed in her scent. "Besides, Ilsa says you shouldn't be on a horse."

Catalina placed the tips of her fingers to his lips.

"My dear auntie," she said, softly increasing the pressure on his lips. "Who is not an obstetrician, I might add. Also says that if I cross my legs, our baby will suffocate."

She slid the tip of her tongue along the outer surface of his ear, and then, for a second, into the space that was trying not to hear.

"Where's the logic in that?" she said.

Diego groaned. He turned his face to take her teasing tongue. But then, his body throbbing, he pulled away.

"Come on," he said, as firmly as his breathless voice would allow. "Let's walk." He blew out a sharp burst of air. "We'll ride another day." Reaching for her hand, he forced his eyes away and looked out over the horizon.

Rain was certain. The sun had cast a long shadow over the tall grass and the sky was now the color of unpolished silver. He could read the land. But Catalina was still a mystery to him. He had known her since they were children, loved her for as long. But he hadn't a clue how to handle her. He returned his gaze to her. Then he lost what little was left of his resolve. Her long-lashed eyes weakened him. But it was her sweet, insistent plea that finally broke him down.

"Please, Diego. Take me to the lake. Nothing's going to happen, to me or the baby. I promise."

He knew that she believed that. Catalina was what her father called a "passionate optimist." He searched her eyes. And then surrendered. *"Está bien.* But only to the north edge."

Catalina threw her arms around his neck and covered his face with kisses.

He grabbed a woven blanket off the fence post, entered the paddock, and walked toward his horse.

Lucero was a bay-colored Andalusian, a gift to him from Don Enrique over nine years ago when he started working with Lorenzo, mucking out stalls.

Lucero was born with a bad leg, and was of little value on the open market. A lame riding horse wasn't worth the money it took to feed him. But he convinced Don Enrique to let him keep the colt, and then spent weeks strengthening its bad leg.

Now, no one could beat Lucero out on the open field.

Diego smiled, slung the saddle blanket over Lucero's back, and led his horse to Catalina.

"Are you sure you won't be uncomfortable?" He grabbed a bale of hay that had been left near a feeding tray and helped her mount.

"I'll be fine." Catalina hiked up her calf-length linen skirt and straddled Lucero's back. "How's it any different than riding along that bumpy road in a car with a sunken seat?"

He frowned. Those bumps had made her nauseous.

"You know what? This is not a good idea. Not in your condition." He moved to pull her down but she shook her head.

"No, Diego. Don't make me feel weak. I don't have a condition. I'm pregnant."

"I know, but . . ."

"Sit behind me. I need to feel your strength."

Diego ignored the flutter in the pit of his stomach and did what he imagined any man would do in the same situation. He swallowed back his fears and deferred to the wishes of his wife. Swinging up behind her, he pressed his heels against Lucero's sides and nudged his horse into a slow walk toward the forest.

"Thank you," she whispered.

He kissed the top of her head. She didn't see him close his eyes. But she would feel his strength, his arms around her. And she would know how much he wanted to make her happy.

A gentle breeze rippled the tall grass, mixing up the colors of the landscape. Light green blades blended with pale yellow tips, creating a soft pastel green. Bright red and yellow wildflowers added spots of brilliance to the multi-shaded green of the meadow. The wind stirred, whistling past his ear and rattling the branches of nearby trees. He shivered. And then hugged Catalina closer.

Gradually, the landscape changed. Lucero broke into a trot as they reached the end of the meadow and approached the edge of a dense grove of eucalyptus. He eased Lucero back.

Then he closed his eyes and inhaled, taking in the woody, camphor-infused aroma of the forest.

Catalina grasped his thighs for support as Lucero started down a small path trampled into the forest floor. They followed the trail until it ended at the edge of a small lake fed by the waters of the Guadalquivir. Groups of African flamingo floated upon the emerald surface. Some dipped their heads below the water in search of food. Others glided serenely across the sparkling lake. Their salmon-colored feathers shimmered in the setting sun.

A loud splash shattered the silence. A male bird jumped on the back of a female.

She spread her wings to receive him.

The male uncurled his slender neck and cawed into the air.

Catalina shifted on the saddle blanket. He wrapped his arms around her belly. A shiver of movement passed under his hands.

"I can feel the baby," he said.

She rested her hands over his. "What're we going to name her?"

"Her? What if it's a boy?"

"She's not." Catalina took his hand and rubbed it over her belly. "We're having a girl."

"What makes you so sure?" He buried his face in her hair. It smelled of lavender, of horses, and the country air.

"I don't know, I just feel it."

"We're going to disappoint the family, then. They're all waiting for a boy."

"And you, what do you want?"

"A girl," he said quietly.

He heard her sigh and knew that she was smiling.

A few minutes passed in silence and then a lone flamingo squawked into the wind.

"*Mira.*" Catalina pointed at the sky. A flamingo had taken off into full flight, showing the black underside of its wings.

He watched the bird disappear, and then dropped his gaze on her. She was happy. That made him smile.

A light sprinkle began to fall, wetting the eucalyptus leaves and spreading their fresh, camphor-infused aroma over the dampened forest. He led Lucero into the shelter of the trees, dismounted, and then helped Catalina down.

Her body brushed against him and he felt her hair, warm with the sun, and soft, so soft, against his face. He pulled her closer and her breath, gentle little wisps of air, tickled his neck. He shuddered, then took her hand and led her to a fallen log.

"Let's see what Tita's divinations tell us about the future," he said, searching the ground. He gathered seven small sticks, and then pulled a jackknife from his pocket.

"Don't make fun of my mother." Catalina pushed against his shoulder. "She really believes those old Romani superstitions."

He smiled, slicing at one of the sticks.

"And who says I don't believe them too?"

Still smiling, he whittled down another stick, and then two more until four of the twigs were longer than the other three.

The way his mother-in-law had taught him.

His heart skipped half a beat.

His mother would be mortified if she ever found out that Catalina's mother—a Portuguese Gypsy who dabbled in divination—had shared some of her "skills" with him.

Unlike his mother, however, Diego saw no harm in the art.

He examined the seven sticks, chose one, and placed it horizontally in front of him. Then he took the other six twigs in his hand and turned to Catalina. Imitating his mother-in-law's voice he said, "What you want sticks to tell you today, my dear?"

"Stop!" She laughed. "You'll alter the power of the sticks."

"Ah-ha." He tweaked her nose with one of the twigs. "So you do believe in divination."

She thought for a moment, and then shifted into character.

"I want to know if our baby girl is going to be as happy as we are right now," she said, acting the part of a wide-eyed *payo* about to be swindled by a fake fortune teller.

He smiled. Rubbing his hands together, he mixed up the sticks, then held them still in his right hand. With his left, he drew one out, letting the remaining five fall to the ground over the large twig already there. There were three short ones and two long.

His smile faded. Quickly, he gathered the twigs.

"Ask something else," he said, suddenly taking the game too seriously.

Catalina's eyes widened. Her hand twitched over her belly. "I don't know. . . ."

"Let's just ask if she'll be healthy." His hand trembled as he tossed the twigs.

Three short and two long. Again.

"Forget it." He pushed the sticks away with his boot. "It's just a stupid superstition. Doesn't mean anything."

"Of course it doesn't, *cariño*." Catalina tossed back her head, promptly dismissing the illogical predictions of the sticks.

A raindrop landed on her lips.

"I love the rain," she said, closing her eyes.

He stared at the raindrop.

Slowly, the pounding in his ears subsided and gradually, his racing heart stilled. He leaned forward. Touched his mouth to hers.

"And I love how the rain tastes on you."

Catalina's mouth curved into a smile when he kissed her lips.

He lifted her hair. Brushed his fingers over the nape of her neck. Gently, until he felt her shiver.

"I want to call our baby Esmeralda," she said, hugging her arms together. The dark hair on her arms had lifted.

He looked at her for a moment, and then down at the ground. A smile flickered at the corner of his mouth. He knew as well as she that their baby was conceived here, at Emerald Lake. *El Lago Esmeralda.*

Catalina brought her hand to his face and touched his cheek. Not removing her eyes from his, she moved her hand down his chest and un-tucked his shirt, then started to undo the buttons.

Her fingers brushed against his skin. And just the lightest touch shot volts of electricity through his charged body. The physical reaction was inevitable. When she reached the last button, he tugged the shirt off his shoulders and ripped it from his arms.

"I've missed being with you," she said, her voice urgent as she loosened his belt.

He closed his eyes, every muscle in his body aching.

"I love you," he said.

Controlling his own desire, he framed her face in his hands and opened his eyes. "Are you sure we should do this?"

"Positive." Her tongue glided over his words as she coaxed open his lips.

Gently, he lowered her to the ground and knelt beside her. After removing her blouse, he unfastened the button of her skirt. Yards of white cloth slid down her slender legs.

He bunched up the skirt and made a pillow for her head.

His breath caught as he gazed upon her, unclothed before him.

"You're so beautiful." He rubbed his hands lightly over the roundness of her stomach, over the new fullness of her breasts. Then he lowered his head and laid his cheek on her belly.

He felt a wave of movement, and then a light kick. Smiling, he closed his eyes.

"I love you, Esmeralda," he said.

Catalina's stomach shifted under his cheek as the baby moved.

"You're going to be such a good father," she said. Then she released his hair from the cloth tie and smoothed it down over his shoulders. "You're already a great husband."

He raised his head. "It's all I ever wanted to be."

A drop of rain fell, landing on her chest. With his finger, he drew the small bead of moisture down to the curve of her breast.

His wedding ring caught a ray of light as a cloud moved away from the trees, allowing a hazy beam of sunlight to seep through the branches. Her skin glowed in the soft sepia light.

"How did I come to deserve this?" He caressed her with the tips of his fingers, running them over her body, feathering them between her breasts, down her belly, past her navel, and to the soft skin of her inner thigh.

Her hand tightened against him when he touched her there.

He brought his head up close to hers, his loosened hair spilling over his forehead and onto her cheeks.

"Are you sure you're okay?" he whispered against her lips.

She nodded.

And then gently, he parted her legs, watching her respond to his intimate caresses.

Life could not be more perfect than it felt right now.

3

Diego

Catalina's mood changed as Diego guided Lucero back to the ranch. She was more serious than when they had left for Emerald Lake. More uncomfortable.

Diego had debated postponing their return to Seville, but ultimately decided against it. Catalina had woken up startled after falling asleep in the forest.

Diego rubbed down and watered Lucero with less attention than he usually gave to the task, but by the time they were ready to leave, it was already 8 p.m.

He hurried Catalina to the car and jammed the key into the ignition. The starter clicked, but the engine did not turn over.

After several unsuccessful tries, he jumped out of the car and opened the hood.

"Do you think you can get it started?" Catalina moved into the dull light of the flashlight resting on the engine. She inhaled sharply, gripped her belly, and then made a low noise that sounded like a muffled groan.

Diego looked up from under the hood.

"Are you all right?" He gripped the wrench tighter in his hand.

She avoided his eyes. "I'm fine," she said.

He swallowed and looked up at the sky.

A storm was closing in and the night getting darker. The moon dimmed behind rain clouds waiting to break open.

He fiddled some more with the wires.

The engine sputtered. And then kicked to life. He dropped the hood and opened the door for Catalina.

He studied her face while helping her inside.

"Let's go," he said, not sure what to make of the crease between her eyes.

He tossed the wrench to the back seat, jumped into the driver's side, and shoved the gearshift forward.

It was only after several kilometers that his fingers finally relaxed on the wheel.

He glanced over at Catalina. She was slumped against the door, her hands on the underside of her belly. Struggling to keep any hint of worry from his voice, he said, "Are you feeling any better?"

"Hmm." She shifted position, rested her head against his shoulder. Her fingers dug into his thigh.

A muscle in his jaw twitched.

He kissed her hair, wondering what that sound meant.

"Just relax." A lump formed in his throat. "We'll be home soon." He swallowed hard and switched on the radio.

The soulful notes of a flamenco guitar floated over the airway. He tried to distract himself by following the chord progressions, but loud static crackled over the speakers. He fumbled with the knob, but the static only grew worse. Finally, he snapped off the radio.

Catalina's elbow pushed into his side as she shifted her hands over her belly. Then she made that little sound again. His brows drew together, lips pressed tight as he searched for the cut off from the country road onto the main highway leading back to Seville.

"Can we stop for a minute?" Catalina's voice was a tired whisper.

"No, mi amor, we should keep going." Get closer to the city, he told himself, afraid to speak his thoughts aloud. *Just in case . . .*

"I feel sick."

Immediately, Diego pulled over to the side of the road, jumped out of the car, and hurried to open the door for her.

"Just breathe," he said. His heart was in his throat, strangling his broken speech. "The fresh air will—"

"It hurts."

"Shh." He helped Catalina from the car and led her to a grove of orange trees lining the side of the road. The air was fragrant with the aroma of orange blossoms and olives.

He yanked off his jacket and spread it on the ground. Firmly, he placed his arm around Catalina's waist to help her sit down.

But she pushed him away, bent forward. A sharp gasp escaped her lips. He reached for her, but she held him back with her hand.

"No, don't touch me," she said.

He backed away, watching her carefully.

After a while, the two vertical lines between her brow faded and she relaxed.

Faintly, he smiled.

"Are you feeling better?" he said.

She nodded, eyes cast down. A few wisps of hair had moistened into curls over her forehead.

"Don't worry." He pushed back the curls. "Everything will be all right."

A bead of sweat formed where the ringlet had been. He wiped it away and kissed her forehead. Then he lowered her to the ground, where she sat comfortably for a while.

But then he felt her flinch. She doubled forward, hands clenched.

"I'm scared," she said, her voice low and unsteady. "Something's not right."

His heart jumped as he knelt beside her.

"Shh," he whispered. "I'm here." He smoothed the hair from her brow. "I'll take care of you." Had he been a convincing actor, his voice would not have trembled.

Catalina gasped. Clamped his hand.

"Lie down." He eased her back on the jacket.

"Maybe that'll help."

With a low moan, Catalina curled up on her side. The soft folds of the skirt wrapped around her ankles shimmered white in the moonlight. He rubbed her back. Then he froze, his fingers paralyzed. A dark stain had seeped into the fibers on the back of her skirt.

"We should go," he said, hoping she didn't notice the fear that had altered his voice. He went to help her up, but she lay folded in a fetal position.

"I think I'm having contractions," she said.

"What?" It took him two seconds to process what she had said, and then he reacted. "No, you can't. It's too early."

He caressed her hair, her face, her arms. A drop of rain fell on his hand and he looked up at the sky. Dark clouds had moved in, hiding the moon and shadowing the night.

She grabbed his hand and placed it over her bulging belly.

"Breathe, just breathe," he said, pressing his hand over her stomach—as if the force of his hand could stop the tragedy that was occurring within.

She tried to breathe, but what came out of her mouth were short gasps. He felt her stomach tighten.

"I'm having another contraction."

She squeezed her fingers tighter around his hand, moaning softly. It was a low, helpless sound that distressed him more than the sharpest cry would have.

"I'm taking you to the hospital." Heart tripping, he struggled to help Catalina from the ground. A trail of blood slithered down her leg and along the back of her soft leather shoe. He gasped in shallow breaths while slowly guiding her to the car.

Please, God, please . . . His silent prayer was a desperate plea. *Help me protect her.*

Catalina stopped suddenly.

"I'm bleeding," she said, eyes fixed on the thick red flow oozing down her leg.

"Tranquila," he whispered into her hair, bracing her against his shoulder. "We'll find help." A light sprinkle of rain began to fall. "I promise." His voice was strangled in his throat. "Nothing's going to happen—to you or the baby." He draped his jacket over her trembling shoulders.

She clutched his hand. And then, her legs collapsed.

"Hold onto me." He scooped her off the ground and carried her to the car.

She dropped her head against his chest and sagged into his arms.

He eased her into the front seat, and then sprinted to the driver's side. Wet drops landed on his shoulder. Then the clouds burst and the rain poured down. He jumped behind the wheel and crammed the key into the ignition.

Click. Click. The starter sputtered. And then it died.

He pushed the key harder, forcing it against the ignition. Nothing. Except that now, all of the dashboard lights were on.

The rain pelted against the windshield, running down in heavy sheets. He tried the wipers.

Swish. They swept across the windshield, cutting two semicircles across the glass.

Fingers trembling, he tried the ignition again.

It was dead.

Panic entered his body and glued his hands to the wheel. The steady rhythm of the wipers beat into his brain. He couldn't move, his body paralyzed.

Swipe. Swipe . . . Swipe. Swipe. The wipers pushed the rain off the glass. Large drops of moisture replaced those that had been driven away. He watched the drops form and then saw them swept away, cruel monotony. Then he snapped out of shock and into action.

Bolting from the car, he grabbed the flashlight and wrench from the back seat, lifted the hood, and began to fumble with the fuse wire. His hands shook uncontrollably. Especially the left—which was supposed to be the more stable one.

He cried out. A loose piece of metal had cut his hand.

He looked up. And then he saw it. A feeble beam of light. Headlights. In the distance.

Dropping the wrench, he ran in front of the car. Waving his arms hysterically, he screamed against the rain.

"¡Ayúdame!" he cried out, his voice lost in the storm. "Help me, please!"

The approaching car braked to a sudden stop. A black Mercedes.

Diego sprinted to the driver's side.

Through the sliver of an opening in the window a young man's voice said, *"Aléjate de mi coche."* Cold, controlled, the voice told Diego to get away from the car.

"Help me, please!" Diego spoke through the crack. "My wife—"

A clap of thunder silenced his voice.

"Lárgate." The driver told Diego to get lost. Then he sealed the window tight.

Diego beat on the glass, desperate to be heard. He pounded on the window, leaving a smear of blood on the tinted glass.

"Please, I need your help . . . my wife is—" His voice rose on a surge of panic that went unheard as the man started to accelerate.

Frantic to stop him, Diego dashed in front of the car.

The driver braked. The engine purred to a stop. And then slowly, the door swung open. A tall, well dressed Spaniard snapped open an umbrella and slid out of the car.

"Get the hell out of my way," the Spaniard said. "Or I'll fucking break your balls."

The rain pattered like percussion against the man's black umbrella.

Diego felt like taking that umbrella and stabbing the man. But for the sake of his family, he held back his rage.

"I need a ride to the hospital," Diego said. That was as controlled as he could be. Then he lost it. He grabbed the man's arm.

"Please—" Blood dripped down his hand and onto the Spaniard's neatly pressed sleeve.

"You're not dying," the Spaniard said, jerking his arm free. "You think I'm letting you anywhere near my car?" There was a slight hint of fear disguised behind the level voice. "So you can steal it?"

"I don't want your car!" Diego shouted, unwanted hostility in his voice. Without thinking, he clenched his fist. "I'm not looking for trouble, please—"

The Spaniard stared at Diego's raised hand, and then shifted his gaze. "Really?" he said, looking Diego directly in the eye.

Diego gazed in horror at his knotted fist, absorbing the devastating reality that he was failing his family.

"No, please." Diego unclenched his hand. "I need a ride— "

"Does my car look like a taxi?"

A surge of uncontrolled rage took over Diego's senses. He dug for the jackknife in his pocket. In a normal frame of mind, he would never have done that. But before he had even taken out the knife, the Spaniard had returned to his car.

The last thing Diego saw before the Spaniard raged past him was a small statue of the Virgin Mary, tilted slightly on the dash.

Diego bolted after the car, screaming for the man to stop, to come back.

Eventually, he stopped running, when running became futile. His heart crashed as he watched the taillights of the Spaniard's black Mercedes fade with his indifference.

Charging back to the car, he saw Catalina crumpled against the door, her skirt no longer white.

"No, Caty . . . *No!*"

He dove into the car and reached for his mobile phone in the glove compartment. Frantically, he marked 1-1-2. Before he could connect, the phone went dead.

He had forgotten to charge the battery.

"Shit!" He hurled the phone and searched Catalina's bag.

"Caty, where's your phone?" His voice trembled, even more when she didn't answer, forcing him to repeat the question.

"Elena has it," Catalina finally said, her voice so weak he barely heard it.

"Damn it!" He cursed his little sister.

"Forget about the phone," Catalina said. "Come." She dropped her hand to the seat. "Sit beside me."

Immediately, Diego ended his rant. He rushed over to the passenger side and took Catalina in his arms.

"You have to hold on . . . do you hear me?" He buried his face into her hair. "I'm not going to lose you." He squeezed her head between both hands, kissing her over and over again. He rubbed her hands, desperate to warm them. He rubbed more vigorously, but her skin remained cold.

"No!" His cry lifted upon the air, heavy with that thin, metallic odor that had seeped into her clothing.

"Just tell me you love me, and I'll be all right." Catalina's voice was no more than a faint, dying whisper.

"I love you," he said. But, she wasn't all right.

In one swift move, he lifted Catalina from the car and gathered her in his arms.

Then he walked and he walked. Until it was useless to walk any farther. Warm tears slid down his cheeks, down the sides of his face, and into the corners of his mouth. They dripped thickly onto his neck and down into the collar of his shirt. And while he walked, the wind blew, stirring up the sickening sweet scent of the orange blossom as it chased away the rain.

Andrés Aragón
Seville, Spain

"When I say, 'I hate you,' it really means,
'You hurt me.'"

Anonymous

4

Andrés

The rain was starting to let up. Fucking finally. Andrés Aragón was in a hurry to get to the hospital. His ten-year-old sister, Adela, had suffered another asthma attack. He would've been there by now if it hadn't been for that goddamn Gypsy. The *tipo* looked like a punk who was out to cause trouble. He had blood on his hands, a wild expression on his face. Like all *gitanos*, he carried a knife.

Andrés admitted to a slight moment of fear when the man raised his fist. Should anything bad have happened out there on that road, there would have been twenty more Gypsy men behind that one man, all of them out for blood. His blood. Those Gypsies had their own laws, their own class of outlaw revenge. No *payo* in his right mind wanted to get too close to a Gypsy. Either he would be robbed of his wallet, his car, or maybe even his life.

Andrés swerved into an empty parking spot and bolted for the Emergency Room. Screw the Gypsy. He was worried about his sister. The attacks were becoming more frequent. And although his eminent father, Dr. Andrés Aragón Navarro, vehemently denied it, Andrés was positive Adela's attacks were not triggered by any allergic reaction. They were provoked, he was sure, by her fragile psychological state. There was no other explanation. Dr. Aragón's luxury penthouse apartment was always spotless, perpetually free of all visible mold and dust. The maid took care of that. Air purifiers eliminated all other invisible allergens.

No, Adela's triggers were not environmental. They were emotional. Andrés was convinced of it. He knew his sister.

Adela was a sweet, vulnerable girl, his mother's last attempt to hold onto a dying marriage. But her birth only put more strain on an already tense relationship. Mother had never really wanted her and Father barely saw her. If it weren't for Grandma Aragón, who came to live with them after his mother died, Adela would still be an emotional train wreck.

Now, two years after their mother's death, Adela was stable. But she was still so sad. Andrés wasn't completely sure if what was bringing Adela to the hospital was her grief over the loss of their mother, her naturally delicate condition, or the lack of affection from their father. But it didn't matter. It was the sadness that was making her sick.

No one needed to tell him his family was fucked up.

Two hours later, Andrés was mentally fried. He hated to see his sister suffer. She was stable now, receiving aerosolized beta-agonist medications through a facemask. His father was at the hospital, monitoring her care. His grandmother was at her bedside. So he left and went to join his lab mates at El Cántaro. There was still one hour left to his twenty-fifth birthday. And despite his dark mood, he was determined to end the night celebrating.

He jerked open the door. Javier was complaining in a loud voice about yet another failed experiment.

"*Joder.* I can't get that damn protocol to work," Javier said. "Matos is never going to approve my thesis."

"Not yours or anybody else's," said Josemaría. "Andrés has been waiting for six months for *El Bocón* to approve his. If he can't make it happen, you have no chance, *cabrón.*"

"Hey, Andrés!" Maricarmen waved to him from across the room. "Get your hot ass over here. You're late for your own birthday."

Andrés sauntered into the bar. He pretended not to notice that Maricarmen, the only female in Dr. Matos's classical genetics lab, was dressed in a tight sweater pulled over an equally tight skirt.

If anyone had a hot ass, it was she.

He pulled out a chair and sat next to Maricarmen, who was sitting next to Rajiv—the new post doc from India.

Andrés observed his new lab mate.

The man was sitting with everyone else, but was completely shut off. He was reading a book propped up on his messenger bag.

"Hey Rajiv," Andrés said. "What're you reading?"

Rajiv looked up. Showed him the title. *Gandhi's Truth.*

Andrés shifted his gaze to Maricarmen. "Has he been sitting there reading all night?" he asked.

"Pretty much," she said.

Rajiv closed the book. He looked like he was about to say something. Before he had the chance, Andrés said, "It's my birthday today. I hope you're ready to celebrate."

Maricarmen took a cigarette from her purse and Andrés snapped open his lighter for her. She smiled and took a heavy drag, blowing puffs of smoke above her head.

"I'm here," Rajiv said. "Am I not?"

Somehow, Andrés did not like the tone of that man's voice. Condescending, but subtly so. Restrained. Understated. So low key that the others had not even noticed.

Andrés leaned in closer to Maricarmen and removed the cigarette from her fingers to light his own. He took a long, slow drag, and then turned to face Rajiv.

"I'm glad you could join us," he said. "I was starting to think you didn't like me."

"Why would you think that?" Rajiv slipped the book back into his bag. "I've known you for less than twenty four hours."

"Ya, ya." Javier waved his hand in front of Andrés. "We're here to party. How about another round?" He motioned for the waiter.

Pepe scurried to the table and took their order.

Andrés continued smoking. Several seconds passed before he spoke again.

"My sister's in the hospital," he said. "Another asthma attack."

"Oh shit," Javier said. "Not again." He turned toward the waiter. "Make that a *cuba libre* instead of a beer for me."

What the hell? Andrés waited for Javier to say something more about his sister. But beyond asking for a gin and tonic, his friend had nothing else to say.

"I think she's getting worse." Andrés downed the shot of Johnny Walker Black the waiter had brought to the table.

"That's tough, man," Josemaría said. "Cheers." He raised his glass.

The others joined him in a toast.

"You must be worried about your sister," Rajiv said.

"What?" Andrés turned to look at Rajiv. He wasn't sure what he was hearing. Support? Or sarcasm.

"Does she have these attacks often?"

Andrés snubbed out his cigarette.

"Every few months or so. Whenever she gets too stressed."

"Living with you'll do it," Maricarmen said.

She smiled. Blew him a kiss. And then finished her wine.

He stared at her. Summoned the waiter.

"Last round," he said. "Then the party moves over to my place."

No one objected. But nor did anyone agree. His colleagues simply continued doing what they had been doing ever since he arrived. They talked. They laughed. And they drank.

All except for Rajiv, who refused all forms of alcohol.

Andrés stared at his new lab mate.

Rajiv Kumaran was a serious man. Intellectual. Highly motivated. He had finished his doctorate in four years. With six publications. Matos was impressed with him. So impressed that he had given the man the only available post doc. The applicant who lost the job to this impressive foreigner was a Spaniard.

With a national unemployment rate of over 24 per cent that hurt.

Andrés picked up the whisky Pepe had left on the table.

"To all my good friends," he said, raising his glass.

"To graduating before your next birthday." Javier tipped his glass.

The others laughed and imitated his move.

Andrés smiled. Nodded. Downed his shot. And then ordered another round. The party had begun.

It was after midnight when he left El Cántaro. Maricarmen left with him. When they reached La Campana, he tripped over the curb in front of the upscale coffee shop. Cursing the curb, he bent down to wipe the scuff mark off his shoe.

Maricarmen fell on top of him. Then started to laugh.

He stiffened. His giddy lab mate was beginning to irritate him.

Finally he stood, helped her to her feet, and then directed her to an outside table. A waiter, dressed in a clean white uniform, approached to take their order.

"What can I get you?" the waiter said.

The mustache that extended across the man's cheeks and to his ears was the only part of his face that smiled.

Chocolate y churros," Andrés said.

The waiter took their order, returning a short time later with two steaming cups of chocolate and two plates of fried doughnut sticks.

Andrés watched Maricarmen dunk one of the *churros* into the hot chocolate. She wasn't a particularly challenging woman. He'd had her before, and remembered nothing special about the experience. In fact, he hadn't really planned on being alone with her tonight. He wanted to still be with his friends, drinking, but the mood in El Cántaro had shifted along with his emotions. Too many jokes at his expense had made him unpleasant. Except for Maricarmen, his friends had all found an excuse to go home.

His phone vibrated. He glanced at the caller ID. "Shit."

"Where the hell are you?" His father snarled into the receiver.

"Why? Is Adela all right?"

"She's fine." His father's voice was hurried, rough. "Did you change the filter on the air purifier in Adela's bedroom?"

"You're calling to ask me that?"

"Adela's sick because of you."

"No. She's sick because of *you*."

A long, heavy silence, and then, "Don't cross me, Andrés."

"What do you want from me?"

"Adela's being released. I want all those filters changed before she gets home."

"It's already done." Andrés cut off the call. Only yesterday, he had changed all six filters.

"You all right?" Maricarmen didn't look up when she spoke.

She was busy texting.

"Bastard." Andrés spewed out all the reasons he was on edge tonight, starting with his father.

Maricarmen listened, but didn't seem to care.

"Hey." She hit *send* on her latest text. "It's your birthday. I thought we were going to celebrate."

He forced a smile. Reached for her hands.

"I'm sorry, you're right."

He kissed the tips of her fingers.

"Forgive me. You don't need to hear all this."

He leaned across the table and whispered in her ear.

"Let's go to my studio." He pitched his voice purposely low with intimacy. "I want to be alone with you."

* * *

Thirty minutes later, they were at the front gate to Andrés's studio—a gift from his father on his eighteenth birthday. Or, rather, a compromise. If he agreed to pursue a career in molecular medicine, his father promised to support his art. Not such an easy deal. He hated science. And had no time for art.

The gate squealed as he pushed it open.

"Entra." He put his hand over Maricarmen's lower back and guided her into the studio. Then he turned up the dimmer switch, just enough to spread soft light into the room.

His studio looked impressive at night, with the moonlight pouring in through skylights cut into the wood-beamed ceiling. The kitchen area was inviting, with a black marble counter and four stainless-steel bar stools topped in black leather. His eyes landed on the wine rack, which he had filled only yesterday with vintage wines and his favorite sherry. Yesterday, he had expected to receive more people.

But whatever. His eyes shifted to the loft on the second floor. At least there was some advantage to being abandoned by his friends.

"I love this place," Maricarmen said. Her eyes darted from the large workbench that doubled as a coffee table, to the black leather sofa, to the wooden easel, cluttered with rolled-up tubes of paint, crusted palettes, and brushes soaking in jars.

Andrés sauntered into the kitchen. He pulled a bottle of Harvey's Bristol Cream from the rack, uncorked the bottle, and poured a single glass. For her. He felt like something stronger. Yanking open the freezer, he grabbed a few cubes of ice and dumped them into a tumbler. He poured himself a shot of Johnny Walker Black, drank it, and then refilled the glass.

Maricarmen wandered over to the easel. She studied the unfinished portrait propped up on the wooden frame.

Andrés came up beside her and handed her the glass.

"Who is she?" Maricarmen said, accepting the sherry.

Andrés swallowed more whisky.

"My mother," he finally said. A muscle tightened in his jaw.

"She's beautiful." Maricarmen raised the glass to her mouth.

"She's dead."

"Yeah, I know, but—"

"Forget about it. I feel good, what about you?" Andrés grabbed her hand and led her to the sofa, plunking himself down beside her. Before she could answer he said, "I have something that'll make us feel even better."

Leaning to the side, he pulled a folded rectangle of paper from his pants pocket and reached for a mirror amidst the clutter on the workbench. He dumped the contents of the paper onto the mirror, took a razor blade from a wooden box on the bench, and cut the fine white powder into two thin lines. Using a carved ivory straw that he pulled from the same box, he snorted a line.

"Here." He offered her the straw. "El Tiburón is bringing some quality shit lately. Expensive, but good."

"No, thanks." Maricarmen looked away.

He nodded, to himself for she was not looking at him, smiled, but not with pleasure.

"I thought you wanted to party," he said.

"Chill out, Andrés, I don't feel like it tonight."

Andrés frowned. He lowered the straw to the mirror and snorted the second line. Then he fumbled for his glass. Before he could down another shot, the tumbler slipped from his hand and shattered to the floor. He cursed, and then bent down to pick up the pieces.

"*¡Coño!*" A splinter of glass sliced his finger.

"Oh God, Andrés, you're bleeding."

Andrés rose from the sofa, looking forward to her sympathy.

"It's nothing," he said. "Just a small cut."

"Go get a band-aid, Andrés. You're bleeding on my purse."

Andrés looked down. A few spots of blood had stained her leather bag.

He stepped on the purse, and then headed for the kitchen.

"What the hell's wrong with you?" Maricarmen snatched her bag from the floor, wiped the blood off with a paint-stained cloth, and placed the purse beside her on the sofa.

Andrés squeezed his bleeding finger harder than he needed to. Strode to the sink. And ran cold water over the cut.

He wanted to shake Maricarmen, to ask her if she felt anything at all for him, if she had even the slightest shred of compassion for what he might be feeling. His sister was in the hospital. His father on his case. All he wanted was a few kind words.

Was that too much to ask?

He watched the water turn red. Immediately, he felt light-headed. The sight of blood did it to him every time.

Wiping his hands on a dishtowel, he searched for a band-aid in the top drawer of the cabinet, taped it around his finger, grabbed the bottle of whisky off the counter, and returned to the sofa.

He sat beside her, sideways so he could face her, and then drew his finger over her tightly drawn lips.

"Give me a smile," he said, forcing a softness to his voice he did not feel.

He brought his face close to hers and teased her with his lips.

Finally, her lips softened into a smile.

He smiled too, then moved away and lit a cigarette, squinting at her through the haze of smoke drifting from his nostrils.

"Your hair . . . " He reached out to touch a strand of her hair, fascinated by the color tones he saw reflected in the light beside the sofa.

Suddenly inspired, he rested his cigarette in the ashtray and rubbed the lock of hair between his fingers, studying its tonality.

"The color," he said. "It's the pale amber of Manzanilla wine. Dorset Gold mixed with Harvest Moon."

Releasing her hair, he picked up a tube of Dorset Gold and squeezed a drop of paint onto a wooden palette. Then he took the tube of Harvest Moon and blended the second color with the first using the tip of a paintbrush. When he lifted the brush and held it next to a strand of her hair, he saw that the color was identical.

Damn, I'm good. The thought both amazed and frightened him. He never said that about himself when it came to science.

"I want to paint you," he said, so wishing he was enrolled in fine arts rather than biology.

With his hands, he traced the curves of her body, like a sculptor molding a figure out of clay.

"Let me paint you," he said. *"Desnuda."*

She held his hand still.

"Oh no," she said, smiling coquettishly, "I couldn't possibly pose naked for a man."

She moved over to whisper in his ear.

"I was raised Catholic, you know."

Andrés stiffened. And then removed his hand. Maricarmen's references to Catholicism offended him, knowing she was a confirmed atheist. While he didn't adhere to all the moral standards set forth by the Church, he was proud of his Catholic heritage. But, he suppressed his irritation for the trade-off he would get if he played the game right.

Sex.

"Oh, I see," he said smoothly, pretending to be amused.

Then he took back the seduction.

"But there's one thing you're forgetting." The corner of his mouth lifted slightly as he unfastened the top button of her sweater. "Art is where the holy and the human are allowed to meet." He slipped open the next button. "And when God created you, He celebrated the beauty of the female form."

She opened her mouth to speak but he pressed the tip of his finger against her lips and shook his head.

"A body like yours needs to be painted." He moved his way down her sweater, unfastening the last two buttons. "And touched." He slipped the sweater over her shoulders and ran his fingers along her skin. Brushing the hair off her shoulder, he kissed his way softly down her neck, his fingers finding and then parting her legs.

Maricarmen pushed him back.

"You're a dangerous man," she said, pulling her sweater back over her shoulder. "Confusing spirituality with lust."

Andrés sat back and stared, studying her intently. What game was she playing now? He reached across her lap, pulled the ashtray closer, and took a slow drag on his cigarette. The air around them filled with smoke as he exhaled. He dragged a few more times, and then ground out the cigarette.

"Looks like you're going to make it hard for me tonight," he said, not removing his eyes from her.

"Maybe I am." She unbuttoned his shirt, but did not remove it.

He nodded. "Just the way I like it."

His lips were tight, but he managed a smile. Then he brushed his lips over her ear. Softly, he wove a strand of her hair around his finger and kissed the nape of her neck.

"Since today you are a self-proclaimed Catholic virgin," he whispered, moving his lips down her neck to her shoulder, and then back up to her mouth. "I'll respect that."

He pushed up her skirt and rubbed his hand along her thigh. By the way she reacted he knew he'd have her.

But then he did something stupid. He laughed.

"Yeah, right!" He squeezed the soft spot between her legs. "My beautiful fucking Madonna."

"Oh that's good, Andrés."

Maricarmen pushed off his hand. "I hate it when you drink too much." She moved away from him.

"Come back here." Still laughing, he pulled her back.

Gently, he flicked his tongue across her lips, and then slipped it into her mouth, softly, until he felt her body slacken. After kissing her the way he knew she liked it, he slid his hand back under her skirt and ran his fingers along the edge of her panties.

"Let me paint you." He unclasped her skirt and lowered the zipper. "I'll call your portrait *The Tainted Virgin*."

He felt her pull away.

"Shut up, Andrés. You're acting like a jerk."

She sat up abruptly, banging her knee against the workbench.

"*¡Coño!*" She grabbed her purse off the sofa and headed for the door. Fumbling with the lock she said, "The party's over. I want to go home."

"*Tranquila.*" Andrés rushed over to the door and crushed his body against hers, framing her with his arms. He pushed the door shut with one hand and whispered against her hair, "I'm sorry, all right? Take it easy."

He kissed the back of her head and turned her to face him.

"Let me see your knee." He bent down and brushed his fingers gently over the pinkish-red spot that had formed on her skin. "I'll get you some ice." He headed for the kitchen.

"Don't worry about it," she said, holding him back. "Just take me home."

"Why?" He really wished she'd stop changing the rules. It made him crazy. And maybe a little vulnerable.

"I'm sorry," he said. "I was a jerk. But you know me."

He returned to her, brushed a strand of hair from her eye.

"I don't mean half of what I say."

He cupped her face and kissed her, sincerely this time.

"But, I'll take you home . . ." He kissed her again, and then deeper. "If that's what you want."

Finally, she relaxed.

He lowered her to the floor.

Running his fingers across her belly, he unzipped her skirt, and then removed her clothing.

It was not the way he wanted it. Nor even the person he wanted it with. But the tension that hardened his body needed to be relieved. Crude, he knew. But he never claimed to be a prince.

Unbuckling his belt, he slid out of his clothes. And then he took what he wanted and gave nothing back. When it was over, he drove her home, both of them silent.

* * *

Later that night, he slipped into Adela's room.

She was sleeping peacefully.

He kissed her on the cheek, pulled up the covers, and turned out the light.

When he was alone in his room, he pulled a picture out of his dresser drawer. He stared at the photo of the woman he was still in love with.

It should have been Rosa with him tonight, not Maricarmen.

He stuffed the photograph back in the drawer, and then turned on the TV. The words *Breaking News* scrolled across the screen.

"At approximately eleven-fifteen p.m.," reported the anchor for Canal Sur's evening news, "what started as a peaceful gathering turned violent as over one hundred friends and family of seventeen-year-old Catalina Meléndez marched from the Tres Mil Sector toward El Virgen del Rocio Hospital."

Andrés unbuttoned his shirt and entered the bathroom attached to his room, only half-listening to the news.

"Earlier this evening, Catalina Meléndez died when the car she was traveling in with her husband, nineteen-year-old Diego Antonio Vargas, broke down on the road from Huelva," Guillermo López reported with his usual, journalistic detachment.

"The young woman was six months pregnant and had gone into premature labor. After failing to start the car, Diego Vargas walked with his wife in his arms toward Seville. A passing motorist stopped and rushed them to Virgen del Rocio Hospital, but Ms. Meléndez died before reaching the clinic."

Andrés removed his clothes and tossed them in the hamper. His mind was still on Rosa. It had been fourteen months and two days since she'd broken up with him.

He was still trying to figure out how to get her back.

"Ms. Meléndez's death has incited the Gypsy community," Guillermo López said. "Allegedly, the young woman, of Gypsy ethnicity, died because an unidentified Spaniard, who had been flagged down by Diego Vargas, refused to drive her to the hospital."

Weird, Andrés thought. A Gypsy had flagged him down, too. But there was no woman. Too distracted to pay any further attention to the news, Andrés yanked on his sweat pants, grabbed the phone off his belt, and proceeded to text Rosa.

Call me, he punched out on the screen, and then hit "send."

"According to eye witnesses," the anchor said. "Family members and friends who had gathered outside the hospital demanded access to the attending physician. When access was denied, a group of four young men, cousins to Diego Vargas, threatened the security guard at the entrance. Apparently frustrated by the guard's refusal to let them in, Antonio Meléndez, uncle to the young woman, attempted to storm the hospital. One witness claims this action was met with a furious response from the guard, who pounded Antonio Meléndez with his baton. Within minutes, the situation was out of control. A riot broke out after a group of enraged young men pushed two parked cars into the street and set them ablaze."

"Holy shit." Andrés sat on the bed and turned up the volume.

"As men hurled bricks, Molotov cocktails, and bottles, officers from the riot squad were deployed to disperse the mob. But their progress was impeded by the burning cars."

A text came in.

Andrés glanced at the message. *What do you want, Andrés?*

He typed out, *I need to talk to you*, but didn't send the message. He was too engrossed with what was being projected over his flat-panel TV.

"As the violence escalates," Guillermo López reported. "The police are monitoring messages being transmitted over Twitter and Facebook, inciting others to join the riot."

Andrés stared at the screen. A burning police car belched black smoke into the air. Dumpsters were on fire. Shop windows smashed. Sidewalks strewn with shattered glass.

Quickly, Andrés erased his previous message and texted Rosa, *Are you safe?* Rosa lived in a flat facing the front entrance to the hospital.

Five minutes passed without a response.

He marked her number. "Answer, goddammit."

A text came in.

He ended the call and checked the message. *Scared but okay.*

Of course she'd be scared. Angry Gypsy men armed with rocks, crowbars and other makeshift weapons now ruled the streets.

5

Diego

Diego stood frozen in the street outside the hospital, an ambulant zombie. Chaos reigned around him. A gasoline-filled Coke bottle exploded in a nearby dumpster. Flames consumed garbage. The odor of destruction poisoned the air.

Burnt trash. Melted plastic. Gasoline.

Around him, Diego heard the furious voices of his friends and family, demanding justice. Shouting for revenge against the unknown Spaniard who had left him stranded. He registered the voices, but it was as if he were hearing them detached from his body. People ran past him, spewing accusations and spitting out curses. Sloshing gasoline and igniting it into fire. The destruction was real but the execution of it was like a slow-motion take in a made-up movie. And while the Coke bottle bombs burst around him, Diego stood like a caged animal only recently captured—wild with fear and agitation.

In the hours that followed Catalina's death, the initial shock had given way to unspeakable agony. Unable to think rationally, Diego reacted. He joined the others as they took out their anger on the streets outside the hospital. But mere destruction of property wasn't nearly enough. What Diego wanted to destroy was not cars and garbage and buildings.

He wanted to kill that arrogant Spaniard who had caused Catalina to die.

Too much blood lost, the doctor said.

Too late arriving at the hospital.

Joaquín pushed a Molotov cocktail into Diego's hand.

Diego grabbed the gasoline-filled bottle and hurled it against the wall of a nearby building. In a flash, flames illuminated the scene.

Then the bad movie went into freeze frame.

Diego saw his brother, Juan José, texting a message on his BlackBerry. Joaquín was doing the same on his iPhone. His cousin, Lorenzo, had just pulled out his mobile and was running video footage. A few others Diego didn't know gripped crowbars. One had a bloody hand. Another a white shirt splotched red.

The image triggered a memory. Diego stared at his sleeve, still stained with Catalina's blood. And then he stepped on the landmine of that memory and detonated an explosion.

"I want blood!" he cried. "Spanish blood!" He wanted to kill every last Spaniard who could possibly be that man.

Joaquín snagged his arm.

"Then go spill some." Joaquín reached into his pocket, produced a switchblade, and pressed it into Diego's hand.

"Go," he said. "Get your revenge."

Diego saw the challenge in Joaquín's eyes. He grabbed the knife. But the action did not seem real. He felt like a ghost, watching a scene he did not want to belong in, and yet somehow was one of the major protagonists. He stared blankly at the knife, as if the weapon held everything—and nothing—he wanted.

In the middle of the chaos, his brother Samuel ran up beside him, an aerosol bomb in his hand.

The duct tape holding down the spray button on the can of deodorant let out a continuous flow of combustible fumes. Samuel ignited the aerosol jet with his lighter. And then all of a sudden, the scene was real. They had about five seconds before the makeshift bomb would blow. Diego snatched the can and flung it away. An orange tree went up in flames. And then he saw Joaquín shift his eyes to the knife—no longer held as tightly in Diego's hand.

"So what, you're not going to take what's yours?" Joaquín shifted onto his stronger leg. "A life for a life?"

Justice is not yours to take. From somewhere deep inside himself, Diego resurrected his father's voice. *"Do not avenge this wrong committed against you."*

Windows shattered in a nearby electronics store. Looters climbed over the jagged holes, grabbing whatever they could carry out of the *payo* business.

Diego turned to run after them, to stop them. This was not supposed to be happening. None of it was.

A hand gripped his arm, holding him back. He looked over his shoulder. Uncontrolled fury blazed in Joaquín's eyes.

"Are you going to let the *payo* get away with one more unjust act against our people?" Joaquín pushed two fingers into Diego's chest, his hand forming a finger gun.

The few seconds between Joaquín's question and Diego's response became one of the most vivid, sobering moments Diego would experience in the first few hours after Catalina's death. There was nothing he wanted to do more than to make some other man hurt as much as he hurt right now. But Joaquín's enraged insistence somehow numbed the very desire, leaving him nauseous from the anger now turned against his friend.

"I don't know which injustice is worse." Diego flung off Joaquín's hand. "The *payo's* prejudice. Or our own."

He pushed past Joaquín, but then Lorenzo ran by, his arms full of gasoline-filled Coke bottles plugged with fuel-soaked rags.

Joaquín grabbed one, lit the cloth stopper, and shoved the bottle at Diego.

"Are you going to forget it was a Spaniard who killed Catalina?" Joaquín said.

"No!" An eruption of anger exploded from Diego's mouth. "You won't let me!" Hatred boiled up in him like molten lava, but he wasn't sure who he hated more at that particular moment—Joaquín, or the unknown Spaniard who had taken Catalina's life.

Just as the bottle was about to detonate, he pitched the cocktail into a parked car.

There was an explosion. Fire. And then a man staggered out of the car. The Spaniard's white lab coat caught on the door. He yanked at it, but was unable to free himself.

Seconds later, his right arm was in flames.

Diego dropped the knife and rushed forward, but Joaquín pulled him back.

"Leave him!" Joaquín shouted. "The car's going to blow!"

"Let go of me!" Diego jerked free of Joaquín and sprinted toward the man.

He threw his jacket over the Spaniard's arm and smothered the flames.

"Help me," the Spaniard said.

"I'll get you to the hospital," Diego said, choking on the toxic air. He put his arm around the man's shoulder to help him up.

But then a blaze of neon blue strobes flashed angry circles through the darkness and a wail of screaming sirens pierced the night. Diego squeezed his eyes shut, whispered a choked apology to the man, waited long enough for a cruiser to get within sight of the injured Spaniard, and then got up and ran. Along with his friends and family, he ran away from the destruction. Away from the *payo* policemen who would never understand. Away from justice. Away from the enemy. But he would never be able to run away from himself . . . or from the tragedy that had just occurred.

6

Andrés

Andrés had not moved from his bed all night, paralyzed with
something greater than fear. As the news reports continued to stream
in throughout the night, the tragedy became clear. A young woman
had died. Riots rocked the city. Chaos ruled.

All because an unidentified Spaniard driving a black Mercedes had
refused to take the woman to the hospital.

That's not how it happened, he had repeated to himself, over and over
again, incessantly throughout the night. *I never saw the woman.*

His eyes were glued to the screen. Broadcasts were still going on,
nine hours later.

"The scenes of open lawlessness which began at approximately
eleven-fifteen p.m. last night have extended throughout the city," said
Roberto Pabón, who had replaced Guillermo López behind the news
desk. "The streets of Las Tres Mil, Las Letanias, and Torre Blanca
are strewn with flaming cars, broken glass and burning buildings. By
midnight last night, the police had managed to break through the
blockades. Firefighters brought in their trucks, but they failed to
contain the rioters. BBM and Twitter messages circulating since Ms.
Meléndez's death have fueled the anger of hundreds of Gypsy youth
and incited new waves of violence."

Andrés scrolled through current Twitter feeds. A picture of
Catalina Meléndez, dressed in her wedding gown, had been re-
tweeted more than a thousand times.

He looked back up at the TV. A news bulletin scrolled over the screen. *Uncle of Catalina Meléndez pleads for an end to the riots.*

"What is going on right now in the streets of our city has nothing to do with what happened to my niece," said Antonio Meléndez, uncle of the woman whose death triggered a riot. "The violence taking place in our city was hijacked by mindless thugs and is not representative of the vast majority of my people. I do not condone this violence. We already have two grieving families. Violence is not going to heal their pain."

Andrés's chest was so tight with tension that for a moment he couldn't breathe. He fell back against the headboard, sucked in a gulp of air, and closed his eyes.

I never saw the woman.

The door creaked open. And then Adela's bunny slippers padded across the floor.

"Are you all right?" she said, her voice small.

He opened his eyes. "*Sí, mi cielo.* I'm fine."

She grabbed a handful of sheet and pulled herself onto the bed.

"Your face is all crumpled," she said, running her fingers over the crease between his eyes.

He kissed the girl's braided hair and slid her to his side.

"Can't a man think without his little sister getting all over his case?"

She giggled, and then grabbed his hand.

"What happened to your finger?" She cupped his bandaged finger in between her hands.

Andrés cringed. She was squeezing directly on the cut. Gently, he removed her hands.

"Forget about me," he said, tickling her tummy. "What're you doing out of bed so early?"

The giggles ended.

"Papá says I have to go to school today." She snuggled into him.

Andrés hugged her closer and then looked up at his grandmother, who had entered the room. His lips tightened.

"What's wrong with her?" he mouthed.

"Carlitos," his grandmother whispered.

Andrés nodded.

Carlitos was a bully. Adela the perfect target. His sister was born six weeks premature, the innocent victim of his mother's addiction. At ten years, she had the height and weight of a child less than half her age. His mother had been too caught up in her own pain to worry about the effects of alcohol on her unborn fetus.

"That's it." Andrés moved Adela aside and slid off the bed. "I'm going to her school." He strode toward the closet. "I'll catch that bully Carlitos by the throat and—"

"Ya." His grandmother squeezed his hand. *"Tranquilo, hijo.* I'm going to talk to the principal."

"Fine." Andrés held up his hands in mock surrender. "You go talk." He yanked a shirt off a hanger. "And then can I kill Carlitos?"

Adela giggled.

"Oh, you think that's funny?" He scooped her off the bed and into his arms.

She dropped her head back in a fit of laughter.

"Spin me around," she said, gripping her legs around his waist.

He did as she asked and she screamed in delight.

"Not so rough, Andrés." His grandmother pleaded for him to stop.

"All right. All right." He kissed Adela's cheek and sat her on the bed. "I'll see you after school, *vale?*"

Her face fell.

He raised her chin.

"And then we'll play *Briscas*, like I promised." He raised his hand and she slapped him a high five.

As quickly as it had come, Adela's sadness turned to laughter and her pain was forgotten.

Too bad it wasn't as easy for him.

7

Diego

A haze of gray smoke hovered over the San Fernando Cemetery. The air smelled acrid. Two days of rioting had left the city smoldering. Charred hulls of cars littered the streets. Shattered store windows were boarded. Broken glass carpeted the pavement. It took the police forty-eight hours to reclaim the streets. But by eight a.m. on the third day, the roads had cleared and police had cordoned off the crime scene. Then the attention of the media shifted away from the streets to the cemetery.

Diego barely noticed the solemn crowd that had gathered behind the hearse. Or the cameramen. Or the policemen. All he saw was the color black. It was everywhere. Men dressed in black suits wearing dark glasses. Woman in black skirts and blouses. The hearse. The mausoleum gifted to him by a wealthy uncle from Badajóz so he could bury his wife and stillborn child.

It was a girl, his baby. An innocent baby girl.

Wails pierced the air. Sobs. Agonizing cries. But Diego neither screamed nor cried. He held firm against the tears that lurked behind his eyes. There was nothing left for him to feel.

The funeral procession began its slow walk down the cypress-lined path of the cemetery. Diego walked too, but he did not feel part of what was going on around him. There was a sense of unreality attached to the movement. It was as if he were sleepwalking, lost in a terrifying nightmare.

An old woman carrying a bouquet of red and white carnations shuffled to the side of the road, allowing the hearse to pass. And then she joined the procession. Others followed her. Others who were neither family members nor Gypsies. The destructive events of the last two days had made what should have been a private event painfully public.

A sharp stab of pain collapsed Diego's heart. His throat tightened. And then unmercifully, his mind spiraled back to the final hours of Catalina's life. And for probably the hundredth time, he replayed the scene, wondering what he could have done differently the night Catalina died.

If he had just charged the battery on his phone. If he'd just fixed the car before they headed out of town. If they'd returned to Seville earlier in the day rather than at night. If he hadn't been so hostile, hadn't pulled out his knife. He might have saved Catalina's life.

Diego blew out a burst of pent-up air, realizing that, not for the first time that day, he had forgotten to breathe.

As the procession got closer to the burial site, his heart beat faster. And faster. Until it felt like it would explode into a thousand tiny pieces. And then suddenly, the movement around him stopped.

They had reached the mausoleum.

A wave of emptiness rolled over Diego's aching stomach. His shoulders drooped and his knees weakened. He felt faint.

Samuel took Diego's limp right arm and draped it over his shoulder. Their cousin Lorenzo did the same on Diego's other side. Between the two of them, they formed a solid body of support as the pallbearers lowered Catalina's coffin to the ground. Beside it, they placed a tiny white casket, adorned with a spray of pink flowers.

Diego choked back a sob.

It caught in his throat. He needed to breathe. He needed to get away. Caskets that small should not even be made.

Reporters spoke into microphones. Cameras flashed. But Diego detached himself from everything that was going on around him and floated upward to a space far, far away.

People receded from sight until they appeared to be standing on some distant horizon. Like an outsider looking in, he saw Catalina's father, Tito Lolo, kneel down and touch his daughter's casket. But it was as if the man moved suspended in another world.

He watched Tita Juana, Catalina's mother, collapse beside her husband. Two of Tita Juana's sons took her in their arms.

The rest of Catalina's family and friends held each other by the hand and made a circle around her grave. Catalina's younger brother, Josué, released a dove into the air. Diego's little sister, Elena, let go of a second bird—smaller and more delicate than the first.

The baby dove flapped its wings and hovered over the casket. Then it flew upward into the clouds, up towards him. Up to Catalina.

After a while, the old woman who had joined the procession took two carnations from her bouquet, one red, the other white, and placed them on top of Catalina's coffin.

Hundreds of other unknown people added their flowers. Some left entire arrangements.

Others placed stuffed animals on top of the miniature casket. Most of them were dressed in pink.

Diego felt himself falling into a black hole of dread and oblivion—his body weighted down by all the "if onlys" in his heart. If only he hadn't taken Catalina to the forest. If only . . .

"Son . . ." His father's voice pulled Diego back. "It's time."

Don Josemi placed his hand on Diego's shoulder.

Diego heard his father, but at that moment could not perform the simplest task of putting one foot ahead of the other and stepping forward. It was as if his body and all its functions had simply shut down.

Lorenzo and Samuel guided him forward, but his legs felt like hundred-pound weights were attached to them. He held onto the two men for a moment, and then asked his family to let go of him. When they did, he fell to his knees before Catalina's casket.

"Te amo," he whispered. *"Mi vida."*

He kissed the cold, polished wood. Then laid his head on the coffin. He spread out his arms. And then, unconsciously, his hands moved over the smooth surface, as if wanting to caress the woman who lay inside.

Eventually, his gaze shifted to the small, white casket. Slowly, he raised his head and sat back on his heels. Hand shaking, he reached inside his jacket and pulled out a small, stuffed lamb. Blankly, he stared at the last gift he had bought his baby girl. And then he placed the white lamb on his daughter's casket.

Unable even to mouth the word *goodbye*, he hid his eyes behind his hand, wondering if anyone, anywhere in the world felt as numb and angry and guilty as he felt right now.

8

Rajiv

Rajiv stared out the window of Javier's battered gray Citroën. They were supposed to have taken Andrés's Mercedes, but for whatever reason, the man decided he didn't want to drive his car.

Rajiv's lab mates talked and laughed around him, but it was as if he were invisible. Words and laughter floated over him, but did not include him. Unable to participate in the jokes or conversation, he turned his attention inward, back to the discourse he had started in his head.

Only eight days after having left India, he was seriously beginning to doubt whether he had made the right decision in coming to Spain. He had enraged his father, disappointed his mother, compromised his God, and made himself miserable in the process.

In hindsight, he should have listened to the keys.

"Rajiv, please. Don't upset your father tonight."

He should have known to keep quiet. His father had arrived at the apartment that night violently twirling his keys. The warning was clear.

Do not confront him.

"I have struggled for thirty years to give you and your brother a good education, the education that was denied to me. And for what? So that you can use it to defy me?"

Appa's words still stung. Rajiv knew all too well the sacrifices his father had made for his family.

"I vowed that my two sons would never have to struggle to get the education I was denied. And the only thing I have ever asked, the only thing I've ever expected in return—"

"Is absolute loyalty and total control of our lives."

Rajiv still wondered how he had dared speak those words that for so long had been safely guarded in his heart.

His father's reaction pained him still.

"You will not humiliate me in front of our community. You will take up the position in Dr. Gobi's lab and get married, or you will no longer be my son."

"Fine! Then I'm no longer your son!"

Rajiv's belligerence was now tempered with remorse.

His heart thumped as he remembered the last encounter with his father before catching the train to Mumbai. He had gone to the bank to change his last 20,000 rupees into euros. There were strict regulations on foreign money exchange, but he thought that with a foreign letter of employment and a valid travel visa, he would be able to convince the bank clerk to make an exception to the rule of no rupees to foreign money and exchange his 20,000 rupees. After all, he was a bright young scientist, educated, honest. He needed those euros to start a life in Spain as a serious professional.

Neither the bank clerk who attended him nor the manager who was called for assistance thought as he did and he left the bank with the same 20,000 rupees untouched in his account.

Then he spent the rest of the afternoon ranting to his brother, not knowing that his father was in his bedroom, overhearing every word.

Two hours later, Appa returned with 300 euros bought, according to what his brother later told him, from a Gujarati who did business in Europe, but made more money in India converting rupees to foreign currency to sell on his own personal black market.

Appa never asked for the 20,000 rupees to pay for the costly exchange. And as hard as Rajiv tried to convince his father to accept the rupees through the persuasion of his brother, the money remained in Rajiv's bank account. Appa refused to take the money as stubbornly as he refused to speak to his second son.

A lump formed in Rajiv's throat.

I may no longer be your son. Rajiv stared out the window of Javier's car. *But you will always be my father.*

Rajiv's stomach churned. The vein in his temple pulsed. His chest felt like an open wound doused in acid. It was three o'clock in the afternoon, well past his accustomed lunch hour.

He just wanted to get something to eat, and then go back to the lab. But, his lab mates wanted a drink first.

What choice did he have but to follow along?

It wasn't his car. It wasn't his country.

His leg cramped. Painfully, he shifted his weight to the other side. Normally, he would have done what he had been doing every afternoon for the past seven days. He would have taken a bus to the center of the city, picked up a potato and egg sandwich at the bar beside his flat, and flopped on his bed for a twenty-minute nap.

But riots had broken out in the city. Bus service was sporadic. The only way to get around was to rely on other people. Which today meant riding with his lab mates crammed into a miniature car.

A bead of sweat broke out on his temple.

He swiped at it and sighed.

The air inside the car was close, stifling. Recent rains had drenched the city of Seville in heavy moisture, and the rank smell of river water rode on a faint breeze that did little to alleviate the muggy heat of early spring.

Andrés cranked up the AC. But the blast of air that came from the console was hot.

"*¡Joder!* When are you going to get the air fixed, Javier?" For whatever reason, Andrés had switched to English.

"Probably never," Javier said, also in English.

"This car is a piece of shit," said Josemaría from the back seat, a half-smoked Fortuna hanging loosely between his lips.

"What do you want from me?" said Javier with a sigh. "I'm just a poor graduate student."

"*Ser estudiante es vivir en miseria,*" said Maricarmen, seated beside Josemaría. *¿Verdad,* Rajiv?"

The one person who addressed him directly chose to do so in Spanish. *Why?* Rajiv frowned.

"Sorry," he said, looking back at Maricarmen, "I don't understand."

"Forget it." Maricarmen shifted slightly. "It wasn't important."

Smiling to mask his frustration, Rajiv stared back out the window as they crossed the Triana bridge.

They were an interesting bunch, his colleagues. They laughed and joked a lot more than his friends back home. All of them spoke to him in adequate English, though made it clear that he needed to learn Spanish.

It was hard to include someone who didn't understand the humor in their jokes.

But no matter. Rajiv was determined not to be defeated.

They crossed over the bridge onto the west bank of the Guadalquivir, where traffic flowed smoothly toward the Plaza del Altozano. No bulls sitting in the middle of the road. No bicycles. How ironic to think he actually missed the obstacles he once cursed.

"Rajiv, this is the Triana district," said Javier, looking over his shoulder. "It's the old Gypsy quarter."

"*¡Cuidado!*" Maricarmen shouted, directing Javier's attention back to the road.

"*¡Coño!*" Javier slammed his foot on the brake to avoid hitting the white Renault in front of him.

The driver ahead had stopped in the middle of the road and gotten out of his car, leaving the door open, ignition running.

"What the hell?" Josemaría leaned out the window and shouted at the driver. "*¡Hombre, coño! ¡Quítate del medio!* Get out of the middle of the road!"

A short, dark-skinned man with greased-back graying hair acknowledged Josemaría with a yellow smile as he raised his palm and motioned for Josemaría to be patient.

A dog, ribs showing through patchy fur, one leg lifted under its belly, limped around the Renault.

"Must be a member of the Street Dog Relief Society," said Josemaría with a grin.

The man scooped the dog off the ground, then shuffled toward the side of the road with the mangy animal in his arms, stroking its matted fur with a sun-weathered hand.

"*Por favor.*" Andrés sank his head against the headrest.

Josemaría laughed and reached over to slap Andrés on the shoulder. "Take it easy, *hombre.*"

Andrés shrugged off Josemaría's hand.

Gently, the man in the road placed the animal away from the traffic, looked at it a few moments, and then strolled back to his car. He thanked his fellow motorists for their patience with a wave of his hand.

"Only a Gypsy would block traffic to save a half-dead dog," Andrés said. His voice was low and carefully controlled.

Rajiv wondered why.

"Don't worry about it." Javier readjusted the clutch. "We'll be out of here in no time."

The engine sputtered and then died.

"Or, maybe not!"

"Oh no." Rajiv groaned. His stomach hurt with each wave that rumbled through it.

"Don't worry, Rajiv. All this baby needs is a little loving, and she'll start like a charm." Javier kissed the steering wheel with mock affection, sending Josemaría into a fit of laughter. Stepping on the clutch, he cranked the key in the ignition. The engine turned over. "She's no Ferrari, but I love my baby!"

"Cut the crap, Javier, and just drive." Andrés mopped the sweat off his brow. "I need a drink." A silver medallion hanging from a clip around his belt clinked against the door as he shifted position.

"Take it easy, brother, I'll get you there." Javier steered his car into the underground parking lot below El Faro de Triana, a yellow brick tapas bar and restaurant overlooking the Guadalquivir River.

The car shuddered to a final stop.

"*¡Puta madre!*" Andrés gripped the dash.

"Hey, Rajiv," said Javier, looking through the rearview mirror. "Stick with Andrés and you'll learn all the bad words in our fine language."

"Shut up." Andrés's irritation provoked a wave of laughter from his colleagues.

Rajiv smiled to be polite, and then painfully unfolded his body from the car, stretching his cramped legs in relief.

He pulled up his poorly tailored trousers, their hand-stitched hems sagging over a pair of black leather boots.

Suddenly self-conscious, he stole a glance at his lab mates, neatly dressed in designer pants and colorful cotton shirts. He wore a white button-down made of cheap but durable synthetic material.

He was painfully aware that his style of dress had gone out of fashion in Europe ten years before. But there would be no extra money to buy new clothes. His tailor back in India took the last of his meager savings in exchange for two pairs of hand-stitched trousers and five dress shirts.

He had thought he was ready to take on the world.

He had no idea then that the world had already left him behind.

Along with his colleagues, he entered El Faro de Triana, a stand-up bar with gleaming surfaces and airy, open spaces.

The room had a salty smell, the air pungent with the odor of fermenting fruit. Blue and white ceramic tiles lined the walls and large windows opened over the river. Rows of crystal glasses hanging from wooden shelves lined the polished bar.

Rajiv followed the others to a table near the window while Javier ordered their drinks at the bar. Four glasses of Manzanilla and one tonic with lime. *Good.* Javier had remembered to order his tonic. He really did not want to explain, yet again, why he didn't drink alcohol. Only those who have lived in Gujarat, or some other dry state driven by religious fanatics, could possibly understand the politics that ruled his current choices.

"¡Salud!" Andrés raised his glass in a toast.

Rajiv picked up his glass as he watched and imitated the others.

The keen art of observation and imitation were essential for his survival outside of all that was once familiar.

As he toasted, Rajiv studied his lab mates.

For the most part, they were a fun group. Except for Andrés, they laughed a lot. Josemaría was telling yet another joke, lost on Rajiv, and Maricarmen was flirting with Javier, who flirted back.

Andrés stood in front of the window, his back turned. Silent. He was a dark, enigmatic man.

A young girl carrying a large wicker basket entered the bar. She hesitated, and then approached them with confidence.

Rajiv observed the girl with interest. She was a thin waif, dark-skinned. Her unwashed hair hung in dull strands around her face, drawing attention to her large, empty eyes.

She reminded him of the child beggars in India. She was dressed in a ragged skirt that tumbled to her ankles in a vibrant display of color. Around her neck the girl wore several strands of brightly painted beads. On her feet she had on a pair of torn sandals, brushed with the dust of the street.

She stopped in front of Javier and took a red rose from the basket in her hand. She offered it to him, but he brushed her away.

"Para la señorita," she insisted.

When Javier ignored her, she moved on to Andrés.

"Lárgate," Andrés said harshly. "Go on, get out of here."

Rajiv dug a few coins from his pocket and offered them to the girl.

"Go," he said. "Get yourself something to eat."

The girl backed away, her eyes wide. She shook her head.

"De ti, no," she said, her voice small and shaken. *"Eres un gitano."*

She shot the rest of the group a proud, menacing look before turning and strutting away.

"What did she say?" Rajiv's eyes followed the girl out the door as he called on his colleagues for translation.

"She called you a Gypsy," said Maricarmen, an uneasy hesitancy in her voice.

"What's that supposed to mean?"

"It means you're going to confuse people, my friend!" offered Josemaría, stifling a laugh.

Rajiv reached for his glass and gulped down another swallow of tonic. He kept his eyes on the table. When he finally looked up, he saw Andrés staring at him.

A deep furrow creased his lab mate's brow. It was as if Andrés was seeing him for the first time. And not liking what he saw.

"What? What is it?" Rajiv said.

He had the distinct impression that Andrés didn't like him.

Andrés squinted, and then dragged on his cigarette.

"You do look like one of them," Andrés said. Words mixed with smoke as he exhaled.

"One of whom?" Rajiv asked, annoyed that he had to.

"The Gypsies." Andrés snubbed out the cigarette, pursed his lips, and looked away.

"And?" Rajiv called his attention back. "Do you have a problem with that?"

"Depends." Andrés raised his eyes and locked them on Rajiv.

"On?" Rajiv wanted to say more, but chose not to.

"On whether you choose to identify with them, or with us."

Rajiv shook his head.

"Incredible. People will always find the opportunity to draw lines over differences rather than unite over similarities."

"Just ignore him, Rajiv," Javier said. He stepped in between the two and asked the bartender to turn on the TV. Then he ordered another round. "It's the only way to stay sane around our friend." Javier slapped Rajiv's shoulder and handed him a glass of tonic.

Rajiv accepted Javier's peace offering. He had seen enough fanatics in his time to know when to keep quiet. Just one more trial. One of many more to come. He swallowed more tonic. No one ever said a journey that begins with so many miserable people was going to be easy or problem-free.

9

Andrés

"Buenas tardes, I'm Susana Soltero, reporting to you live from La Iglesia del Buen Pastor in Tres Mil Viviendas where the Meléndez/Vargas families are holding a memorial service for Catalina Meléndez, the young mother whose life is being remembered today in Gypsy churches throughout the country."

Andrés looked up at the plasma screen behind the bar. Susana Soltero was one of the city's most respected field reporters for Canal Sur News.

"The city of Seville grieves today with Diego Antonio Vargas as he remembers his wife and child in a special service being held at the church where Diego and Catalina were married. The mood is somber but reverent as family, friends, neighbors, and sympathetic observers mourn the loss of Diego's young wife. With us now is Don José Miguel Vargas, Diego's father."

The camera swerved to a distinguished-looking man dressed in formal clothing.

"Don Josemi," the reporter said. "The entire city grieves with you today. What would you like to say to them, and to the Spaniard who allegedly was the cause of your family's pain?"

Andrés stiffened, his hand glued to the glass.

Don Josemi shifted a tasseled walking stick to his other hand.

"We are all trying to understand this tragedy," Don Josemi said, "even though right now understanding is difficult. My son will never return to the man he once was. But, with time, he will be stronger."

Slowly, Andrés raised the glass to his lips, drained it. Sitting there, listening to a man capable of responding to personal tragedy with nobility rather than rage was agonizing for him.

"You have spoken out against the violence that occurred after your daughter-in-law's death," the reporter said. "As the family patriarch, how are you now advising your loved ones?"

"Every member of the family under my authority has been told not to seek revenge or harm another person. And all those who were involved in the rioting will respond for their actions. Tomorrow, all three of my sons, and my nephews, will turn themselves over to the authorities. We seek justice, but not revenge."

"*Joder,*" Javier said. "The man's incredible."

"The morning paper called him Gandhi," Maricarmen said.

Andrés lowered his empty glass to the table. Don Josemi's dignity tortured him. Why couldn't the man just be violently angry? That would be a normal reaction, especially for a Gypsy.

"The Gypsies don't want justice," Andrés said, feeling like he had to say something that sounded right. "They want revenge. Some innocent Spaniard is going to get whacked." He threw a few bills onto the table. "I'm out of here."

His lab mates were too engrossed in the news to say goodbye.

"Many have commented on your quiet strength in this time of trial for your family," continued the reporter. "Where does that strength come from, Don Josemi?"

"Any strength I have comes not from me," Don Josemi said. "But from my faith in a loving, merciful God."

Sadistic saint. Andrés cursed Don José Miguel Vargas as he staggered onto the street.

He fell back against the wall, his heart beating wildly. While he had been able to feign indifference while surrounded by his colleagues, he was far from in control of his emotions.

His phone rang. He loosened his collar, which suddenly felt too tight, and answered the call. Adela was on the line.

"*¿Qué pasa, mi cielo?*" he said, successfully forcing the tension from his voice.

"When are you coming home?" Her voice sounded lost.

"Soon," he said, flagging down a taxi.

"Two beats of a heart?" She recited the phrase he had taught her.

"Two beats of a heart," he said. "I promise."

He pocketed the phone and jumped into an approaching taxi.

When he reached the apartment building, he threw open the door to the lobby and sprinted for the elevator.

The doorman marked the eleventh floor and the elevator glided up to his father's penthouse apartment.

"Andrés?" His sister's small voice called out when he entered. "Is that you?"

"Sí, mi cielo." He walked into Adela's room. *"Soy yo."*

The girl smiled and took his hand as he sat next to her on the bed.

"Are you sick?" she said. "Your eyes are all red."

He turned away from her.

And then came back with a quick cover.

"You mean like a monster?" He drew close to her face and made clawing movements with his hands.

Adela giggled and nodded her head.

"And your nose looks like it has a cold," she said, touching the outside of his nose.

Andrés cringed. And then gently removed her hand.

"Forget about me. What are you doing in bed?"

"I don't feel well."

"I see."

He moved his hand to her forehead.

"Oh yes, you feel terribly warm."

Her skin was smooth and cool.

"Guess I can't go to school tomorrow," she said.

"I guess not."

Andrés lowered his eyes and sighed.

"Is Carlitos bothering you again?" He brushed her hair back behind her ears.

She nodded, her eyes large and sad.

"That's because you haven't evaporated his words with your magic stone."

"My what?" Adela sat up in bed.

"Wait here." Andrés rose from the bed and headed for his room.

When he came back, he placed a smooth turquoise stone in her hand.

She looked up at him, her eyes bright.

"This stone has magic powers," he said, sitting next to her. "It can wipe away any painful words faster than you can blink your eyes."

Adela blinked. Then she giggled. The corners of her nose crinkled as she smiled.

"Keep this stone in the pocket of your school uniform, and the next time Carlitos says something ugly to you, reach into your pocket. Slowly—you can't let him know you're reaching—and say to yourself, because if he hears you, the magic will be broken, 'I'm a beautiful girl and your words don't hurt me.' Those are the magic words. And while you're saying the magic words, rub the stone between your fingers, like this . . ."

He took the stone from her hand and held it against his thumb, passing his forefinger over the glassy surface.

"The warmth from your finger will heat up the stone and release the magic. But never show Carlitos the stone. If he knows you have it, he'll want it, and the magic will be gone."

Adela looked up at the ceiling and let out an amused laugh.

"What, you don't believe me?"

She shook her head.

"Go ahead, try it." Andrés placed the stone in her hand.

Adela rubbed the stone vigorously between the palms of her hands, as if she were preparing to throw a die onto a gaming table.

"No, no, no."

Andrés held her hands still, and then lowered them to her lap.

"You can't let anyone know you have the stone. It's your secret weapon. You have to rub it very gently. And, it has to stay in your pocket." He brought her hand to the pocket of her nightgown and helped her release the stone.

"Now go on, touch the stone like I showed you. Then say the magic words."

"I am a—"

"*Shhh.*" Andrés lifted his finger to his lips. "Remember, you can't say the words out loud."

Adela's eyes opened wider.

"I am a beautiful girl," she mouthed, her hand moving slowly inside her pocket.

"And your words don't hurt me," he whispered.

"And your words don't hurt me," she repeated, silently, forming the words with her mouth.

Andrés nodded. "Good."

He pulled her to his chest and kissed her hair. He prayed that she would remember those words the next time Carlitos, or their father, decided to take out his frustrations on her.

Why was it that family was so often the enemy?

10

Diego

Diego sat at the edge of the sofa, wedged against the armrest by his older brother, Juan José. Every inch of floor space, the sofa, and every chair was occupied by family, with the unspoken but obvious intention of surrounding him with a protective wall of unconditional love and support. Everybody was physically and emotionally exhausted. But no one could sleep. They were all on silent vigil, making sure he felt safe.

Diego hunkered down further into the sofa. He was in a deep, dark place. Wearing Catalina's embroidered shawl around his neck, he sat unmoving, his expression blank. He felt numb, frozen into pain. It was as if his heart had stopped beating. For a moment, he wished it had.

Why was he alive when the woman he loved was dead?

Twisting away from his brother, Diego yanked the pillow out from under his head and crushed it over his face. Maybe if he pressed harder . . . and harder. He could suffocate his life and live as a ghost with Catalina.

His breath heated the pillow. Rapid short breaths that would be easy to extinguish . . .

"Diego, are you all right?" His little sister, Elena, pulled at his sleeve.

He eased up on the pillow, his heartbeat now wild and erratic. Breathing heavily, he sat still on the sofa.

"Diego?" Elena pulled harder on his sleeve.

"What?"

He was only half-aware of his sister standing beside him. His mind was still trapped in the horror of a wish he had not fully let go of yet.

"*Tranquilízate, hijo.*" His mother came over and sat on the armrest. Her fingers trembled as she brushed them through his hair.

A lump formed in his throat. His hands tightened on the pillow he now clutched in his lap. Water formed in his eyes.

"*Hijo . . .*" His mother knelt, rested her head on his lap. "I love you," she said, her voice strained.

Amara, Joaquín's cousin, crouched beside his mother.

"You'll get through this," she said. "I promise."

Diego shook his head, unable to speak.

"Listen to me," Amara said. "You're going to be all right."

Diego stared at her. "Tell me how that is even possible."

"You're strong, Diego."

"Way stronger than me," Elena added.

"*Silencio.*" His father silenced the women, and then rose slowly from his chair. "Our family has suffered a terrible loss. But we will not let the Enemy rob our Diego of anything more." He took his wife's hand and raised her from the floor. Doña Magdalena stood beside him.

Diego knew that right now his mother could only see a few feet in front of her. He was glad for that. If she could see any further, she would not have the strength to start the journey that lay ahead.

"We must now unite as a family," his father said. "Diego must never feel alone. Or unprotected."

He turned to Diego and said, "Come here, son."

Don Josemi extended his hand. And then he asked the family to enclose Diego in a circle of prayer. He was taking back his family.

"Though we are grieving, confused and hurt," his father said, "we must ask God to honor our pain and surprise us with joy that can only come from Him."

Diego stiffened. Any joy he had could *never* come from Him. Even though his father would try, with every breath he had, to pray Diego back from the edge of hopelessness and despair, Diego knew those prayers would not be answered.

He was not going to find his peace in a God that made no sense.

In a God that wasn't as all-powerful as his father claimed.

While his father and uncles prayed over him, begging God to help him, to heal him, to prevent the Accuser from whispering lies of guilt into his hurting heart, Diego remained rigid.

His brothers and sisters embraced him. The women wept. The children squirmed. But Diego was frozen silent.

Until his father said, "I'm here for you, son. For whatever you need."

A single tear rolled from Diego's eye.

Abuela, Diego's grandmother, broke away from the circle and waddled into the kitchen. When she came back into the living room, she was carrying a basin of water, a bottle of *agua de azahar*, a washcloth, and a towel. She stood still for a moment, studying the scene. Her long gray hair, twisted into two thick braids tucked into the waistband of her skirt, rose and fell over her chest. She took in one painfully short, ragged breath. And then she pushed her way through the huddle, shoved off the obstacle of arms, and grabbed Diego from his family.

"You come with me." Abuela led him back to the sofa.

She pushed him down and then sat beside him, the basin perched precariously on her lap.

His mother went to steady it, but his father held her back.

"*Déjala*," his father said. Let her be.

"Why my son cry?" Abuela's voice was thin and unsteady, cracked with age. "No more crying." She dipped the washcloth in the basin and then splashed it with orange water. "Mama is here."

Abuela, I'm not your son, Diego thought but didn't say. *I'm your grandson.* But did it matter? Abuela wouldn't register the correction anyway. Dementia was a cruel, confusing disease.

Tenderly, Abuela wiped his brow. And that one small act, that one small gift of comfort, touched him deeply. It was like a speck of light on a dark, endless path—showing him where to walk.

11

Rajiv

At the bar across the street from the university, Rajiv gathered with his colleagues to watch the evening news. Like them, he was following the tragic story of Catalina Meléndez with interest. Not only because of what had happened to the young mother, but also because of how the boy's family was responding to the tragedy.

Javier had translated the headline on the morning edition of *ABC Sevilla: First there was Gandhi. And then there was Don Josemi Vargas.*

Rajiv watched as Don Josemi entered the police station. The man was silent, dignified. His son, Diego Vargas, walked with him—as well as a handful of other young men wearing jackets and dark glasses. Today the patriarch was handing over his family, in honor of his promise. Only eight days after his daughter-in-law's funeral, the man could already find the strength to do what was right.

The news went to the commercials and Rajiv mulled over what he had just seen. The reporters were relentless, trying to extract a story from someone else's pain. But Don Josemi didn't lose his composure. Nor did any of his sons. They answered the reporter's questions briefly, politely. Rajiv didn't understand any of what they were saying, but his colleagues were good about translating.

Supposedly, one of the sons, Samuel, said that if it weren't for his father, he and his brothers would have acted on their impulses at least a dozen times since the night Catalina died. But because their father had demanded peace, not one of them would act any further on their anger. Out of respect for their father, they would obey his instructions. Revenge would not be taken.

Hunh. Revenge on whom? Rajiv wondered. Vengeance must surely be difficult when there is no identifiable target.

But, having lived through several Hindu/Muslim riots, he understood the hysteria. Like many of his countrymen, Gypsies were considered a vengeful people. Supposedly, it was not uncommon for a posse to form whenever one of their own was threatened or wronged. Like in this case, Diego Vargas.

The media had quickly picked up on the allegation that a racist Spaniard had refused to drive Catalina Meléndez to the hospital. Diego Vargas was immediately labeled "the victim." At least that's what Rajiv's colleagues were saying. According to Javier, a small pocket of Gypsy hotheads—most not even related to the Meléndez/Vargas families—were now looking for a Spaniard to avenge the woman's death. But since the offending Spaniard could not be identified, any Spaniard would do.

Just like any Hindu caught in the middle of a Muslim riot could be the next murder victim. Or any Christian in the wrong place at the wrong time could be martyred. People could change countries, assimilate into foreign cultures, convert to a different faith. But human nature would never change. Man was irrational. Volatile. Reactive. Fortunately, there was always someone, in this case a father, willing to restore order to chaos.

Rajiv's thoughts drifted to his own father. He could relate to the respect the younger-generation Gypsies were giving to the patriarch. It was a value his culture had made sure he understood as well.

But when respect was not returned, and crossed over into control, he struggled with the concept.

"There's a matter of importance we need to discuss." Appa had been on a mission that night. *"I have come from speaking to Mr. Sundaram. He wants to—"*

"Sell his daughter." A disrespectul answer, yes. But he had told his father—several times—that he no longer wanted to discuss the subject of an arranged marriage.

He had stood firm. Which was good. But that didn't mean he felt right about this particular internal battle.

As obstinate as Appa was, however, Rajiv would not stop trying to communicate with him. Just yesterday, he had written his father a long letter, trying overly hard to explain his decision.

It was a good opportunity for advancement in his career, he had written. Fascinating work was being done here, in Seville. He would have a good future—once he published. And then he could offer a woman something better than what he had when he left India.

The woman he fell in love with, he had thought but did not add.

Nobody would know that secret desire; he barely acknowledged it even to himself. But some day, he would happily fall in love with the right woman.

"Rajiv, I ordered you a hamburger," Maricarmen said.

A potential candidate for the future Mrs. Kumaran?

Rajiv quickly discarded the possibility. He used to hate it when his mother imposed food on him. Why would he want that same torment from his wife?

"*Ah*, okay," he said. "You ordered my food."

"She does that sometimes," Javier said. He leaned toward Rajiv, pretending to be discreet. "They say it's part of her OCD."

"Shut up, Javier." Maricarmen removed the top bun from her sandwich, and then reached for a knife and fork.

While Javier and Josemaría laughed, Rajiv looked around the table. Everybody else had a hamburger, too.

He stared at the sandwich. A hamburger had meat, he knew. But how long could he remain a vegetarian? Then not to seem impolite—or odd—he resolved to try the foreign food.

He loaded the greasy patty with a thick glob of ketchup. It was the only way he could tolerate eating what he did not dare to taste.

Cautiously, he took a bite, and then put down the sandwich.

His mind revolted.

He swallowed the bite without chewing, praying that Appa would be eternally safe from the knowledge that his son was eating the holy flesh of a slaughtered cow.

His stomach cramped. The cow was sacred in his religion.

And that was one of the few traditions he had actually revered.

Silently, he rose from the table—plate in hand—and left the unfinished burger on the bar.

Some traditions were simply meant to be respected.

The door opened and Andrés sauntered in. The usually social always-ready-to-take-a-break-from-work chap had stayed behind while the others took off to watch the broadcast. Now he was looking like a man with an agenda.

"What's up, Andrés?" Rajiv said, "Something on your mind?"

Andrés frowned. Then, calling the waiter, he ordered himself a whisky on ice. He lit a cigarette. Then he turned and spoke to Rajiv.

"Have you done any work with RNA virus replication?" Andrés dragged, and then blew smoke into the air. His eyes narrowed behind the blue-gray haze that billowed around his face.

"I've published a few papers on RNA virus mutations," Rajiv said. "What do you need to know?"

Andrés knocked back a swallow of whisky.

The ice clinked when he set down the glass.

"I'm working with a fungal virus," Andrés said. "I'm trying to get the virus to infect the fungal cell, but I can't get it to replicate."

Andrés drew his finger down the glass, trailing a drop of moisture. "I need to know why."

Carefully, Rajiv considered his response. Andrés Aragón was still a mystery to him.

"Fungal viruses are considered unconventional, unstable," he said, keeping his tone low-key. "They lack an extracellular route of infection. That could cause potential attachment problems."

Andrés dragged on his cigarette. A crevice appeared between his eyes.

"What're you working on?" Rajiv said, now more than a little curious. RNA replication with fungal viruses was fascinating stuff.

"The impact of asymptomatic viruses on fungal pathogenesis," Andrés said.

"Interesting."

Rajiv mulled Andrés's project over in his head.

If Andrés were somehow able to identify the virus-encoded determinants responsible for altering fungal host phenotype, he would effectively be able to understand and modulate fungal pathogenesis. An intriguing concept. He leaned back in the chair.

"Tell me more about your project," he said.

Before Andrés could answer, Josemaría shouted across the bar.

"Pepe, turn up the TV."

"Buenas tardes," the reporter said. "I'm Lourdes Fagundo, reporting to you live from the Bucharest University Hospital in Romania."

Rajiv glanced up at the screen. An attractive woman held a Canal Sur microphone.

"I'm here with Dr. Andrés Aragón Navarro," the reporter said, "who has just come out of a grueling, ten-hour surgery to repair the heart of the young Romani girl, Sophie Beklea."

"Hey, Andrés," Pepe said. "They're interviewing your father."

Andrés remained silent, his eyes hard as they stared at the screen.

"Dr. Aragón," the reporter said. "Another successful surgery. What was it like in the operating room?" She turned from the camera and held the microphone up to the doctor's mouth. Her smile was now inappropriately beyond professional.

Rajiv would have paid for even half of what Dr. Aragón had.

"This one was touch and go," Dr. Aragón said, his voice loud and dramatic. As if it belonged on stage. "But I thank God and *Nuestra Madre Santísima* for their love and protection over this child."

"Amen! Hallelujah!" Javier said, clearly mocking the man.

"Cállate," Maricarmen said. Shut up.

Rajiv sat on the edge of the seat, his eyes shifting from Andrés to his celebrity father and then back to Andrés. The resemblance was uncanny. The older man could easily have passed for the younger if it hadn't been for the silver hair at the temples, the slightly larger girth.

He looked back at Andrés. Both he and his father were handsome men, with sharp, angular faces and chiseled features. But the confidence the older man projected made the younger man seem almost . . . insignificant.

"Cardioplegia is a revolutionary technique by which a patient's heart is stopped from beating for precisely the time it takes to perform complex cardiac surgeries, such as open heart." Lourdes Fagundo reported knowledgeably on the risks and challenges of cardioplegia, but Andrés had clearly tuned out her well-researched accolades. His eyes were closed, his balled fist clenched against his right ear.

"Tell us, doctor," the reporter said. "How is young Sophie doing?"

"Sophie is still in critical condition," Dr. Aragón said. "But she's stable. I ask you all for your prayers over this special little girl."

Andrés punched his fist into the table.

Again. And again. And again.

"Our prayers are certainly with young Sophie," the reporter said. "And with Dr. Aragón and his team, who will be traveling to Bulgaria next week to perform open heart surgery on a three-year-old Romani girl. Dr. Aragón's commitment to improving surgical techniques is certainly changing the way heart surgery is performed and his humanitarian work in marginalized communities has made a positive difference in the lives of hundreds of people."

Andrés stood abruptly and turned off the TV.

The screen faded into darkness.

"Hey, what gives?" Josemaría said. "Your father's a hero."

Rajiv noticed what probably no one else recognized. The momentary look of pride immediately suppressed by pain that flashed over Andrés's face.

"My father may be an excellent cardiologist," Andrés said. "One of Spain's finest."

A muscle tightened in his jaw.

"But he doesn't know a fucking thing about the human heart."

12

Diego

Diego leaned back against the hard wall of the holding cell. Every breath hurt. It felt like someone had ripped a hole in his chest with a broken bottle laced with acid, twisted it deeper as he bled, and then reached into the open cavity and seized his heart.

Five days had passed since he, along with his brothers and cousins, had been incarcerated. They were waiting for their preliminary hearing in a dingy jail cell in the prison outside the city.

The harsh jangle of keys alerted him to the jailer's approach. He stared at the cinder-block wall, ignoring the keys. He knew that one of those keys would open the cell, and that he and his family would be taken before the judge, found guilty of whatever crime was attached to inciting a riot, and then sentenced to a long jail term. It's what happened when you were a Gypsy on the wrong side of the law.

The guard thumbed through his keys.

Diego shot a glance at Samuel, but his brother had his eyes closed. The bump in his throat moved up and down several times as Samuel swallowed.

"You." The jailer pointed at Diego. "Come with me."

Diego rose to his feet. Samuel stood, too.

The jailer cuffed Diego's hands.

"The judge wants to see you," he said.

Diego nodded.

Samuel moved to follow, but the jailer stopped him.

"Not you," the guard said. "Sit down." He pushed Samuel back.

He probably would have spat, too, if he did not have to represent his uniform. With his lips set tight, Diego followed the jailer to the courtroom, prepared to hear his fate.

"All rise," the bailiff said.

A man dressed in a suit and tie, the court stenographer, Diego and his father rose to their feet. Besides them, the courtroom was empty.

Diego glanced over at his father. Don Josemi's eyes looked tired, but they projected strength. For his father, Diego stood a little taller.

The honorable judge Edna Cardona looked stern behind her half-frame reading glasses. Her lips were pressed together, deepening the wrinkles that drew down the corners of her mouth.

"When you and your family turned yourselves in," Judge Cardona said, not looking up from her paperwork, "I thought there would be more rioting." She tapped her pencil on the waxed surface of the bench. "I activated one hundred civil guardsmen." *Tap. Tap. Tap.* "There was not one incident. Not one fire. Not one single act of violence." The tapping stopped. Judge Cardona set down her pencil and looked up at Diego over the frame of her glasses.

"Look out the window," she said.

Diego turned and looked outside. He saw a throng of people, *gitanos* and *payos*, carrying placards, demonstrating for his release. The signs they held before them read "*Libera a* Diego Vargas" or "Free Diego and his family." His throat worked under his collar. When he glanced over at his father, he saw Don Josemi wipe his eyes.

Judge Cardona motioned for him to return to his seat and then asked the suited man to come forward.

"State your name for the court," the bailiff said.

"*Licenciado* Mauricio Ferrer," the man said, "representing Dr. Rubén Rosario, in absentia."

Diego's stomach clenched.

Dr. Rubén Rosario was the man whose arm had been burned on the night of the riots. He was still in the hospital, undergoing a series of skin grafts to repair the damage.

"Proceed." Judge Cardona handed the lawyer a piece of paper. "Read your client's statement aloud to the court."

"On behalf of my client," the lawyer said, "I hereby deliver to the court Dr. Rosario's wishes in the matter of the State vs. Diego Vargas."

He read, "It is my wish that Diego Vargas be exonerated of all charges placed against him. This young man, who expressed his anger with violence, did not act in accordance with the law, but I do not wish to hold any charges against him. The losses he has suffered are far greater than my own. My only request is that Diego extend the same forgiveness to the Spaniard who did not come to his wife's assistance. This will make all the wrong done that night be forgiven."

Diego slumped back into his chair. How could it be that the doctor, whose life Diego had irrevocably altered when he threw a firebomb into a parked car, refused to press charges?

Judge Cardona rose slowly from behind the bench. She did not blink. She did not move. Then finally, she spoke.

"Dr. Rosario's sentiment is reflective of that of our city," she said, looking directly at Diego. "You are free to go." She collected her papers and slipped them between the covers of a black leather portfolio. Then she turned to the guard and said, "Release him."

Without a backward glance, she turned and disappeared through the chamber door.

Case closed.

The two weeks after Diego's release were nothing more than a blur of sleepless nights, caffeine-fueled days, and a steady diet of nicotine instead of food. The doctor had freed him but left him chained. In exchange for that freedom, which extended to his brothers and cousins, the doctor had required that he offer the same forgiveness to the Spaniard who had not come to his wife's assistance. Diego couldn't do that.

And he was starting to feel the strain.

He flopped back against the wall of a nearby building. Lit a cigarette. He was supposed to be meeting Joaquín at the plaza. But all of a sudden it felt like bad idea. Something was churning inside of him, like a low-level fever. He was nervous. Angry. And feeling like he had to do something, anything, to remind himself that he was still alive. Out of the corner of his eye, he saw Joaquín approach.

"Punch me," he said, and then landed the first blow. If he was going to be in pain, he wanted the wound to be physical. And real.

His fist sunk into Joaquín's gut.

"What's wrong with you?" Joaquín gasped.

"You have to ask?"

Four weeks after Catalina's death, Diego felt like a zombie awakened from the dead. Confused. Disoriented. Murderous.

"My life has been ripped out from under me!" He attacked Joaquín again. For no other reason than that he was there.

Joaquín fought back, lobbing a solid right hook into Diego's left eye.

"Hit me again!" Diego shouted.

The physical pain was welcome. It gave him a reason to believe it hurt so much to simply breathe.

"Back off, *primo!*" Joaquín shoved him back.

Diego charged forward.

"You want to get angry?" Joaquín wrestled Diego to the ground. "Then get angry at the right person." He pinned Diego to the sidewalk. "I'm your friend, not your enemy."

Diego surrendered, his emotions and his energy spent.

Joaquín unpinned him.

"You want to feel good again?" Joaquín wiped the back of his hand over his mouth, swiping at the blood. "Then stop wallowing in your pain and do something about it." He rose to one knee, offered Diego his hand. "Find the man who left you stranded."

"How am I supposed to do that?"

"By hunting him down." Joaquín pulled Diego to his feet. "Through his black Mercedes."

Joaquín was right. Diego had to find the man who had stolen his life.

In honor of his father's wishes, he would not avenge Catalina's death. He would, however, prove right what Don Josemi always said. That some men are born thieves, raised into criminals by the random chance of birth, while other men are made into criminals through the power of choice.

He gazed out over the street—not of his *barrio*, but of one of the richest neighborhoods in Seville, Los Remedios. Dozens of citrus trees lined the immaculate sidewalk. A light breezed stirred, smelling of orange and night-blooming jasmine.

Diego flinched.

Catalina was dead. The whole world should be ugly and dark. Nothing should look so peaceful.

Or smell so sweet.

"Look over there." Joaquín pointed at a black Mercedes convertible parked in front of a towering high-rise.

Diego shot a nervous glance at his accomplice, who stalked the dark street like a panther ready to take its prey. Then he shifted his eyes to the targeted Mercedes.

"She's a beauty." Joaquín whistled softly.

Diego stared at the luxury vehicle.

Its value and beauty meant nothing to him. But the fact that the car was black, and a Mercedes, did.

Reaching for the blue and white pack of Ducados in his shirt pocket, he pulled out another cigarette. Black tobacco was a potent anesthetic. Fingers shaking, he stuck the crumpled cigarette in the corner of his mouth and lit the tip. Slowly, he inhaled the bitter narcotic, exhaling the acrid smoke into the dusty air, its harsh scent mixing with the musty odor of rain-drenched cement.

"Stay here." Joaquín pulled him against the building. "And keep your eyes open."

Joaquín slithered over to the car, popped open the hood with his switchblade, and then went for the fuse wires.

Easy money, Joaquín always said, stealing cars. Diego took a deep drag, tilted back his head, and blew smoke up into the air. Instant cash. He dragged again, and then flicked his half-smoked cigarette to the ground. Unlike his pumped-up accomplice, Diego found no joy in the money, no thrill in the hunt for the next vulnerable target. Stealing luxury vehicles was a morally repulsive activity—one he had consistently refused to take part in ever since Joaquín turned away from more honorable ways to make a living to become the *barrio*'s most talented thief.

For years Joaquín had tried to convince him that grand theft was more lucrative than training horses. Less work than street vending. Diego had always agreed that was true, but had firmly refused every request his friend made to get in on the action.

Until now.

Now he had a purpose and the motivation to become a criminal.

If he could find the Spaniard who had left them stranded through his black Mercedes, he could restore "order" to the universe. He could track down the man who had thrown his life into chaos and bring the coward to justice. He could make that man suffer. Pay the price for what he did. A wrong had been done, leading to irreversible loss. And that wrong must be made right. Punishment had to be meted out. The score evened. Restitution made. Only then would the moral order that had been violated be restored.

And all Diego needed to restore that order was what he would find in the glove compartment of the cars he was targeting: ownership papers that would lead him to an address, link a name to a face. And, ultimately, to a deep, unjustified loss.

"Date prisa." Diego scanned the street. "Hurry up."

He heard a muffled click as the central locking system disengaged the doors.

"¡Móntate!" Joaquín slid into the driver's seat. He pulled up his crippled leg and yelled for Diego to get in.

Diego sprang into the passenger side as Joaquín raised a steel hammer and smashed down on the steering lock, freeing the wheel. Then, with a simple connection of the right wires, Joaquín started the car. Whooping and hollering like a cowboy, he gunned the engine and sped away from the upscale neighborhood.

"Slow down, Joaquín."

Diego gripped the handle above his head while his eyes searched the dash.

The tilted Virgin wasn't there.

"Don't worry. Everything's cool." Joaquín zigzagged the wheel, like an adolescent showing off his driving skills in a borrowed car.

Diego glanced at Joaquín, and then turned away.

"Let's just get out of here," he said. "Stop fooling around."

"Take it easy, *bro.*" Joaquín straightened the wheel as he accelerated. "I've got your back."

Within the hour, Diego and Joaquín delivered the stolen Mercedes to El Tiburón, The Shark.

El Tiburón was one of the richest men in the *barrio*, but he did business in the rat-infested, lawless neighborhood of Las Vegas. Blocks of deteriorated apartment buildings loomed over piles of festering garbage. The skeletons of vehicles stolen for parts remained beside mounds of burnt ash.

By day, the *barrio* looked abandoned, uninhabited. By night, the roaches crawled out of the cracks in the walls—the drug addicts for their fix, the runners to provide it. Nobody from outside the *barrio*, not even the police, wanted to enter the neighborhood at night. The cops stayed away, unless somebody got shot, and sometimes they stayed away then, too.

Diego stepped around a pile of rotting clothing and followed Joaquín up to The Shark's unofficial "office."

Rafa León lived in a chalet in El Aljarafe, but he conducted business from the ruin of an abandoned building in Las Vegas. Outside the crumbling entrance he parked his car—a Lexus convertible. Inside the dilapidated building was a luxurious executive suite.

Built into a broken wall was a sophisticated audio-visual unit with a flat-screen TV, the latest home theater equipment, and a complicated sound system that would have been the envy of any serious musician. The floor was destroyed, but on top of the exposed cement there was a leather sofa, an intricately carved wooden desk.

It was across this desk that the business transaction was completed. Joaquín reported their latest acquisition. The Shark unrolled a wad of bills and paid them too little cash for someone else's hard-earned car.

Twenty-four hours later, that car would be in Morocco, repainted and resold. Joaquín would be on the lookout for another easy target. And Diego would be alternately agonizing over what he had done, and feeding into his obsession.

He knew the risks he was taking when he signed up for a life of crime. He had been a front-row witness to the consequences of that choice as Joaquín's friend. Once inside the underworld, it was difficult to get out. People got hurt. People died.

But Diego didn't care.

El Tiburón could hurt him. Maim him. Kill him if he wanted.

What did it matter? God had already blown a hole in his chest and left him hollow. He might as well open the target wide.

Maybe the next blow would leave him dead.

13

Andrés

Andrés had no idea how to get himself out of the dark place he was in. Thirty-one days had passed since the night he had gone from concerned older brother to closet criminal. And in those thirty-one days he had tried everything to help him forget. Alcohol. Sleeping pills. Painting escapist fantasies. None of it worked.

He was still an unhappy, tortured man.

A glass of whisky in one hand, his mobile phone in the other, he sat down on the bed and scrolled through his contacts, pausing only on the women. Gisela. *No*. She doesn't put out. Isabel. *Tampoco*. Too uptight. Lissette. Can't hold her liquor. Maricarmen. Still not talking to him. His thumb stopped moving when the bar landed on Rosa.

All thoughts of the other women evaporated. Rosa was the one he wanted to be with. She understood him. She listened. It was why he had fallen in love with her. She had believed in him when no one else could.

He hit the "option" button, and then "send message."

I miss you, he texted. *Please, call me.* He needed to talk to her. It was hard to keep dark secrets without deteriorating inside.

"Andrés!" His father took possession of the room.

Andrés stumbled off the bed.

Some of the whisky from his glass sloshed over onto his latest work of art—a painting he had begun two days ago and then left, favoring the bottle to the palette.

"What?" Andrés pocketed his phone.

"What the hell are you doing in here?" His father's voice was angry, stern. Unyielding. "It smells like a distillery."

"I was painting." Andrés hurried to remove the canvas from the easel. He placed it against the wall, painted side facing inward.

His father glared at the empty easel.

"It helps me relax," Andrés said, feeling like he had to.

"There's been a tragic shooting in El Vacie," his father said. "I'm going back to the hospital—"

"And that is relevant to you . . . how?"

El Vacie was a Gypsy ghetto. Gang violence. Murders. The famous Dr. Aragón didn't do emergency surgery.

"A boy was shot in the chest." His father stared over his gold-rimmed glasses. "Caught in the crossfire of a drug deal gone bad."

"So? What's that got to do with you? I thought you were going to Adela's school with Grandma."

Slowly, his father removed his glasses.

"What I do, or don't do, is none of your goddamn business." He looked coldly at Andrés. "And let me tell you something. If he survives, that boy's life is going to be much more miserable than yours or Adela's ever will be. You might want to think about that the next time you are tempted to feel sorry for yourself."

"Whatever." Andrés walked back to his bed.

His father turned to go, and then he stopped, the crease in his brow deepening as his gaze fell back on Andrés.

"How's the work on the thesis going? Are you almost finished?"

"No, not really." Andrés looked away.

"I don't have time for this!" His father set down the rich leather briefcase he had bought on his last business trip to Italy.

"What is that supposed to mean?"

A knot formed in the pit of Andrés's stomach.

"I'm having trouble with the last set of experiments."

"It's only a masters degree," his father said. "What the hell is taking you so long?"

Only the fact that I hate what I'm doing, Andrés thought but would not dare say. At least not now. He was on edge and his father volatile. A dangerous combination.

"When are you submitting your thesis?"

"I'll be finished by the end of next semester."

The lie seemed bigger once it was exposed. But maybe with Rajiv's help the lie could become the truth.

"Don't let me down." His father snatched his briefcase off the floor and then walked away.

Andrés shuddered under the power of his father's words.

Then he slammed the door and closeted himself in his room with the only two things that came close to therapy: an artist's palette and a bottle of Scotch.

It was in his room that Andrés first discovered the companionship of alcohol, learning from his mother the deceitful solace of the bottle. Growing up with a father who drove his two children as furiously and as mercilessly as he drove himself, drinking and painting became vital to holding on to his sanity.

Andrés downed another shot. Someday, when he finished his degree, what was now his therapy was going to become his life. He would go to Paris and finally study art.

It was a promise he had made his mother only days before she died.

He grabbed his keys off the dresser and went to get his car out of the garage. But when he got down to the underground parking, he opted for the scooter instead.

The Mercedes brought back bad memories.

Fifteen minutes later, Andrés was at the only place that offered him any sense of peace. The chapel of the Esperanza de Triana.

The chapel was home to the brotherhood of men who worshiped the Virgin called the "Hope of Triana." There were women, too. But they mostly were there to support the brothers. Not in a *machista* way, but in a way that brought softness to what would otherwise be a less functional, less organized male world.

He reached for the brass knob on the chapel door. Hesitated. And then withdrew his hand.

Would God even want him here? A fuck-up like him?

He took a deep breath, and then slowly returned his hand and opened the door. If God didn't want him here, He wouldn't want him anywhere. And right now, Andrés needed a place to feel safe.

He stepped over the portal and entered the sanctuary.

An old woman dressed in black shuffled up beside him, dipped her gnarled fingers into the basin filled with holy water, and then dragged them over her face in the sign of the cross.

Andrés did the same and then slipped into an empty pew.

He watched the woman in black genuflect before the altar, then hobble to the bank of votive candles set beside it. She lit one of the candles, dropping a coin into the offering box.

Andrés studied the old woman as she prayed. Her face glowed with the dancing light reflected from the flickering candles that hopeful parishioners had placed on the stand. She looked peaceful. As if she had found some sort of comfort at the altar.

For him, the sanctuary offered no sense of peace. The comfort he once found in the chapel did not reach that small spot at the bottom of his heart that refused to allow the rest of him to feel good.

He had killed someone. Not intentionally. But the woman was dead. It wasn't like he had committed a crime or anything. He hadn't broken any law.

Then why did he feel so fucking bad?

He watched the old woman cross herself, slip her rosary around her neck, kiss it, stand, and then waddle away. Her left ankle twisted outward. Her gait was slow. But the old woman smiled as she dragged her lame foot across the floor. She smiled because she could. She was at peace.

Andrés contemplated finding his own peace through prayer, but quickly gave up the thought. It wouldn't work. Every time he tried talking to God, he ended up in monologue with himself instead. And the lines he rehearsed would definitely not bring him peace.

But talking to Rosa might.

He snapped open his phone and glanced at the time. It was almost five-thirty p.m. Time for the women to gather upstairs. There were only two weeks left until Holy Week and lots of details to attend to. Silver candlesticks had to be polished. Tunics mended. Gold thread re-stitched to the Virgin's processional garments. The women worked every night, from five-thirty until eight p.m., to make sure the vestments were clean and in order for Good Friday.

Rosa was one of those women.

Andrés stood slowly. Debated for about two seconds whether he should march up those stairs or not, and then strode across the chapel. His relationship with Rosa was not where he wanted it to be yet, but she was coming around. At least she was talking to him now. And answering his texts. Soon, she'd take him back.

Climbing the stairs two at a time, he skidded on the landing, and then rapped on the door at the end of the hallway.

"Who's there?" called out Doña Inés, *la camarera.*

"It's me, Andrés."

"*Entra, hijo,*" said Doña Inés.

Andrés entered, nodded at the women. The clean, fresh smell of starch filled the room with the odor of women at their work.

"*Pasa, pasa,*" said Doña Inés. Her thick glasses searched out his voice by the door. When he approached her at the table, she pointed to the floor. "Would you please pick up that brush for me?"

"*Sí, como no.*" Andrés hurried over to find the toothbrush that had fallen to the floor. "*Toma.*" He placed the brush in her hand.

"*Gracias, mi'jo.*" She continued polishing the gold embroidery of the ceremonial robe spread out in front of her. The thread was made of fourteen-carat gold. The robe was velvet. The brotherhood dressed their Virgin in this robe only once a year, on Good Friday.

"The embroidery gets so dull after being in the treasury." Doña Inés rubbed her fingers lovingly over a freshly polished spot of gold, accidentally knocking over a bottle of bicarbonate.

Andrés picked up the bottle and placed it back on the table.

"What would I do without you, Andrés?" Doña Inés smiled as she polished the gold thread.

Andrés smiled too, and then looked around the room. Rosa was stitching loose threads back in place on an expansive piece of emerald velvet. Her expert fingers guided the threaded needle across the robe as she kept her eyes steady on her work.

He frowned and looked closer. Her forefinger was raw.

"Are you walking as a *costalero?*" said a young woman named Génesis. Steam hissed from her iron as she pressed out the wrinkles on a white frock.

"Not this year," Andrés said. He no longer had any interest in walking with the other brothers with the float of the Virgin on his back. A lot of things had changed since his mother died.

"As a penitent, then?"

His attention was drawn to another young woman working hard to remove spots of hardened wax from a long, white tunic. He had no idea who she was. Or why she cared if he was going to dress as a *nazareno,* one of the robed penitents who walked in the processions.

"No," Andrés said. "I'm not. Why?" he had to add.

"Just wondering." Her cheeks turned pink as she placed a piece of paper over a blotch of hardened wax, allowing the steam from the iron to lift it off the soiled material.

The tunic was left spotless, the air infused with the pasty smell of melted wax.

"*Señoritas, ya, por favor,*" Doña Inés said. "Concentrate on your work."

"It's hard to concentrate when Andrés walks in the room," Rosa said, subtly sarcastic.

Girls giggled around him, but Andrés kept on his poker face. Why did she have to hurt him?

"Can I talk to you?" he said.

"I'm busy," she said, not looking up from her work.

"*Ya. Ya.*" Doña Inés made a disapproving, clucking sound. Her filmy eyes searched in the direction of Rosa's voice. "Go," she said, her gaze well placed. "Talk to Andrés."

Rosa stiffened. And then followed him into the hallway. She was obedient that way.

Her lips formed into a tight, straight line.

"What do you want, Andrés?"

"To talk to you."

"About what? There's nothing left to say."

He floundered. Now that she was there, standing in front of him, all the words he wanted to say froze inside of him.

"I brought you something," he said instead.

He dug into his pocket and produced the silver thimble he had been carrying around for the last two weeks.

"Wear this," he said. "It'll protect your finger."

She looked up at him, flustered.

"Thank you," she said, her voice wavering slightly. Then she reached behind her for the door-knob. "I have to get back to work."

"Wait." He reached for her, but she had slipped away.

With her went his heart.

14

Diego

Ignoring the fact that he had found no tilted Virgin on the stolen Mercedes, Diego felt the need to check out the car's ex-owner. The statue could have fallen off. Or been removed. It didn't really matter. What mattered was that he investigate all possible leads.

He glanced at the address written on his clipboard, the address he had copied off the registration papers from the stolen Mercedes. He looked up at the high-rise that loomed before him, not far from where they had hot-wired the luxury car.

It was eight-thirty in the morning, a working day. The owner of the stolen vehicle, a Mr. Hostos Sotomayor, would most likely be at home, getting ready to go to the office. He probably would still not have noticed that he no longer had a car. Suspecting no foul play, Mr. Sotomayor would have no reason not to open his door, and once he did, Diego would know if Mr. Sotomayor was the man who had devastated his life.

Diego blew out a lungful of air, clipped the tape measure to his belt, and smoothed back his hair. Then he climbed the five steps to the front door of the building, pressed the button on the security monitor, and announced himself to the guard. The monitor crackled as the doorman requested his identity.

"Ernesto Ramos," Diego said, using the alias that had become his alter ego.

"Who you here to see?" the attendant asked.

"Señor Hostos Sotomayor." Diego modulated his voice to mask the fear. If he got caught in this risky charade, jail time was sure.

He was a Gypsy, posing as a handyman, approaching the owner of a stolen car very near the actual crime scene.

The Spanish police would quickly come to the right conclusion and he would be arrested for the criminal he was.

"What is your business with Mr. Sotomayor?" The doorman's voice broke over the wire.

Diego swallowed and looked down at his tan-colored work boots. He had never before worn a boot or shoe that wasn't black.

"I've come to take measurements for Señor Sotomayor's new kitchen cabinets," Diego said, still staring at his boots.

He had learned to lie so easily.

The door buzzed open and Diego stepped into the lobby of the luxury apartment complex. The walls were dressed in rich wood, inlaid with beveled glass and mirrors. The security attendant sat behind an ornate desk topped with marble.

"You have some ID?" the attendant said, looking at Diego suspiciously.

Diego presented a laminated card with his photo, assumed name, and the invented company Torres Contractors, SA.

"Work orders." The doorman gave back the card as Diego handed him the clipboard with what looked like a convincing work order. It helped to have contacts in the underground.

The attendant crunched his brow, scrutinized the fictitious papers, then handed the clipboard back to Diego.

"*Está bien,*" he said. "You can go up."

Diego nodded, strolled to the elevator, stepped in, and then blew out a sigh of relief. He hit the button for the eighth floor where Mr. Sotomayor lived, according to papers he was no longer in possession of. The elevator slid to a stop and Diego stepped out onto the marble tiles of the hallway. He followed the numbers down the corridor until he landed at apartment number 832 at the far end of the hallway. He hesitated, and then knocked on the door.

A young boy answered almost immediately, eyes wide in silence.

"Is this . . ." Diego cleared his throat. "Is this the home of Mr. Sotomayor?" His heart pumped wildly.

The boy nodded.

"Would you please tell him that . . ." A bead of sweat formed on Diego's brow. "That I'm here to take measurements for the kitchen cabinets he commissioned." He swiped at the sweat, wiping it away with fingers equally wet.

"We didn't order any cabinets," the boy said, without a flicker of doubt.

"Is this apartment 832?" Diego looked down at his clipboard, feigning confusion.

"I am Señor Sotomayor." A tall, middle-aged man, hair brushed gray at the temples, appeared at the door. "Can I help you?"

Diego stood mute as he studied the man's face. Mr. Sotomayor was not the man he sought. He was at least twenty years too old.

"I'm sorry." Diego swallowed against the lump that blocked his throat. "I think I have the wrong apartment." He pretended to consult his clipboard. "I'm actually looking for a Mr. Omar Perez. Do you know where he lives?"

"There's no one in this building by that name." Mr. Sotomayor's face was kind. "Are you sure you have the right address?"

"*Mi amor . . .*" An attractive woman approached the door, one hand on her rounded stomach, the other reaching out to her son. "We'll be late for my doctor's appointment."

Diego's heart stopped for a beat, and then began to pound. He stared at Mr. Sotomayor's wife. She was rubbing the top of her belly.

Catalina used to do that, too.

"*Sí, sí, sí.*" The man put his arm around her shoulder. "Let me try to help this young man find the apartment he's looking for."

"No, that's okay." Diego fell backward, the breath knocked out of him. "I'll find it."

Mr. Sotomayor stared at Diego. A small crease appeared on his brow.

"I think I've seen you somewhere." Mr. Sotomayor scrutinized Diego's face. "But I can't place where."

A cold chill ran up Diego's spine. *He recognizes me from last night. He must have seen me standing outside the building.*

"Yes, I'm sure I've seen you," Mr. Sotomayor said again.

Diego tried to speak, but all that came out of his mouth was a choked gag.

"Aren't you the young man who brought food to the community hunger drive at the church last night?" Mr. Sotomayor's wife stepped closer to the door. "In Las Tres Mil Viviendas?"

"No, I . . ." Diego was thrown so far off guard he didn't know what to say. No one was supposed to know about the donation he had made with El Tiburón's money. "You must be thinking of someone else," he said, desperately trying to maintain his composure.

"Pastor Rivera says you . . . I mean the young man who brought in the donation," said Mr. Sotomayor's wife, "collected food and money from the community. It was a sizable donation." Her smile was warm, her voice kind. Making his lie all the more intolerable.

Lies! What you heard are the lies I told! Diego wanted to scream his confession. His donation was bought with money tainted by the pain of someone else's loss.

"God bless you, young man," Mr. Sotomayor said.

Diego recoiled. Why would God ever bless him after what he had done to these people? After what he would do to so many others.

He felt hot, asphyxiated. He grabbed at the collar of his shirt, pulling it away from his throat.

"Are you all right?" The woman reached out her hand.

Diego backed away.

"I'm sorry," he said.

And then he was gone, down the elevator and on the road to Southside. Mr. Sotomayor and his wife would never know what he was sorry about. Nor how horrible he felt about what he had just done to their lives.

15

Rajiv

Three months had passed since Rajiv landed in Seville. It was June now and he was seriously starting to wonder when he was going to do what he needed to do and finally assimilate into Spanish culture. He was still avoiding alcohol. Still surviving on frozen vegetables. And still communicating in English because he couldn't take the time from work to learn Spanish. His lab mates suggested he find a girlfriend, an assuredly foolproof method of acquiring the language. Would have taken care of his chronic loneliness, too. But he highly doubted that any woman would tolerate his almost habitual melancholy. He had sunk into the insufferable habit of yearning for his homeland.

He longed to hear the familiar sounds that used to define his days. Bicycle bells. The low bellow of cows that refused to budge from their place among the traffic. The horns of cycle rickshaws negotiating their way around crowded streets. He wanted to smell his mother's cooking, hear her voice again. Hers was the only voice he had heard before he left for Spain, though in that one voice there were actually two. Appa spoke to her the words he could not speak to his son. And she became his mouthpiece.

"*But, son,*" she had said, her eyes full of unanswered questions. "*If you go to Spain unmarried, you'll have no one to cook for you. What will you do for food?*"

Appa had gone out that afternoon and bought a kilo of lentils and assorted bags of spices. Mother packed them in his suitcase as her husband instructed.

A lump formed in Rajiv's throat. It hurt to think of home.

Brushing off the memory, he focused on something safer.

He had joined his lab mates for lunch. Which meant, of course, a round of drinks. He had ordered tonic. But, truthfully, he was getting tired of tonic.

He watched with fascination as the bartender poured four glasses of pale white wine out of a massive oak barrel behind the bar. The man served the wine, along with Rajiv's tonic, and then scribbled the tab on the wooden counter with a piece of white chalk.

Not really wanting to, Rajiv heard the sermon Appa had perfected with the help of Hindu seers: *"Alcohol is an evil substance, an immoral indulgence frowned upon by God and, wisely, banned by the state of Gujarat."*

Alcohol may have been banned in the state of Gujarat, but it had always looked so tempting in the programming beamed into India via British broadcast TV.

Rajiv looked away, focused on his glass. The scene before him brought back bittersweet memories.

He swirled the lemon round and round with a plastic stirrer as images of his past flashed over his mind. He saw the small shack across the street from the university where he and his friends gathered for tea every afternoon after organic chemistry class. He was usually the last to arrive, but Kumar always had a cup of cardamom-spiced tea waiting for him. Sometimes they talked. Sometimes they laughed. Sometimes they said nothing at all, understanding that the strength of friendship often resides in the silence.

And in a cup of tea.

Rajiv smiled as he remembered the ritual: one cup shared between two friends. The Spaniards would probably not understand this comforting ritual of friendship, where one would drink from the saucer, the other from the cup. He missed his friends. He missed the laughter. But most of all, he missed the comfort of belonging.

Javier left the group and approached the bar.

"We'll have four more," he said, returning the empty glasses to the bartender.

"Five," Rajiv said.

"Yes!" Josemaría pumped his fist. "Guru Gandhi is finally going to have some fun."

"This I have to see." Javier snapped his fingers at the barman. "Bring us another glass."

"You know what, forget it." Rajiv stood. He was not going to be the object of his lab mate's fun.

"Hey, where you going?" Maricarmen said.

"Home."

"No, you're not." Andrés stood beside Rajiv. "You wanted a glass of wine." He handed Rajiv a glass of Manzanilla. "So that's exactly what you're going to have." He stared first at Josemaría, and then at Javier. "And you two are going to shut your mouths. You got it?"

Stunned, Rajiv sat back down. And then, surrounded by his now more serious friends, he tasted his first sip of the famous Spanish sherry, Manzanilla.

The dry white wine initially shocked his system, but the next several swallows glided down his throat, creating a sensation of warmth and giddiness he had never experienced before. He began to relax, something he hadn't done since boarding the plane in Mumbai twelve long weeks and a lifetime ago.

Twenty-four hours after his initiation into the "inner circle" of the lab, Rajiv was still experiencing the effects of his first foray into Spanish wine. He squeezed his aching head as he opened the lid to the incubator. Like most initiates, he had not understood the wisdom of moderation until the time for moderation had both come and gone. He collected his plates from the incubator.

In retrospect, he had always considered himself a level-headed man, not prone to obsession or excesses. The only thing he might consider mildly obsessive was the driving force that pushed him to succeed in the lab. But that drive was not so much an obsession as it was a necessity. If he hoped for any kind of future in science outside of his country, he had to have the drive to find it.

He couldn't remember his last day off, or ever calling in sick. Idleness was a luxury he could ill afford. Which probably explained why he had been in the lab almost round the clock for the last two weeks—feeling miserable and now nursing a hangover.

It was Saturday evening and he was back in the lab, running on adrenaline rather than food and rest. He sat at the bench and opened the lid of the first plate, allowing himself the indulgence of one final thought before returning fully committed to his work.

How was it that for a man not prone to addictive behavior (outside of cigarettes), he could not stop thinking about how he, a once avid tea enthusiast, wanted nothing more than another taste of Spanish wine.

Maybe there was something to Appa's tedious lectures.

He could still hear them so clearly in his head: "*Even though alcohol and certain drugs can bring a man to a higher level of consciousness, that chemically induced higher consciousness is momentary and dangerous. After a few moments of chemical paradise, the mind crashes into chemical hell. Hours and days of mental agony follow.*"

How the bloody hell did Appa know that? Rajiv sighed, and then formed his own hypothesis.

Now that he had a few days perspective on his first experience with "chemically induced higher consciousness," he figured that the hours of physical and mental agony he had experienced were attributable to the error of having mixed fish with wine.

He had sampled a small piece of fried fish, and though it seemed to go down well, it must have upset the balance of acids in his stomach, thus causing a reverse reaction when combined with the wine. A useful theory, he thought. And while he would try not to mix fish with alcohol again, he would indulge in the smooth intoxication of Manzanilla wine. The wine had relaxed him, which was a welcome seduction. He felt only a small pang of guilt as he concluded his hypothesis. He knew better than anyone that a theory was no more than an abstract thought often used to justify a belief. The fish had nothing to do with the after-effects of his seduction.

Rajiv quickly pushed the abstraction of alcohol seduction from his mind and concentrated on what he knew in concrete, measurable terms: his work.

He felt a sense of relief, having returned to the lab. Dr. Matos's laboratory had become his sanctuary, the only place he felt confident, in control. It was time to get back to work, to focus his thoughts, to plan his experiments for the following week. He liked thinking about the intricacies of molecular genetics. When nothing else made any sense, there was comfort in the familiar.

Rajiv settled back into his work on the bench. The others wouldn't return to the lab until Monday morning, giving him precious time without any distractions. Saturday and Sunday were his most productive days.

He heard a key at the door. Then a voice shattered what had been welcome silence.

"Hey, Rajiv." Andrés entered the room, still wearing his dark glasses. His pants were stained with paint.

"Andrés."

Rajiv snatched the pipettor off the table and sucked buffer into the plastic tube. He kept his eyes focused on his work rather than on his lab mate, carefully monitoring the thoughts that wanted to spill out in words from his mouth. Even though Andrés had defended him, Rajiv was still not sure what to think of the man.

"What's up?" was all he finally said.

Andrés said even less. Silently, he cleared a spot on the cluttered workbench and hoisted himself up.

"Just came to check on an experiment I started." Andrés spoke coolly, but there was a note of tension in his voice.

Rajiv pressed his thumb down on the plunger of the pipettor and ejected fluid into a thin glass tube. Something was up.

Andrés never came in to check on his experiments.

"What're you working on?" Rajiv spoke slowly as he sucked liquid into the pipettor. He had not had another conversation with Andrés about his work since they were interrupted by the Canal Sur news broadcast. Carefully, he measured the liquid out into a tube and then put down the instrument. He rubbed his eyes.

"You look like hell, Rajiv."

"Is that a professional opinion?" Rajiv leaned back in his chair. "Tell me about your project," he said.

Andrés shuffled through a stack of papers on the bench.

"We're looking at new avenues for enhancing biological control potential." Andrés removed his dark glasses, pressed his fingers against his eyes, then squeezed his hands over his unshaven face.

There was a spot of white paint on his left cheek. A red one under his eye.

"Bad night?" Rajiv said.

Andrés looked up. His eyes were hard.

"Can I see the protocol?" Rajiv said, before Andrés could go into any details. Supposedly, Andrés painted when he was either drunk or mad.

Andrés stared at him oddly, and then pulled a black three-ring binder from his desk.

"It's the third one," he said, handing over the notes.

By the way he continued staring, Rajiv knew. Andrés had something other than science on his mind.

"Do you know anything about the Gypsy migration from India?" Andrés said.

Rajiv stiffened. "No, Andrés," he said curtly. "I don't."

"Well you should. It involves your people."

"My people?"

"The Gypsies. They migrated to Europe from India in the early fifteenth century."

"And that relates to me . . . how?" Rajiv exhaled a burst of pent-up air. The conversation now officially annoyed him.

"Forget it." Andrés snatched his glasses off the bench and put them on. "Just be careful with those people. They're all liars and cheats. They make their living robbing the *payo*." He pushed his glasses tighter against the bridge of his nose. "They're either drug runners, car thieves, whores, or pimps."

Rajiv shook his head. He was not going to respond to that rant.

"Let's talk science," he said quietly.

Andrés drew his brows together, and then motioned at the binder.

"This is the protocol I'm using. But I can't get the virus to infect."

Rajiv detected an unusual urgency in Andrés's voice. And then he understood. Andrés was so desperate for his help that he'd come in on a Saturday to get it. What he didn't understand was why.

He scanned the notes. And then it occurred to him. Maybe Andrés should try a different buffer.

"Try different temperature sets," Rajiv said. "Bacterial viruses require maltose for infection. Maybe you should look for a cofactor."

Andrés pulled over a swivel chair and plopped himself down, lifting his feet onto the workbench.

"Tell me something, Rajiv." Andrés's voice hovered between joviality and reproach. "Why are you so obsessed with all this?"

"With what, Andrés?" Rajiv fought to keep his voice low and steady.

"With work. And experiments. The lab. There is life outside this dreary place, you know."

"You wouldn't understand." Rajiv put a stained plate on the microscope and pretended to study it.

"No, I probably wouldn't." Andrés lowered his feet off the bench and stuck a toothpick between his teeth. "You think you can help me with my experiment?" The flippant tone to his voice clearly stated his indifference toward the work.

Rajiv did not look up.

"Depends," he said.

"Let me guess. On whether I'm willing to devote the time and effort to—"

"On whether you are willing and able to treat me as your equal."

Andrés frowned.

"Yeah, sure. Of course," he said.

"Good." Rajiv pulled off his lab coat. "Then let's go get a cup of coffee." He folded the flap over his messenger bag. "It's how I like to talk science."

Hopefully, he would be able to separate his enthusiasm for the science from his loathing of Andrés's personal philosophies. If he heard him say one more time that all Gypsies were violent criminals, he would probably strangle his lab mate. There were few things that bothered him more than blatant racism and all-inclusive stereotyping.

16

Diego

It was summer now. The fifth of June. A date that marked two significant events in Diego's life: the one-year anniversary of his wedding, and the three-month mark of life without his wife.

Emotionally, he was in a dark, unforgiving place. He had been robbed. Of happiness. Of direction. Purpose and meaning. Without Catalina to care for, to love, he was lost. And for the first time in his life, he felt an emotion he had never experienced before. Hatred. An overwhelming, devastating hatred toward the unidentified Spaniard who had caused his world to shatter.

Ten stolen Mercedes later, he had still not found the man.

But he would.

Because now he was a seasoned criminal.

"Toma, hijo." His mother handed him a cup of coffee.

He thanked her. And then went to the van to pull out the tarp.

It was eight o'clock Sunday morning. And just like every other morning, he was at the market, setting up the tarp and tables and displaying the merchandise his family had brought to sell. He had stopped training horses. Negative emotions, such as anger and impatience, had no place in the training arena. He knew that, even before his boss asked him to take some time off. A few weeks away became a few months. The shoes and skirts he offered for sale eventually replaced the lariat rope he once held so confidently in his hand. The work was exhausting, but he was grateful for it. Because at the market, he found the unconditional support of his family and the numbing distraction of routine.

He grabbed the metal poles from the van and, along with his brother Samuel, helped his father set up the first tarp. Mechanically, he twisted the poles together. Silently, he raised the tarp. Then he started on the second one. After both tarps were assembled, he hauled out bags of blouses, boots, shoes, and stockings from the van and displayed them on the tables. Then he unfolded a chair and sat behind the merchandise his family hoped would sell today.

"You look tired." His mother pushed back his hair, then sat beside him. "Are you sleeping well?"

"I'm sleeping."

"And are you eating?"

"I eat."

"Not at home you don't."

Diego took in a deep breath.

"I'm eating, Ma, okay? Don't worry about it."

"Don't worry about it? Diego, you're my son. How do you expect me not to worry?"

Diego stared straight ahead. Their neighbor had just sold a baby's christening gown. It had tiny pink and white flowers sewn onto the collar. He set his jaw firm and closed his eyes.

"Hijo . . ." His mother touched his arm.

Slowly, he opened his eyes.

"There's going to be a special service tonight, at our church. Maybe you—"

He stood to attend a customer. The transaction was smooth. Five euros for a pair of stockings. He handed his mother the money.

His mother added the five-euro bill to her money belt, and then continued to press her point.

"There're going to be guest musicians from Madrid. I know how much you love music. I think you'll enjoy it. . . ."

"Ten euros," he told a woman who asked the price of a blouse.

"Diego, are you listening to me?"

"Sí, Mama, I'm listening."

"Please, will you go with me tonight? It might help you . . . be more at peace."

Diego sighed. He could hear the desperation in his mother's voice. Her longing for him to feel whole again. And her despair made him feel even worse.

A nervous agitation came over him. His fingers trembled as he took twenty euros from the woman who had asked the price of the blouse. A tremor started deep inside as he gave the money to his mother. It grew to a violent quake as he waited for her to hand him the change.

His mother's eyes stretched wide as she handed him ten euros.

"Are you all right?" she said nervously.

"I'm fine," he said, turning away from her.

But he knew she knew he was far from fine. He was tired all day, yet at night, he couldn't sleep. He would lie awake for hours, feeling the torment of a darkness that no one could see but him. He had trouble concentrating. Even the simplest tasks, like choosing what shirt to wear or what merchandise to buy, seemed monumental decisions. He had become apathetic. Indifferent. He could not taste food, see beauty, or touch anything with pleasure. But still he told the world that he was fine.

When two o'clock arrived, he helped his father dismantle the tarps, pack up the unsold merchandise, and clean the lot. Then he opened the door to the van, flopped down on the seat, and closed his eyes. He did not open them again until his father parked along the curb in front of their apartment.

And then the routine continued. By three, he was staring at his lunch, leaving most of it untouched. By five, he was ready to hit the streets. Usually to hook up with Joaquín.

His family knew nothing about his criminal activities and understood little of his relationship with Joaquín. They objected to his going out. But neither their lectures nor their love ever stopped him.

He stood, ready to leave. But then the kitchen door squealed open. Manolito, a young boy from the neighborhood, charged into the room.

"Diego, I finally got it!" Manolito plunked his beat-up guitar case on the table. "I got the four-stroke *rasgueo*." He unsnapped the locks and pulled out his instrument. "Let me show you."

Don Josemi entered the room with Manolito's father, Pablito. They pulled out chairs and sat down at the table. Diego's little sister, Elena, soon followed, a dustpan and broom in her hand.

Diego managed to smile. Sweeping the floor worked for his little sister today. And every day someone pulled out a guitar.

"Vale." Diego nodded for Manolito to sit down.

The boy pulled out a chair and hooked his right foot on the rung. Then he placed his guitar on his thigh in the flamenco position.

Manolito had become Diego's unofficial student. He didn't know quite how that had happened, but assumed Don Josemi had something to do with it. Diego had learned to play the guitar from his father, who had learned from his father before him. Manolito's father had no musical talent. But somehow, Manolito had inherited a special gift for rhythm.

A few months ago, Pablito had bought Manolito a used guitar. Don Josemi then encouraged the boy to show it to Diego.

At first, Diego only pretended to be excited. But soon he found Manolito's passion contagious. And the more he helped Manolito learn what his father had taught him, the easier it became to find small moments of joy in what had become his new normal.

"Wait a minute." Diego stood and moved toward the boy. "Rotate your arm, like this." He repositioned Manolito's arm over the guitar. "It's like turning a key in a lock."

"Like this?" Manolito followed Diego's instruction, successfully modifying his rotation.

"*Sí.*" Diego adjusted Manolito's hand to better position it over the fret board. "That's it. Now play what you wanted to show me."

Manolito nailed the four-stroke *rasgueo*.

"Excellent!" Diego held up his hand and Manolito slapped him a high five. "Now let's see if you remember the arpeggio I taught you the other day."

Manolito correctly found the right chords.

"Good." Diego snapped his fingers and cocked his head, listening for any slip in rhythm. "Remember," he said. "In the second and third measures, you're going to use your middle and ring fingers on the same string to finish the arpeggio."

Manolito nodded.

"*Ya,* Manolito, stop for a moment." Diego took the guitar from the boy and pulled up a chair. "Your technique is good, your finger work excellent, and you have an intuitive sense of rhythm, but something is missing."

"What?" said Manolito, his eyes wide.

Diego positioned his hands on the guitar.

"Passion," he said, his fingers shifting as he found the first chord. "You're playing well, but without emotion."

He picked at the strings, eyes glued to the fret board.

"Every time you take up your guitar, Manolito, think about making love—"

"Ahem." His father coughed loudly into his hand, jerking his eyes toward Manolito.

Diego looked up at his father, and then saw Manolito's bright young face. Quickly, he said, "Think about all the people you love. See that love in your mind and play to it. Think of your guitar as . . ." He stopped talking and thought . . . *your lover's body, responding to your hands*. His fingers shivered, then stopped their restless movement, lying motionless over the strings.

"Are you okay?" Manolito said.

Diego blew out a heavy breath, eyes fixed on the guitar.

"Love is a powerful emotion, Manolito. Feel it, in the very depths of your soul." He returned his gaze to the boy. "Then you will be playing flamenco guitar."

Diego stood and handed Manolito his guitar.

"Me voy," he said, carefully masking the emotions that wanted to spill from his heart.

"Before you go . . ." A cautious hesitancy had edged out the former lightness in his father's voice. "Joaquín was looking for you."

Diego stiffened. "What did he say?"

"Wants you to meet him tonight." His father paused. "Says you know where to find him."

Diego turned his back to his father and an uncomfortable silence came between them. It happened every time their conversation turned to Joaquín.

"My friend." Pablito began to speak, then hesitated before continuing. "I'm an old man. Seen and done many things." He coughed, a harsh, sickly sound. "Will you listen to some advice from an old man with many regrets?"

Back still turned, Diego punched his arm to his side, fist clenched.

"Stay away from Joaquín." Another cough wracked his body, but Pablito continued. "He's not your friend."

What did Pablito know? Diego fell back onto the sofa and turned on the TV. Joaquín was a good friend.

Sort of.

At least he didn't keep nagging him about getting his life together. Or wreck his mood just when he was starting to feel better.

Why did Pablito have to go and say that?

He was having fun with Manolito.

Now, he was agitated. And alone. Unable to sleep.

"Diego." Joaquín rapped on the window. "Come outside. I need to talk to you."

Diego stared at the TV.

"I know you're in there." Joaquín peered through an opening in the black-and-white-checked curtain.

Was Joaquín's late-night visit God's way of proving a point?

Rap. Rap. Rap. Joaquín knocked harder on the window.

"Come on, Diego. I don't have all night."

His father always said that no good things happen after 12 p.m.

Diego rose from the couch and went outside. It was 2 a.m.

He lit a cigarette. "What is it?" he said.

"I need cash." Joaquín followed Diego down the stairs and out into the street. "I owe The Shark some money." He spoke fast, his speech accelerated. In rapid-fire sentences, he told Diego how he was a dead man if Diego didn't help him.

Diego took a drag. It felt like he was sucking up sparks of hot ash. A slow fire burned inside him. He was mad at his friend. The last time Joaquín owed El Tiburón money, and didn't pay it back in time, he acquired a permanent limp. El Tiburón worked like that.

It was the price too many paid when they got hooked on The Shark's expensive cocaine.

"Please, Diego, I need your help." Joaquín's eyes were black, the pupils dilated. How many lines had he snorted tonight?

Diego sighed. "Another car?" he said. Smoke from his cigarette cut into the early-morning air.

"No. I have a different plan."

Diego tossed the cigarette. And then he followed his friend out into the cold, dark night.

Joaquín's plan, when it was finally executed, came in the form of a Japanese car.

They had spent the last hour in a borrowed BMW, circling El Bar Fandango. Joaquín was quiet now. Not reeling out the mad, flowing monologue Diego had come to expect from him when on a mission. Instead of flapping his mouth, he used his eyes, searching the streets for his next victim.

He finally stopped circling when a red Toyota Corolla ended up both behind them and in front of El Bar Fandango.

Joaquín slammed on the brakes.

The BMW came to a sharp halt, skidded, and then there was a loud bang as the Corolla crashed into the rear of their car. With a lurch, they shot several feet forward across the road.

Before the BMW had even come to a stop, Joaquín was already out of the car, half-running, half-limping toward the other driver.

Then the shouting began.

The driver of the Corolla, a short, pudgy Spaniard with more hair on his face than on his head, was gesturing with his arms, accusing Joaquín of not knowing how to drive.

"I'll have your license revoked," the bald man screamed. "You bastards drive worse than women"

He glanced at Diego, who had come up beside Joaquín. Looking confused, the man was quiet for a moment. But he had found his theme, and promptly went with it.

"You two gay or something?" the Spaniard said.

Every muscle in Diego's body tensed. If you really want to infuriate a Gypsy man, and land yourself in a major fight, call him gay. There is no bigger insult.

It was the perfect incentive for Diego to let out his rage.

Diego sprang forward. His left fist landed in the man's face. His right dug the switchblade from his pocket. He snapped open the knife. Something so deep, so raw inside wanted to hurt this man.

In less than two seconds, the knife was at the man's throat.

"No, Diego!" Joaquín caught him in a choke-hold. "Drop the knife."

Diego fought back, but Joaquín had immobilized his arm.

"Let go of me, Joaquín." He felt like a madman about to take the plunge into insanity.

"You're ruining my plan." Joaquín hissed into his ear while tightening his hold on Diego's neck. "Back off!"

The door to the bar creaked open.

All three men looked around.

Four large Gypsy men stepped out and stood in the road. It was then that Diego realized. The accident had been set up.

"What's going on?" The apparent leader spoke directly to Joaquín.

"Just sorting out a little problem here," Joaquín said.

The four men stood with their arms crossed. Then the leader moved forward, his eyes on Joaquín.

"This bastard doesn't know how to drive," the Spaniard said, foolishly deciding to defend himself. "He braked in the middle of the road."

The lead thug spat out a wad of tobacco, then grabbed the *payo's* collar. "Get your papers," he said.

"Papers?" The Spaniard stared, petrified, into the Gypsy's eyes.

"Your insurance papers." The Gypsy was in the Spaniard's face, his grip tighter on the man's crumpled collar.

"I . . . I don't have any . . ." The Spaniard was struggling, but he knew he was trapped. It was clear he wasn't completely on the right side of the law.

The perfect target for extortion.

"Look, can we . . ." The *payo's* voice trembled as it trailed off.

"That BMW's worth twenty-three thousand euros," the Gypsy said.

The others from the bar lumbered forward, their approach perfectly timed.

The *payo* took one more look around. His face showed fear.

"I don't want any problems," he said.

"Give me your wallet." The Gypsy held out his hand.

The *payo* fished out his wallet.

The Gypsy took out a credit card and tossed the wallet to Joaquín. "You owe me one," he said. Then he turned toward the Spaniard.

"Take him to a cash machine."

After robbing the man at the nearest ATM, intimidating him into agreeing to repair the BMW, and forcing him to agree to a 5,000 euros "compensatory damage" settlement to be paid within thirty days, Diego and Joaquín drove back silently to the *barriada*.

It was 5 a.m. But Diego was as far from sleep as he would ever be. Over the last three months he had done bad things. *Felt* bad things. But he had never threatened a man. If Joaquín hadn't stopped him, he might easily have hurt the Spaniard.

That thought terrified him. But what frightened him even more was the knowledge that every moment he spent with Joaquín was one step deeper into the underworld of crime.

"How did you know the *payo* didn't have insurance?" Diego felt compelled to ask. If for no other reason than to understand the criminal mind.

"I didn't," Joaquín said. "Sometimes, you just get lucky."

17

Andrés

Andrés pulled over to the side of the road in front of his apartment complex. He cut the engine. The Mercedes purred to a stop. He sat still for a minute, rubbed his eyes. It was eight o'clock in the morning. He was half-asleep. But, he wanted to see Adela before she left for school. He'd been away from home for the past week, sleeping at the studio.

Avoiding his father.

He glanced over at the newspaper on the seat beside him.

"Dr. Aragón Triumphs in Medical Matters of the Heart" screamed the week-old headline.

A nerve pulsed behind Andrés's right temple. And then neurotically, he read again what he had already memorized.

Behind the door of operating room two, on the cardiac surgical wing of Hospital Universitario Virgen Macarena, Dr. Andrés Aragón Navarro leads a team of three surgeons, two anesthesiologists, and two nurses through a delicate surgery to repair the heart of a three-month-old Gypsy boy born with a deformed left ventricle. Soft, classical music plays in the background and a monitor beeps steadily. A TV screen mounted from the ceiling reveals a magnified view of pink, pulsating tissue. It's the heart of the child on the operating table.

Andrés stared out over the dash.

As hard as he tried, and he had tried for the better part of one week, he couldn't erase the image of the fragile infant lying unconscious on a cold steel table, his heart exposed.

Even more unfathomable was how the healing of that damaged heart was now in the hands of a man like his father.

One week of substance-sustained self-pity had left Andrés weak, his body clumsy, and his mind lethargic. He had spent the past seven days in seclusion, with his whisky and his palette, staining the studio black. But he couldn't stay away forever. Rajiv was waiting for him to start the experiment they had planned over coffee. And of course there was Adela. She had called him twice a day, her small voice sad. If it weren't for her, he'd be lost to his addiction.

If it weren't for her, he'd be his mother's son.

He dropped his head back against the seat, removed the keys. It pained him to think about his mother.

Antonia del Río had been a beautiful woman once. Slender, with patrician features. And when she was sober, a good mother to him and Adela. A practicing Catholic, it was she who had introduced him to the Church. And it was because of her he had met Rosa Sánchez.

It was a Friday night, the day he met her. Only two weeks before Holy Week. He was in the chapel, helping prepare for the Good Friday procession. Rosa was there too, polishing silver.

At 9 p.m. the work stopped and he followed his brothers up to the women's workroom, where the sisters had prepared a light supper. Rosa smiled at him when she handed him a cup of orange juice and a ham and cheese sandwich. His mother noticed and quickly arranged an introduction. Rosa was everything his mother wanted for her son. Beautiful. Faithful. A good Catholic. She had promised to save herself for him. And he respected that.

For two wonderful years, everyone believed his mother's dream would come true. That Rosa and he would someday be married.

But then, his mother died.

And he became an angry man.

All because, on the last day of her life, Antonia Del Río had a change of plan.

His mother was supposed to have been in Madrid that day. But an ETA terrorist threat on the AVE line grounded the train and sent her home. His father didn't know that the National Guard had decided to take ETA's threat seriously and had already invited his Gypsy whore into his bed.

When his mother returned home, she found them together. And then she drank, and she drank, and she drank—until she could drink no more. When the paramedics arrived, she was seizing.

They rushed her to the hospital and hooked her up to life support but she slipped into a coma. That part of her brain that controlled life function had become so depressed that it simply turned off. She died that night. Poisoned, the doctors said, by the alcohol that coursed through her blood and shut down her life.

Andrés kept his eyes steady on the street. His chest constricted. And then he felt it, that oozing, festering ulcer that gnawed away at his insides, chewing a hole into his heart.

After his mother died, something snapped inside him. He became hard, intolerant. Hateful. And then when his father's mistress showed up at his mother's funeral, the hatred became maniacal. She sat in the back row, her face covered with a black veil. But through the holes in the lace he could see her dark skin. And those haunting Gypsy eyes.

His father ignored her. But Andrés could not. He cornered her after the service. Threatened her. Told her to get her adulterous cunt back to the ghetto.

Rosa overheard him. The shocked expression on her face that day, the anger that followed, drove him to act like a madman. The rage. The betrayal. His own self-loathing. Andrés felt it all as he pushed Rosa to the wall.

Two days later, Rosa left him.

Two years later, he was still using his mother's pain-reduction technique. And still feeling guilty. For being weak.

But as guilty as he felt for having succumbed to his mother's weakness, he was proud of the one correct decision he had been able to make today. He had returned for Adela.

He shifted out of the car, entered the building, and took the elevator up to the eleventh floor. After opening the door to his father's apartment, he stepped into silence. Adela, his father, and his grandmother were seated around the kitchen table, eating breakfast.

"Andrés, you're home!" Adela sprang from the table in a frenzy of flying feet. She leaped into his arms and he hoisted her over his hip. She hugged him, then took his face between her hands.

"Why did you stay away so long?" she said.

"Had things to do."

She combed her fingers through his hair.

"Your hair is too long," she said. "You look like a girl." A chortle escaped through her nose and she made a gleeful, happy sound.

Andrés tweaked her nose and smiled.

"Your sister's right." His father glared over his spectacles.

And, just like that, Andrés wasn't smiling any more. He flinched as if someone had slapped him, marveling, not for the first time, at how badly his father could sting him with so few words.

"Where the hell have you been?" his father said.

Adela drew back his face and looked into his eyes, distracting him from answering.

"Papá's going to buy me a horsey," she said, with no particular enthusiasm. Just the facts. "He said I can ride with you next year at the Spring Fair."

Andrés lowered Adela to the ground.

"What are you talking about, *mi amor?*" Andrés's voice faltered. "You know you always ride with Papá."

"I'll be on a business trip," his father said, sounding annoyed. "Sit down." He gestured with his glass.

That's fucking bizarre. He knows his schedule ten months in advance. Andrés shook his head. And then he pushed back the dread that hovered around his heart.

"I don't do the April Fair," he said.

His father put down his glass.

"You'll *do* it next year," he said. And then he played the ace card. "I know you don't want to disappoint your sister."

"But I will." Andrés grabbed the keys he had only minutes before thrown on the side table. "It's in my nature. Part of my DNA."

Two hours later, Andrés strolled into the lab.

"Where've you been?" Rajiv moved over to the dissecting microscope, focused the lens on the plate. "I've been waiting for you all week."

"I was busy." Andrés threw his briefcase on the workbench.

Rajiv stiffened. "Your plates are in the incubator," he said, not looking up from the scope. "I inoculated them two days ago."

"You're kidding, right?" Andrés sauntered toward the coffeemaker.

Rajiv had already set up the experiment they were supposed to be working on together.

"Just get the plates." Rajiv's tone was sharp.

Andrés poured himself a cup of coffee.

"Somehow, I don't like your tone today, Rajiv."

Andrés swaggered to the incubator and removed the plates.

"It sounds almost . . . condescending."

A chair scraped against the floor.

Andrés stole a glance over his shoulder.

Rajiv had returned to the bench.

Slowly, defiantly, Andrés collected the last plate, pulled a stool over beside Rajiv, and rolled up his sleeves.

"Now what?" Andrés set the trays down on the bench.

A deep crease cut gouges between Rajiv's eyes.

"You need to make heterokaryons from the two fungal mutants," Rajiv said, his voice clipped and even.

Andrés unscrewed the lids from the top two Petri dishes. Rajiv's tone threatened a confrontation. But as he couldn't afford to make an enemy of Rajiv, Andrés forced himself to adopt a professional, businesslike reaction to his lab mate's perceived threat.

"Are the strains ready?" Rajiv picked up the plates, observed them. "This procedure is tricky. Have you ever done it before?"

"Yep." Andrés had never performed the operation, but he'd observed it. He was sure he could fumble his way through it.

He took a pair of forceps and pulled a mycelium from one plate and drew it onto a slide. He took another strain from a different plate. Then he hesitated. He knew he had to insert one mycelium into the other, but wasn't sure how to go about it.

"You need to cut the corners at an angle," Rajiv said. "One strand has to be thicker than the other to go in."

"I know that." Andrés snipped the ends. Then he inserted one strain into the other under the dissecting microscope.

"Impressive. You got it on the first try." Rajiv sounded amazed. "You have good hands." He handed Andrés another set of plates. "A surgeon's hands."

Andrés repeated the procedure.

"Should've been used for medicine."

Andrés frowned as he pinched the forceps around the second strain.

"Why aren't they?" Rajiv did not look at Andrés as he prepped another plate.

Andrés finished the procedure.

"Medicine is my father's field, not mine." Andrés's hand jerked and the scissors clinked to the ground.

Rajiv bent down to pick them up. Then he took his own tray of samples and headed for the incubator.

"Your father made the headlines again," Rajiv said. "That must be tough." He opened the incubator and inserted his samples. "To live behind such a huge shadow."

Andrés took a double take. He stared at Rajiv's back. No one had ever understood that about him. Not even Rosa.

"It's not so much that he's famous, you know. I can handle that." Andrés sprinted to catch up with Rajiv.

"What is it, then?"

"What bothers me is that the reason he became famous was because he chose to heal Gypsy hearts."

18

Rajiv

Rajiv was beginning to see Andrés more clearly, but understand him less. He grabbed a stack of Petri dishes from the supply cabinet, wondering why Andrés was so intolerant and judgmental toward the Gypsy community. His lab mate had obviously not inherited bigotry from his family, at least not from his father, who seemed an active champion of the Gypsy cause.

Appearances could be deceptive, he knew, but Dr. Aragón's service to the marginalized communities of Eastern Europe did not seem forced. He had no apparent reason to travel to Bucharest to perform pro-bono surgery on a sick Romani child, having abundant opportunities right here in Seville to elevate himself to hero status, if that was what he wanted.

Rajiv sat down at the bench and placed the stack of Petri plates in front of him, refusing to cede credibility to Andrés's harsh accusation against his father. While he had often felt intimidated by his own father's power, he could not understand Andrés's angry arrogance. Appa had, on countless occasions, made him feel the lesser man, even as he became the more educated. It was a phenomenon he understood well. No matter how successful he became, his father always managed to appear shrewder, cleverer, and infinitely more resourceful than his better-educated son. Rajiv knew, better than Andrés could possibly imagine, the painful pull of a powerful father.

"Rajiv!" Dr. Matos's gigantic voice invaded the room.

Rajiv looked up sharply.

His boss was standing at the door to his office, head cocked, brow creased.

Dr. Matos took one step forward and closed the office door.

"I need to talk to you," he said. The man's English was accented—a sharp, authoritative bark.

Oh no. Rajiv groaned silently. *There goes the morning.* Dr. Matos's "discussions" could go on for hours, effectively interrupting any work that might have been planned for the day.

Dr. Matos approached Rajiv at the bench.

"Walk with me," the professor said.

Dr. Jaime Matos Alameda insisted that all scientific experiments be discussed walking, round and round the outside corridor that circled the lab.

"I hear you've been helping Andrés with his experiments." Dr. Matos led Rajiv out the door and into the hallway.

"Oh, that," said Rajiv, trailing behind him. "I've just been giving him a few ideas."

"Do not interrupt me," Dr. Matos said, with the authority of one who had worked hard to earn the title of lab director.

Rajiv could hear the laughter of his colleagues stifled behind their hands. To him, there was nothing funny about the compulsive control his boss held over the lab.

Professor Matos walked with his hands folded behind his back. Rajiv followed along beside him, his hands stuffed into his pockets.

"I'm curious," Dr. Matos said, eyebrows drawn together. "Why did you change the protocol on Andrés's experiment?"

"Sorry . . . I just thought I'd try—"

"I did not ask for an apology. I asked you why you changed the protocol."

Rajiv stared straight ahead. A vein pulsed on his temple.

"Trying different temperature sets seemed to be a logical alternative to get the virus to infect," Rajiv said, quietly holding back his anger. "Andrés has been—"

"Andrés has been wasting resources on that experiment for over a year," cut in Dr. Matos. "With your modification to the protocol, however, we may actually see some results."

The professor's voice boomed into the empty corridor, only to be absorbed into the hollows of the cinder-block walls that formed an echo chamber around him.

"This could be a nice piece of work," Dr. Matos said. "I want you to finish Andrés's experiment."

"What?" Rajiv stopped walking. "I have my own experiments—"

"Andrés needs this experiment to finish his thesis." Dr. Matos picked up the pace of his already accelerated stride.

"Then let him do the work." Rajiv sprinted into step behind his boss.

Dr. Matos froze into place.

"I did not invite you to my lab to challenge my authority." The professor kept his voice low, little above a whisper, but there was strength in the softness of his tone. "What do you think I'm running here? A summer camp for misplaced refugees?"

Rajiv's face tightened. His brow furled into a deep crevice—the same one that marked his father's face when he was angry or unstable. Professor Matos Alameda was a brilliant scientist, but a miserable human being. Rajiv clenched his fists but remained silent. He was well aware that one precipitous comment or ill-timed response could send him on a plane back to India.

"You will stop work on your experiments until you finish Andrés's work," Dr. Matos said, resuming his obsessive walk. "He needs to graduate this year."

"And who's going to write his thesis?" Rajiv said, before he could stop himself. "Do you expect me to do that as well?"

A growing sense of dread invaded his body as Rajiv anticipated Professor Matos's response.

"You will do whatever I tell you to do. Andrés's father is on the board of trustees of the university. If Andrés does not defend by December, I will hold you personally responsible."

"You can't be serious."

Dr. Matos stopped dead in his tracks, his face a study in cold, hard indignation.

Rajiv searched desperately for a way out of the corner Matos had pushed him into.

Forcing back his temper, he was about to offer the professor what he believed a reasonable compromise when his mouth froze, words stuck on his muted tongue. Andrés was sauntering down the corridor like a rock star on parade.

Rajiv tensed as he anticipated the many things that could go wrong with the scene unfolding before him.

"Hey, Rajiv," Andrés said. "Are the cells ready for harvesting?"

An ominous silence filled the corridor that had not long ago been overpowered with words.

"Get your ass into the lab, Andrés." Dr. Matos's gigantic voice effectively shattered the silence. "Rajiv is not available right now." Dr. Matos's cold eyes stopped any further comment.

But then something inside Rajiv snapped. He heard his father's voice—piercing and spiteful: "*You do not leave my presence until I have instructed you to do so. Tell your friends that you are unavailable at the present time.*" The words stung as if spoken for the first time, propelling him into action that was ill advised.

"Excuse me," he said, turning his back on his boss and walking away.

"*Oye,* I'm not finished with you!"

"But I'm finished with you," Rajiv decided, speaking the words carefully under his breath as he hurried down the corridor and into the stairwell. It wasn't until he crossed the portal of El Cántaro that he was finally able to let out his breath.

A stupid move, he acknowledged. He might not have a job tomorrow.

But at least he would have the one thing he left India for.

Control of his own life.

19

Diego

As the numb months of summer turned into oppressive fall, Diego alternated between bouts of violent anger and overwhelming sadness. It was as if his brain had taken the catastrophic event and then blasted the experience into a million pieces like shrapnel, wedged into his head. One minute, he was coping okay. The next, a chance association would detonate a memory, trigger a flashback, and send him sinking into sorrow. And there was nothing he could do to stop the cycle.

"God the Father can fully share your sorrow." A strong voice boomed through a microphone. It carried over a set of speakers and out into the streets of Tres Mil Viviendas. The voice had come from the white tent.

Diego stopped abruptly, turned, and started walking in the opposite direction. That tent was full of *Gitanos Pentecostales*, Evangelical Christian Gypsies, who were convinced that becoming like them was a good thing.

"Sometimes when death comes," continued the voice, "our brothers cry in anger, 'Where was God when my loved one died?'"

Diego froze. But he kept his back to the tent.

"I tell you now, brother . . ." The voice was persistent and unrelenting. "He was where He was when His son was crucified. He understands the pain you feel. He understands your anger."

"No, he doesn't." Diego kicked a stone into the gutter.

"He may feel far away, and you may feel abandoned, but He is with you, *hermano.*"

Diego's heart pounded. He wanted to turn around, but was afraid to move. It sounded like the man with the microphone had come out of the tent to speak to him directly.

"Couldn't God have prevented death?" The voice would not let go of him. "Yes, he could have. But he chose not to because His purpose for that life was bigger than our understanding."

Diego rubbed his neck and then, eventually, glanced over his shoulder. There was no one standing outside the tent.

"And now I ask you. . . ." The voice grew louder. "In whom, or in what, do you place your trust? Do you place your trust in human understanding? In the strength of your own hand or in violent retribution? Oh, *mi hermano,* think about what you are trusting."

Diego sighed and started to walk. He was tired, hungry, and sick of the voice coming at him from the tent.

"As King David wrote in Psalm twenty, verse seven . . ." The pastor's voice, loud and fervent, carried through the speakers and stalked Diego down the street. "'Some trust in chariots and some in horses, but we trust in the name of the Lord our God.'"

"*¡Gloria a Dios!*" The crowd offered its support with shouts of glory to God.

Diego picked up his stride. He didn't need any Alleluia Christians to tell him he had made the wrong choice when he decided to hook up with Joaquín. He lived with the guilt of it every hour of every day, of every month that crawled by.

Had six months already gone by without Catalina?

He swiped his sleeve across his face. And then strode the length of Calle Manuel Falconde, consumed by guilt, anger, and fear.

When he reached the end of the street, he kicked at a pile of garbage left rotting on the sidewalk and detoured into Pablito's bar, a place he'd been avoiding. Pablito was Amara and Manolito's father. Amara, his childhood friend. He used to spend hours at Pablito's bar, playing his guitar for Manolito, talking with Amara. But somehow, it didn't feel right to be there now.

It was hard to pretend to be okay around the one man outside of his family who knew him like a son.

His entrance was greeted with silence. For probably what was the first time in their lives, Armando and his brother Emilio, the cornerstones of Pablito's place, were at a loss for words.

Grief seemed to do that to the people around him.

Armando was the first to speak.

"Where you been?" Armando's voice was tentative. "Haven't seen you around for a while." He pointed his *Cruzcampo* beer bottle at Diego. "You all right?"

Diego flopped onto a chair at Armando's table. He debated what to say, and then just came out with, "Do I look all right?"

"Well, no, actually . . ." Armando's voice trailed off.

Diego immediately regretted his hostility. Armando was in his late fifties, but the tired wrinkles that creased his face gave him the appearance of twenty more years.

How could he have been so rough with the man?

"Sorry, *tío*." Diego placed his hand on Armando's shoulder. "I'm doing okay."

"*Basta, ¡ya!*" Amara approached the table and stood between Armando and Diego. She shot a warning glare at Armando and immediately the two men fell silent. Armando smoothed back the few wisps of hair he had left. Emilio straightened his collar. Diego rolled down and rebuttoned his sleeves. Amara had that kind of effect on men. They always wanted to look and act a little better when she was around.

"Can I get you something to eat?" She shifted her eyes to him.

Diego held her gaze. Her eyes were soft and offered comfort.

"No thanks," he finally said, looking away. "I'm not hungry."

"Eat, you look famished." Emilio slid a small plate of Spanish *tortilla* in front of him.

"Yeah, like you haven't slept in days," Armando said, adding to the observation Emilio had offered.

"That's not what famished means," Emilio said. He let out a loud, exasperated sigh.

"I know what famished means," Armando said, hands waving in the air. "But what I think you meant to say was fatigued. That's the word you're looking for."

"No, I'm not. I meant what I said. Famished. He looks fa—"

"*¡Ya!*" Amara stopped the discussion with her hand. "Will you let the man eat?"

Diego managed a faint smile as he played with the potato omelet.

He had known Amara since pre-school and had yet to see a man able to counter her. Not quite eighteen, she already had the power and presence of a woman twice her age.

Unlike Amara, however, he welcomed Emilio and Armando's lively banter. It distracted him from himself.

Amara returned to the bar and prepared an infusion of chamomile tea. She brought it to him, along with a piece of toast.

Diego rubbed his hands over his face and then drank the tea.

He choked. The herbal infusion burned as it traveled down his throat and past his heart.

"Con calma, hombre." Armando leaned forward over the table. "You all right?"

Diego squeezed his fingers into the middle of his chest.

"Got this pain . . . right here." His fingers traveled to his heart.

"Might be having a heart attack," Armando said.

"He's only nineteen years old," Emilio said, exasperated. "I never heard of no nineteen-year-old ever dying from no heart attack."

"Could happen," Armando said. "I knew this boy once, in Triana, done up and died, heart stopped cold while we was betting on the roosters. Not more than twenty years old, maybe—"

"You're crazy, *hermano*." Emilio stared at Armando with a look of amused disbelief.

Diego pushed away the tea.

"Me voy," he said. I'll see you later.

"Tranquilo, hijo." Emilio clamped his hand over Diego's arm. "What's your hurry?"

"Maybe he needs to get away from the two of you." Amara marched across the room. "How can you be laughing and telling jokes, and drinking . . ." She grabbed the beer bottle away from Armando. "When Diego is in mourning?"

Diego looked down at the table. The ritual of Gypsy mourning had never made much sense to him. Friends and family refrained from drinking, or singing, or dancing, or doing anything fun that might show a lack of respect to the person who had lost a loved one. When maybe all that person wanted to do was to have everybody forget that he was supposed to be grieving.

"It's all right," he said. "People don't have to stop living because I died."

Amara sat beside him. *"You* didn't die," she said.

Diego snapped. Blame it on lack of sleep, or too much caffeine, or one too many cigarettes. Whatever it was, he couldn't control the sudden surge of anger that erupted inside of him. He shoved the chair out from under him, sending it crashing to the floor.

"Didn't I?" He pushed the toppled chair away with his foot. "Tell that to my dead heart!"

Armando exchanged a nervous glance with Emilio. Amara lowered her eyes.

"Pour me a beer, Amara." Diego picked up the chair and slammed the legs against the floor as he stood it upright.

"Are you sure that's what you want?" Amara said.

He stared at her without responding.

"Fine." She stood and pushed herself away from the table. "If that's what you want, go ahead. Drown your sorrows. Be like every other Gypsy man with no place to go and no hope for the future. Worship the golden Virgin of Cruzcampo." She marched toward the door and yanked it open. "But pray to your idol away from here."

At that moment, Diego felt so desperate, so disoriented, that he wanted nothing more than to saturate his senses with the *barrio*'s answer to all those unanswered prayers. A beer shared with friends. A forced smile. Sometimes it was the only way to forget about life among the living.

"However," Amara said, pulling him back from the edge, "if you are the Gypsy man I know you are, then pull yourself together and finish your tea."

Finish my tea? Unexpectedly, Diego laughed. Amara had given him exactly what he needed. A swift kick in the butt.

And the genuine concern of a friend.

20

Andrés

Andrés reached for the knob on the chapel door. He was nervous. Upset. Dr. Matos had given him an ultimatum. Either finish the work, or get the hell out.

His boss was furious. After a heated discussion with the professor, Andrés pretended to work for the rest of the day, and then took off for the only place that still offered him some semblance of meaning. The small chapel on Calle Pureza.

He yanked open the door, strode into the sanctuary, and sat down in a corner pew.

A shadow passed over him. A light, familiar scent followed. A perfume that was not too overpowering, but distinctly feminine, with hints of jasmine, orange, and musk.

Rosa. He looked up, his heart pounding.

She walked by, engaged in conversation with Ignacio Torres.

Andrés glanced quickly from his fraternity brother to his former girlfriend.

They both avoided his eyes.

A sharp twist constricted his chest. Ignacio was the treasurer of the fraternity. A devout, well-respected man. Only twenty-six years old, he was already a successful businessman.

All he needed to complete the profile was a perfect, pious wife.

Andrés stood, and then grabbed Rosa's wrist, stopping her.

"I was sitting right there," he said, feeling like a wounded dog who had just been stepped over. "It would've taken you two seconds to stop and say hello."

"*Suéltame.*" She struggled to break free. "You're hurting me."

"I'm hurting *you*?" He let go, flinging back his hand.

"Is there a problem?" Ignacio stepped in front of Rosa, shielding her from Andrés.

That move hurt. As if the noble knight needed to protect the fair maid from him.

"Yeah, there's a problem. *You*." He pushed Ignacio back.

"Stop it, Andrés!" Rosa pulled Ignacio away from him.

"Go to hell." Seething inside, Andrés turned and walked away. "Both of you."

He headed for the exit. At the portal, he ran into a young woman who had opened the door from the opposite side. He stumbled back, allowing her to enter.

"Is this the chapel of the Esperanza de Triana?" she said, in slightly accented Spanish.

He nodded, and then fell back against the wall, watching her.

Another woman. Another challenge.

Another way to get back at Rosa.

The woman slid into a back pew, reached into her bag, and pulled out a black leather notebook. She looked American. Her informal clothing, jeans and a printed T-shirt distinguished her from the European women who visited the city. Her T-shirt read "UMass," and sported a university logo on the left pocket.

Rosa strutted past him, stiff-backed and silent. Her bodyguard escorted her outside.

Andrés pressed his lips together and acted as if he didn't care.

He stared blankly at the woman who would make an interesting diversion.

The artist in him visualized a fascinating watercolor portrait. She definitely looked American, but she didn't have that pale, pasty pallor of East Coast tourists looking for sun after a long, cold winter. Her skin was light, but not white. More like the flaxen gold of Manzanilla wine. Her hair was dark. Wild black curls framed her face, like the porcelain dolls he bought for his little sister.

He wondered if she would allow him to paint her. The corner of his mouth lifted slightly and his pulse quickened. She would be a provocative model. He continued to observe the woman.

She had the book in her hand, still closed. But then slowly, almost hesitantly, she slid a photograph out from between the cover and the first page of what now looked to him like a journal.

She took the picture in her hand and studied it so intently Andrés knew this was no ordinary photograph.

He pushed back his hair, and then prepared to make his move.

The door creaked open behind him and Andrés looked over his shoulder. Don Francisco, the president of the fraternity, walked across the portal. Very soon, that young American was going to be kicked out of the chapel. Public hours were almost over.

As if on cue, Don Francisco passed by, stopped, and then looked back over his shoulder.

"I'm sorry, *señorita,*" Don Francisco said, "but the chapel is now closed to the public. I'm afraid I'm going to have to ask you to leave."

Leaving seemed the last thing the woman wanted to do.

"Five more minutes?" she said.

"I'm sorry," Don Francisco repeated, politely but firmly. "The public is not allowed at this time."

Andrés nodded and a slow smile formed. And then like a cat ready to pounce on its prey, he made his move.

"It's okay, Don Francisco," he said, "she's with me." He placed a hand on Don Francisco's shoulder. "Give us a few more minutes." He turned to the woman and smiled.

She looked like she wanted to say something. To him. But wisely, she remained silent.

Don Francisco glanced warily at the woman, and then back at Andrés. *"Está bien,"* he said. "Five minutes." Then he turned and walked away.

Andrés watched Don Francisco depart, and then he turned toward the woman.

"Forgive me," he said, suppressing his anger and digging out the charm, "but I've not seen you around here before."

She stood abruptly. In her haste, the photograph fluttered to the floor. She bent down to pick it up, but he was faster. His hand brushed against hers as he scooped it off the floor. He did not stand immediately.

"Where did you get this picture?" he said, still examining the photograph. It was an old black and white of a fraternity brother dressed as a penitent

She ignored his question but thanked him quickly as she snatched the photo from his hand. She slipped it back inside the journal. Then she glanced up and looked into his eyes.

He stared back at her, intrigued. She was the first American he had met with black hair and blue eyes.

"Do you belong to this fraternity?" she said, forcing her voice to sound casual.

"Yes, I do," he said, eyes fixed firmly upon her. "May I sit down?" He waited for her nodded consent before sliding into the pew beside her.

"My name's Andrés," he said.

"Do you have a last name?" she said.

"Do you have a first name?"

"Crystal." She looked directly at him, eyes unwavering.

The corner of his mouth lifted.

"Aragón," he said, sitting back against the pew. "Andrés Aragón Del Río."

"Great name." Her eyes flickered for a moment and then steadied again. As if Aragón was not the name she was hoping for.

"What brings you here?" He did not break her gaze.

She heard the question but did not answer it. Her gaze had shifted to the silver medallion he wore clipped to his belt loop.

"Can I see that?" She pointed at the medallion. And then quickly withdrew her hand.

"What?" she said. "Why are you looking at me like that?"

The corners of his mouth twitched as he fought to contain a smile. He did not remove his eyes from hers as he unclipped the medallion and handed it to her, making sure that his fingers grazed hers as he placed it in the palm of her hand.

The fingers didn't seem to faze her. The medallion, however, did. She stared at the silver medal as if it were a priceless relic. And then slowly, she ran her finger over the embossed surface, over the crown at the top, the cross that ended in an anchor at the bottom. Over the wine challis and host. Then she passed her hand down over the braided band that wove together three colors. Gold, the color of royalty. Purple of kings. And green . . . the color of hope.

That woman wanted something. Badly. He wasn't sure what it was she wanted, but he knew he had something she was interested in.

The Medallion.

He smiled. There was nothing he loved more than a woman who wanted what he had.

21

Rajiv

Rajiv felt the tension melt from his face as the warm water of the shower fell over his tired body. The pulsing stream was seductive, working like some nautical siren to lure him away from his goal of returning to the lab.

It's already seven o'clock, teased the water nymph. *Why go back now? Just relax . . . you must be exhausted.*

Rajiv lathered his body, surprisingly attentive to the whisperings of the water.

Just take the night off—rest, continued the seductress. *You've been working so hard.*

Rajiv felt himself start to weaken. It was true. He was tired, both physically and mentally. He had worked through the last two nights, trying to finish a few experiments that might lead to a nice paper and hopefully . . . a permanent job.

Fate had worked in his favor over the last three months. Dr. Matos had scheduled a mini sabbatical in Bilbao, beginning the day after Rajiv had acted on his ill-thought-out decision to walk away from their discussion.

Over the professor's three-month absence, Rajiv continued with his own work while helping Andrés with his experiments. Not because he was forced to, but because in some kind of odd, unexpected way, he actually liked Andrés—when the man was sober.

Away from alcohol, Andrés was tolerable. At times, even pleasant to be with. He saw the world differently from most, more creatively. But when he had to, he conformed. He shifted from his dominant right brain to successfully tap into his left-brain logic. When he did that, he became an impressive scientist.

Matos was back now and Rajiv wanted to present him with the last set of results from their latest experiment, hoping it would be a suitable peace offering to placate his boss. He was sure Professor Matos would be sufficiently satisfied with the work to forgive his blatant—and in retrospect, foolish—act of disrespect.

Rajiv inhaled the fresh scent of sandalwood soap. It was the last bar from home and he wanted to savor it.

But unfortunately, thinking of home made him remember why he was here. He cranked off the shower. The renewal of his one-year contract with Professor Matos depended on this work.

"Enough." He grabbed the towel from a hook on the wall. "I'm going back to work." Resolved, he conquered his mind and silenced the temptress of the water.

The sound of loud knocking startled him as he stepped out of the shower. He wrapped the towel around his waist and moved into the living room, peering out the torn curtain that only partially covered the window. It was his neighbor, Pili, holding a bottle of wine and two glasses.

"Oh God." Rajiv dashed back to the bathroom and shoved his right leg into his trousers. His left caught on the stitching that had come undone from the hem, and he tripped, falling forward onto the bathroom floor. "Bloody hell." He untangled his foot and thrust it into the leg of his pants. Still on the ground, he zipped up the fly, then searched for his shirt. He spotted it on the kitchen chair and after pushing himself off the floor, grabbed his shirt, and hastily began to fasten the buttons.

"*Buenas tardes.*" Pili called out from the other side of the door.

"Just a minute," Rajiv said, still fumbling with the buttons. Finally, he opened the door, his shirt open at the chest, one side longer than the other. He felt her eyes as they moved slowly over his chest and down to the misaligned buttons.

"You like one drink?" she asked, not taking her eyes off the opening in his shirt.

"Ah . . . no . . . thanks." Rajiv looked at his watch. "I have to get back to work."

"I can come in?" Pili stepped across the threshold before waiting for an answer.

"No, I have to . . ."

Rajiv felt her hip brushing against him. He stepped back, making room for her to enter. Some temptations were harder to resist than others. He pushed the door shut behind her with the heel of his hand.

"*Toma*," she said, handing him the bottle of Campo Viejo and two smudged glasses.

Rajiv snatched the bottle and wine glasses from her hand and placed them on the table.

"Let me fix." Pili took his shirt in her hands. With extremely nimble fingers, she unfastened the buttons—having reached the bottom before he had gotten over the shock that she had started at the top. His shirt now open, she began to refasten the buttons, allowing her fingers to feather across his chest in amazing intimacy.

Shocked, Rajiv backed away. He fumbled with his shirt.

"*¿Qué te pasa?*" She took a glass off the table and poured wine from the bottle she had already opened.

"*Toma.*" She handed him a glass.

Rajiv accepted the wine and downed it in a single gulp. She plunked herself on the sofa and he poured himself another glass.

"So . . ." Rajiv pulled over a chair and sat opposite her.

"Are you . . . do you . . ."

"*¿Fumas?*" She pulled out a lighter and pack of cigarettes from a small purse on her lap. "You want one cigarette?" She crossed her right leg over the left. Her dress rode up higher on her thigh.

"Ah . . . yes." Rajiv forced his eyes away from her legs.

She handed him a cigarette and then leaned forward to light it. She did not sit back immediately. Instead, she reached out her hand and pushed a strand of wet hair off his face.

"You very handsome," she said.

"Oh . . . ah . . ." Rajiv was suddenly aware of his uncombed hair. He pushed his fingers through the wet locks, attempting to smooth back the dark tangles. He had no idea what to say to her next.

"You like take pictures?" she said, reaching for the camera on the side table.

"Yes, yes I do," he said, relieved. At least one of them was still conversant.

"Take my picture." She handed him the camera, then struck a Marilyn Monroe pose against the sofa.

Rajiv smiled and snapped the shutter. *Now that'll be a photograph to send home to father.*

Pili patted her hand on the sofa, inviting him to sit next to her.

"Vente," she said, "I wan' to talk with jew."

Her slow, painfully enunciated English sounded like it had come off an "English made Easy" tape.

Slowly, Rajiv rose from his chair and sat next to her on the sofa. Work could wait . . . at least for a little while.

"Are you a student?" he asked, clutching the armrest.

"Jess," she said, her mouth lifting in a Colgate commercial smile.

"Be careful, there's a nick on your glass." Rajiv took the chipped wine glass from her hand. "I'll get you another one." He stood up, but she caught his hand and pulled him back down. "Your glass is broken," he insisted, showing her the cracked glass.

"Jess," she said, tilting her head slightly, flirting with her eyes. She took the wine glass back and wrapped her lips around the rim.

"Okay, suit yourself." He felt like one of those bumbling fools in a Bollywood movie who had absolutely no idea how to relate to the opposite sex. "What do you study?" he stammered, trying to muster some small semblance of intelligence to his words.

"Jess," she replied, crossing over him to grab an ashtray off the end table.

Rajiv felt her breasts press against his chest as she reached across his body.

"You have no idea what I'm saying, do you?" A well-formed question, he thought, considering his mind was still on the breasts. But she did not answer it. She just smiled.

A playful smile twitched the corners of Rajiv's mouth as his eyes landed on her shoes. The laces criss-crossed her legs, binding her calves in leather. His mind put her in a Roman coliseum, a female gladiator ready to conquer. He shook his head to brush off the image. Then he allowed for a little fun, praying she would not understand.

"Your shoes are ugly," he said.

They were actually quite sexy.

"Jess."

"And your dog just died." He put on a serious face to hide what otherwise would have been an idiotic smile.

"Jess. That is good."

Rajiv closed his eyes and shook his head, forcing himself to stop. Don't be such a cad, he told himself sternly. You're acting like the village virgin. Get a grip, man. At least, don't make it so obvious.

"Mira, Pili," he began in Spanish. "I need to get back to work."

"No hables tanto." She crushed out her cigarette in the tar-stained ashtray. "Shh, no more talk." She removed the cigarette from his lips and extinguished it in the ashtray. Then she edged her hips nearer and ran her fingers over his face.

Rajiv brushed his hand over hers, suddenly aware of the coarse stubble that had roughened his face.

"It's kind of rough, isn't it?" He smiled self-consciously.

"Jess," Pili said, rubbing her hand along his cheek.

Rajiv felt her lips brush against his, upsetting what had been twenty-six years of carefully regulated, culturally controlled sensuality. Camera cut-offs before the kiss was Bollywood suppression at its best. But Rajiv decided that he liked Western cinema infinitely more. Running his tongue around the outside edges of her mouth, he felt decadent, as if tasting for the first time the forbidden flavor of an imported sweet.

She started to unbutton his shirt, and then stopped on the second button. Her eyes landed on the white string that crossed his chest.

"¿Qué es eso?" She slid her finger under the string and lifted it up. "What is this?"

"Oh, nothing." Rajiv removed her hand. "It's just something they make you wear after becoming a Brahmin."

"¿Un qué?" She laughed. *"¿Un Brahma?* Like the bull?"

"No, a Brahmin. It's a caste . . . in India."

Rajiv rose from the sofa, turned off by her laughter.

"Are you hungry?" He moved away from her and into the kitchen.

He realized how stupid he must have sounded as he opened the door to the refrigerator and pulled out some leftover vegetables, but he didn't know what else to say.

Things were not quite working out the way he had imagined they would in the fantasy he had created in his mind.

"No gracias." Pili followed him into the kitchen with her glass of wine. She pushed him up against the counter. Removed the dish from his hand. "I no like potatoes." She crinkled her nose and placed the curried vegetable on the counter. "But you I like." She passed her tongue lightly across his lips and then into his mouth.

"*Vente,*" she said, leading him back to the sofa. She brought the glass to her mouth. "Why you nervous?" She raised her glass to his lips. "*Relájate.*" She parted his lips with the glass. "Relax."

He tilted the glass with his fingers and swallowed a generous portion of wine.

"Good." She smiled. Then she reached out and took his hand, placing it upon her bulging cleavage.

Rajiv jerked his hand away, spilling wine on her dress.

"I'm sorry," he stammered. "I'll . . . just wait there."

You're really blowing this. He ran to the kitchen for a paper towel. There was only an empty roll on the holder. Looking around, he saw the bath towel he had thrown on the floor and picked it up. He shoved it into Pili's hand.

She took the towel, sashayed into the bathroom, and lifted her dress up to the tap, running cold water over the burgundy stain. She didn't bother to close the door, allowing Rajiv a clear view of her shapely legs. Pinching the two sides of the stain between her knuckles, she scrubbed hard. Then she bunched the dress up further into her hands, giving Rajiv an uncensored shot of her satin panties.

Rajiv sank back into the sofa and closed his eyes. His body throbbed. She had achieved the response she was looking for.

The sex that followed was clumsy and unsatisfying. Mostly because of him. It wasn't the way he thought his first intimate encounter would be.

Somehow, it felt like he had cheated love.

22

Diego

Even though six months had passed since Catalina died, Diego was determined to remain faithful to their love. He stubbornly refused to let go of anything that reminded him of her. Memories, dreams, bits of intimate conversation that only the two of them had shared. All of her possessions. He kept the memory of her torturously alive by playing the unfinished script of their life over and over and over in his mind. Their bedroom was the stage. Her possessions the props to the play that he would not allow to end.

But when denial finally led to an empty reality, there was no will or desire left in him to resist what was ultimately inevitable. It was time to close the curtain.

And so, one sad September day, he walked into the bedroom he had shared with Catalina and prepared himself to clear it of every painful reminder of their life together. Samuel offered to help, but Diego told his brother it was something he had to do alone.

He began with the shelf on which Catalina had placed her skirts, blouses, and shawls. Tentatively, he picked up the stack and brought it to his nose. The material still smelled of her—a light, lavender scent. He placed the clothes in a large plastic bag but lingered on one final piece—a white top still stained with chocolate. His throat tightened. He and Catalina had stopped for a cup of hot chocolate almost every evening during those early months of her pregnancy. He hesitated for a moment, and then crumpled the shirt, violently stuffing it into the bag.

And then, his hand shaking, he moved on to the next shelf.

He filled the bag with stockings, panties, and bras. He stuffed in a few purses. Then he crammed in the doll Catalina had made for their baby. The booties, tiny sweaters, and pajamas. His chest tightened and it hurt to breathe. He reached up to the last shelf. And then he stopped. His heart hammered a blow to his chest. His hand trembled, but finally he took Catalina's wedding crown off the top shelf. He closed his eyes. The crown slipped from his hand. A pearl bounced to the floor. He fell back on the bed. His heart thumped once, and then beat faster. This was a memory he had not wanted to revisit but now had no choice. Against his will, his mind replayed the memory.

"You look so beautiful." He remembered whispering those words to Catalina when she stood before him at the altar. Dressed in white chiffon, she was his fairy-tale princess come to life. He took two steps forward, raised her veil. Her crown tipped slightly. She reached up, but he had already straightened it. With one hand on her crown, the other on her cheek, he kissed her. Not wanting to stop. Not able to. Until the pastor pulled them apart.

"Enough," the pastor said, separating them with his Bible. *"No more until we give this union up to God."*

There was a sharp snap and Diego's eyes flew open. Samuel had entered the room.

"Oh, man, I'm so sorry." Samuel looked down at the floor.

Diego followed his gaze. The crown was in two pieces under his brother's right foot. Slowly, Diego sat up. Then he bent down, picked up the pieces, and threw them in the bag. And then he rammed in the veil, Catalina's white high heels, her perfume, and her jewelry. The only thing he could not hurl into the bag was her wedding ring. He glanced at it briefly, and then looked away. A lump formed in his throat. He swallowed against it and pushed the ring into his pocket. Then he tied up the bag, brought it to the trunk of his father's car, and tossed it inside. He flung open the door, flopped into the driver's seat, and waited for Samuel to get in. And then he drove outside the city limits to burn the bag.

That day was the second worst day of his life. And like the first, his eyes were dry.

* * *

When Diego returned to the city, he was in a worse state than when he left. He drove directly to Pablito's place, planning to leave Samuel there, and then to have a mini breakdown in private. He cut the engine and parked in front of Pablito's bar.

"Why don't you come in?" Samuel said. "Our family's inside."

Diego's fingers tightened over the wheel. He usually avoided his family's nightly ritual of gathering together after church—a ritual that had become as sacred as the church service that preceded it. Every night after *el culto*, his parents, Elena, and several other family members joined Pastor Pedro to eat, pray, and talk—sometimes about him, sometimes about others, sometimes about God. So close had their association become that Pastor Pedro was now considered part of the family.

Diego had known Pastor Pedro all his life. And when he was young, even attended the pastor's services. But by the time he had reached adolescence, he had too many questions to accept the simple faith of his parents. And then after Catalina's death, he saw no purpose in worshipping a God that let bad things happen to the people he loved.

Samuel gripped Diego's shoulder.

"Come on, I can't leave you like this."

Diego stared out the windshield.

"I'll be okay. Please, just go."

Samuel didn't move.

"Come inside, Diego. If not for yourself, then do it for me. I don't want you to be alone tonight."

Diego let out a long sigh.

"Fine." He jerked open the car door and followed his brother into the bar.

"Diego! ¡Hombre! ¡Qué bueno!" Pastor Pedro jumped from his chair and offered it to him. *"Siéntate, mi'jo."*

Reluctantly, Diego sat down.

"Hijo, what would you like to eat?" A spark of hope lightened his mother's face.

Diego shrugged. *"Un serranito de pollo."* He avoided looking at his mother. He didn't want his face to take her hope away.

Glancing over at the bar, he caught Amara's eye.

She looked down, smiling.

"Amara, *mi'ja,* bring Diego a chicken sandwich," Pastor Pedro shouted across the room.

"*Sí*, Pastor," she said.

"You doing all right there, Pastor Pedro?" Diego's father deftly redirected the family's focus off him to a stronger, less volatile member.

"*Estoy malito, hermanos,*" Pastor Pedro said. I'm not well.

He unwrapped a disposable syringe from its packaging, sucked insulin into it from a small vial, lifted his shirt, and injected the medication into his stomach. He complained some more about how ill he felt, but then he smiled—because whether he was healthy or not, his life was in God's hands.

If it was God's will to heal him, *gloria a Dios*, he would be healed. If it was not God's will then, like the apostle Paul, he would suffer the thorn in his side and continue to serve the Lord.

Pastor Pedro had tried to share that and similar philosophies with Diego on several occasions after Catalina's death, but Diego refused to listen to what he could not possibly understand.

The pastor lowered his shirt and dug into the food Amara had placed before him—a double ration of fried squid.

Diego ate his sandwich in silence, listening to the conversation floating around him, but hearing very little.

"Do you know what David did on the worst day of his life?" the pastor said.

Diego looked up sharply. Why was it that whenever his mind was burdened with thoughts and feelings he could not possibly understand, someone—usually associated with God or His church—would torture him with a message from the Bible?

"He cried, brothers," Pastor Pedro said. "On the worst day of David's life, he cried."

Diego dropped his unfinished sandwich to the plate and pushed it away.

"In 1 Samuel, chapter thirty, verse four, the sacred Scriptures tell us that when David returned from battle and found his village ransacked, burned to the ground, all the women and children gone, he wept out loud until he had no strength left to weep."

The pastor speared another ring of fried squid, placed it on top of a small slice of bread, and brought it to his mouth.

"On the worst day of *my* life, *hermanos*," Pastor Pedro said, "I know what I'm going to do. I am going to cry, brothers, and then, like David, I will find my strength in our Lord, Jesus Christ."

"Amen, amen," Don Josemi said.

Diego pushed back his chair.

"Estoy cansado," he said. I'm tired. Straining to smile, Diego took leave of his family and sprinted for the door.

Outside, he fell back against the wall and closed his eyes. Seconds later, he felt Amara beside him.

He shook his head and held up his hand, forbidding her to speak.

She was silent for a moment, but then voiced the question he did not want to hear.

"Have you ever cried for Catalina?" she said, hesitating only slightly.

Slowly, Diego opened his eyes.

"Back off, Mara. I can't go there right now."

She looked down. Her eyelids fluttered.

"Sorry, I didn't mean to . . ." She turned to go.

"No, please don't go." His body convulsed. The feel of her skin, the softness of it, caught him by surprise.

"Are you all right?" Amara withdrew her hand.

"No, I'm not."

His throat burned and his body ached to be held.

Amara sensed his unspoken need. She put her arm around him. Rested her head on his shoulder.

And before he could stop himself, he slumped into her arms.

23

Andrés

Andrés pushed his fingers through his hair, trying to concentrate on the protocol set before him on the workbench. He was distracted by thoughts of Crystal. Even though he had never intended to see her as more than a diversion, he had found himself getting into the girl.

The night they met, she had accepted his invitation to have a drink in the bar across from the chapel. They talked for over two hours. She said she was a writer, doing research for a story about Holy Week in Seville. She asked him a lot of questions about the brotherhood, about the chapel.

Her questions were well researched, those of a journalist interviewing her subject. But at the same time, they were guarded. She was always on the defensive. And the one time he asked her a question, about the old photograph she had stashed in her journal, she stopped talking. Who was that man? The mystery of it appealed to him. He wasn't the only one keeping secrets.

Intrigued by her fascination in all things related to Holy Week in Seville, Andrés gave her bits and pieces of what she wanted, but held out the more important information. The brotherhood was a secret order. Inside information was guarded. He toyed with her, thinking she would play the game. But when he invited her to come back the following night, she turned down his invitation.

He threw down the pen. Exercised his fingers. Then he forced his attention back to the protocol.

What was he doing wrong that the experiment kept failing?

He ran his hand back through his hair.

What could he do differently to make this experiment work?

He dug his fingers into his scalp, feeling the pressure at the back of his head. Too much pressure. It was filling his head, bringing out those feelings.

He shot up, pushing the chair away from the bench. Then he sprinted to the bathroom at the far end of the lab, closed the door, and splashed cold water on his face, desperate to shock his father's words out of his head.

"You're never going to amount to anything."

The water wasn't working.

"After all the opportunities you've been given."

Panic surged as the splashing became more vigorous.

"Hey, Andrés." Josemaría barged through the door. "Have you figured out that experiment yet?"

Andrés cranked the faucet off, wiped his face with a paper towel, and found his composure.

"No," he said. "I haven't."

Josemaría moved over to the sink to wash his hands. "You should talk to Rajiv—"

"Screw work, I have other plans." He couldn't ask Rajiv the same question he had already asked him three times.

Andrés threw open the door and walked out into the lab.

"Don't tell me." Josemaría followed behind. "You're meeting a woman." He pulled up a chair and sat beside Maricarmen.

"Maybe I am." Andrés went with the lie.

"And this will be the one," Maricarmen said. "The woman who will make you happy." A slight touch of emotion weakened the sarcasm in her voice.

Andrés shrugged. "Maybe." He shot a cold stare at Maricarmen. "Why, you jealous?"

"Hardly." Maricarmen glared back at him. "Let *her* deal with your lunacy."

"One is only as mad as the world around him."

Andrés tugged off his lab coat. There was still an hour left to the work day, but Matos wasn't around, and no one else would care if he left early. Hell, Rajiv hadn't even come back to work after the afternoon siesta. He hung his coat on the hanger above his desk. Then he grabbed his satchel and walked out the door.

When he was alone, he pulled out his iPhone and logged onto Facebook. Now friends, he could scan her profile.

He scrolled down through her recent entries. Crystal Webb posted regular status updates. Her current mood, new things she discovered, different people she had met. Their brief encounters in the chapel after that first meeting were accurately documented. Time, place, what new fact she had learned.

But for all the postings, there was no indication in her writing how she felt about him—beyond the obvious. He was a good source of information. But, he wasn't talking.

About to log off, he noticed a new entry. She was leaving now for the Paseo de Cristobal Colón.

Perfect.

Andrés pocketed his phone, jumped onto his scooter, and headed for the public promenade along the Guadalquivir River.

When he arrived, the promenade was bustling with people returning to the streets after the afternoon siesta. He strolled the sidewalk with them, searching for Crystal. Finally he saw her, sitting on a bench, writing in her journal.

"Oye, guapa."

Andrés looked over his shoulder, following the voice that was meant for her. An old man leaned against the counter of a nearby cigarette stand, blubbering perverted comments.

"Que cuerpazo tu tienes," the old man said, his voice slurred by missing teeth and too much wine. That's a hell of a body you have, in colloquial Spanish. He stuffed a pack of cigarettes into his pocket and shuffled toward her, adjusting his crotch.

She told the old man to back off. But *el viejo* edged closer to the bench.

Andrés moved in. It was creeps like that who gave Spaniards a bad name.

"Te quiero comer, nena," the old man said, now almost on top of her. I want to eat you.

Andrés was about to grab the old man when Crystal rose from the bench.

"To eat me," she said, her voice controlled but on the edge of anger, "you need teeth."

Andrés stopped short. He almost choked on a laugh as he watched the old man's eyes grow wide.

Then he heard Crystal say, "Get going, old man."

El viejo took two steps back. And then without a word, he turned and shuffled away.

"Remind me to never get on your bad side," Andrés said, walking up beside her.

"You are reminded," she said, following the old man's retreat with her eyes.

"*Oye*, back off. I'm not the enemy here."

"Sorry." She collected her book bag from the bench. "It's been a bad day."

"Do you want to talk about it?"

"No, thanks." She turned to leave.

"Hey, where you going so fast?" He skipped out in front of her. "Let's have a drink—"

"Not interested," she said.

"Oh, really?" Her response irritated him, but he would never let her know that. "Let me see if I can change your mind."

"And how do you propose to do that?"

"By giving you access to the story you are looking to find."

Her eyes fluttered.

"Come on." He took her by the hand. "I'll answer all your questions, honestly this time."

She took back her hand.

"Trust me," he said.

She blew a curl off her forehead with a long, drawn-out sigh.

"All right, one drink."

He smiled. And then dug the keys to the scooter out of his pocket. Ten minutes later, they were in front of Bar Garlochi, a veritable shrine to Spanish Catholicism and its most sacred celebration, *La Semana Santa*, Holy Week.

He pushed down the kickstand, and then escorted her into a small room designed to look like one of the floats paraded around the city during Holy Week.

The golden light of hundreds of flickering candles illuminated the area. Incense floated on the air, mixing with the sweet aroma of fresh carnations. On the walls, dozens of gold-framed pictures of the Virgin and her Son hung in holy tribute.

"Two house specials," Andrés said, approaching the ornate bar.

Silver candelabras lined the shiny countertop, their melting candles throwing eerie flickers across the room.

The barman nodded. Then he turned up the ambient music. The familiar funeral dirge all *Sevillanos* associated with *La Semana Santa* bled through the speakers on the wall. Andrés stiffened. That dirge was the same one he had heard the night his mother died.

He looked up at the ceiling. Purposefully, so that he could forget. He had become a master of the mask. All it took was a little distraction.

He stared intently at the gothic chandelier hanging from the ceiling, noticing how it dispersed a tremulous ray of light onto the brightly painted, royal blue walls. Large gold mirrors reflected the light, which bounced off red velvet ecclesiastical draperies. With his mind lost in color, the music soon faded. After a few more minutes, the dirge no longer affected him.

The barman returned with two gold chalices.

"*Sangre de Cristo*," Andrés said, sliding one of the cups in front of her. "The Blood of Christ."

"Interesting." Crystal ran her finger over the religious symbol engraved on the chalice. "I feel like I'm supposed to be taking communion, not drinking wine at a bar."

"Try it." He lifted the chalice to her mouth, like a priest offering the sacrificial wine.

"Not bad." She sipped from the cup. "It's sweet, almost like sangría."

"But it's not sangría," Andrés said. "This cocktail contains a secret recipe that few people know how to prepare."

He took a long swallow.

"Speaking of secrets . . ." He returned the chalice to the counter. "What's yours?"

She looked up sharply. "Who says I have any?"

He smiled slowly, revealing nothing. "Everybody has secrets." He squashed the butt of his cigarette in an ashtray, keeping his eyes on the counter. "Especially those who come to a foreign country, looking for answers."

He glanced up again, but she looked away, her attention skillfully diverted to the wooden bust carved into the corner of the bar. The bust was that of a dark-skinned woman wearing a white bodice trimmed in gold leaf.

"That's an odd carving," she said, eyes moving from the woman's chest to her wild, gold-painted hair. "For a shrine to the Holy Virgin."

Andrés grabbed a small notepad off the bar, noting her reaction.

"Art is where the holy and the human are allowed to meet," he said, this time actually meaning it. He knew what she was thinking. The wood carving was erotic. The folds of the woman's sculpted blouse outlined the underside of her bust rather than covering it, exposing a pair of very ample breasts.

He started to sketch a woman on the notepad he had pilfered from the bar. It was what he did when he struggled with emotions he didn't know how to release.

"You draw really well," Crystal said, watching him bring the woman's body to life. He had chosen to draw the woman reclining, lying on her side, with her head resting on her arm.

"I paint, too." Andrés did not look up from his work.

"Let me guess. Nudes?"

"If I have a willing subject." Andrés moved his pencil along the pad, forming the curve of the woman's hip and then outlining a long, slender leg. He shadowed the curves under her breasts, and the place where one leg rested on top of the other. Then he brought out the details of her face. He really wanted to impress this girl. That bothered him. It gave her the control.

Crystal looked closer.

"Hunh." Her surprise slipped out.

She had recognized her own features in the woman's face.

It was a good likeness, he had to admit. He had captured the slight downward curve to her mouth, and the high, distinctive bridge of her nose. A Roman nose. Or maybe Spanish.

"You have an amazing talent," she said.

Andrés brushed his pencil lightly over the figure, adding shadows to create the appearance of cheekbones.

"My studio is just outside the city."

He added another layer along the lids of the eyes.

"I can take you there. . . ."

"Some other time, Picasso. I still don't trust you."

A nerve jumped in his jaw. But he continued to sketch. The afternoon had taken an unexpected turn. He had lost control. Of something as simple as a woman.

24

Rajiv

Everything Rajiv once knew about his life no longer had any meaning. Logic. Order. Scheduled eating. None of this was part of his new reality. He had joined his colleagues for a late lunch, but ended up drinking instead—something that made him feel horribly, pathetically lost. For a man who had never done anything out of order, never been allowed to, the imposed shift in paradigm was disturbing. When his lab mates finally decided it would be a good idea to eat something, he offered up silent thanks to whatever god might still be listening to him. And then he followed his friends to El Kiosco de las Flores for what was now a very late lunch.

"El Kiosco is *the* place for fresh fish," Javier said, opening a large door with glass windows framed in metal. Round tables covered in white linen were set with wine glasses and cloth napkins. All the tables were empty. There was only a solitary patron seated at the bar, downing a tall glass of golden Cruzcampo. The waiter was leaning against the back counter, shirt cuffs rolled up, arms folded across his chest.

"*Buenas tardes,*" the waiter said, coming up to the front of the bar.

"*Buenas,*" Javier said, approaching the counter. "What've you got to eat? We're starving."

"Dinner's not being served yet," the waiter said.

"Forget dinner, we need lunch. What've you got left?" said Javier.

"Fried fish," the waiter said, pouring his red-faced patron another glass of beer.

Javier turned to his lab mates, who nodded their approval.

"*Vale,*" Javier said. "We'll have four *raciones* . . . *espérate.*" He looked back over his shoulder. "Rajiv, you want a salad?"

Rajiv hesitated before replying. Except for that one unpleasant occasion with the fried fish, he had been eating the Spanish version of a salad—lettuce and tomatoes, and bread, lots of bread, every time he joined his lab mates for lunch. It wasn't so much that he liked salad. In fact, he had grown to detest it. But for a Hindu vegetarian, eating the flesh of once living creatures was as repulsive as it was taboo. Spinach and garbanzo beans were always an option, as well as potato omelet. But he was growing tired of those choices. They always left him hungry.

The fried fish in itself wasn't bad, he remembered. It had no strong odor or unpleasant taste. And he liked the fact that it was served in small, manageable nuggets that were first breaded, and then fried. He stared at the framed picture of a victorious football team on the far wall. If he was going to remain in Spain, he was going to have to learn the cost of victory. He was tired of being hungry. Of being defeated. And so with five simple words, he rejected a lifetime of careful teaching.

"Just order me the fish," he said, his voice strong enough to hide his repulsion.

"Fried fish at this hour," the barman said, shaking his head. "You boys are crazy."

"We're obsessed," Andrés corrected. "With our work." He smirked at the lie.

"Mad," added Josemaría, twirling his index finger in circles around his right temple. "Totally and absolutely mad."

"And in need of more wine," added Javier. He slung his arm over Rajiv's shoulder. "To celebrate with our new friend."

Tentatively, Rajiv smiled. He finally felt . . . accepted. Although he was not sure that feeling was meant to last.

The waiter served the wine first, then brought five plates of fried fish to the table.

Rajiv's stomach cramped. There was a whole fish, scales and all, lying on the plate in front of him.

"Hey, Rajiv . . ." Andrés stabbed his fish with the fork. He ripped off a chunk of flesh and brought it to his mouth. After chewing the morsel and swallowing it completely, he continued speaking. "Why aren't you eating?" He pointed at Rajiv's plate with his fork.

"I am. I will." Rajiv stared at his plate. He swayed slightly, but doubted it was because of the wine.

"¿*Qué te pasa*, Rajiv?" Maricarmen said. "Are you all right?"

Rajiv held up his hand to hold off the question and picked up his fork.

He stared at the dead fish, at the shriveled, scorched eyes that stared back at him from the plate, taunting him.

Ugh. He shuddered. What an utterly revolting thing to do. Fry a once-living creature and then eat it. His stomach lurched. He fought to push off the image of those dead, sunken eyes.

You can do this. He looked up to see if anyone was watching, and when he saw that they were not, covered the fish's eyes with a paper napkin. Then he plunged his fork into the scaly outer layer and gouged off pieces of skin, as he had seen the others do, to get to the softer inner core.

Struggling with his fork, he managed to yank off a small chunk of flesh and place it into his mouth.

It's actually tasteless, he thought.

He dug into the white meat to pull out another bite. Then he reached for his glass, washing the fish down with a gulp of wine.

"How's the fish?" asked Javier.

"Not bad." Rajiv shoved a large piece into his mouth with increased confidence.

Two glasses of wine later, he had managed to eat almost half the fish when something sharp, like the prick of a dull needle, pierced the back of his tongue and caused him to gag.

The wine that had relaxed him turned violently against him and Rajiv felt an intense, overwhelming wave of nausea invade his body.

"Excuse me."

He pushed himself away from the table and stood up sharply. The chair flew out from beneath his legs as he stumbled his way to the restroom at the far end of the bar. His stomach churned in painful spasms as he exploded into a stall and threw out all the contents of his stomach. Panting, he crouched with his head over the foul-smelling toilet, wondering how his life could get any worse than it felt right now.

25

Diego

Diego looked over his shoulder, and then stepped into the lobby of his apartment building, hoping to go unnoticed. Joaquín had left him several messages through his father, all of which he ignored. He did not need any more unproductive activities like extortion and robbery. That was not supposed to be the plan. Nine months had passed since Catalina died and he was no closer to finding the man he sought. Joaquín had become distracted. Unpredictable.

It was time to cut him out.

Diego had managed to avoid Joaquín all day, and had no intention of meeting up with him now.

He slipped past Tito, who sat on guard at the entrance, legs crossed on the scratched metal desk, arms folded over his chest. His eyes were closed, mouth open. Diego moved quietly to the elevator and went to push the button but it was already illuminated.

"Eh, Diego *¿qué pasa?*" Tito stirred and Diego looked back. A toothless grin spread across the doorman's ruddy face.

"What's up?" Tito said.

"Not much." Diego said the first thing that came to his mind—something that did not require any further comment—and then turned back toward the elevator. The door shuddered open. About to step in, he felt himself pushed back instead.

"*¡Amigo!*" Joaquín wrapped his arm around Diego's shoulder, then turned to Tito and flashed a smile. "Let's take a walk."

Diego played along with Joaquín until they were outside.

"Get your hands off me." Diego shoved Joaquín back.

Joaquín lunged forward.

"Where you been?" Joaquín grabbed Diego's arm. "I left a message for you." He threw Diego back. "Tiburón has a job he wants done. And you're coming with me."

Joaquín looked over his shoulder, and then lowered his voice.

"It's a black Mercedes," he said.

Diego looked past Joaquín.

"Está bien," he said.

He hated Joaquín for threatening him, but he hated himself more. Both El Tiburón and Joaquín were ruthless, and wouldn't think twice about eliminating any obstacles to their lucrative business. But Diego was equally as driven. He still wanted that Mercedes.

He stood straight, pushed his hands through his hair, and followed Joaquín down the street.

A few hours later, they were in Heliopolis, one of the wealthiest neighborhoods in Seville, with one of the highest concentrations of luxury cars in the city.

The routine was the same as it always was. Joaquín wire-stripped the targeted Mercedes. Diego made sure they did not get caught.

"Woo—eee! I'm good!" Joaquín fished into his jacket pocket and pulled out the stopwatch he had set before moving in on the black Mercedes. He clicked the button and glanced at the dial, trying to read the time as he sped through the light of a street lamp. He squinted and brought the watch closer to his eyes.

"Two minutes and twenty seconds." Joaquín's face twisted in a triumphant smile. "I beat my own record!" The car swerved to the right, tires hitting the curve.

"Cuidado, Joaquín." Diego gripped the dash.

A silver medallion swung furiously on the beaded chain wrapped around the rearview mirror.

"What's wrong with you?" Joaquín accelerated. "I've got this baby under control."

Diego clenched his teeth, glanced away, and said nothing.

"I'm worried about you, *primo,"* Joaquín said. "You're starting to lose your edge." Briefly, he turned his eyes on Diego. "That may cost us."

"I'm glad to see you're worried about me." Diego stared through the windshield. They were approaching the Alameda.

"Don't fuck with me, man. I'm starting to feel I can't trust you anymore."

"How many cars has it been, Joaquín? How many people's lives have we hurt?"

"Fifteen, to be exact," Joaquín said, sounding too proud. "Sixteen if we deliver this one safely to El Tiburón." Violently, he gunned the engine. "Why all of a sudden do you care? You're getting what you want from this. Fuck me if I know what that is."

"What I want has nothing to do with you—watch out!"

Joaquín swerved to avoid the car speeding toward them in the opposite lane. He pulled hard on the wheel, braked, and the Mercedes went into a spin. It flew across the road, hit the curb, and smashed sideways into a lamppost. The lamp went out, the other car sped away, and then everything went black.

Diego lifted his head. He reached up, felt the gash on his forehead, and looked over at the driver's seat. It was empty. His eyes shot to the road. He caught a fleeting glimpse of Joaquín just before he disappeared into a dark alley. Diego staggered out of the car. The Mercedes was destroyed, a huge dent in the side. Broken glass glistened over the tire marks etched into the road. A costly loss. But he didn't care that El Tiburón would be furious. Or that The Shark would make Diego and Joaquín pay dearly for that loss. Ripping open the glove compartment, he searched through its contents until finding what he was looking for. He snatched the registration papers and ran as two wailing sirens in the distance closed in on the crime scene.

26

Rajiv

Rajiv stumbled off the bus in front of El Corte Inglés. He had no food in the flat, and there was a supermarket in this upscale department store. Only hours after the latest food-related fiasco, he had determined that he would learn how to cook—even though the concept of cooking for himself alone was completely foreign. The taking of food had always been such an elaborate, communal affair in his father's house. Nobody ate until everybody was at home. Which, of course, often obliged him to ditch friends for dinner. Now that the ritual of food intake was no longer binding, he sadly found that he had no real friends to skip dinner for.

The nature of Spanish friendships was still a mystery to him. His lab mates were good company, but they kept him at a distance. They included him in their lunch plans, but did not invite him to any of their after-hours gatherings.

He had thought about inviting himself, but doing so was against his nature. He had never had to work at friendship before. Making friends had always come easily to him.

Now there was nothing easy about his life.

He chugged more tonic from the bottle Andrés had handed him before he staggered from the bar.

Unlike all his other lab mates, Andrés was the only one who didn't laugh at him when he returned to the table.

Rajiv was grateful for that. But still he wondered how far he could go in depending on Andrés as a friend.

While Andrés and he had established a congenial rapport, the confidence of friendship was not yet there. They shared some decent conversation, about both intellectual and personal matters, but the relationship had its limitations. For the most part, he liked Andrés—despite their rocky start. The man was smart, even though at times he failed to use his intellect. He was brash, abrasive even. But he was also capable of being a decent friend.

Rajiv hoped Andrés would develop that capability. He longed for the company of a decent friend.

He waited for a police car to speed by, then crossed the street and entered the department store. He picked up a few groceries, a gallon of water, and a large bottle of Pepto-Bismol to soothe his up-until-now-treatable ulcer. Then he trudged down the narrow street in front of the building toward his apartment in La Alameda.

Panting for breath, Diego stopped running as he stumbled into a narrow alley near the Alameda. He doubled over, hands on his knees, head bent. God only knew how he had eluded the police. Relief washed over him. Then came the guilt.

His eyes landed on the crumpled papers gripped in his bloody hand. He was messing up so any people's lives. And to what purpose? Was it worth the misery? What if he never found the right black Mercedes? What if he did? Then what? Would he kill the man? Torture him? Execute Gypsy judgment? Nine months ago, those thoughts would have been inconceivable.

Nine months ago, he was a different man.

He crushed the papers. Tossed them to the ground.

There had to be a better plan.

A light breeze crawled through the alley, blowing the crumpled papers in the air. He looked up. Followed the papers as they tumbled down the alley.

A man at the other end leaned against the building on the far corner of the narrow passageway.

Rajiv stopped for a moment. Leaned against the wall of a nearby building. He rummaged through the bags, dug out the Pepto-Bismol, and poured a generous portion of pink relief down his throat. Two more blocks, one more alley, and he would reach his dreary flat.

Lost in his own misery, he did not see the young woman slink out of the shadows until she stepped in front of him. She was light-skinned, and wearing a short skirt. Her breasts strained against the laces of her low-cut black bodice.

"Hola, guapo," she said, striking a provocative pose.

Her tight skirt inched up even further along her thigh.

Rajiv did not avert his eyes. Western fashion was certainly more intriguing than the Indian sari.

"Western women are indecent, immoral." His father's words bounced around in his head. *"They dress shamefully and flaunt their bodies."*

The corner of his mouth turned up in an involuntary smile.

His father had a point. But they sure looked good while they were flaunting it.

Suddenly, he could envision a pleasant end to his lonely nights.

His smile seemed to encourage the woman.

"¿Qué haces aquí solito?" she said, parting her lips provocatively.

Rajiv stared at the woman's lips. They were bright red—as brilliant as a burst of fresh blood from a newly opened wound.

"Sorry, I don't understand you," he said, his eyes moving from her lips and feasting upon her breasts—two firm mounds of flesh that looked like they were aching to be released from the lace ties.

He turned his eyes away, a culturally conditioned response, but then returned them to the laces.

"You like to come home with me?" the woman asked in broken English, shifting her weight to the opposite hip. Her lips spread into an inviting smile.

Rajiv smiled back, debating whether he should set down the bags, or simply try to ignore the cramp in his right arm.

He decided to ignore the cramp.

If this were one of the classic Hindi movies he used to watch with Appa, this was the part where he would look into her eyes, twirl her away, and run down the rain-drenched street in carefully controlled ecstasy. He could easily imagine a Bollywood ending to his solitary nights.

"Vente." She reached for his hand. "I charge you only fifty euros, special price."

Rajiv sighed. The only good thing about old Bollywood movies was that he had shared them with Appa.

Ignoring the sudden weight in his chest, he turned and walked away, letting go—though reluctantly—of the illusion of intimacy.

"Hola, guapo."

Rajiv glanced back over his shoulder.

The woman with the red lips had already forgotten about him, having promptly engaged another man, a few years younger than himself. She brushed up against him and wobbled for one unsteady second on her stiletto heels, the falter a temporary lapse in an otherwise carefully orchestrated plan.

The man studied her for a moment, and then he said, "Go home, *linda*. Save that beauty for a man who really deserves it."

The woman's eyes widened and she relaxed her provocative pose. Then she turned to go, a young girl's laugh parting her painted lips.

Rajiv stood amazed. He looked back at the girl. She had moved off the street, but was still staring at the man who had made her feel, probably for the first time, like the beautiful young woman she was.

Another cramp gripped his stomach. He bent over slightly. Then he tripped over the curb and stumbled into the gutter. The bags landed on the street beside him.

"¿Estás bien, hermano?" The man he had seen with the young woman steadied him with a bloody hand.

"What?" Rajiv stared at the man. He looked like a younger version of his friend Kumar, long hair falling wildly over his shoulders, the same aura of unsettled energy.

"Forgive me, *pensé que* . . ." The man fumbled for the words in English. "I thought you were . . ." He stared at Rajiv, and then finished what he had started to say, "One of us." He pulled a pack of Ducados from his shirt pocket, tapped two cigarettes from the pack, and offered one to Rajiv.

He looked about as miserable as Rajiv felt.

"Thanks." Rajiv pulled a plastic lighter from his pocket, lighting the stranger's cigarette first, and then his own. He tried not to notice the blood that had stained the white wrapper red.

The man inhaled deeply on the rolled black tobacco. A cloud of smoke escaped his mouth as he exhaled.

"You are not from here," the man said. "Where is your home?"

"India." Rajiv pulled a handkerchief from his trouser pocket and handed it to the stranger. "I'm Rajiv."

"Diego," the man said, nodding.

Diego. Rajiv pondered the name. It was familiar to him.

He studied the man. And then, instant recognition.

It was the young Gypsy from the news. The one who had lost his wife. Diego Vargas.

"And your family?" Diego said. "Where is your family?" He pressed the handkerchief against his forehead. A bright red spot grew into the fibers.

Rajiv thought the question odd, but he went for a casual response.

"They're in India," he said. "I'm here alone."

"Alone?" The man sounded amazed.

Rajiv had the distinct impression that Diego felt sorry for him.

"You traveled alone?"

"Yes." Rajiv shifted uncomfortably. "Why is that so difficult to understand?"

"No one travels alone."

"Apparently I am the one and only." Baffled, Rajiv went to pick up his bags.

Diego bent down to help him.

"You look like you need a cup of coffee," Diego said, handing him a bag.

Rajiv stared at the man.

"You look like you need a doctor," he said, his gaze fixed on the nasty cut on the man's forehead.

Diego pressed the handkerchief harder against his wound.

"I'm fine," he said.

"Brilliant," Rajiv said. "Let's go get coffee, then."

What a colorful life he was starting to lead.

27

Diego

Diego stole a glance at the man keeping pace beside him. What strange affinity had drawn him to this foreigner? Identity? Compassion? With his dark complexion and sharp features, the man did look like one of them. But he wore foreign clothes, and spoke English with an accent neither British nor American. Diego had learned fairly good English through his years on the streets, but this man spoke differently, with an unfamiliar lilt. No, he determined, they definitely did not share a common identity.

Was it compassion, then? Maybe. The man was all alone. Diego pondered this. The thought of being alone was incomprehensible to him. No matter how deep a Gypsy's pain, he would never be cursed with the sadness of solitude. A cup of coffee seemed the appropriate gesture. What harm could come of that?

Diego yanked open the door to a bar that was unfamiliar to him. The sound of raucous laughter bounced off the walls, and he noticed that a few of the patrons had turned around in their chairs. He excused himself and headed toward the bathroom.

Opening the tap, he splashed cold water on his face and washed the dried blood from his hair. With the edge of his shirt, he wiped his face dry. Then he looked at himself in the mirror.

His thick hair provided sufficient cover for the wound on his forehead and he had washed off most of the blood. Only his red-stained shirt could give him away for what he truly was.

Diego pushed open the bathroom door and joined Rajiv at a table near the bar. He slipped off his jacket. Then, motioning to the next waiter that passed by, he ordered two cups of coffee.

The waiter glanced his way, but did not acknowledge the order.

A group of four men, *Madrileños* by their accents, sat down at the adjoining table. They ordered a round of beers from the same server, and within minutes, the waiter returned with four glasses of Cruzcampo and placed them on the neighboring table. His tray now empty, he headed back toward the bar.

"Oye." Diego raised his hand to call the waiter. Still willing to believe he had not been intentionally snubbed, he would ask, politely, why they had not yet been served their coffee.

Before he had the chance, Rajiv called out, *"Perdóneme, ¿Qué pasa con nosotros café?"*

Diego cringed. Rajiv's grammatically incorrect Spanish sounded unintentionally rude.

The waiter halted in mid-stride. An arrogant look of defiance soured his face.

"¿Qué pasa?" the waiter sneered. "You Gypsies can't even speak Spanish anymore?"

A man seated at the table beside them looked up from his beer.

Diego met the man's eyes, and then returned his gaze to the waiter. "He's not a Gypsy."

Almost imperceptively, the waiter took one step back. But he did not let go of the menace in his eyes. He stared at Diego, and then shifted his gaze to Diego's bloodstained shirt.

"Aquí no se sirven ni gitanos ni moros," the waiter said, his voice low, threatening. He spat out the words *"gitanos"* and *"moros"* from the left side of his mouth. The butt of a cigarette hanging out from the right bobbed up and down with the energy of his attack.

A muscle spasmed against Diego's tightened jaw. Had he not been in a foreign environment, he would have beaten the arrogance out of that man. He no longer had tolerance for ignorance.

"What did he say?" Rajiv looked to Diego for translation.

Diego crushed his cigarette into the ashtray. He felt the crease deepen between his brows as he concentrated on extinguishing the wasted butt. "He say that Gypsies and Moors no are served here."

"Ah-huh." Rajiv's eyes darted back to the waiter, who was standing by the adjacent table. "Excuse me, what is your good name, sir?" He spoke in English now, with much more confidence than when he had tried to communicate in Spanish.

"What?" The waiter turned to face Rajiv, his lips curled into a snarl.

"Your name, sir. What is your good name?"

"No entiendo." The waiter took the cigarette from his mouth and blew smoke at Rajiv.

Rajiv frowned and picked up a napkin from the table.

"Tell me, good sir . . ." He folded the paper napkin in half, and then in half again, ignoring the fact that the man had said he did not understand English. "How does one distinguish between a Gypsy and a Moor . . . and a Hindu, for example?"

"No importa. They're all criminals."

So he did understand.

Diego gripped the edge of the table. He wanted to not react, but the man was so insulting, so rude. So like the Spaniard who had destroyed his life. He sprang to his feet, shoving the chair out from behind him. The wooden back hit against the adjacent table.

"¡Fuera mierda!" Diego clenched his hand into a fist, but Rajiv grabbed his wrist and held him back.

"You want to give him a reason to believe his accusation?" Rajiv rose to his feet, eyes fixed on Diego. Then he turned to the waiter and said, "Please sir, we would like our coffee." He sat down, pointing with his head for Diego to do the same.

"Go to hell," the waiter snarled in Spanish, his back already turned as he stormed away.

Diego froze, halfway between sitting and going after the man.

"Take it easy," Rajiv said.

Diego sat down, but he was on the edge of the seat.

"You going to let that *payo* walk all over us?" Diego said.

Shit. He sounded exactly like Joaquín.

Snatching his jacket off the back of the chair, Diego stood.

"Let's go," he said.

"We're not going anywhere." Rajiv leaned back against his chair. "Not until he serves us our coffee." He folded his hands over his chest and looked up at Diego.

Diego stared back in disbelief. *"¿Qué? ¿Estás loco?* You crazy?"

"You with me?"

Diego did not answer immediately.

Eventually, he lowered himself back onto the chair, yanking the pack of Ducados from his pocket.

He fumbled to light a cigarette, but his cheap plastic lighter refused to ignite. He clicked several times, and then slammed the lighter on the table, the cigarette clenched between his fingers.

"Toma," said a young woman from the opposite table, flicking her silver lighter into a steady flame. "Looks like you need one." She offered a pleasant smile.

"Gracias," he said, cupping his hand around the flame and lighting the cigarette.

"Don't pay any attention to him," the woman said, glancing at the surly waiter. "His wife took his manners with her when she left."

The slight trace of a smile brushed over Diego's face. The woman smiled back.

Diego glanced over his shoulder at the Spaniards at the neighboring table. They were staring at him, whispering to each other. It seemed as if they were trying to place him.

Slowly, he turned to face Rajiv.

"I am with you," he said, holding onto Rajiv's eyes.

Rajiv nodded. "Good. Get ready for a long night."

One hour had ticked by and still no coffee. Rajiv lowered his eyes, bringing yet another cigarette up to his mouth. What the bloody hell was he doing here? While the waiter's attitude offended him, was it worth the fight? The man was a bigot. So why bother with him? There were bigots and racists all over the world. But they were usually the minority of a population. So why did he feel compelled to make a statement with this one?

He dragged again. Blew smoke out the side of his mouth.

Maybe it was because this bigot had attacked him personally.

"The *payo* don' like us," Diego said, drawing Rajiv out of his thoughts. "The Spanish, they hate us."

Rajiv looked around the room. It didn't seem that any of the Spaniards in the bar—apart from the waiter—felt such hatred.

"Do you really believe that?" Rajiv turned back to face Diego.

Diego lowered his eyes. Traced his finger along a crack in the table. "I never used to," he said quietly, "but, things change."

"Sometimes," Rajiv said, knowing the man's mind was still focused on one word, "hatred is only fear disguised."

Diego looked up.

"It's true," he said. "They're afraid of us. They think we're all criminals. That we steal and sell drugs." He stared past Rajiv at the group of Spaniards who were enjoying their fourth round of beer. "The *payo* don' understand us, our customs, our way of life. They don' trust us and we don' trust them."

Rajiv looked down at the table and spun the lighter with a flick of his fingers. He was amazed at how well Diego had been able to express himself in English. Confident that Diego would understand him, he proceeded to tell a story that his father had once told him.

"Reminds me of the story of the two peacocks looking down on the world from their nest in a banyan tree," he said. "The first peacock says to the other, 'Look at all those people fighting, afraid of each other, unwilling to get along. One day we peacocks will be the only ones left. Then we'll rule the world.'"

He looked up, slid the lighter across the table toward Diego.

"The second peacock says, 'Which one of us, the ones with blue feathers, or the ones with green?'"

"Peacocks?" Diego let out an unexpected laugh. "That's good." He stopped the lighter with his finger before it fell off the ledge.

Rajiv shook his head and smiled as the waiter passed by with a tray of drinks for yet another table.

"Excuse me," he said politely, "would you be so kind as to bring our coffee?"

"*Jódete.*" The waiter turned to face Rajiv, then spat on the floor. A glob of brown spit landed on Rajiv's boot.

"*Hijo de*—" Diego shot to his feet.

"Would you mind lending me your towel?" Rajiv pulled a stained cloth from the waiter's arm. "Nasty stuff, this phlegm." He wiped his shoe, folded the soiled towel in upon itself, and dropped the cloth on the waiter's empty tray.

No one spoke. There were a few muffled laughs, some sharp intakes of breath, and then the room stilled into dead air.

"Get out of here, now!" The waiter's booming voice shattered the silence.

"As soon as we have our coffee." Rajiv leaned back in his chair.

"You'll get your coffee when I fuck your mother." The waiter stormed away.

Diego slammed his fist into the table. His nostrils flared as he tracked the waiter with his eyes.

"How can you let him get away with that?" Diego said.

"Get away with what? Embarrassing himself with threats that make no sense?"

Rajiv lowered his head, rubbing his fingers methodically over the crease in the middle of his forehead.

"A man by the name of Mohandas Gandhi once asked, 'What takes more courage, blowing others to pieces from inside a moving tank, or trying to stop the moving tank by standing, unarmed, in front of it?'"

In the silence that followed, Rajiv sensed that Diego was not alone in contemplating the answer to his question.

He tensed. The waiter was approaching from behind, his gait heavier, angrier than before.

"I told you to get out!" The waiter grabbed Rajiv's arm and shoved him off the chair.

Diego jumped up, helping Rajiv off the floor.

"Déjalo ya, Fernando," said one of the Spaniards. "That's enough."

Rajiv met the Spaniard's eye, straightened himself, brushed off his clothes, and then turned to face the waiter.

"As soon as we have our coffee." Rajiv swayed slightly as he spoke. His head felt as if it were about to burst.

Diego tightened his grip on Rajiv's arm and guided him to the chair. *"Siéntate,"* he said.

Rajiv sat down, opposite his new friend.

"¡Cabrón!" The waiter slapped the table with his note-pad, turned, and stomped away.

Rajiv closed his eyes for a moment, then opened them and said, "Since it looks like we're going to be here for a while, tell me about yourself. I'd like to get to know the man now sharing the evening with me."

Diego took a slow drag, and then puffed out a cloud of gray smoke into the dusty air.

"Not much to tell," he said. The muscles in his jaw were taut with tension. "My life is simple."

He took another drag. Smoke escaped from his nostrils and lifted into the air.

"I live day to day, sometimes moment to moment . . ."

He paused, eyes focused over Rajiv's shoulder.

Rajiv looked back. The waiter had two cups of coffee on his tray, and was heading in their direction.

"I jus' try to get along," Diego continued. "That's all." He snubbed out the cigarette without removing his eyes from the waiter, who had approached their table.

"Su café." The waiter's tone was exaggeratedly polite.

Then in a flash, the smell of coffee was on Diego's shirt and in the air.

"*¡Maldita sea!*" Diego jumped from his chair.

"Enjoy your coffee," the waiter snarled, his smile triumphant as he swaggered away.

"*¿Estás loco*, Fernando?" Rajiv heard the woman shout at the waiter. "Are you crazy?"

"Come with me." Rajiv pushed Diego toward the bathroom. "And keep your head up. Nobody can take away your self-respect if you don't give it to them."

"*¡No puedo más!*" Diego unbuttoned his soiled shirt and threw it on the bathroom floor. "I can' do this!"

He splashed water on his face, then snatched his shirt from the floor.

"What am I doing here?"

"Living." Rajiv began to unbutton his shirt. "From day to day. Here, put this on." He handed Diego his shirt. "Sometimes living means standing up and being counted."

Diego slid his arms into Rajiv's shirt and fastened the buttons. He glanced at himself in the mirror. Then he followed Rajiv—who was stripped down to his undershirt—to the same table, where they asked the same waiter for a cup of coffee.

"You two just don't give up, do you?" The waiter's lip curled up in a snarl.

"Not until we are properly served," Rajiv said, his eyes firmly upon Diego.

"Well, that's not going to—"

"*Oye, mesero.*" One of the Spaniards at the next table called out to the waiter. "Bring me two cups of coffee."

"*Voy,*" said the waiter with an ugly scowl before storming off into the kitchen.

A short time later, he returned with the coffee and placed it on the Spaniard's table.

"*Gracias,*" the Spaniard said, standing up. He took the two cups, walked over to Rajiv and Diego, and placed the coffee in front of them.

"The coffee's on me," he said, placing one hand on Diego's shoulder and another on Rajiv's.

The room stilled into absolute silence.

28

Andrés

Andrés stepped out onto the balcony off his bedroom. There was a quiet stillness to the air. The Prado de San Sebastián was deserted, a ghost town of buried memories. Lighting a cigarette, he stared out over the expansive fair grounds, which a few months from now would be transformed into a tented city, crowded with *casetas*, food stands. And horses.

He dragged, searching for a way out of what Adela wanted him to do today. She had been after him all morning to take her up to El Rancho del Cielo to see the young Palomino their father had bought her. Apparently tired of renting other people's property, Dr. Aragón had entered into negotiations to buy the young filly to parade his daughter on at the Spring Fair. The colt still needed to be trained, but with the money his father was shelling out, Adela's horse would be docile and obedient for the April Fair. It had to be. After all, *La Feria* was all about appearances.

His heart lurched. And then against his will, his mind reeled back eighteen years, remembering what he wished it would not.

It had been hot that day, back in April of his seventh year. The sun beat down upon the city as work came to a halt and those who craved to be seen lined up at the Prado de San Sebastián for the traditional start of the Spring Fair, *el paseo de caballista*. The horse parade.

The parade was once his favorite part of the fair. Thousands watched *el paseo*, but only those with the means to hire a horse, and the money to look good mounted on it, could participate in the gala event.

And according to his father, Andrés and he looked good, riding together on Guerrero. Just turned seven, Andrés felt on top of the world—even though, secretly, he didn't like horses.

The smell of the horse's sweat sickened him. And he didn't like the feeling of his trousers turned wet where they came into contact with the horse's hide. But, he endured the offensive odor, the moisture around his crotch, for the greater pleasure of having his arms wrapped around his father's waist. It wasn't often his father took notice of him, let alone allowed him an embrace. He wasn't about to waste such a special moment on disgusting odors or wet underwear.

"A good-looking boy you got there," one of his father's friends had called out as his father guided Guerrero to a canvas-covered *caseta*.

"Takes after his old man," his father said, pulling back on the reins as he accepted a glass of *fino* from a pretty woman who had emerged from the makeshift house. He thanked the woman for the wine, drank it, and returned the empty glass. And then with a light nudge, he eased Guerrero into an even trot.

His father was an experienced equestrian, his study full of framed blue ribbons, gold cups, and trophies. Before he be a doctor, he had wanted to be a professional polo player. It was his grandmother, not his father, who had told him that. Andrés was always learning things about his father from other people.

According to his mother, his father knew his son would follow him to equestrian glory. Just like he would follow him into medicine. After all, what else was having a son all about?

"Come on, Andrés, let's go." Adela bounced out onto the balcony.

Andrés took a final drag on his cigarette, extinguished the butt against the wall, and then allowed Adela to lure him back inside.

"Can we go now?" Adela was wearing her coat.

He shut the balcony door, and with it, a memory that should have been forgotten long ago.

He had screamed that day when Guerrero bucked. His foot caught in the stirrup. Guerrero tried to shake him off. Pitched him from side to side like a dog fighting with a rag doll between its teeth. When he was finally freed from the stirrup, he was scraped and scared. Ten days later, he was back in the saddle.

As his father ordered.

"Come on, Andrés. Take me to the ranch." Adela pulled him toward the front door.

"You know what," he said, suddenly thinking of a way out. "It's December fifteenth. You know what that means?"

Adela shook her head.

"The camels are at La Plaza de la Encarnación."

"Really?" Adela's eyes lit up.

"Come on, I'll take you." He grabbed his car keys.

Fifteen minutes later, they were at the plaza, now transformed into a Christmas playground. Stalls had been set up, selling everything from cheese to freshly baked breads, to sausage, hand-bags, and jewelry. A small Ferris wheel turned in a slow circle. Children carried balloons. Hot chocolate, *Buñuelos*, and cotton candy were all available for purchase around the square.

He bought Adela some cotton candy, and then mounted her on a camel. There were three of them, tied together. For five euros the handler would take up to six children for a ride around the square. Adela waved to him as she passed by, secure in her basket seat.

After petting the resting camels, and feeding a few sheep, they walked down Calle Cuna toward La Iglesia del Salvador. Then they waited in line to see the church's elaborate Nativity.

While waiting, it occurred to him that maybe Crystal would enjoy seeing the Nativity, too. It was a typically *Sevillano* Christmas tradition. He dialed her number.

"Hey," he said when she answered. "Why don't you come to La Plaza Salvador? All the Christmas lights are on. It's—"

She cut him off with some excuse about being tired.

That bothered him. How many times over the last three months had he stayed late at the chapel to talk to her? Or took her phone call when he would rather have been painting? Being tired was not a good enough reason to say "no."

"Couldn't you come up with a better excuse?" he said.

She argued that she didn't need an excuse to say no.

"Whatever." He ended the call.

"What's wrong?" Adela moved in front of him. Looked up. Crystals of pink sugar dotted her face.

He took out his handkerchief and scrubbed at the sticky sugar.

"No." She turned her face away. Unlike him, Adela didn't care about being dirty.

"Why is the top of your nose all crunched up?" Adela said, avoiding his handkerchief.

Andrés squeezed his eyes, releasing the tension.

"Is it because of that girl on the phone?"

"How did you know I was talking to a . . .?" *Forget it.* He let the question trail off. "You don't know what you're talking about."

"You sounded mean."

"What?" Andrés pocketed the handkerchief.

"You talked like a grumpy bear. That's why she doesn't want to be with you."

Andrés processed what he was hearing from a ten-year-old. Then he said, "Well, since you're so smart, tell me. How do I get this girl to go out with me?"

"Bring a friend with you, silly. Girls don't like to be alone with boys. It makes them feel funny."

"Oh really?" He edged her forward in line.

"He might give her cooties," Adela said, pulling off a strand of cotton candy and stuffing it in her mouth.

"Ah, now I see."

Maybe his sister had a point. Fear of cooties was age-related. But, maybe meeting Crystal in the company of someone else might ease the tension. The woman was so damn difficult. She mistrusted everything he said, challenged every invitation. It wasn't like he was going to steal her precious virginity. That was surely already given to some other lucky man. All he wanted was for her to like him.

Was that too much to ask?

He had to find some way to make himself seem trustworthy.

Immediately, he thought of Rajiv.

That would work.

Mostly because Rajiv was not a threat to him. While brilliant in the lab, the man was an idiot around women.

But he was smart. And could make Andrés look smart as well.

Perfect. He'd try to arrange something "casual" with Rajiv. And then invite Crystal to come along.

Ironic. Andrés never would have thought he would need another man to help him with a woman. But he liked the challenge. He was tired of easy conquests.

29

Rajiv

Glad to put the events of the past forty-eight hours behind him, Rajiv reflected upon the unexpected turn his life had taken over the last few days as he strolled down Calle Peral en route to his apartment. He certainly had a deeper admiration for Mohandas Gandhi. And a sadly more profound realization that he lacked the emotional strength that had made Gandhi great. He had gotten through the ordeal in the coffee shop with only mild irritation to his ulcer. But he hadn't slept in two days, thoughts of all that could have gone wrong in the coffee shop robbing him of much-needed sleep.

When he wasn't torturing himself with the knowledge that philosophy was easier on the pages than it was out on the streets, he was building a theory about why he, a dreadfully confirmed intellectual, felt more comfortable in the company of a Spanish Gypsy with little formal education than in that of his university-educated colleagues.

He stole a glance at Diego, who walked beside him.

Analyzing the situation logically, he had come to the conclusion that subconsciously, he wanted to live vicariously through his passionate new friend. His scientific goal had given him a purpose, but left him dully predictable. To himself, at least, if not to others.

Of course, there was nothing dull or predictable to a man like Diego Vargas.

A Gypsy, all the way.

Rajiv finally understood why people thought he was also of Gypsy origin. Dr. Matos, besides being a scientific genius, was also an avid historian. Over the course of several hours, he had explained the migration of the European Gypsy from the Punjab region in India to Egypt, to their arrival in Europe in the fifteenth century. According to Dr. Matos, because their history was not written or recorded, much of what is known about Gypsy history today is based on linguistic research. Their language, Romani—called *Caló* in Spain—shows evidence of an eastern origin containing elements of Punjabi, Hindi, and Dardic languages. Fascinating stuff.

They had reached his flat. It was a dreary place, one of a group of units designed around an open courtyard. Rajiv saw his neighbor, Pili, standing outside her door.

His heart jumped and then beat faster. He had been avoiding the woman since their last disastrous first meeting. But now he found himself shamelessly watching her. She was cleaning her exterior windows, dressed in very short, very tight pants.

When they approached, she rubbed the sooty panes with unusual energy. Then she bent over to dip her cloth in the bucket of water.

Rajiv squirmed, trying hard not to notice her beautiful . . . windows.

"Buenas tardes," she said, water dripping from her cloth into a puddle on the floor.

A toy poodle nipped at her feet, chewing on the laces wrapped high above her ankles.

"Buenas tardes," Rajiv said, stepping around the puddle. He felt like a schoolboy who had stolen his first peek at a clandestine men's magazine.

Pili dropped her wet cloth into the bucket and wiped her hands on the back of her shorts. She reached up to her shoulder, slowly pulling up a strap that had fallen over her arm.

Rajiv felt himself following her hand as it moved from her shoulder, across her chest, and to a pen that hung from a chain between her breasts.

"Oye." Pili smiled at him, twisting the pen between her fingers. "You come visit me? Tonight?" She seemed to want him to notice her plunging neckline.

He respectfully obliged.

"*Um*. Well—" Rajiv's non-response was cut off by the shrill barking of the woman's dog. Startled, he dropped his keys while fumbling to open the door to his apartment.

Trying to appear nonchalant, he picked the keys off the floor, managed to open the door, and then shut it quickly behind him. In between a few short breaths of air, he invited Diego to sit down.

Tossing the keys on the table by the door, he moved into the kitchen area and placed a bottle of San Ascensio on the counter.

He pulled the corkscrew he had bought out of his front shirt pocket and attempted to uncork the bottle. Fumbling with the unfamiliar tool, he ground the cork to pieces.

Diego rose from the couch, took the bottle from his hand, and jabbed the corkscrew into the shredded plug. After a few twists and a gentle tug, he pulled out the mangled cork.

Rajiv bobbed his head in the traditional Indian way, which this time meant *I would have gotten it, eventually*.

He smiled sheepishly, then grabbed two cloudy water glasses from the kitchen cabinet—the only two glasses he owned—and poured out the wine.

Diego set down his glass and picked up a colored print Rajiv had left with a pile of photographs on the counter. He studied the print, but it was clear his mind was on another subject.

"Why you think men are so intolerant of each other?" Diego said. Two deep crevices appeared on his brow. "Why do they fight? And kill? And hate so much that they destroy lives?"

All of a sudden, Diego was in a deep, dark place that Rajiv had no access to.

"Who is the woman in this picture?" Diego held a print of the goddess Lakshmi in his hand.

Rajiv took the print and studied its familiar details. Lakshmi sat inside the petals of a large white lotus blossom, floating in a tranquil pool of water.

"It's a depiction of the goddess Lakshmi," he said, wondering how much more he should say, or whether he should share the message behind the image.

Some people liked it when he gave deeper, more philosophical answers to simple questions. Others detested it.

He hesitated for a second, and then decided to verbalize the metaphor. Diego had already allowed for it. How many people can ask the question, *Why are men so intolerant?* without expecting to receive at least a semi-philosophical answer?

"Do you see the flower Lakshmi is sitting on?" He showed the print to Diego. "That's the lotus blossom."

Diego stared at the print, and then up at Rajiv.

"The lotus is an interesting flower," Rajiv said, thinking back on what he had once been taught. "It grows out of the mud at the bottom of a dirty swamp, and only blossoms when it rises above the murky water, when it reaches the light."

He studied Diego's reaction before going on. His friend was listening intently.

"There is good in all people," he said, continuing with the metaphor. "Sometimes it's just buried in the mud."

Diego looked up sharply.

"My mother believes that the lotus is God's favorite flower," Rajiv said. "She says that the lotus is one of the white flowers from heaven that comes to dwell within the heart." He looked up and then quickly returned the print to the counter.

Diego looked ready to run out the door.

"Yes, well . . . right then," Rajiv said with a nervous laugh. "That's enough philosophy for one day." A photo fell from the pile and tumbled to the floor.

Diego picked it up and studied it for a while.

"I know what you're trying to say," he said, not looking up from the photo. "About the flower." He frowned and then fell silent. "About darkness and light. And how it exists in every man."

Rajiv did not interrupt his friend's reflection because whatever Diego was thinking beyond what he was saying seemed to have brought him meaning.

"Who is this woman?" Diego asked, still looking at the photograph.

Rajiv concentrated on refilling the glasses, debating whether to answer the question. He really didn't want to get into how that photograph had arrived from India, sent to him by his brother on his father's behalf. Who else but he and his brother could possibly understand how a father could sever a relationship with his son, but not surrender control? But then he finally decided to trust his new friend.

"That's a girl my father selected for me to marry," he said. "The latest one, that is."

"*¿Cómo?*"

"You don't want to know." Rajiv flicked his hand in the air to brush off the question.

"She's very pretty," Diego said.

"She is." Rajiv offered Diego a glass. "But I'm not interested in marriage right now, although I wouldn't mind falling in love."

Diego's hand stopped in midair as he reached for the wine. His face took on an odd, pained expression and his eyes grew dark. His hand shook as he took the glass.

Rajiv looked away, uncomfortable with the silence that followed.

Diego was the first to speak again.

"It is painful to love, my friend." Diego twirled the wine slowly around the inside of the glass. His brow creased and his lips stretched thin.

"Perhaps." Rajiv glanced back at Diego, then quickly turned his eyes away. He no longer felt the older, wiser man. "But it can't be any more painful than not being allowed to love at all."

"What?" Diego's expression changed from melancholy to confused, an emotion Rajiv was much more comfortable, and definitely more familiar with.

Rajiv lowered his eyes.

"I had this classmate once," he began, but then stopped.

He hadn't spoken to anyone about Mira since the day he chose to no longer be her friend.

"We were inseparable," he continued, cautiously allowing the story to unfold. "She was beautiful, even though her legs were crippled by polio." He brought his hand to his mouth, a tight fist that wanted to silence the memory. "And smart. She could outwit any one of us." He smiled. "We were happy together, until my father caught on and ended our relationship."

Diego raised his glass to his mouth.

"You were in love with her?" he asked.

Rajiv heard the question but did not answer.

"Have you ever had to make a choice between your heart and your life?" Rajiv said.

"Aren't they the same thing?" Diego's voice had taken on an urgent, almost angry tone.

"They should be, shouldn't they?" Rajiv rubbed his fingers over his brow. "I turned my back on Mira in exchange for the title of Dr. Rajiv Kumaran, PhD." His heart jolted. "I was a coward."

Diego focused on the glass, then reached inside and dug out a piece of cork floating on the surface of the wine.

"At the time," Rajiv continued. "It seemed like my only choice." He pushed his keychain back and forth along the tabletop. "I wasn't in control of my life."

Diego looked up from the glass. "Who is?"

"I am, now. That degree I couldn't give up, it was my freedom. My ticket out of India."

Rajiv stuck his finger through the ring on his keychain.

"Do you know . . ." He lifted the keys and swung them against his fingers. "My father never allowed me or my brother to have our own keys to the flat. My mother wore the only key to our home on a string around her neck. Our every move was known by, as Sanjay used to say, 'She who wears the key.'" Rajiv wrapped his fingers around the keys and held them in his hand. "Now I have more keys than I know what to do with." He threw the keychain on the table. "And I can choose my friends, and . . ."

"And?"

"And be with any woman I want."

"Like your beautiful neighbor, perhaps?" A flicker of mischief erased Diego's formerly somber demeanor.

"Like my beautiful neighbor." Rajiv sighed and shook his head. "Only problem is, I have no idea what to say to her."

"Las mujeres . . . they are not so difficult to understand."

"Not for you, perhaps," Rajiv said. "In all of your, what, seventeen? Eighteen years?"

"Nineteen." Diego set down his glass. *"Mira, hombre, te reto.* I . . . how you say in English? I challenge you."

"Challenge?" Rajiv smiled. "You challenge me to what?"

"To *conquistar* your lovely neighbor." Diego spoke quickly, like young people do when they get excited.

"To conquer Pili?" Rajiv sounded painfully old in comparison.

"Sí." Diego jumped off the sofa. "All right, Rajiv, I'm Pili." He thrust out his chest and balled his left hand over his hip. "Now, how're you going to seduce me?"

"Don't move." Rajiv snatched his camera from the table. "This photo's going to *Entertainment Weekly.*"

Diego laughed, brushing Rajiv off with a wave of his hand.

"*Dale*, say something."

Rajiv rolled his eyes.

"Oh God, you're going to insist on doing this. All right." Putting down the camera, he faced Diego. "Hello, Pili. What nice breasts you have."

"*No, amigo, en serio.* Seriously, what're you going to say to her?"

"All right. All right." Rajiv wiped the smile from his face. "Hello, Pili. How are you?"

Diego's eyes opened wide in an expression of bemused astonishment.

"That's it?" He dropped his hand from his hip. "That's what you're going to say?"

"What's wrong with that?"

"No." Diego shook his hands in the air. "You're going to say, *Buenas tardes, Pili, que guapa te ves hoy.*" Then you smile, and repeat in English. "You look beautiful today—jus' in case you mess it up in Spanish."

"*Buenas tardes*, Pili . . ." Rajiv mimicked Diego as he retreated to the kitchen.

"No . . . no . . . no." Diego pulled him back. "You have this beautiful woman living next door and you don' even try to talk to her."

"I'll tell you what. I'll just watch you in action and learn from the best."

Diego shook his head. A slight smile appeared at the corner of his mouth.

"*Creeme,*" he said, plopping down on the sofa. "I am no better at this than you are."

Rajiv poured more wine. Then he picked up the photograph from India and turned it over on the table, so that there was nothing to see but a name and date scribbled on the back of the Kodak paper.

"Someday, I will get married," he said, placing his keys on top of the photograph. "With the woman I fall in love with."

And this time when he said it, he actually believed what he was saying. With a young, passionate friend like Diego acting as his love guru, why shouldn't he finally be able to fall in love?

30

Diego

Diego left Rajiv's apartment different from the way he entered. A little lighter, less burdened. He had drunk wine with a friend for the first time since losing Catalina. And for the first time since her death, he didn't feel guilty about doing something other than grieve.

"Diego, where you been?" Manolito ran up the sidewalk as Diego reached for the door to his apartment. "I've been looking all over for you."

"Why?"

"They're having a *juerga* tonight." Manolito gestured behind him. "They've lit a huge *candela* near the Centro Infantil. Everybody's there, singing and dancing. It's the biggest bonfire I've ever seen!"

Diego groaned, and then fell back against the wall. One too many glasses of wine.

Manolito folded his arms across his chest, brow furrowed.

"What's wrong with you?" he said, taking two steps closer. "You're acting like Armando when he drinks a lot of beer."

Diego pulled himself straight, trying hard for sobriety.

"You go on," Diego said slowly, over enunciating his speech. "I'm just going to stay home tonight."

Manolito pulled on his sleeve. "No, Diego, come on, you have to go."

"No, I don't." Diego shook off Manolito's hand. "What's wrong with you?"

Manolito pulled him away from the wall and pushed him onto the sidewalk.

"You *have* to go," Manolito said, with such determination that Diego could not refuse him.

Reluctantly, he agreed. He slung his arm around the young boy's shoulder and walked with him down the street.

The community had already begun to congregate around the fire. The *barriada* was alive with the sights and sounds of the impromptu flamenco jam session. Men drank and women danced, seducing their partners to do the same. Lone voices rose above the boisterous crowd and broke out into song. Frenzied shouts and happy *oles* filled the air as Diego's uncles, Raúl and Alejandro, prepared a makeshift stage in front of the fire. They set up microphones and speakers on a raised platform, then tested the sound system. A spontaneous energy filled the open air.

"A mi me llaman el loco . . ." Samuel strolled toward them, arms spread wide, singing loudly. "They call me the crazy one, because I love to sing." Samuel lowered his arms, poured a thin stream of wine into his mouth from the flask in his hand, then offered the suede pouch to Diego. *"Toma, hermano,"* he said.

Diego stumbled as he reached for the flask.

"Steady, brother." Samuel put his hand on Diego's shoulder, then handed him the wine.

Diego glanced sideways at Manolito, and then turned his back to the boy before swigging from the flask. An unconscious move. He wiped his mouth across the back of his hand, then poured more wine down his throat, lips never touching the rim.

"Can I have some?" Manolito pulled on Diego's sleeve.

Diego stiffened, flask still high in the air.

"Tú no," he said, quickly lowering his arm. He tousled the boy's hair while shoving the wine back at Samuel. If he never did anything right in his life again, he would at least make sure that Manolito never lost his future to the slow, dull seduction of either drugs or alcohol.

A group of four men surrounded Diego, their brotherly embrace separating him momentarily from Manolito. Diego turned to pull the boy in, but quickly pushed himself away from the group as he saw a leathery adolescent with oil-slicked hair hand a lit joint to Manolito.

"Forget the wine," sneered the adolescent. "Take a hit of this."

The sweet flowery scent of hashish floated on the air.

Manolito reached for the joint.

"No, Manolito!"

Diego snatched the weed from Manolito's hand and crushed it under his boot. The young dealer turned and ran as Diego grabbed Manolito by the arm.

"Don't you *ever* start smoking, you hear me?" He shook Manolito hard. "If I ever see you with . . ." He stopped, breathing heavily, as he saw Manolito's eyes. Wide and wet, they had taken over his face.

Diego forced his voice to a gentle calm. "That stuff is poison, do you understand?" Manolito nodded and Diego let go of his arm. "All right, come on, let's go find your father."

Diego moved unsteadily along the plaza, but he did not release the hand he had clamped into Manolito's shoulder. He searched until he found Pablito, surrounded by his friends and family.

Armando and Emilio called out and offered him a flask.

Diego brushed it away as the men continued with their lively prattle, their voices warm and loose with wine.

"I'll see you later," Diego said, delivering Manolito into his father's care. He was still not sure how to re-integrate into the activities he once enjoyed.

"No, I *told* you," Manolito said. "You have to stay."

Diego sighed, then closed his eyes. For a long time, he hadn't felt entitled to fun. But then something changed in Rajiv's apartment today. It no longer felt wrong to be light-hearted.

"All right, Manolito," he said, slowly opening his eyes. "I'll stay for a little while."

"Yes!" Manolito pumped his arm in victory.

And then suddenly, the guitarist on stage broke into a familiar improv. Diego turned toward the music. He knew that pattern of rapidly repeated thumb-strokes like he knew his own hand. His father, Josemi *"el monstruo"* Vargas, sat on the platform, the heel of his shoe hooked on the bottom rung of an old wooden chair. His fingers moved deftly over the strings in a three-stroke *alzapúa*. Diego's heart beat faster as he absorbed the emotion transmitted through his father's guitar.

And then, his father leaned into the microphone.

"Diego . . ." His father's voice choked and he paused a moment before going on. "This party is for you, son. Your family and friends have gathered here tonight to tell you how much we love you, and--" He swallowed, his Adam's apple bobbing up and then down. "That we will always be here for you . . . no matter what it is you need."

Diego choked against a sob.

And then he stared into his father's eyes.

"Thank you," he whispered.

Someone put an arm around his waist. It was his mother.

He turned to her and smiled. She kissed his cheek and he put his arm around her shoulder, pulling her closer.

"Weren't you supposed to be somewhere else tonight?" he said. "At church, or some other place like that?"

"I'm right where I'm supposed to be," she said.

He nodded. And then he smiled.

A flurry of movement from the back corner of the platform caught his attention. He inhaled sharply as he saw Amara lift her flounced skirt in a brilliant rustle of red and sashay onto the makeshift stage. Amara was a beautiful woman, with the kind of looks other women envy and most men don't know how to handle. But he tried not to see her that way. Amara was like a sister to him.

A quiet expectancy settled over the crowd. Diego's father struck a chord and Amara raised her arms above her head, flexed her fingers, and struck a powerful pose. She leaned slightly forward, chin resting on her chest. And then she lowered her left arm to her side, tensed open her hand, and raised both arms back over her head. She stamped her heel and in a flurry of movement, began to dance.

His father joined her, following Amara's steps with the appropriate chords and notes.

And then Alejandro stepped up to the microphone.

Diego's pulse quickened as his uncle released a gut-wrenching cry.

Alejandro's raspy voice resonated within him, stirring up startling, uninhibited emotions. Pain, love, guilt, and fear. Each emotion shot through him with equal force as he focused on Amara.

She began to dance harder, beating the floor with her heels. Beads of sweat perforated her brow.

"*¡Guapa! ¡Toma que te toma!*" Raúl cupped his hands and clapped them together. In his role as the unofficial *palmero*, Raúl brought both Amara and the crowd to new heights of frenzy with spontaneous shouts of encouragement and praise.

Amara responded with added fervor, twisting her body, arms circling above her head. The expression on her face intensified and she became lost in the trance of the charged flamenco atmosphere

As she danced, her hair came loose from the knot at the back of her head until it was flying wildly in all directions. Her comb flew across the floor and landed in front of Diego. He reached out to pick it up. The bottom of her skirt brushed over his outstretched hand as she swirled away from him.

Then almost without warning, her movements became more sensual. Her skin, damp with sweat, glistened in the firelight. Her hair, gleaming with moisture, clung to her flushed cheeks in wet, twisted strands. Diego felt a hot shaft of tension rise through his body. And then suddenly, she ended the dance, spinning around at violent speed to come to an abrupt stop. The last low note of the *cantaor* lingered in the air, held in suspension to then die with the guitar at the perfect moment, leaving nothing but the raw emotion of absolute silence.

A slow, quiet *ole* broke the spell. A roar of praise followed that first *ole*. Diego released his breath as a chill shuddered through him. Amara lowered her arms and her eyes fell on him. She walked forward a few steps to the end of the stage, and then stopped. Diego looked up and she extended her hand.

"Vente," she said, breathing heavily. "Play us a song."

Diego tried to speak but found he could not even breathe. After a few moments, he placed his hand in hers and climbed onto the stage. The crowd roared their approval, shouting for Diego to take up his father's guitar.

"Toma, hijo." His father got up from the chair and handed Diego his instrument.

Diego accepted the guitar, and then sat on the vacated chair.

"Amara's going to try to get Elena to dance," said Raúl, pointing with his chin.

Diego saw his sister struggling with Amara, her dance teacher.

"Come on, you know the steps," he overheard Amara say.

Elena held back, using her weight against the numerous arms and hands urging her onto the platform.

After a few moments, he called out, *"Dale,* Elena. You can do it."

Elena glanced over at him and stopped her struggle. She pushed the hands off her body, found her composure, and walked resolutely to the center of the stage. Wisps of black hair masked her eyes.

Diego struck his first chord slowly, waiting for her to begin.

She raised her arms, arched her wrists, and began to dance.

Diego followed her with his guitar, but something was wrong. Elena was moving with the music, but she was off rhythm. Her face portrayed fear rather than confidence. He looked briefly at Amara, then at Raúl, who fell quickly into his role.

"*¡Arsa, eso es!*" Raúl encouraged Elena with shouts of praise.

Elena responded with bolder movements, but it was not to be. She slipped and fell forward, her legs folding beneath her. A stunned silence followed her fall. Diego put down the guitar and rushed to help her up, tripping over the chair before he could reach her. She ran off the stage and he followed behind, catching her as she crumpled to the ground. He knelt beside her.

"*No te preocupes,*" he said, caressing her tangled hair. "Nothing happened."

Amara knelt beside him. She took Elena's hand in hers.

"*No importa,*" she said. "What you have to do is pick yourself up, dry your tears, and try it again. I'll dance with you."

"Go." Diego brushed a tear from Elena's eye. Then helped her to her feet.

"*¡Aye bendito, mi nena!*" Diego's grandmother pushed her way through the crowd. Her two hair ropes bounced fitfully, thumping up and down with the energy of her stride.

"*No llores, mi'ja,*" she said, gasping for breath. She enveloped Elena in her ample arms, crushing her youngest granddaughter firmly against her heaving bosom.

No longer needed, Diego turned to walk away.

"*¡Eh!*" Abuela's shrill voice stopped him before he had taken two steps. "*¡Un momento!*" She panted heavily, catching her breath. "Where you going?"

Diego rolled his eyes, turning to face her.

Under normal circumstances, he had unlimited patience with his grandmother. But when she was overstimulated, her tongue took on a mind of its own, making it intolerable to be around her.

"To see my friends," he lied.

"Friends? You forget friends. They bring only trouble. You go with Amara." Abuela yanked Amara to her side.

"Abuela." Diego glanced nervously at Amara, who had lowered her eyes. "*Por favor.*"

"Amara, she nice girl." Abuela continued relentlessly. "She will make good wife. She have big hips." Abuela patted Amara's hips. "Good for making babies."

Amara flinched.

"You go with her." Gently, Abuela pushed Amara toward him.

"Ya, Mama." Diego's mother appeared beside Abuela. She pulled Amara away. "That's enough."

Abuela rolled out her lower lip and looked away. But she did not remain silent.

"I feel my heart . . . pounding." Abuela thumped her fist against her chest. "You send me to my grave. Is that what you want? You want to send me . . ." She paused and looked up into the starry night.

"What did I do, *Querido Jesús,* to deserve such a *disrespectful* daughter-in-law?" Abuela raised her hands along with her eyes. "Do you see how she treats me? Oh why must I carry this *heavy* cross? Take it from me, Lord. The burden is too great!" Abuela clamored to her Savior with thick palms offered up to heaven in fervent supplication. *"¡Aye! ¡Aye! ¡Aye! Mi Señor,* see how I suffer. Why my daughter-in-law torment me so? Why, *mi Señor?* Why?"

"Está bien, Mama. Está bien." Diego's mother soothed her agitated mother-in-law with a calm, gentle voice. She had the grace and patience of a saint.

Diego's father appeared quietly by his wife's side.

"Vente, Mama," he said, placing his arm around his mother's heaving shoulders. "Let's go home." Abuela's theatrical tension was well known in the *barrio,* but his father was, as always, a blessed calm in the storm. He put one arm around his mother, the other around his wife. Elena folded herself under her mother's free arm, and then the four of them walked home together.

Diego sighed. Then he reached into his shirt pocket and pulled out a pack of Ducados. Tobacco, strong and black, seemed a logical antidote to an encounter with Abuela.

Amara glanced over her shoulder at Diego's family.

"Abuela has spirit," she said, smiling. "I like that."

Diego shook his head. "Tell that to my mother. Mama would prefer if Abuela was filled with a different kind of spirit."

"The Holy Spirit," they said simultaneously.

Amara laughed and touched his arm. Her long-fringed shawl slid over one shoulder and slipped down her arm.

Diego shivered. And then hugged his jacket closer.

"Come on," he said. "Let's go get something to eat."

He hadn't planned on doing that. On inviting Amara out. But somehow, it just felt right.

He started walking, but then stopped abruptly. Joaquín was heading toward him.

"Go," he said quickly. "I'll meet you at Pablito's."

"Why? What's going on?" Her eyes shifted from him to Joaquín, and then back again.

"Go," he repeated, more urgently this time.

"Are you in trouble? If you are, let me help you."

"You can't help me, Mara. Nobody can." He pressed his lips together. "I started something that only I can end."

31

Rajiv

Rajiv jumped off the bus in the Arenal sector of the city. Andrés had invited him for a drink at what was supposedly his favorite bar—a place called El Café Modernista. Rajiv wasn't exactly sure what was going on, but it was definitely not that Andrés had developed a sudden desire to be social. It was more like he needed something. And this time, his need had nothing to do with work.

Andrés had said something about wanting to convince a girl that she could trust him. Highly unlikely, Rajiv thought, but the premise was interesting. Andrés had instructed him to sound smart, but more importantly, to make Andrés sound intelligent too. And, of course, trustworthy.

Rajiv promised he would try.

In addition to the strange turn of events with Andrés, things were slightly confusing right now. Instead of looking forward to work, Rajiv found himself searching for any excuse to leave the lab, which had definitely worked in Andrés's favor.

He had invited Pili to join them, which of course he had Diego to thank for. His love guru's instructions had actually worked. He had spent a few pleasant evenings with Pili.

The sex had gotten better, but while he couldn't deny Pili's seductive beauty, or her alluring sexuality, he did not feel truly comfortable with her.

The truth was, he was looking for something more than sex.

Not since Mira had he thought about women in terms of a relationship but now it was almost all he thought about. He had even mentally identified his "ideal woman."

She would be intelligent, able to carry on a conversation— preferably in English, as he had not yet perfected Spanish enough to sound more than brutishly coherent. And she would be fun, to counter his—sometimes dull—lack of social grace.

Unfortunately, what he was looking for was not what Pili offered.

He turned off La Avenida de las Delicias and continued down a side street until coming to the bar. Reaching for the knob of the wooden-framed door, he stepped into what looked like an art deco coffee shop.

He could see why Andrés favored the place. The walls were decorated with framed art and the windows covered in heavy velvet drapery. Veneered wooden tables were lined up against the wall, their surfaces spotless.

Rajiv glanced around the room. The place was definitely Andrés. Orderly. Artistic. Upper class.

He searched for Andrés, finally spotting him at a table in the back of the room. He was sitting with a young woman. A beautiful, modestly dressed, refreshingly lovely young woman.

Rajiv hesitated.

And then he moved over to the corner, hiding himself behind a group of well-dressed older men. He couldn't just go over and join Andrés. Not yet. He wanted to study the woman from a distance first, so as not to appear a fool when he saw her close-up.

The woman could be Spanish. She had black hair and a tanned complexion. But, she didn't dress like the women here. Instead of heels and dress pants, she wore tennis shoes and jeans. Instead of a scarf, she had a silver butterfly dangling from a chain around her neck.

A waiter approached Andrés and asked for his order.

Rajiv noticed that the woman already had a glass of red wine in her hand. But, Andrés turned to the waiter and said, "Bring us two glasses of Manzanilla . . . La Gitana."

The waiter nodded and walked over to the bar.

The bartender poured two small glasses of pale white wine, placed the glasses in front of the waiter, and scribbled the tab on the green marble counter with a piece of chalk.

As the waiter served the wine, Andrés stared at the woman. Then he reached over, took the red wine from her hand, and replaced it with the white.

"This is the best sherry in the world," he said, holding his glass up to the light. When the light passed through it, the flaxen yellow color of the wine turned gold. "It's made right here in Andalusia, in San Lucar de Barrameda."

"That's a pretty high claim," the woman said, smiling but reserved. "Tell me, what's so special about this wine?"

Her question was more of a challenge than a request. And surprisingly, Rajiv had understood it. His understanding of the language was definitely better than his ability to speak it.

"Close your eyes," Andrés said.

"Why?" she said.

"Trust me."

She did not close her eyes.

The corner of Rajiv's mouth lifted slightly.

"Come on, just close your eyes." Andrés reached over the table, and with the tips of his fingers, closed her eyes.

Then he took the glass she had put down and placed it in her hand. "Feel how cold the glass is against your hand."

She nodded, and then smiled lightly.

"Breathe in." Andrés raised the woman's hand and brought the glass close to her nose. She inhaled.

Then Andrés dipped the tip of his finger into the wine and passed it over her lips. "Now taste."

She ran her tongue over her lips as he raised the glass to her mouth. Her lips parted slightly.

Andrés smiled and dropped a trickle of wine into her mouth.

"Some swear they can detect a hint of the sea in this wine." He raised the glass again and poured a few more drops into her mouth.

"Can you?"

Rajiv continued to watch, intrigued. Not by Andrés's obvious attempt at seduction, but at the woman's response to it. Behind her reactions, there was something intelligent. The light trace of a smile never left her face, as if she were on to the game—and playing one of her own.

Her eyes fluttered, but remained closed.

"Yes," she said, in an eager, breathy voice that did not seem to belong to her. "It tastes salty and . . . a little tangy."

The corner of her mouth twitched, and then it was steady. But the smile was still there.

Andrés nodded. Then he offered her another taste.

"Imagine yourself next to the sea," Andrés said. "On the warm sand, your skin caressed by a moist ocean breeze." He tipped the glass and trickled more wine down her throat.

She swallowed and a light crease appeared on her brow.

"Feel the sun on your skin," he continued, "and your lover's hands, spreading warm oil across your body. Your lips . . ." He glided his finger across her lips, "ready to receive his kiss."

A small laugh escaped her lips, but she did not open her eyes.

Rajiv smiled. *Did Andrés really think that whatever he was doing was actually working?*

"Okay," she said, controlling the laughter. "I agree. There's something . . . special . . . about your Manzanilla wine."

Finally, she opened her eyes.

"Now will you trust me?" Andrés looked like a Sherpa who had just conquered Mount Everest. For the 550th time.

Rajiv couldn't take it anymore. He jumped out of hiding and burst into their space.

"Sorry I'm late." He dropped his bag beside the table.

"Rajiv." Andrés acknowledged him, rather coldly, and then he turned to the woman and said, "Rajiv works with me in the lab."

Rajiv pressed his palms together under his chin and bowed his head. "It's a pleasure to meet you . . ."

"Crystal," she said, offering him a polite smile.

Not meaning to, but unable to help himself, Rajiv found himself staring at the woman. The color of her eyes captivated him. They were like the sky after a monsoon rain, a hazy shade of blue brushed with flecks of gray.

There was an awkward moment of silence.

"So, what're you drinking?" Rajiv finally said.

Crystal raised her glass. "*The* best sherry in the world."

The right side of Andrés's mouth curled upward.

"Oh, really?" Rajiv called for the waiter. "Says who?" He shifted his eyes to Andrés. "Are you sure you verified your sources?"

"I always do."

Her eyes lingered for a moment on him, and then held steady on Andrés.

"Manzanilla La Gitana," she said, "is a dry white Palomino wine from Jérez produced by Winery Vinicola Hidalgo. It is currently the best-selling wine in Seville." She set down the glass. "But I prefer red wine." She slid aside the Manzanilla and picked up the glass of red wine. "Vega Sicilia is a rich, aromatic wine that generates respect by nothing more than simply naming it."

Oh shit. Didn't see that one coming. Rajiv had already bungled "The Plan."

Andrés emptied his glass. Then he reached into the pack of cigarettes in his pocket and snapped the lid open on his silver lighter. A crease knotted between his eyes.

"Vega Sicilia is a Spanish classic." Andrés flicked down on the flint and stuck the tip of his cigarette into the yellow-blue flame. The tip slowly ignited and he inhaled. "I'm glad you have come to appreciate it."

He turned and motioned to the waiter. When the waiter approached the table, Andrés ordered a full bottle of Vega Sicilia.

Two hours later, Pili showed up.

"Hola, mi amor." Pili landed on Rajiv's lap. Her tongue was in his mouth before he had a chance to say hello. Embarrassed, he pushed her off. Standing quickly, he pulled out a chair, encouraging her to sit down. When she was safely seated, he reclaimed his chair.

"Pili, these are my friends," Rajiv said. "Andrés and . . ." He caught her hand, which had moved to his thigh, before introducing her to Crystal.

Crystal raised an eyebrow, smiled at him, and then greeted his date.

"Rajiv, who would have thought?" Andrés sounded not only impressed, but surprised. He turned to Pili. "Can I get you a glass of wine?"

Wasn't that supposed to be his question? Rajiv drew closer to Pili, turning his back on Andrés.

"What would you like to drink?" he said, hoping she would not say wine.

"You know what I like." She ran the tip of her finger over her lower lip.

The double meaning was not lost.

Andrés whistled under his breath.

Crystal sipped her wine. Then she cocked her head and said, "It's nice to find a man who knows what a woman wants."

"Oh, believe me," Pili said. "He knows exactly what I—"

"Yes, well . . . *okay*." Rajiv flagged down the waiter. "Bring me a *cuba libre*," he said. "For the lady."

One hundred and twenty painful minutes later, Rajiv followed Andrés to the bar, hoping to talk him out of ordering another bottle of wine They were already on their third one. Andrés had consumed most of the second, and a good portion of the third.

Rajiv had never seen Andrés drunk, but from what he'd heard from the others, it wasn't pleasant. And with just one more glass of wine, Andrés would be there.

"So, what do you think about my *date?*" Andrés slurred.

Before Rajiv could answer, Andrés continued, "I have a feeling I'm going to get lucky tonight. You know what I mean?"

"No, actually I don't." Rajiv hoped his lab mate would now just stay quiet.

"Rosa can go fuck herself. I don't need her."

Rajiv rubbed the crevice that had formed between his eyes. He had no idea who Rosa was. The random shift in focus was disconcerting.

"I'm going back." Rajiv turned to leave, but Andrés grabbed his arm.

"You know what, Rajiv . . ." Andrés's face was only inches away. "That Pili's hot." He grinned. "Where the hell did you find her? In a brothel?"

Rajiv inhaled sharply. *Why won't he just shut up?*

"No, seriously, Rajiv." Andrés fell back against the bar. "She looks like she can put out." He slapped Rajiv on the shoulder. "You lucky dog!"

"I think the dog here is you." Rajiv gripped the counter, wondering why he was even answering his lab mate's drunken rambling.

"Why? You're not a man? You don't care about getting laid?" Andrés's speech was so slurred it was almost incoherent.

"What do think being a man is supposed to mean?"

"Fucking as many women as possible."

"Oh, that's good, Andrés."

Rajiv knew he should just shut up, but the man was provoking him.

"I'm sorry," he said. "But I have a different definition."

"And what might that be?"

"Being a man means being faithful to the *one* woman he falls in love with."

"That's bullshit. Being a man is fucking someone before they fuck you. Speaking of which . . ." He glanced over his shoulder at Crystal, and then back at Rajiv. "She's kind of giving me a hard time." He lowered his voice, as if he and Rajiv had some kind of fraternal friendship. "It makes me want her even more."

"That's enough, Andrés. I do *not* want to have this discussion with you."

"All right. All right. I'm going to take a leak."

"Good, why don't you do that."

While Andrés headed for the bathroom, Rajiv took advantage of his absence to think about what he'd wanted to reflect on all night: Crystal Webb.

He had to admit an increasing attraction to her. In the couple of hours since they'd met, he'd enjoyed their conversation—in English, free of the burden of having to search for words or trying to understand meaning. And he had discovered that she had a sharp wit and quiet intelligence that engaged him. But he noticed that while she volleyed with him intelligently, she flirted with Andrés. And why wouldn't she? Andrés was surely the more handsome man, and he seemed to intrigue her, as men like Andrés always did. Andrés could be charming—when he wanted to be.

He looked over his shoulder for Andrés. His lab mate was at the other end of the bar, paying the bill. *More of his charm.*

Rajiv pushed himself away from the bar.

Andrés had money. Lots of it. But Rajiv was determined to pay his part. He wouldn't eat for the next week, but so be it. He was not about to let Andrés flaunt his wealth in front of him.

But by the time he pulled out his wallet, Andrés had already taken his change from the waiter.

"Don't worry, I got it," Andrés said, pocketing his wallet.

Rajiv tensed. Andrés had gotten the better of him. That was not going to happen again.

"I'm pushing off." Rajiv rubbed his forehead. He could feel the veins bulging against his temples.

"Where you going?" Andrés stumbled into a chair as he followed Rajiv back to the table. "Let's go somewhere else and have another drink."

"That's *not* a good idea." Rajiv's voice was sharp. Then he looked at his lab mate, dispassionately. *Dammit.* He knew he was going to have to drive Andrés home.

"How about I take you home?" Rajiv said, fuming inside. He wasn't ready to leave yet.

He dug into his pocket and fished out a roll of Tums. Acid reflux was his body's habitual response to stress. He unpeeled the wrapper and popped a tablet in his mouth.

"Can I have one?" Crystal held out her hand. "Must have been the wine."

He stood like a deactivated robot.

"Hello?" She waved her hand in front of him. "Did someone turn off your switch?"

"Sorry." He snapped back to life, offered her an apologetic smile, and handed her a Tum.

He pulled himself together enough to ask both ladies if they needed a ride home. Crystal said she'd catch the bus. Pili had her scooter.

"Come on, Andrés, let's go." Rajiv gripped Andrés's arm, steadying him as he stood. "Give me your keys."

"Why? You think I can't dri . . . drive?"

"Just give me the damn keys." Rajiv's voice rose along with his anger.

"Tranquilo, hombre." Andrés pulled the keys out of his pocket and handed them to Rajiv.

Rajiv puffed out an irritated sigh as he steered Andrés out the door behind the two women.

How nice. He gritted his teeth. Both Crystal and Pili would soon be gone and he, babysitter to a drunken fool.

"Where're you parked?" Rajiv did not even attempt to hide the frustration in his voice.

"Oh, I don't know. Somewhere around here." Andrés gestured wildly with his arms. A row of scooters lined the street.

"What color is your scooter, Andrés?" It was getting harder and harder for Rajiv to remain calm.

"Black. No, I mean . . . red. My *car* is black. My *scooter* is red." Andrés grinned like a drunken jackass.

"Is that it over there?" Rajiv pointed to a red Vespa parked across the street.

"Yeah, that's it." Andrés stumbled against the curb.

Rajiv grabbed Andrés's arm and pushed him onto the seat. He straddled the scooter in front and clamped down on the handle-bars.

"Tell me where we're going," he said, pacing his words as steadily as he could.

"Los Remedios,"Andrés said.

"Thank you, Andrés, that was very helpful."

Rajiv jammed the key into the ignition and started the scooter.

And then, cautiously, he drove toward La Avenida de las Delicias, painfully aware that he was driving on the right-hand side of the road when all his life he had only ever driven on the left.

"Here, Rajiv, right here!" Andrés gesticulated wildly. "Why aren't you turning?"

Rajiv squeezed on the brake and made a sharp turn, ending up in the left lane of an extremely narrow street.

Brakes screeching, the car approaching in its proper lane slammed to a halt, the driver cursing and shaking an angry fist.

"What're you doing, Rajiv?" Andrés grabbed his arm. "You trying to kill us?"

"Shut up, Andrés." Rajiv swerved the scooter back to the right lane. "I don't want to hear you speak again, unless it is to tell me where I need to take the next turn."

Miraculously, Andrés sobered up enough to guide them to his father's flat in the exclusive sector of Los Remedios.

"Here." Rajiv tossed the keys to Andrés. "That is the last time I'm going on a scooter with you."

"But you were driving, not me," Andrés protested with a cocky smile. He stopped smiling when he saw the expression on Rajiv's face. "Want to come up for a drink?"

"Oh yeah, that'll be a whole lot of fun." Rajiv was ready to leave. But then he thought better of abandoning his lab mate, who had just tripped over the curb and was sprawled on the sidewalk, mumbling and laughing.

Rajiv hoisted Andrés to his feet.

"All right, let's go." He felt like shoving Andrés against the wall and leaving him to rot. But, unfortunately he would not be able to do that.

Just once, he would love to act on his instincts.

Andrés staggered into the lobby of the elegant Edificio del Presidente, an upscale apartment building overlooking the fair grounds.

Rajiv followed him to the elevator in the lobby where the doorman, dressed in a crisp blue uniform and wearing a cap, waited to take them up.

"Good evening, sirs," the doorman said, holding the door open for them. Following along behind, he marked the eleventh floor, eyes staring straight ahead, trained not to notice the comings and goings of the residents of the building.

"Good night, sirs," he said as Andrés and Rajiv stepped out of the elevator. His face had all the expression of a department-store dummy.

"Maybe for you." Andrés fumbled with his keys, then opened a carved wooden door that led into an ornate foyer. He flicked a switch. A crystal chandelier illuminated the entryway. Large works of art decorated the walls. And a carefully arranged collection of oriental vases graced the polished elegance of the table that separated the living from the receiving area. There wasn't one item out of place—until Andrés kicked off his shoes and left them in the middle of the floor.

"Nice place," Rajiv said.

The designer room looked more like an art gallery than a home.

"Andrés, is that you?" A sleepy voice, belonging to a child, called out from a room at the far end of the hallway.

Immediately, Andrés's face softened and his voice lost its sharp edge.

"*Sí, mi amor, soy yo.*" Andrés quickly regained his composure, flopped down on the richly upholstered sofa in the center of the room, and closed his eyes.

"Go back to sleep," he said. "I'll be in to see you soon."

"I love you," the young voice said.

Andrés swallowed, slowly opening his eyes.

"I love you too."

For a moment, there was silence.

"Andrés, listen to me," Rajiv said, glad for the unexpected reprieve from Andrés's drunken intensity. "I'm going to make you a cup of tea."

"Why?" Andrés's eyes glassed over, unable to focus on Rajiv, though he tried. "I don't want any . . ." His words ended as his eyes drooped and his mind shut down.

Rajiv let out an exhausted sigh as he started down the hall to the kitchen. A door opened and an old woman peered out at him from sleep-heavy eyes.

"Is he drunk?" she said, looking past Rajiv and into the living room.

"Ah, well . . . yes, actually. I'm sorry . . . I was just going to make him . . ."

The old woman shook her head.

"Thank you for bringing him home." She sighed, and then disappeared behind her bedroom door.

Entering the kitchen, Rajiv tried to make some sense of Andrés's erratic behavior, but found no way to understand it—beyond the excess of alcohol.

He had seen Andrés intoxicated before, but never so crudely unpleasant.

Something serious was going on.

"Hey, Rajiv. Come're. I have to tell you something." Andrés called to him from the living room.

Now what? Rajiv searched through the cabinets, found a box of chamomile tea, and put a bag into a mug.

"What is it, Andrés?" He set the microwave for two minutes and headed back into the living room. Andrés had his iPhone out, and was scrolling through a list of Twitter feeds.

"I have to tell you something . . ." Andrés enlarged the screen on his phone, isolating a single tweet.

The microwave dinged. Rajiv took that as an excuse to leave. He turned to go.

"I'm the one the Gypsies are looking for."

"What?" Rajiv spun back. "What are you talking about?"

"I'm the man who didn't stop for Catalina Meléndez." Barely conscious, Andrés stared at the Twitter feed.

Rajiv's stomach dropped. He glanced at the Tweet from JusticiaGitano. *Still looking for the Spaniard.* His body froze.

Damn you, Andrés. For putting me in this position. Of all the people you know, why did you choose me as your confessor?

What the bloody hell was he supposed to do now?

32

Andrés

Andrés squinted as a harsh ray of light stabbed his eyes. He groaned and ran his fingers back through his hair. He hated the day after.

Eyes half open, he surveyed his surroundings, still hazy in the morning light. He was lying on the living-room sofa, a china teacup on the table in front of him. Gradually, painfully, the fog in his mind lifted and he remembered sporadic details of last night.

Drinking wine with Crystal. Vega Sicilia. Rajiv. There was another woman too. Big breasts. Leggy.

His head throbbed and his eyes drooped, half-focusing on the floor. On the shoes he had tossed off and left in the middle of the room.

"Shit!" His eyes flew open.

He pushed himself off the sofa, knowing that he should remove the shoes. Father hated disorder. He stood up. Too fast. The blood drained from his face and he staggered. His arm shot out. And then his father's prized vase crashed to the floor.

"¡Joder!" Andrés's stomach flipped violently as his eyes fell on the broken shards of china littering the tiled floor.

Frantically, he bent down to pick up the hand-painted remains of what had been a collector's piece of priceless porcelain. A sickening wave of nausea rose up through his body as he worked feverishly to collect the broken pieces off the usually spotless floor.

"¡Coño!" A jagged piece of china punctured his skin, opening the flesh of his hand. Drops of blood soon began to mix with the broken shards.

Andrés squeezed his eyes shut, desperately trying not to see the blood. *"The son of a doctor, weakened by the sight of blood. It's pathetic."* His father's cruel words echoed in his head.

Bong . . . Bong . . . Bong. The antique pendulum clock on the wall marked the hour. Andrés counted seven ominous chimes. Grandma Aragón's clock sounded as morbid as the bells that tolled in the cathedral when they heralded death.

He'll be home any fucking minute. Andrés's stomach contracted into a painful spasm. It was Saturday morning. His father always came home early on Saturday morning to change his clothes after spending the night with his mistress.

A key clicked into the lock. Andrés felt his heart stop, as if a heavy hand had closed around it.

A terrible coldness iced down his aching body.

"¡Joder!" His father tripped over the shoes. "What the hell happened here?" His eyes darted from the shoes to Andrés, taking on a deep, black intensity when they landed on the shattered vase.

"It was an accident." Andrés struggled to control the quivering of his voice as he moved toward his father in the foyer.

"An accident?" His father's voice was gigantic. "You son of a bitch! That vase is irreplaceable!"

Andrés attempted to defend himself, but the wave of acid welling up from his stomach provoked vomit instead.

"You idiot! That's my new carpet!"

A pungent mess soiled the hand-woven threads of the oriental rug in the foyer, mixing with the blood that dripped from Andrés's hand.

"Get the hell out of here!" his father shouted.

Andrés heard the door to his grandmother's bedroom creak open. Then he heard the click when it closed, only seconds later.

"Go back to your whore," he said, purposely lowering his voice. "Fuck with her, not me."

"Get out of my house." His father moved forward, finger pointed at the door. "I should have kicked your ass out a long time ago. If it hadn't been for your mother—"

"Don't talk about my mother! You don't deserve to mention her name."

"You insolent fool! I loved your mother. You are not the only one here who misses her."

"Love!" Venom oozed through the word. "What do you know about love? You never loved my mother. If you did, you wouldn't have hurt her with your Gypsy slut."

"Get out." His father's voice was chillingly controlled. "You make me sick." He took two steps forward. "You are a pathetic—"

"*¡Toma*, Andrés!" Adela ran into the room, her tiny feet stumbling to reach him. "*¡La piedra mágica!*"

Frantically, she shoved the turquoise stone into Andrés's hand.

"Say the magic words, Andrés." There was desperation in her voice. "Hurry," she insisted. "I'm a beautiful boy, and your words don't hurt me."

She clamped both hands to her mouth, her eyes wide, as if she had suddenly remembered that the magic words were not supposed to be spoken aloud.

His father gripped Adela's arm and thrust her aside. "Go back to your room . . . *now!*"

"Come on, Andrés!" She dodged their father and tugged Andrés's sleeve. "Say the magic words!"

"*Shhh*, Adela, *está bien.*" Andrés's voice trembled as he took his sister by the hand and pulled her away from their father. "Don't say anything more," he said desperately. "I have the stone. I'll be all right."

"But Andrés, your hand is bleeding. It looks hurt."

"No, it's not hurt," he said, forcing his voice to an urgent whisper. "Just go back to your room." Andrés pushed gently against Adela's back to hurry her away. It was not until he heard the door shut behind her that he breathed again.

"What the hell are you teaching that child?"

Andrés pushed past his father and grabbed the keys off the table.

"Don't you dare walk away from me."

"You taught me how." Andrés crammed his feet into the shoes he had kicked off the night before and yanked open the front door. "And to think I once admired you, wanted to be just like you." He punched his fist into the solid wood doorframe. "Now, I want to be anyone but you." The hallway echoed the thud of the heavy door as he slammed it shut behind him.

Andrés hit the elevator button, his hand dripping blood on the marble tiles of the hallway. Pulling a handkerchief from his pocket, he pressed the monogrammed linen against his palm. The white cloth turned red as he entered the open elevator.

Arnaldo, the doorman, shifted his eyes to Andrés's hand, then quickly turned away, looking forward as he had been trained to do.

"What the fuck are you looking at?" Andrés said.

"Nothing, sir." Arnaldo responded mechanically. "I'm sorry if I have offended you."

The elevator glided to a stop in the lobby, its door sliding open into a mirrored entryway.

With mirrors all around, Andrés dared not look anywhere but straight ahead. He pushed his way through the double glass doors, turning left onto Calle Asunción.

The morning air was brisk. An unusual wind stirred up loose pieces of everyday life: pages of newspaper, cigarette butts, paper napkins, and crumpled cigarette packs with names like Winston and Fortuna. The streets of Los Remedios were usually spotless, but the wind had made it more difficult for the street cleaner to do his job. What the wind made difficult, Andrés made unpleasant, knocking his elbow against the man who was busy sweeping dust and debris off the side of the road.

"Watch what you're doing," he growled at the street sweeper, pushing his way through the doors of Cafetería La Asunción.

In the immaculate cleanliness of the upscale bakery he felt disheveled. So he made his way to the men's room, dropping his blood-soaked handkerchief to the floor.

Staring at his swollen face in the mirror, he let the cold stream of water from the faucet wash over his hand, eyes glued to an image he had grown to detest: his own reflection.

Eventually, he bent down over the sink, using his hands to cup cold water over his face. He buried his wet face in a paper towel. Then he raised his eyes to the mirror.

"Do not let him weaken you," he told his reflection in the glass. "Stay strong. For Adela."

33

Diego

The night of the *juerga*, Diego finished what he needed to do with Joaquín—another car-theft—and then he spent the next twenty-four hours planning a way out.

He was taking back the control he had given away. First to the Spaniard. Then to Joaquín. And finally, to the Shark.

Joaquín would be easy to blow off. Despite a friendship that went back almost fifteen years, he could walk away from what they had. Which had deteriorated to a series of stolen cars, extortion, and life lived in the shadows. The good times they once shared were gone. There was nothing there he would miss.

The Shark was not going to be as easy to dismiss. Getting into the underworld was ten times easier than getting out. But he could do it. He'd offer El Tiburón a pay-off. From money he would borrow from his uncle in Badajoz, which he would pay back by returning to his work at the ranch, or playing his guitar, or helping Pablito in the bar. He bolted up the stairs to the rooftop of Pablito's place. He needed to talk to the man. Urgently. Maybe Pablito would agree to give him a part-time job.

Yanking open the door, he was about to rush out onto the roof when he stopped short. Amara was crouched in a corner, tending her rooftop garden. He pulled back the door, leaving it half open.

He watched her snip a leaf from the stem of a red carnation. Then move over to a pot of Spanish lavender. After shearing off a few dead branches, she bent over and buried her nose into the plant's purple petals, absorbing their sweet perfume.

"You look so much like your mother." Pablito stepped out of the rooftop apartment he once shared with his wife. He stood outside the door, gazing at her.

"How long have you been there?" Amara looked down, eyes fluttering.

"Long enough to see how unhappy you are."

Diego flattened himself against the stairwell. The moment was too intimate for him to invade. But, he didn't want to leave.

He wanted to know why Amara was unhappy.

He peeked through the crack. Pablito had moved forward, taken Amara in his arms.

"This was your mother's favorite place." Pablito scanned the rooftop sanctuary—from Amara's garden to the studio apartment he had shared with his wife when they first got married. It was still furnished the way his wife had left it when they moved into the larger apartment above the bar. Someday, the studio would belong to Amara and her husband. Life goes on, Pablito always said. Even though his wife's life did not.

"I still miss her." Amara settled into her father's arms.

Pablito laid his hand on the back of her head.

"So do I, *hija*." He ran his fingers over her hair. "But whenever I get sad, I remember her in all the small things that once brought joy to her life. "Like the butterfly that dances on the wind . . ."

"Or the colors of a rainbow that brighten a stormy day." Amara finished his sentence.

The exchange seemed to be something they shared often, something private between the two of them, something that must have started when Manolito was an infant, from the day the boy's first breath was his mother's last.

Why had Amara never shared these feelings with him?

"That's right, baby," Pablito said. "Every time you find beauty in the world, you will feel her presence."

Probably because he was so self-absorbed with his own pain that he had never taken the time to understand hers.

Amara turned toward her father, took his hands in hers.

"Why can't I help Diego see that, Papa?"

Oh no. No. Please, don't go there. Diego's heart pumped like a bass guitar wound too tight.

"He will see it," Pablito said. "When he's ready."

"I'm worried about him." Amara turned away from her father. "He's spending too much time with Joaquín."

Diego did *not* want to hear this, but he was glued to the ground.

"He's confused, Mara. Angry." Pablito rubbed his hand over the shiny spot now prominent on top of his head. "Death ends a life. It does not end a relationship."

Amara turned to face her father. "Why don't you talk to Diego, Papa? Maybe you can help him."

"He won't listen right now, baby. He has to come out of the darkness first, before he can appreciate the light."

I'm trying, believe me, I am.

Diego's chest hurt. While he never doubted that people were talking about him, he had never been forced to actually confirm it.

"Is there anything I can do to help him?" Amara said.

"All you can do is wait for him." Pablito kissed her lightly on the forehead. "And help him enjoy the small things that once brought happiness to his life."

He walked slowly toward the landing where Diego stood hidden, stopped, and then turned around.

"When he is finally able to return to the country, Mara, and see the beauty he once saw there . . ." He paused, smoothing down hair no longer there. "When he is finally able to go back to the forest, then he will begin to heal."

Diego's heart jumped. He backed down the stairs, barely able to breathe. *That's never going to happen.*

"He won't go back," Amara said. "It's too painful for him."

Diego's chest felt like it was about to explode. Painful was too mild a word.

"He has to go back, Mara. He has to come to the end of one journey before he can begin another. Listen to me, *hija*." Pablito's voice moved further away from the door. "Do you know when I was finally able to say goodbye to your mother?"

Silence.

"When I finally learned how to let her go."

Diego slunk down the last stair, his purpose forgotten. He felt like a dead man walking. Ten steps back from where he had come.

34

Rajiv

Rajiv collapsed into his office chair. It was 8 a.m. and he was alone in the lab. Of course he would be. It was Christmas Day.

Exhausted from another sleepless night, he desperately wanted coffee. But, consuming caffeine right now would be self-inflicted torture. His chest was on fire.

Jerking open the top drawer of his desk, he searched through the contents of his drawer. Like an idiot, he had left his last roll of Tums on the nightstand beside his bed. He tossed aside a few paperclips. Some rubber bands. Far too many pencils. But no Tums. He shoved back the drawer. Andrés was turning his acidity into a burning ulcer.

Over the last ten days, Rajiv had become a living wreck. Besides being perpetually acidic, he now suffered from chronic insomnia. Burdened with the knowledge that he might possess information a lot of people desired, he debated, with each sleepless minute that ticked by, what to do with that information. Keep it to himself? Tell someone? But tell whom? Diego? The police? If he told anybody what Andrés had confessed, what would be the result of that choice? Would somebody else get hurt? Or die? Would Andrés be arrested? Killed by vengeful Gypsies? By Diego, even?

Diego was certainly capable of violence. That Rajiv had seen in the coffee shop. But what if the information wasn't even true? Andrés had been drunk. Rambling. What if what he said was just a drunk man's blabbering, something glued to his subconscious from a TV news report? Or his own vengeful fantasy.

Rajiv had contemplated broaching the subject with Andrés, but how does one go about confirming a confession? One made not consciously, but under the influence of too much alcohol. Surely, sober, Andrés would not have made the dubious admission of being a heartless villain.

As if that wasn't complicated enough, there was also the issue of friendship. How could he betray one friend's trust by ratting on him to another? Over the last few months, Andrés had become a friend. Not, perhaps, one he was totally comfortable with, but a friend nonetheless. Granted, the relationship had become strained over the last few days. Mostly because Andrés didn't remember much of that night and Rajiv remembered all of it. There had been a few tense moments when Andrés either made or received a call from Crystal. But Rajiv always diffused the conflict by assuring Andrés that he had no interest in the woman.

On the other hand, how could he not tell Diego what might finally bring him closure? In the few weeks since he had known the man, Rajiv had come to sincerely appreciate Diego's friendship. They had met several times. Shared the details of their lives. Developed trust. How could Rajiv betray Diego's confidence? Just yesterday, Diego had invited him to spend Christmas Day with his family. A rare invitation. From what he had learned from his colleagues, few Gypsies opened their homes to outsiders. Rajiv needed to honor the invitation.

Four hours later, Rajiv left the lab. He had spent the morning pretending to read scientific literature. After so many hours of unproductive reading, he called Diego for directions, and then caught a connecting bus to El Prado. A half-hour later, bus 31, tagged with the destination Polígono Sur, hissed to a stop before him. He hopped on. Then rode the bus to Las Tres Mil Viviendas. To Diego's home on the Southside of Seville.

Rajiv glanced out the window. The Southside was said to be a dangerous place. He believed that, though the streets were probably no dirtier or less safe than those of any major city, including Mumbai. The buildings were dilapidated, the roads full of potholes, but at least most of the forty-thousand inhabitants of one of Seville's poorest neighborhoods enjoyed the luxury of concrete housing. Most of India's poor lived under sheets of rusted tin or yards of old cloth—and those were the lucky ones.

Rajiv continued to gaze out the window as the bus passed in front of a cement-housing complex. Each building looked the same as the next—dull, monotonous structures with chipped plaster and a faded façade. But no one building was the same. Each unit boasted its own unique graffiti—some colorful, others only splotches of black paint. He wished he could understand the Spanish written on those walls.

The bus slowed to a stop in front of the frame of what used to be a covered bus stop. Diego was there, waiting for him. Rajiv greeted his friend with a hug. A completely uncharacteristic move for him. Then he followed his friend down the street. The road was lined with rows of large white vans. *Furgonetas* they were called in Spanish.

They stopped in front of a yellow building. Diego took out his key and opened the door to the front lobby. A man snored behind a metal desk at the entrance, his fleshy double chin resting on his chest, cushioned by a tuft of gray hair sprouting from the top of his shirt.

"Despiértate, Tito." Diego spoke sternly to the sleeping doorman, but there was a hint of tenderness beneath his words. "Wake up!"

"*Coño*, Diego." The man snorted. "*¿Qué pasa?*"

"Go back to sleep, Tito." Diego strode past the doorman and pushed the button to bring down the elevator. The door shuddered open, the floor a few inches below ground level. Diego stepped down into the elevator before looking over his shoulder at the doorman. "Don't work too hard," he said.

Tito guffawed loudly, his belly shaking over his belt.

Diego glanced at Rajiv, smiled, and shook his head. Then he pressed the button marked number five.

The elevator shuddered as it ascended.

As they stepped out of the elevator, sounds drifted toward them from inside the apartment. Family sounds. Shouting. A voice that sounded like a mother on the verge of losing control.

"Jus' ignore all the noise," Diego said. "Abuela can get . . . loud."

Then with yet another key, he opened the door into his world, inviting Rajiv to enter.

The homey scent of food cooking on a stove greeted them as they entered. Rajiv couldn't identify all the smells, but he detected the pungent odor of frying garlic. Onions boiling in a stew. Roasted tomatoes. The spices were unfamiliar. But warmly welcoming.

A thin adolescent girl came in off the balcony, struggling with a black lamb that was trying to get at the bottle she held in her hand.

Diego introduced her as his little sister, Elena.

The girl's eyes doubled in size as she stared, silently, at Rajiv.

"Elena, *¡saca ese cordero!*" Take that lamb out of here. A generously plump woman dressed in black descended upon the room.

"Tranquila, Abuela.*"* Diego moved over to the woman and kissed her on the cheek.

"Dios te bendiga, mi'jo," she said, her voice barely audible as she glanced warily at Rajiv. Methodically, she wiped her hands on a multicolored apron.

"Abuela, this is my friend, Rajiv," Diego said.

Rajiv went to extend a hand, but then quickly pulled it back. The old woman's brows were drawn together in a fierce glare.

She studied him intently. The braids she wore tucked into her apron rose and fell with her labored breathing.

"No, you cannot be friend of my grandson," she eventually said, resolute in her declaration. "You no are from here."

She drew closer to Rajiv, squinted, and then scrutinized his face.

"Where you from?" she finally asked.

"He's from India, " Diego said.

"India?" Her eyes bore into Rajiv's face. "And you *bata?*"

Completely intimidated, Rajiv turned to Diego for translation.

"She's asking where your mother is."

"In India, with my father."

"And you wife?"

"I'm not married." Rajiv shifted his weight uncomfortably.

"Then you are alone. How can a mother send her son away to be alone?" She shook her head and immediately her demeanor changed. "Come." She grabbed hold of Rajiv's hand. "Now you have new mother." She pointed to the sofa. "Sit. I bring you food."

"No, that's okay. Really, I—"

Rajiv's new "mother" brought her index finger to her lips, made a shushing sound, and then turned toward the kitchen.

Rajiv saw no choice but to follow Diego into the living room.

Carefully, he stepped around piles of schoolbooks, notepads, and loose-leaf papers that covered the tiled floor. A varied assortment of pencils, protractors, and rulers hindered his progress, but he finally made it over to a tattered brown vinyl sofa—part of a three-piece set that completed the modest furnishings of the room. Diego sat in one of the overstuffed chairs, seemingly comfortable with the disorderly confusion of his home.

"*¡Fuera, Elena, al balcón!*" Go to the balcony, Abuela shouted on her way down the hallway. "Out! *¡Y saca todo eso de aquí!*" She pointed with a bloated finger at the mess on the floor, ordering the girl to pick it up.

Elena struggled with the sliding door to the balcony, placed it back on track, then walked out with her baby lamb, ignoring her grandmother's orders to collect the books from the floor.

"She's obsessed with that lamb," Diego said. "She drives Abuela crazy."

"I bet." Rajiv was as overwhelmed as Diego had said he would be.

Elena peered over her shoulder. Then turning to her lamb, she stuck the nipple in its mouth, cradling the animal tenderly while it drank from the bottle.

"Whose books are these?" Rajiv noticed a biology textbook in a pile on the floor.

"Elena's," Diego said. "Her books make Abuela almost as crazy as the baby lamb."

"No doubt." Rajiv sat back on the sofa. Interesting. The girl was several years past puberty and still in school. From what he had heard from his Spanish friends, "all Gypsy children dropped out of school before the age of twelve."

Rajiv looked around him. The walls were covered with framed photographs of what he assumed was Diego's extended family. There were several group portraits, composed of numerous individuals ranging in age from infancy to several decades past midlife.

He shifted his eyes to a wooden table against the far wall, some kind of makeshift altar. There were several small cups containing flowers. Dozens of tiny candles flickered across the table. Above the altar, a framed picture of a Gypsy caravan hung on the wall.

Abuela returned with two heaped bowls of food.

"Eat," she said to Rajiv. "You too skinny. *Se te caen los pantalones.* Your pants . . . they fall down. This *caldo*, it put meat on you bones. I go get bread. Bread good for make you more fat." She pointed at Rajiv. "You eat. *A jalar.*"

"What language was your grandmother speaking?" Rajiv watched Abuela disappear down the corridor.

Diego looked up quickly.

"English," he said, almost defensively. "And Spanish."

"No, I know . . . but I heard some words that didn't sound like Spanish . . . or English."

"Sometime Abuela uses *Caló* words," Diego said.

"Caló," Rajiv repeated. "Yes, I've heard of that."

"It's the language of our people. We don' use it much . . . only a few words."

Rajiv studied the contents of the bowl Abuela had placed before him. He could identify the chickpeas and the potatoes, but there was something dark floating on top of the broth, trailing a rusty red stream of grease. It looked like black rubber tubing. He took a deep breath, then ladled a spoonful of the broth into his mouth, avoiding the large, unidentified chunk.

"You no eat." Abuela had returned from the kitchen. "Why you no eat?" She hovered over him. "You no like *cola de toro?*"

Rajiv's stomach turned a tiny flip. He thought he had heard Abuela say something about a bull's tail. But he pretended not to have heard anything. It was safer for his psyche that way.

"Eh, you no like my *caldo?"* Abuela repeated.

Rajiv swallowed, then looked up at Abuela and smiled.

"Sí, Señora . . . está muy rico, pero . . ." His spirit rebelled. He could not maintain the lie.

"I'm sorry," he said. "It's against my religion to eat meat."

"What religion! If you mama see you like this, she cry!"

You have no idea. Rajiv lowered his eyes.

The door creaked open. Rajiv looked up. A tall, middle-aged man who looked like Diego walked in with two bunches of red and white carnations. Rajiv recognized him from the news. It was Don Josemi Vargas. Abuela waddled over to the door and greeted her son.

"Gracias, mi'jo," she said, accepting the bouquet he offered. "You bring flowers for my altar. Maybe now *Mi Señor* be pleased and answer my prayer. Maybe now my Diego will make me a baby."

Diego inhaled sharply as his grandmother shuffled to the altar with her flowers.

"No, mama." Don Josemi followed her across the room. "The flowers are not for your altar." He scooped up the bouquet. "They're for you. Merry Christmas." He kissed her cheek, and then placed the carnations in a vase he had taken from a nearby china cabinet.

Diego introduced Rajiv to his father, but kept a wary eye on his grandmother, who had pulled a deck of Tarot cards from her pocket.

Don Josemi wished Rajiv a merry Christmas and welcomed him to their home. Then he gave Diego a sideways glance.

"Don't let her get out of control," Don Josemi said. "Your mother's in the next room."

With that, he opened the door separating the living from the sleeping areas and disappeared with the second bunch of flowers.

Abuela glanced over her shoulder. When Diego's father left the room, she shuffled the cards, her lips moving in silent incantation.

"Let's see what stars say today," she whispered, her eyes shifting to the door Don Josemi had just walked through. She lay three cards face down on the altar, side by side. "Will my grandson marry and make baby with Amara?" Her chest rose and fell as she focused on the cards set out before her. Then she turned the first one over to reveal the past. "The Hermit," she muttered. "Desire for peace, quiet and solitude. Why the Hermit? My grandson no need quiet and solitude. He need sex." She turned over the next card. "No, Moon card no good." A deep crease appeared between her eyes. "Moon card bring high emotion and confusion. No good . . . no good. Moon card big problem for my Diego. He need Hierophant card. Hierophant card bring desire for marriage and family."

Elena came in off the balcony as Abuela laid her hand over the final card, her fingers hovering over it in dramatic, exaggerated expectation. Sliding the nail of her thumb under the card and grasping it from the top with her swollen forefinger, she paused . . . and then let out a loud sigh. Finally, she flipped over the card.

It was the Death card.

There was silence. And then there was the explosion.

"*Aye, Aye, Aye, Mi Señor,* my misery continue! Why you show me Death card? Death card mean no baby. Nothing change. My grandson resists too much. *¡Aye, aye, aye!* Why you not give me Hierophant card for my grandson? Why, *Mi Señor,* why?"

"Mama, *por favor.*" An elegant but plainly dressed woman appeared at the living room door. She held the other bouquet of carnations in her hand. "Stop all this nonsense."

Rajiv understood the woman to be Doña Magdalena, Diego's mother, from the way his friend had once described her. A devoted wife and mother who loved her family fiercely, but hated anything that separated them from the love and grace of God.

Which included Tarot cards.

Doña Magdalena stepped into the living room. Diego introduced her to Rajiv and she welcomed him to their home. But unlike Don Josemi, Doña Magdalena apologized for her mother-in-law's "theatrics." She seemed irritated when she shifted her eyes to Abuela's makeshift altar. She mumbled something about Abuela and her pagan practices, and how such rituals were displeasing to God. And then she marched into the kitchen.

Rajiv returned his attention to Abuela, who was beating her fist on the altar and crying, *"Aye . . . Aye . . . Aye . . ."*

The shimmering flames of the votive candles nearest her bunched hand vacillated with the energy of her anguish.

"Why you not give me card that give my grandson desire for marriage? Why, *Mi Señor*? Why?"

"Mama, stop!" Doña Magdalena had returned with her flowers in a vase of water. "The cards are not going to give you anything. Not the future. Not the past. Not any kind of healing for Diego!"

Diego sprang from the chair and stepped out onto the balcony, shaking his head as he walked past his hysterical grandmother and agitated mother.

Rajiv joined him, lighting up a cigarette while offering one to his friend. They blew gray smoke into the air as they looked out over the enclosed patio. While Rajiv did not believe in the Tarot, he did recognize that God had given him the opportunity to speak to Diego about the event that now linked them together: Catalina's death.

From this conversation, he would decide what to do with the information he had.

"Is it always like this?" Rajiv began the discussion discreetly.

"Siempre. It never ends."

Rajiv looked back at Abuela, now with her head bent down over the altar, supported on her folded arms. She held a white carnation in her hands.

"My mother used to sprinkle jasmine flowers in water," Rajiv said. "That was her favorite offering to Lord Krishna."

Diego did not respond. Holding his cigarette between clenched lips, he grimaced as he pulled out a small plastic bag from the pocket of his jeans. It was filled with delicate white jasmine flowers.

"I picked these for Abuela," he said, opening the bag and handing it to Rajiv.

Rajiv brought the bag to his nose and inhaled. The sweet aroma of jasmine scented the air, reminding him of home.

Handing back the flowers, he summoned his courage and dug deeper into the meaning of Abuela's dramatic reading.

"So, tell me," he said. "Is there a particular reason why your grandmother reacted so strongly to the Death card? I don't know much about the Tarot, but it's the first time I've heard the Death card interpreted as *no baby*."

A light smile lifted the corner of Diego's mouth. He looked down at the ground, flicked burnt ash from his cigarette.

"She's an eccentric old woman." Diego dragged, blew smoke into the air. "Nobody pays any attention to what she says."

"Yeah, I know, but . . ." Rajiv hesitated. He hated giving credence to cards, but he was not against using what he had to get where he needed to be. "Sometimes," he said, digging out from his memory bank something he had once heard from a traveling charlatan, "the Death card appears in a reading when a person needs to make changes, but is resisting. The death imagery sometimes serves to remind us that the more we hate something, the more we become bound to it. The symbolic death that the card offers may allow us to move forward."

"There is no truth in a plastic card," Diego said.

"I agree, but there is truth in what God leads us to understand."

Rajiv pushed on.

"For example, perhaps you are holding onto friendships that are no longer supportive. Or maybe you are harboring hatred toward someone for some offense against you that is keeping you from being free."

"I will never be free." Diego's voice deepened and grew hollow. "Not until I find the man who destroyed my life."

"And then? What will you do?"

"I will destroy him." A shadow passed over Diego's eyes.

Rajiv nodded. He had his answer.

The Christmas Day celebration extended into evening. The apartment filled with visitors. Family. Friends. Neighbors. Guitars were pulled out. Extra tables. Raw meat was grilled over charcoal on a rack assembled on the balcony. Rajiv could now identify the smoky, carbon-heavy odor of barbecued beef. And, surprisingly, the scent no longer made him sick.

The only nauseating residual of his first Christmas celebration was the troublesome fact that he harbored a secret.

Andrés's skeleton in the closet was now his.

35

Andrés

The Christmas holidays came and went without any particular joy or special memories. On December 24th, Andrés's father carved the Iberian ham. His grandmother prepared the caviar. On the 25th, Andrés waited for the bars to open and drank shots with his friends. On December 31st, he endured his father's annual New Year's Eve party by playing board games with Adela.

He never drank on New Year's Eve.

Because his father always did.

On January 5th, he shopped for presents. That night, he left hay in a box under Adela's bed to feed the Wise Men's camels. On January 6th, he watched her open the presents he had wrapped after she went to bed.

Despite the traditions he once enjoyed, however, the twelve days of Christmas were as depressing as the ten months that had preceded them. Now almost the end of February, it would soon be *Semana Santa*. Holy Week. His favorite time of year.

He stepped through the chapel door.

Holy Week in Seville was everything he liked about the city. Death became a work of art. Grief became beauty. Sensuality and *Semana Santa* went hand in hand. Holy Week was the highlight and harbinger of spring. A time for new beginnings. New life. Last year, there was no spring. Death was everywhere. In his mind, on the news. In the memories of his mother. But this year, things were going to be different. When he popped twelve grapes into his mouth at the strike of twelve on December 31st, he made his New Year's resolution.

He was going to stop with the obsessive brooding.

Catalina Meléndez was dead. His mother was dead. No amount of drinking or obsessing was ever going to change that.

It was time to move on.

"Andrés, go help Lucas with his *costal*." Don Francisco breezed by, pointing at the young boy who had become Andrés's charge.

"*Sí, hermano, como no.*" Andrés strode deeper into the chapel. With only four weeks left until Holy Week, the brothers were in full preparation. Tonight, the *costaleros* were scheduled to practice carrying the float. Lucas, the youngest among them, was still learning how to bear the weight on his neck and shoulders. Andrés approached the boy, who was having trouble adjusting his headpiece. "Let me help you," he said, taking hold of the bottom edge of the *costal*.

Lucas bowed his head, holding the cloth firmly over his forehead. Standing behind him, Andrés pulled down on the white linen, tugging and yanking until a small, cylindrical pillow cushioned the boy's neck.

"*Ya, hermano.*" Andrés rubbed the boy's shoulder. "Be careful, you hear me?"

"I'll be fine." Lucas stood a little straighter.

"I'm worried about you. You're too young to be doing this."

"I'm sixteen. Just like you when you first walked as a *nazareno*."

"Yeah, but that's different."

Walking as a *nazareno* during Holy Week was a tradition as old as the Catholic Church in Spain. Faces masked to protect their identities, the *nazarenos* walked in silence, covered from head to foot in dark robes, called to reflect upon their sins. And, hopefully, to be moved toward repentance. Last year was the first and only year Andrés had not walked as a *nazareno* since he joined the brotherhood.

Andrés fought to regain his composure. "Serving as a *costalero* is a much more dangerous form of penitence."

Toc. Toc. Toc. Marcelo, the team captain, gave three claps with a hammer on the front of the massive wooden frame of what would become the decorated float paraded on the streets during Holy Week.

"*¡A la igualá, muchachos!* Time to start the alignment."

"Go." Andrés pushed the boy forward. "Marcelo's ready to start the practice."

The boy ran off to join the others.

"He looks up to you." Crystal walked up beside him.

"I've known him since he was five years old." Andrés smiled. "He comes to the chapel with his uncle, but I've always sort of looked out for him. His parents are divorced, you know, he comes from a troubled family." His smile disappeared. "I just want to make sure he grows up . . . all right."

"Lucas, where are you?" Marcelo looked around for the boy, who quickly came forward. "You go first. Juan, next to Lucas." Marcelo placed Lucas in the right front corner of the *parihuela*, where he would receive the least amount of impact from the weight.

"Why are there sacks on top of the float?" Crystal asked.

"They're sandbags, to give weight to the *parihuela*. When all the candelabras and flowers are mounted, the float weighs over a ton. The *costaleros* have to get used to the weight little by little." Andrés's eyes returned to Lucas. "That's why I'm worried about Lucas. He should've waited a few more years, until he's stronger."

"*¡Quieto todo el mundo!*" Marcelo ordered silence from his men with three strikes of the hammer.

A hush fell over the chapel.

"Lucas, you ready?" Marcelo called out to his youngest *costalero*.

"Ready!" Lucas shouted in response.

Marcelo turned to their leader.

"Don Francisco, your men are ready for the first lift."

"*¡Vámonos, hermanos!*" Don Francisco clapped one of the *costaleros* on the back. "Let's go, brothers! *¡A la calle con ella!*" To the street!

Upon hearing the command from their leader, the *costaleros* assumed a forward lunge position, extending their left legs forward, right legs behind to gain momentum. Then, in one perfectly coordinated, unified moment, they released the flexion and jumped into the air. The wooden structure vibrated with the effort, then landed smoothly on their waiting shoulders.

"*¡Magnífico!*" Don Francisco applauded. "That was perfect!"

"*Vamos ya, a pulsera.*" Let's walk gently. Marcelo guided the *costaleros* toward the narrow, arched door of the chapel.

The *costaleros* followed Marcelo's orders, the men in the back standing still, marking time, moving their feet from one side to another without advancing. They maintained the rhythm while the *parihuela* swayed from side to side. The *costaleros* in the front made small sidestepping movements to rotate the wooden structure.

"*Vale,*" Marcelo said, moving backwards towards the door. Good. "*Vale saliendo.*"

The *costaleros* continued moving in a slow, steady shuffle.

"*¡Sin correr!*" Marcelo held them back with his hands. "There's no hurry. *¡Poco a poco, valientes!*"

It took them half an hour to clear the door and reach the street. Once the *parihuela* passed through the door, Andrés asked Crystal if she'd like to join him for a drink.

"At the bar, across the street," he said. "It's where all the brothers hang out." Somehow, he felt like he had to add that.

"Sure, but let's stick to coffee this time." She studied him for a moment and then said, "And only if you promise to tell me everything there is to know about your fraternity."

"One of my favorite subjects." He stared at her intently. "But definitely not the only one. Nor the most . . . provocative."

"And what subject do you find more *provocative* than the Church?"

His lips turned up in a slow smile.

"Why don't you come with me and find out?"

She left with him. And while he waited for Juan Carlos to brew two cups of coffee at the bar, Andrés dialed Rajiv's number. He was supposed to have met the guy at El Cántaro, but what difference did it make? Rajiv could meet him here.

"Hey, it's me," he said when Rajiv answered the call. "Something's come up. I'm at Bar Delicias on Calle Pureza. I'll meet you here."

While Rajiv complained about the change in plans, Andrés stared at the framed photograph of the Virgin Esperanza de Triana that hung on the far wall. The dark-skinned Virgin wore a crown of gold over yards of ruffled lace. Someone had draped a silver medallion over the side of the frame, tilting the picture slightly.

"Just chill out, all right? And get your ass over here." He ended the call, and then took the coffee from Juan Carlos. That was one anal Indian. Couldn't the man ever do anything outside "the plan?"

He returned to the table where Crystal was sitting, set down the two cups of coffee, and sat opposite her. She barely noticed. Her eyes were fixed on a group of fraternity men at the bar.

"What's so interesting over there?" Andrés looked back over his shoulder. The men at the bar had turned around and were watching them. A few of the guys smiled, the way men do when they see another man about to get lucky.

"Probably the same thing that's interesting over here," Crystal said. "Are those men also *costaleros?*"

"No, they're just some of the brothers." He paused, and then said, "Did you know that serving as a *costalero* is considered an act of penitence?" He drew closer, lowered his voice. "For all the sins committed over the past year." He traced his finger slowly over her hand. "Like drinking too much wine . . ." He kept his gaze fixed solidly on the table. "And weakening to too many beautiful women."

Slowly, he looked up. Her lips, finely sculpted and perfectly formed, broadened into a sexy smile.

"No, that I didn't know," she said. "At least not that version of what it means to be repentant."

"Hey, Andrés," one of the men called out from the bar, "you gonna join the *costaleros* under the *parihuela* this year?"

"Not my kind of penitence," Andrés shouted back. "I have a . . ." He returned his gaze to Crystal. "Less stressful method of remembering my sins."

A shadow passed over the table. Crystal shifted her gaze to the window. An old woman peered through the heavy glass. Her face was wrinkled, like that of a dried-apple doll. The grey streaks in her long braided hair had yellowed with age. She looked like a portrait on the cover of *National Geographic*. The woman turned away, and then hobbled through the door. She stopped for a moment to catch her breath, and then shuffled into the bar.

"*¡Aye, Virgen!*" The old woman bent forward, squeezed her hand over her hip, and readjusted the basket hanging over her arm. While hobbling from patron to patron, soliciting their charity by attempting to talk them into buying her homemade *magdalenas,* she complained about how painful it was to walk circles around the city plagued with an arthritic hip.

When she approached them, Andrés waved her off, but Crystal wanted to know what she was selling.

"*Magdalenas,*" he said. "Mini muffins."

"Oh, those look good." Crystal asked the woman how much and then pulled two euros from her pocket.

"*Gracias, mi'ja,*" the old woman said. "*Dios te bendiga.*" She placed a bag of *magdalenas* in Crystal's hand.

"What did she say?" Crystal turned to him for translation.

"God bless you," Andrés said.

Crystal nodded, turned to the woman, and returned the blessing.

The old woman's face broke into a hundred wrinkles. And then she turned and shuffled away.

"I had trouble understanding her accent," Crystal said.

"That's because she's a Gypsy. The Gypsies, they . . ." He stopped, wiped his fingers across his mouth. "Forget it," he said. "Just stick with me." He cocked his head and smiled. "I'll teach you all you need to know about Castilian Spanish."

"Oh, I'm sure you will."

"You don't believe me?" Andrés grabbed a pen from his shirt pocket. "Mira." Look. He pulled a napkin out of the stainless-steel holder on the table and began to write. He held up the scribbles. *'Te quiero*. In English, 'I love you.'"

Crystal looked up. "Or, 'I want you,'" she said.

The corner of Andrés's mouth lifted slightly. "Exactly."

A woman's laugh snapped his attention away. He glanced over at the bar. Rosa glided up to the counter, hanging on Ignacio's arm.

Slowly, Andrés turned his attention back to Crystal. He drew his chair closer. His left knee touched her thigh.

She shifted her leg.

He shook his head.

"Please, don't pull away from me." His voice was cool. It was only on the inside that he quaked.

He edged closer.

"Kiss me," he whispered.

"What?" She leaned away from him.

"Please." His mouth was on top of hers.

She twisted away from him. "Don't do that," she said.

"Do what?" His voice was rougher than he intended. "All I wanted was one kiss. Not your fucking virginity."

"Sorry, but you're not getting what you want tonight." She unhooked her purse from the back of the chair.

"You know nothing about what I want." He gripped her wrist.

"Maybe not." She struggled free of him. "But one thing I do know. It certainly isn't me."

She pushed back her chair. "I'm leaving."

Andrés stared straight ahead. No, he was not going to get what he wanted. Not now. Not ever. The story of his life.

36

Diego

A taunting wind blew, saturating the city with the scent of citrus. Diego turned his face away. Spring had come early this year.

With his back to the wind, Diego strode down the street, aimless and agitated. The orange blossom breeze drifted upon the crisp morning air, lifting with it the raw reminder of a time when spring smelled sweet.

He picked up the pace. Couldn't God have waited a few more weeks to torment him with the unwelcome scent of spring?

It was eight in the morning. He was exhausted, but too restless to sleep. Truth was, he hadn't slept in over four nights—ever since February moved forward into March, winter into spring.

Diego was painfully aware that today was March 5th, the one-year anniversary of Catalina's death. For a long time he had dreaded this day. He had not wanted to come to the end of a year because when March 5th became March 6th, there were no more memories of his life with Catalina. Because on March 6th, Catalina was dead.

He flopped down on the stairs outside his house. He had tried hard over the last year to cope with his loss. And had actually started feeling better over the last few months. But there was still so much he didn't understand about death. About how long it took for the ones you loved to die in your heart. Or if they ever did.

Or ever should.

He felt for the silver ring on his left forefinger, rubbing it mindlessly under his thumb as he stared out over the barrio.

Was it normal to feel conflicted?

He twisted the ring round and round his finger, finally removing it. He sat up and studied the polished silver of the tiny horseshoe crafted into the metal band. Then he angled the ring slightly to see the engraving inside. *Te camelo.* The carefully scrolled lettering was tarnished, in danger of being worn completely smooth with the passing of a few more years. Catalina had inscribed the words *I love you* in *Caló*.

He slid the ring back on his finger, wondering if it was ever going to be possible for him to get close to another woman again. If he could ever love another woman in the same way he once loved Catalina. If he would ever *feel* her in the same way he used to absorb the woman who was once his life. Catalina had made him sense every emotion more acutely than he ever had before. But now what he felt mostly was a vague sense of emptiness. It was as if his heart had been encased in its own dark tomb and buried along with Catalina. And he had no idea how, or if, he could ever dig it back out again.

He hugged his arms around his chest, his fingers pressing into the worn leather of his jacket. Even with the warmth of spring, he still felt winter's chill. He couldn't seem to ever get completely warm.

"Alfarero . . . Alfarero . . ." Faintly, Diego heard the sound of singing in the distance. It was the "Alleluia Christians," singing something about a potter.

Suddenly, the music stopped and Pastor Pedro shouted, "Isn't it a beautiful day?"

The crowd cheered and shouted "Amen."

"I love the spring!" Pastor Pedro said.

Diego frowned, stood up, and started to walk.

"I love the *scent* of spring." The pastor's voice grew more excited.

Diego kicked away a loose stone and picked up the pace.

"Do you know what I found today, *hermanos*? I found one small, delicate orange blossom lying on a branch of green leaves." He paused. "Do you see this tiny flower?" Another pause. "The beauty of God's creation comes alive in the spring. We are blessed, *hermanos*, to live in an area that has so many flowering trees."

Diego slapped the side of an abandoned phone booth, wishing the people in the tent would just go away.

"Spring means new life. A change of seasons. Growth. Sometimes, when things are changing and growing around us, we may sense a need for changes that need to take place *inside* of us."

Diego continued walking, but Pastor Pedro's voice followed him.

"A new season brings changes. A new season brings challenges and exposes champions."

"*¡Aleluya!*" the chorus shouted.

"Today, I want to talk about one man who is a champion of change—King Solomon, the son of King David." The pastor's voice followed Diego into Pablito's bar, condemning him.

"*¡Amigo!*" Armando called out from the far side of the room.

"Come join us," Emilio said.

"*Voy.*" Diego scanned the room. "Where's Amara?"

"Went over to the tent," Pablito said, twisting the filter off the espresso machine.

Diego stood beside Armando. "Why?"

Pablito shrugged. He packed the filter with ground coffee and set the machine to brew.

"In 1 Kings, chapter two, verses one to three, Scripture tells us that when the time drew near for David to die, he gave a charge to Solomon, his son." The pastor's voice boomed over the amplifier and into the bar—making Diego wonder why anyone would have to go to the tent to hear what could be heard in every apartment, business, and alley of the *barriada*. Frowning, Diego watched Pablito steam the milk, and then pour it into the brewed coffee.

"I am about to go the way of all the earth, King David said to his son, so be strong, show yourself a man, and observe what the Lord your God requires."

"There are better ways to show yourself a man," Emilio said, slapping Diego on the back. His face opened into a wide, fraternal grin. "Right, my friend?"

Diego only pretended to share the old man's humor.

"*Toma.*" Pablito set the cup on the counter in front of Diego.

"Change, *hermanos*," Pastor Pedro continued. "Change was happening in Solomon's life. His father was dying. The man who had led Israel successfully for so many years. The man the people loved. The man who was after God's own heart. Now Solomon was expected to fill his father's shoes. For Solomon to grow, for him to please God, he needed to experience change. David needed to die so Solomon could grow and become the king God wanted him to be."

Diego pushed away his empty cup.

"Since I am not a king," he said dryly, "I have to get ready for work."

"Relax." Emilio placed his hand on Diego's shoulder. "You work too hard."

"That don't leave much time for *socializing*," Armando said.

"Or to show yourself a man," Emilio added, snorting with laughter.

Emilio's twisted reference to the pastor's sermon evoked loud chortles from his friend.

"Amigos," said Pablito sharply. "That's enough."

Still laughing, Emilio said, "Sorry, *hermano*, didn't mean no disrespect."

"So . . ." Armando said, carefully swallowing his coffee. "Considering we're on the subject . . ." He gave a gap-toothed grin. "When are you and Amara going to make things *official*?"

A muscle twitched in Diego's jaw. He knew this conversation would eventually come up. He just didn't think it would be today.

"Déjalo, Armando." Pablito avoided Diego's eyes as he gathered the dirty dishes. "Leave him alone."

Pablito knew the meaning of today. But like most everyone else, he didn't know what to say. Or how to react.

"Might not be a bad idea," Emilio said, ignoring Pablito. "Marriage is good for a man, stabilizing."

"Amara would make a good wife," Armando said, as if the thought had just occurred to him. "She's a great girl."

"Beautiful too," Emilio added.

Pablito shook his head, washed the dishes, and then stacked them neatly behind the counter. His silent dignity clashed with Armando and Emilio's hen-house banter.

"I think she'd marry him," Armando said.

"I think she would," Emilio agreed. "Problem is, our man Diego don't know what he wants."

Diego looked away, and then quietly he said, "I know *exactly* what I want, Emilio." He stared at the floor. "You don't know anything about what I want. Neither of you do."

Neither Armando nor Emilio would ever understand how much he wanted to get away from the oppressive sameness of life in Tres Mil Viviendas. They would never understand how much he wanted to start a new life, or how guilty he felt for wanting that new life. They did not understand because he had never told them.

And they had never asked.

A few minutes later, Diego left Pablito's bar, and then he did something he had not done since Catalina died. He entered a church. El Monasterio San Clemente. And then, far from his family and friends, alone, he remembered Catalina.

He remembered everything he loved about her. And everything he missed. And everything he knew would never be. Then he reflected on the choices he had made, about his alliance with Joaquín, his sickening obsession. He contemplated how he wanted to put an end to the crime, to the secret life he had been living. And then finally, he thought about his future.

The last conversation with Armando and Emilio had flustered him. They had not said anything he hadn't heard before, but maybe today he had simply chosen to listen.

Marriage would stabilize him, many said—including his family. And Amara was a logical option for him to consider as a wife.

Had he been a woman in his culture, remarriage would not have been suggested for at least another year. But he was a man. The rules were different. Men were more vulnerable, more volatile. Marriage would temper him, his family said, as well as stop the gossip.

Amara was a *moza,* the neighbors whispered, loud enough for all to hear, untouched by a man and set aside for marriage. And according to the gossip, Diego was making it difficult for Amara to find a man to marry. At eighteen, it was time for her to think seriously about becoming a wife and mother. Diego either had to move out of the way or move forward with their relationship.

Diego thought carefully about those two options. He could not envision his life without Amara in it. But to marry her did not seem completely right. Marriage meant so many things he wasn't prepared to face again. First and most importantly it meant that he would have to crack open his heart, to expose himself to love—only to possibly lose it again.

The love he felt for Amara right now was that of a man holding back his heart. He loved her, as a brother loves a sister, but he was not allowing himself to be in love with her. Who in his right mind would ever want to feel such an intense emotion again, only to set himself up for the possibility of an equally intense amount of pain?

And yet, he could not imagine not loving again because choosing not to love would be like living without a soul. Without love, he was only a lifeless, empty body.

But, love led to other things. Passion. Desire. Physical intimacy. And, of course, marriage.

Marriage meant family. Family meant children. Children meant babies. And babies meant a pregnancy. He was not prepared to risk another woman's life by getting her pregnant. And yet, wasn't that the natural progression of love?

He was confused, yes, but of one thing he was sure. He was not going to stay like this. Stagnation was only a different kind of death. Finally, after two hours alone with his thoughts, his fears, and his grief, a plan became clear. He was going to take charge of his life. To go forward. He was going to open his heart. One painful crack at a time.

Tomorrow, he would take out the chisel. But today, he was going to celebrate the memory of his wife.

37

Andrés

Andrés dragged slowly on his diminishing cigarette, blowing smoke against the dirty window of the taxi he had hired to take him to María Luisa Park. It was March 29th. Palm Sunday. His father was home. Adela with Abuela. Rosa with Ignacio. And he, all alone.

On the two-year anniversary of his mother's death.

Life couldn't get any more fucked up than that.

"Going to see the processions?" the driver said.

Andrés blew smoke into the already acrid air, his only response.

The taxi driver slowed to a stop in front of the park just as the scheduled procession was entering the gates. A long line of robed men snaked along the tree-lined path. The metallic clinking of the silver staffs of the lead *nazarenos* marked the rhythm of their walk. The penitents were dressed in purple robes and carried five-foot tapers. The flames of the *cirios* hissed in the wind, joining with the silver staffs to create an eerie acoustic.

Andrés focused on a young boy struggling to adjust the cloth that covered his face. The boy's *capirote* had slipped to the side, the eyeholes knocked out of place. Andrés watched as the boy tugged furiously on the headpiece. And then he heard a small, frightened voice beneath the heavy drapery.

"I can't breathe," the child said, his candle slipping to the side. "I can't breathe!" The boy's voice had become louder, more frightened and insistent.

Andrés rushed toward the boy. "Take off your *capirote*," he said, kneeling so that he could be eye level with the boy.

"No, I can't." The boy's candle tilted further to the side as he fought with the sweaty material covering his face. "It's my penitence."

"I know, brother, I know, but what's going to happen if you faint because you can't breathe?" Andrés steadied the taper in the boy's hand, then helped him remove the pointed cap. "They'll take you out of the procession and you won't be able to finish the *recorrida*."

Andrés reached into his pocket for his handkerchief, wiped the child's face, then smoothed his fingers through the young boy's hair.

"Just catch your breath," he said. "And then keep walking. When you're feeling a little better, put the *capirote* back on. Now go ahead, get back in line." Gently, Andrés pushed the boy back into the row of *nazarenos*.

Then continued his mad observation of the festivities of the night.

Twelve hours later, Andrés was exhausted. He had spent the night on the streets, moving from one procession to another, from one bar to the next. His head was dull, the after-effect of whisky mixed with too much wine. He stepped into a nearby coffee shop, ordered a cup of black coffee, and lit his last cigarette, crumpling the empty packet and throwing it to the floor.

After several bitter swallows of coffee, he took his iPhone from its cover. *You awake?* he texted Rosa.

The phone buzzed her reply. *No. It's 7 a.m. Go away, Andrés.*

I need you today, he texted back.

He had debated all night whether or not to contact Rosa. Most every argument he came up with ended with a solid *no*. But if anyone could be sympathetic to him today, it would be Rosa. She had loved his mother deeply. And like him, still honored the woman's memory.

Andrés waited, but she did not reply. He sent another text.

Will you go with me to my mother's grave?

The phone rang.

He dropped the device in his rush to answer it.

"Let it go, Andrés." Rosa sounded half asleep. "It's not what your mother would want."

"Yes, she would." He switched the phone to his other ear. "She would want us to remember her."

"Not like that. You know what happened last year when you went to the cemetery."

Last year, after visiting his mother's tomb, he left distraught. Then he went to the Southside, bought some potent cocaine, got high, and provoked a fight. With his father. It was the first time he had actually struck the man.

"That's not going to happen," he said. "I'm past that."

Rosa sighed. "I'm going back to sleep."

"No, please. Come with me."

"I'm not going through that again."

"It won't be like that, I promise."

"You can't make that kind of promise, Andrés, I know you." Rosa sounded awake now. "You sabotage everything you do. Everything you say."

"What if I don't? What if I can prove to you that I've changed?"

"It's too early in the morning, Andrés. Call me later."

The line clicked off.

Andrés lowered his phone. Returned it to its case.

The hell with it. He didn't need her.

The door swung open, ushering in a gust of wind that carried the heavy smell of yesterday's incense. A young girl entered the coffee shop, holding a basket of red roses on her arm. Andrés looked over at her. And then called her to the table.

"Dame una." He dug a leather coin purse out of his pocket and handed her a few euros.

The girl accepted the coins, but did not give him a rose. She stood before him, her hand outstretched.

"You're a thief." Andrés grabbed a long-stemmed rose from her basket. *"Vete."* He flipped her off.

She turned away from him. The rings around her ankles clinked together as she jingled toward a group of tourists drinking coffee against the far wall.

Andrés pushed the stool out from under him and threw some change on the bar. Then flagging down a taxi, he instructed the driver to take him to the San Fernando cemetery.

Silently, the driver made his way up the cypress-lined avenue into the heart of the cemetery. They drove past the bronze statue of the bullfighter, Francisco Rivera, his last fight immortalized in cast metal. Beyond the neatly trimmed hedges were the mausoleums and monuments, including the Aragón Del Río family tomb. The driver stopped and Andrés got out, fumbling in his pocket for the key to his mother's final resting place.

An alabaster angel guarded the heavy door, her wings spread over the portal. He pulled back the bolt and the railed door opened into a dank, musty chamber.

"*Ugh* . . ." He shivered. The smell of moldering wood and stale dust accosted his senses. He brushed a cobweb from the doorframe and entered the burial chamber.

Something rustled in the shadows, scurrying away as he approached. The wind invaded the cracks between the walls. A chill crawled down his spine as a cold draft crept along the back of his neck. A thin stream of light filtered through the dust of the window, but was too hazy to illuminate the shadows of the room. He stood at the door for a moment until his eyes adjusted. And then tentatively, he approached his mother's tomb.

"*Para ti,*" he whispered. Gently, he placed a red rose on the white sarcophagus. A tear formed in the corner of his eye. "For you." His hand lay still upon the cold, marble tomb. "*Te amo*, Mamá." The tear that had formed in his eye rolled slowly down his cheek, catching and twisting on the stubble of his unshaven face. Life at times seemed unmercifully unfair.

Slam! The door flew shut with a sudden rush of wind. Andrés jumped. He moved toward the door. He needed to get out. The darkness. The morbid stillness of stale, dead air crept through his pores, filling him with fear and loathing. Hate and despair.

Thud. Something hit the door. Its dull *thwack* resounded through the ghostly chamber. Andrés grabbed for the iron latch. With a heavy shove of his shoulder, he pushed the door open. But before going through, he turned back to address the spirit that lived within the shadows of the room.

"I will never forget what they did to you," he whispered. "Father and his Gypsy whore. I will never forget."

38

Diego

Diego reached into his jacket pocket and fished out the piece of rope he had stuffed inside. He leaned back against the counter of Pablito's bar, summoning the courage to talk to Amara. Now that he had decided to dig into his chest, he found it easier to work with the rope he was familiar with than with the chisel he needed to learn how to use.

"Start by folding a loop under the rope to make two loops," he told Manolito, demonstrating with the rope in his hand. The boy wanted to learn how to make a slip-knot. "By beginning the knot this way, you can choose which side of the knot will slip to tighten, or to untie." He showed the rope to Manolito. "Which side do you want to slip?"

"The left," Manolito said, eagerly.

Diego passed the left loop through the right one and handed the rope to Manolito.

"Go ahead, tie something up."

Manolito searched the room, his eyes landing on an empty wine bottle on the back counter. He rushed over and roped the bottle, tightening the knot securely.

"There, I did it." He lifted the bottle and swung it by the rope.

"Good. Now slip out of the knot."

Manolito pulled the long end of the rope and the slipknot slid through easily.

Diego glanced over at Amara. She lowered her eyes and smiled.

"Bring me that rope," Diego said. A hairline crack had opened in his heart. He felt as if he were fourteen years old again, learning how to flirt. The corners of his mouth turned up in a smile. He tied another knot and then looked up at Amara. "You're getting the hang of it, Manolito," he said, his gaze still fixed on her. "But now you have to try something a little harder." He slid off the stool, rope in hand. "You have to try to rope something moving, like a . . ." He pretended to be thinking. "Like an animal." He moved closer to her, so close that he could absorb her scent. She smelled of baby powder and shampoo, a light, fresh odor that wrapped itself around his senses. "Or a woman, perhaps." He grabbed Amara's hands and before she could resist, he had her hands tied at the wrist in a secure knot.

She struggled with the rope but pulled the wrong tie, tightening rather than loosening the cord.

"Get this off of me," she said, pretending to be irritated.

Manolito howled with laughter.

"You got her Diego! That was good!"

Diego took Amara's bound hands in his. He hesitated, unsure whether to continue with the playfulness he had started. But then he took a deep breath and said, "Tell me you love me."

It felt good to be light-hearted.

An expression that looked like fear passed over her face.

Diego's heart pounded. He was crossing the boundary of discretion.

Amara looked shocked. Mechanically, she shook her head.

"Tell me," he said, feeling as scared as she looked.

"Kiss her on the lips, Diego," Manolito shouted. "Then she'll tell you."

Diego leaned in as if to kiss her, but Amara stopped him with the tip of her finger. "Not until you untie me," she said.

A shiver passed through him. Amara's little brother was too young to understand the rules of friendship. Amara, on the other hand, knew exactly what she was doing. She was flirting with him.

Diego prayed her father would not walk into the bar anytime soon. Because now he wanted to kiss her. He slipped the knot with one smooth pull and the rope tumbled to the floor. He took two steps forward. His gaze met hers as he drew closer. Then he hesitated. It was as if he had stepped into a room and wanted to open a window, but hadn't yet closed the door behind him.

But then he decided to kiss her.

It was one of the sweetest sensations he had ever known.

He did not want the kiss to end, but Manolito's wild applause made them aware that they were not alone.

Diego backed away, his mouth open, eyes wide.

Amara brought her hand to her mouth, her eyes equally as wide.

His heart beating wildly, Diego snatched a leather cord from the bar. "Slip knots are used for many purposes," he said to Manolito, his voice trembling slightly. "Including jewelry-making."

He moved behind the bar and pulled out a box of colored baubles and beads, spreading a few silver charms on the counter.

"It's a perfect knot for finishing off a cord necklace." He bit down on his lower lip, purposely avoiding Amara's eyes.

"Now," he continued, striving for playful. "Who was that pretty little girl you have your eye on?" He glanced over at Manolito.

"Cristina," Manolito said, eyes bright.

"Ah yes, Cristina." Diego spread his hand over the charms. "Pick one for the young lady."

Manolito sifted through the silver-plated charms, contemplated the selection, and then chose a small butterfly.

"Good choice."

Diego threaded the leather cord through the loop on top of the butterfly, centered the charm on the cord, and then tied an overhand knot on both sides of the butterfly.

"Here." He handed the necklace to Manolito. "Give this to Cristina." He smiled at the boy. "But I will not be responsible for what happens once you present the young lady with such a powerful necklace."

Manolito's eyes grew big. "What's going to happen?"

"Oh, I can't tell you that." Diego busied himself collecting the beads from the counter, pretending to ignore Manolito. "All I can say is . . ." He did not look up from his task. "When I gave a similar necklace to your sister . . ." He snapped down on the plastic lid and returned the box to its place under the counter.

"What? What happened?" Manolito pulled on Diego's sleeve to get his attention.

Diego's mind flashed back to Christmas Eve, when he had presented a small silver cross necklace to Amara. He leaned down and whispered in Manolito's ear, "She kissed me."

He heard a sharp intake of breath.

"I did not," Amara said.

"But you wanted to," Diego said, still not looking at her.

Or was it I who wanted to kiss her?

Diego's heart fluttered as he sat beside Amara on the park bench. It was the third day of Holy Week. Something that meant nothing to him. But he liked being out tonight. Away from the pressures of home.

A light tinkling sound skittered over the air. The gentle breeze lifted the delicate aroma of fresh flowers and melting wax, then played with an arrangement of loosely fitted silver poles attached to an approaching float. Diego's anticipation built as this light, musical effect heralded the approach of the Virgin Mary.

The subtle acoustic continued with the gentle swishing of fringed tassels and then *La Estrella* appeared at the arched entry to the park. A profound silence fell over the night. The Virgin's silver float shimmered, reflecting the glow of at least a hundred candles. The arrangement of the tapers caused a delightful play of shadow and light. A warm trail of golden flames burned upwards, enveloping the agonized face of the grieving Virgin in the soft golden glow of candlelight. Crystal tears fell from the depths of pain-filled eyes, evoking from the multitude a cry of passion that exploded into ecstasy.

"¡Estrella! ¡Estrella!" the multitude shouted, breaking the silence that had heralded the Virgin's approach. A spontaneous surge of emotion welled up from the depths of her people, erupting into frenzied shouts of uncontrolled passion.

"¡Guapa! ¡Guapa! ¡Guapa!"

"Increíble," Amara said. Her voice was reverent.

"¡Qué bonita eres!" shouted a single voice. *"¡Nuestra Esperanza!"*

"¡Eres la mujer más bella de Sevilla!" came another voice, floating above the crowd.

The enthusiasm of the crowd grew into unbridled passion as *La Estrella's* devoted public offered words of love and adoration to their cherished mother. It seemed as if the animated spectators would certainly lose their voices, so passionate had their shouts of praise become.

"¡Estrella! ¡Estrella!"

"¡Guapa! ¡Guapa! ¡Guapa!"

"It's been one year since Our Lady has greeted her people." The deep, rich voice came from a man bent over the metal grating at the front of the float. His back was turned to the public as he talked to the *costaleros* hidden below the elaborate structure. "Let's give *Sevilla* the best greeting we know how! *¡Al cielo con ella!*"

In one fluid motion, the *costaleros* lifted their heels off the ground, and in perfect harmony, began to shuffle their feet in a difficult movement perfected over many weeks in their late-night practices. The candelabras swung with their movement. The tassels swirled, and the Virgin of the Stars danced as she greeted her frenzied public.

"*¡Olé!*" shouted the crowd, encouraging the *costaleros* to continue their intricate dance.

"*¡Dále!*" cried the *capatáz*. "For your people."

"*Vamos a dar un poquito más.*" The captain pushed the *costaleros* to give a little more.

They responded, dancing with even more fervor than before.

As the float passed by, a fleeting sense of wonder enveloped all. The intricate structure smelled sweetly of spring flowers and fresh air. The exotic aroma permeated the park, mixing with the charm of a perfect Andalusian night.

The float continued to open its way through the crowd, dispelling the seductive aromas of Seville in springtime. The much-beloved presentation of the Virgin was over, but the mysterious, bewitching ritual of Holy Week in Seville had only just begun.

Diego glanced back at Amara. She seemed nervous, as if she wanted to say something to him, but couldn't find the right words.

He feared what it was she couldn't say. That she was sorry about what had happened. That he shouldn't have kissed her. That it would never happen again.

His heart dropped. He could still feel the hungry intensity of his kiss, the desire in it, and then ultimately, the restraint. When he had pulled away from her, he had been tempted to draw her back. But ultimately chose not to. Any step forward in their relationship had to come from her.

"Amara, I . . ." He hesitated. "I have to talk to you."

She swallowed and nodded her head. "I know," she said. "It's okay. You don't need to apologize. Manolito was encouraging it."

"What?" He watched her turn her face away. "I don't want to apologize." He drew her face back and encouraged her to look at him. "What happened between us had nothing to do with Manolito."

"Diego, please . . ." She took his hands in hers and looked directly at him. "Let's not make more of this than—"

"Why? Didn't it mean anything to you?"

"It's not about me, *cariño*. It's about where you are emotionally right now, and I don't think—"

"Please, Amara, don't take away what little control I have left. I don't need you to think for me. I don't need you to justify my actions, or to interpret them. I wanted to kiss you. And hold you. And love you. I still do, but I'm afraid . . ."

"Afraid of what?"

He swallowed, not wanting to go where she was leading him.

"Afraid to allow myself to love again." He forced himself to chip away at the small crack he had opened around his heart. "Afraid I might hurt you."

"You could never hurt me," Amara said. "You don't have it in you to hurt another human being."

The absolute belief in her voice made him feel like the lowest of traitors.

"Mara, please, listen to me. I don't know if I will ever be completely whole again, or capable of loving you the way you deserve to be loved. But I do know one thing. I need to be honest with you. I have fears and insecurities. A lot of anger. Pain."

He took a deep breath, drawing from somewhere deep inside the courage he needed to ask her the question that weighed on his mind.

"Can you love a broken fool?"

Her eyes grew wide.

"I can love a broken man," she said, "who is in no way a fool."

For a moment, he stopped breathing. And then slowly, he found his voice.

"I can't promise you the same, intense love I felt for Catalina, because the intensity of that love brought me so much sorrow, but I can promise to cherish you, and—"

"You have very little faith in yourself." She leaned forward and brushed her lips over his—softly, not really a kiss, merely contact. "You have the capacity to love deeply, you always have." She paused, keeping her lips so close he could feel her breath on his face.

"The only thing I ask," she said, staring at him intently. "Is that you continue to be as honest with me as you are right now. And . . ." She leaned in and kissed him, a gentle kiss, tentative but lingering. "You ask both your family and mine for their official blessing."

39

Diego

The meeting of the two families was only a formality. Pablito had always loved Diego as if he were his own son. And Diego's family felt the same way about Amara. Both sides counseled a slow but steady period of courtship. No extremes of passion. No rash decisions. Both Diego and Amara agreed. The relationship had to develop naturally.

Diego walked quietly beside Amara, his mind in thought. He reached for her hand. Something was stirring within him, a small light—a tiny seed of hope growing through the darkness. He had felt it first with Rajiv, then with Manolito, and now with Amara. He brought back the image of Rajiv's lotus blossom. He could visualize it, creeping upward toward the light.

"*Amigo*, where've you been?" Joaquín fell into step beside him. His voice was harsh and mocked the word *friend*.

Diego let go of Amara's hand.

"I thought I told you to meet me tonight." A nerve twitched in Joaquín's jaw. "Where were you?"

"Around," Diego said.

"Around." Joaquín turned and spat. "Is that right?" His eyes hardened as he nailed them on Diego. "I need you tonight." His voice was threatening, but carefully controlled. He shifted his eyes to Amara. "Meet me in half an hour." He moved forward half a step.

"Not tonight." Diego raised his hand to stop Joaquín from getting any closer. "I have other plans."

"Did you not hear what I said?" Joaquín's tone threatened a challenge. "Tiburón has a job for us. Meet me—"

Diego lunged forward and grabbed Joaquín by the collar.

"Maybe it's you who has trouble hearing." He tightened his grip on Joaquín's shirt. "You tell Tiburón—"

Joaquín broke free and shoved Diego back.

"Nobody tells El Tiburón anything, ¡primo! He tells us what jobs . . ." He shifted his eyes and locked them on Amara. "And what people to take care of."

Diego's heart tripped and he grabbed Amara's hand.

"Vámonos," he said. "Let's get out of here." He knocked Joaquín back with his shoulder and continued down the street.

"Tranquilo," Amara said. She reached for his hand.

Diego looked at her, and then away. The confrontation with Joaquín had unnerved him. He had never blown off El Tiburón before, never dared to. When a man with as much power as The Shark asked you to be somewhere, you made sure you were there. If you weren't, there were always consequences.

A pair of headlights broke through the darkness of the street. Diego continued walking, but noticed that the headlights did not advance. He felt the car following him, but did not look back.

"Is someone following us?" Amara looked over her shoulder.

"Just keep walking," he said sharply. "And don't look back."

He quickened his pace, released her hand, and placed his arm around her shoulder.

The car approached, a gold Lexus, and then idled beside them.

The right-side window rolled down and a voice from within said, "Get in the car."

Diego froze. The car belonged to El Tiburón.

"Keep walking," he said, tightening his grip around Amara's shoulder.

He heard a door open and then Joaquín was in front of him. He did not precisely see the man move. There was only a blurred sensation of being grabbed, and then whirled back against the wall of the adjacent building.

"Who the fuck do you think you are?" Joaquín grabbed him by the collar. "You think you can just walk away from all this?"

Amara screamed and ran to him but Joaquín caught her by the waist.

"Stay out of it, Mara." Joaquín pushed her back.

Enraged, Diego reached for a beer bottle lying on the sidewalk, smashed it against the wall, and held it to Joaquín's throat.

"Back off, Diego. Or your girl gets hurt." El Tiburón had Amara restrained against his body, his arm around her neck.

Diego dropped the bottle.

"Let her go," he said, raising his hands to show El Tiburón that he held no weapons against him. "I'll do whatever you say."

"No, Diego!" Amara struggled against El Tiburón, but he held onto her.

"Let her go!" Diego shouted. "I said I'd go with you!"

El Tiburón released Amara, but kept a tight hand on her upper arm. "Take her home," he said, shoving her toward Joaquín. "And you . . ." He turned to Diego. "Get in the car."

Diego avoided Amara's eyes. Flinging open the door, he sat in the front seat of El Tiburón's car.

El Tiburón got behind the wheel and started the engine. Slowly, they drove past Joaquín and Amara, who walked with her arms folded, head held high. Diego's heart ached and he had to close his eyes. He had told her, only hours ago, how things were going to be different, how he had changed. He had promised her that the distance between them, the secret life he led, would not come between them. He had told her not to worry. That Joaquín was not a threat to him. That everything was under control. And for the first time in a long time, he saw hope in her eyes.

"A nice girl you got there." El Tiburón's voice was deadly cool.

Slowly, Diego opened his eyes. "Leave her out of this," he said.

"Oh, but I guess you don't get it." El Tiburón's voice was menacing, sarcastic. "She's *in* the minute you step out." He angled the rearview mirror so that he could see himself, and then slicked back his hair with fingers adorned in gold. "You know what I'm saying . . . *amigo?*"

Diego's heart plunged. "What do you want with me?" His voice was a low, guttural snarl.

"Your allegiance." El Tiburón readjusted the mirror and then turned down a dark alley. Someone bolted from behind a dumpster and ran away. "You're either with me, or you're against me." He stopped the car. A medallion of the Virgin, a crucifix, and a gold-plated shark's tooth, chains all entwined, rose and fell heavily on his chest as he breathed. "And if you're against me . . ." He brushed back his jacket to reveal a small handgun. "I will consider you, and all of your loved ones . . ." He pulled the gun from its holster. "My enemy." He put the gun to Diego's temple. "Do we understand each other?"

Diego stared straight ahead, unflinching.

"I said," El Tiburón repeated, smoothly, confidently. "Do we..." He clicked the trigger. "Understand each other?"

Diego gritted his teeth, then snarled an angry *"sí."* He despised himself for having handed over the one thing he had always valued—his freedom—to another man.

"Good." El Tiburón released the trigger and holstered the gun. "Now get out."

Diego threw open the door and stumbled into the alley. How had ever allowed himself to believe that he could escape the consequences of the choices he had made?

40

Andrés

Andrés slipped the white tunic of his *nazareno's* robe over his head. The fabric slid down his body and fell to the bedroom floor. Tonight, at midnight, he would join his brothers as the fraternity made its processional march through the streets of Seville.

Reaching over to the bedside table, he took his glass and downed a shot of whisky. Then he grabbed the hemp rope off the hook on his closet and tied the coarse strand around his waist. Good Friday had arrived, and he would walk in penitence. As was the tradition.

He rubbed his fingers along the shiny silver of his fraternity medallion, then hooked it around the rope that cinched his waist. He shouldn't have gone to his mother's grave. Rosa was right. The visit always altered him. In a dark, negative, non-repentant, anti-Holy Week kind of way. He took another swallow of amber poison.

As if it was possible for him to exist any other way.

He stared at his reflection in the full-length mirror attached to the door. And then carefully, he placed the *capirote* over his head. Still looking at himself in the mirror, he tugged on the emerald green material until it completely covered his face.

And then slowly, he slipped into his brown leather sandals. He found his white gloves and adjusted them over his hands, the right one first, and then the left. He was ready. Tonight, he would be part of the heightened frenzy of Holy Week in Seville. A night of passion.

A night that could lead to madness if passion were allowed free reign.

Andrés's hand shook as he raised the stub of the cigarette to his mouth and dragged deeply. He shifted on the stool along the outside bar that looked over the Guadalquivir River. A soft breeze was blowing in the air, carrying with it the delicate perfume of orange blossoms and jasmine. The sky had turned a deep, rich blue, almost purple, as night fell over the city.

Bum . . . Bum . . . Barumum. Bum. Bum. The hollow beat of a drum echoed in the air. Then the piercing cry of a solitary bugle screamed, lifting its funeral dirge up into the night sky. It was the same solemn herald of death Andrés had heard the night his mother died. He slid an ashtray closer and crushed out his cigarette. He should have been in the chapel by now, but he needed one more shot.

The air had grown pungent with the aroma of burning incense. Clouds of smoke billowed, adding a mystical, dream-like quality to the night. The foggy haze of ash-gray smoke obscured the scene before him, blurring the boundaries between what was real and what was an invention of his mind.

Slowly, magically, the mysterious transformation of the city began. In the distance, an eerie procession of black-hooded figures crept forward, following behind the lead *nazareno* carrying a gigantic cross. Specks of yellow light grew into tiny, visible flames. The soft flickers emanated from giant tapers held in the gloved hands of scores of hooded men. It was the brotherhood of the Vera Cruz. He recognized the fraternity immediately. The *penitentes* were dressed all in black and walked in silence.

The gloomy specters ahead were shuddering reminders of the somber years of the Spanish Inquisition. Andrés could easily go back in time and conjure up frightening images of fifteenth-century Spain.

In the blackness of the night, the illusion seemed frighteningly real. Hooded. Dark. Ominous. The mysterious men created an uneasy tension and warned of impending doom.

Andrés watched the *nazarenos* of the Vera Cruz as they continued on their way. They were many in number and their rows seemed endless. All was black. All severe. All silent. The tired shuffling of their feet on the harsh pavement and the crackle of soft flames flickering in the night breeze heightened the emotion of the bewitching procession of shadow and light.

The walking slowed and one of the masked men stopped in front of him. The golden flame of his candle sputtered, darting back and forth with a sudden gust of wind.

And then an unexpected rush of air extinguished the feeble flame. The man stared at Andrés through the holes in his mask.

Andrés stared back. And then his mind began to displace reality.

The hooded face before him slowly transformed into a Gypsy woman shrouded in a sheer, black veil, her eyes hidden behind the thin cloth, but cold upon him, staring at him, unblinking and uncaring. The hiss of the newly lighted wick sent the *nazareno* on his way, leaving Andrés with a strange feeling of unease and apprehension. Grabbing his *capirote* off the bar, he pushed his way through the crowd to get to the chapel. There were only four more hours left until the departure of his fraternity. It would probably take him that long to squeeze through the chaos that had exploded on the streets.

Rajiv detested this week-long celebration the Spaniards called *Semana Santa*. Once-quiet streets had been transformed into a teeming, relentless wall of people. Vendors hawked their wares, selling everything from beer to sandwiches to *churros* and *chocolate*. The very reverent and the not so spiritual shared the sidewalks together. Rajiv allowed his body to be pushed along with the crowd, knowing he would eventually reach his destination: the bar across the street from the chapel of the Esperanza de Triana—where he was supposed to meet Andrés, who was said to be meeting Crystal.

At least that's what he said.

"*¡Trianera!*" shouted a solitary voice somewhere off in the distance.

"*¡Guapa! ¡Guapa! ¡Guapa!*" came a chorus of voices in reply.

It was midnight when Rajiv finally reached the bar. Of course, Andrés never showed up. And now, it was impossible for Rajiv to leave. The streets were wall-to-wall people.

So he stayed and drank. And then drank some more.

Andrés would do well to stay clear of him tonight.

At precisely 2 a.m., the arched door to the chapel of the Esperanza de Triana creaked open. Everybody in the bar rushed outside. Rajiv went with them.

A sudden hush fell over the crowd. The eerie silence magnified the groaning of the ancient chapel door. Framed by the Moorish-inspired portico, one man stood. He wore a flowing white tunic and green hood. In his white-gloved hands he held a large wooden cross. Behind him stood the others, all identically robed, all faces covered. Andrés was allegedly among them.

The man with the cross began to make his way out onto the street, followed by a white trail of robed *nazarenos*. The crowd parted before them, leaving not more than a few inches of separation between the hooded penitents and the spectators gathered around them. The white line grew longer, snaking its way through the crowd like a serpent freed from its cage.

Andrés's eyes burned under the dark drape that covered his face. He had been walking the streets beside his brothers for over four hours. He was tired. He hadn't slept for days, and his body was beginning to feel the strain. His mind, however, refused to shut down. He pulled the hood away from his mouth. His face was flushed with alcohol and sticky with sweat. The heavy cloth clung mercilessly to his skin. His feet ached. Part of the penitence, he knew. A penitence he felt no conviction to observe.

Yanking off his *capirote*, Andrés pushed his way out of line. He heard three sharp clacks and looked back over his shoulder. The *capataz* had ordered his men to "dance" the *paso de misterio*—the lavishly adorned float of the fallen Christ they carried on their shoulders. Andrés turned around and watched as the *costaleros* swayed from side to side. As they moved, the statue of the Christ, fallen under the weight of the cross, moved with them. The float danced above the multitude, Christ's agonized gaze fixed upon the people below . . . upon Andrés.

"*Santo Dios.*" Andrés turned his face away. "*No me mires.* Don't look at me!"

"*¡Adelante, valientes!*" the captain shouted. "Let's go! *¡Vamos a andar!*"

In one smooth movement, the *costaleros* jumped into the air. The *paso* vibrated with their effort. The candelabras trembled. The flames of the candles flickered. Then slowly, heavily, the *paso* advanced down the street.

Andrés watched the *paso* disappear into the distance. And then he stood alone, outside of the fraternity, his face unmasked.

Andrés strode into El Café Modernista and ordered a shot of whisky. Carefully, he wiped the counter with a paper napkin before placing his *capirote* on the bar. He dug into his pocket for his phone. Glanced at the missed messages. Rajiv had called him ten times.

"Shit." He scrolled to the last entry.

A muffled voice answered the call.

"Where are you?" Andrés said.

"Screw you." Rajiv clicked off the call.

Andrés called again. "Look man, I'm sorry." He spoke quickly before Rajiv could hang up again. "I couldn't get through the crowds. Where're you now?"

"Still in the center of the city, waiting for a bloody bus."

"Forget the bus. Come join us. I'm at Café Modernista." He hesitated, and then went with the lie. "With Crystal."

"I'll think about it." Rajiv hung up.

Andrés grinned. He knew the man would come. Rajiv Kumaran was infatuated with Crystal Webb.

Thirty minutes later, Rajiv stormed through the door. Andrés was sitting at the end of the bar, a glass of half-drained scotch in his hand. He motioned for Rajiv to join him.

Unlike the last time he was in this bar, this time there was no hesitation. Rajiv headed directly for Andrés. He had a few words to share with his arrogant friend. He was almost at the bar when something brushed up against his leg. His eyes shot to the floor. He saw a black flash disappear under the folds of Andrés's robe.

Annoyed, Andrés shook his foot.

A small black dog skittered out from under his robe.

Andrés kicked the dog out from under him and sent the animal sailing across the floor. The dog squealed as it crashed into the hard wood of the adjacent wall.

Then all hell broke loose. A young girl screamed. Ran after the dog. A man flew across the room. But before the man had the opportunity to attack Andrés, Rajiv did the job for him.

"You bloody worm!" Rajiv landed a solid right hook into Andrés's left cheek.

Andrés reeled under the attack.

"You hurt that dog!" Rajiv shot off another wild punch. "Like you hurt everybody around you."

Andrés swung back. "What the hell's wrong with you?"

"You! That's what's wrong. You're a bloody bully."

Rajiv grabbed Andrés by the collar of his *nazareno's* robe and wrenched it tight. To hell with Mohandas Gandhi. Sometimes, violence just felt right. He landed a punch that cracked open the skin below Andrés's eye.

Andrés reeled back, the force of the blow knocking him against the wall.

"Does it make you feel like a man . . ." Rajiv was at Andrés's throat, hands wrapped around his neck. "Kicking a young girl's dog? Fight me, you miserable piece of—"

The man who had first lunged for Andrés scrambled to pull Rajiv off. Thanks to the man's interference, Rajiv loosened his grip, giving Andrés the advantage over him.

"No, but fucking the girl you want does." Andrés curled up his fist and sank it into Rajiv's stomach.

Rajiv doubled over. He gasped, clutching his stomach. Then he rose up and threw a staggering left hook that connected, snapping Andrés's head back with the force of the blow. "Where is she?"

Andrés fell. Hard. Spurts of blood flew from his sliced lip and splattered on his white tunic. He lay dazed, gasping for breath.

"You have no chance with her." Andrés panted, wiped blood from his lip. "Do you really think she's going to choose you over me?"

Angry shouts and a mad rush followed as the people in the bar mobilized. The man who was with the little girl pulled Andrés off the floor and knocked a solid blow into his stomach.

Andrés doubled over, clutching his gut. He grabbed at the hemp rope cinching his waist. As if, all of a sudden, it felt too tight. His silver fraternity medal clinked to the ground. He stumbled, stepped on it, and was thrown off balance.

Rajiv crouched. He looked Andrés directly in the eye. Never had he felt such power, such control over another man.

"If I take you out of the picture by telling the world what you did to a young woman named Catalina," Rajiv said, calmer than he should have been. "I am guaranteed my chance with her."

For the first time in his life, Rajiv had the upper hand.

It felt good.

Someone grabbed Rajiv and pushed him away.

"Let me at him." The man lunged forward. He had a knife. "You think you can hurt my sister and get away with it?"

The man fought against hands that now restrained him. He broke away and went after Andrés. But Andrés did not move to defend himself. It was as if the shock of what Rajiv had said now rendered him paralytic.

An armed policeman burst into the room. He grabbed the man by the arm, twisted it behind his back, and forced him to drop the knife. The crowd responded. Some with cheers, others with outrage.

"You all right?" the policeman said, turning toward Andrés.

"What?" Rajiv protested. "He's not the offended party."

Rajiv stepped forward, but a number of hands held him back.

"Cállate," someone hissed. "Be quiet. You're not the one who should be arrested."

Slowly, Andrés reached out and picked his silver medallion off the floor. He squeezed it in his hand, then rose to his feet, eyes landing on the girl. She was huddled on the ground, cradling the dog in her arms, head bowed over its trembling body.

Rajiv watched the two officers cuff the man's hands behind his back, then push him to the door.

"Get the girl," one of the officials said. "Take her to the squad car." The officer looked back at Andrés. "Maybe you should have stayed with your fraternity tonight. It's Good Friday . . . or have you forgotten?"

"What's so good about Friday?" Andrés snatched his cap off the bar. "This one or any other."

41

Diego

Diego paced La Avenida Reina Mercedes, nearing and then distancing himself from the biology building at the University of Seville where Rajiv said he worked. He strode back and forth, back and forth, his right hand opening and closing at his side, the left pressing a cigarette to his lips, then away. Back to his lips, and then away again. Nothing had changed. He would never be free. He would be forever tied to a gold Lexus and stolen Mercedes, to hatred and fear. To the dark, ugly side of life.

He stopped, squeezed his fingers to his temple. The smoke from his cigarette curled up into the clear blue sky. He needed to talk to Rajiv, though he wasn't quite sure why.

He had made so many mistakes over the last year, hurt so many people. Amara was furious with him. Though she had always suspected it, she never fully understood the extent of his involvement with El Tiburón. Now she knew that he was not only a criminal, but also a lowlife, a nothing, a man subject to the control of a more ruthless, more dangerous, more powerful man.

And she knew what he had not wanted to acknowledge. That Joaquín, his life-long friend, had become his enemy.

How had it happened that he and Joaquín had grown so far apart? That the man with whom he had once shared everything, every thought, every dream, now only shared half a wad of bills paid out for a crime? More incomprehensible still, how had he grown to hate this man he once loved?

If, as Rajiv had said, hatred was only fear disguised, then what was he afraid of? Was it easier to hate Joaquín than to hate the criminal activity Diego had brought into his own life? Was it easier to hate the Spaniard he blamed for Catalina's death than to hate and blame himself? He should have listened to his instincts that day and kept Catalina safe. Her death was as much his fault as the Spaniard's who left them stranded.

He had only a vague memory of the Spaniard. He remembered a man of about his age. Tall. With a black umbrella that hid his face. The only detail he remembered clearly about the man was the car he drove, the tilted Virgin on the dash. Beyond that, the man's features were unclear. He could be any man, any Spaniard. And for so long, every Spaniard had been a threat to him.

Diego flicked the butt of his cigarette to the ground.

"Not anymore," he said quietly as he crushed out the wasted butt. The cigarette couldn't get any flatter, or any more extinguished, but he kept grinding it into the pavement. And in an odd, totally disjointed way, he remembered his grandmother who, with an old, rolled up newspaper, would seek out and kill the cockroaches in the kitchen. *"Kill them good,"* she would say, swatting and then squishing the captured roaches. *"Or they come back and multiply in kitchen."*

He stared at the pulverized butt. Shreds of black tobacco stuck out between the ripped, nicotine-tarnished paper. He had spent the last year hunting for roaches, but he was tired of feeling weak. He wanted to capture the triumph he had felt when he stood proudly beside Rajiv in the coffee shop. He wanted to feel strong again.

He forced himself to stand a little straighter. All he had to do now was conquer the fear that was keeping him from entering the building that loomed before him. For a man who had only studied until the tenth grade, the University of Seville was an intimidating place. Taking a deep breath, Diego summoned his courage and threw open the door. His heart beat wildly as he climbed the three flights of stairs to the department of genetics.

He would fight for that triumph again.

An imposing door prohibited entry to the department. Diego raised his hand to knock, then hesitated, standing with his fist suspended in the air.

Some small part of him, the part that had failed in school, wanted to tell him that he did not belong in this institution designed for smart, successful people.

A woman in a white lab coat appeared from around the corner.

He smiled nervously, then knocked on the door.

Another, larger part of him told him that he did.

He knocked again but no one answered.

He contemplated leaving, but then the woman passed by and said, "They're always engrossed in their work in there. You have to knock louder than that."

He knocked again, louder, but still no answer.

An eerie feeling crept over him. As if somehow, he was not meant to go through that door.

About to walk away, he looked back over his shoulder.

Someone had opened the door.

"*¿Eres analfabeto?*" A well-dressed Spaniard stood on the other side of the door. He tucked his hands into his pockets, his white lab coat pushed behind his hips. A silver medal hung from a loop around his belt.

Diego lost his breath. That voice. It sounded so familiar.

"Are you fucking illiterate?" The man's voice was not so firm now. His face had lost its color. But his Spanish was more hostile as he repeated the question.

Diego fought the urge to grab the man's throat.

"*¿Sordo también?*" The man had recovered both his voice and his composure.

Diego turned his head to the side in an unconscious reaction against the insult. Of course he wasn't deaf. He had heard every ugly word of what the Spaniard said. But the man's voice sounded far away, as if it belonged to another place and time.

"Read the sign." The man pointed to a notice on the wall. "That is, if you can."

It was only then Diego noticed the laminated sign instructing all visitors to call from the reception desk located on the first floor.

"I'm looking for Rajiv." Diego spoke slowly, though his heart was racing.

Through the partially open door, he caught a glimpse of Rajiv, throwing rubber balls into a wastebasket, surrounded by a group of boisterous men.

"He's not here," the Spaniard said. And then he slammed the door in Diego's face.

"What's wrong with you, Andrés?" Rajiv yanked open the door, talking to someone Diego couldn't see.

"He's not allowed in here." The voice behind the door sounded more desperate than condescending.

A cold chill shivered down Diego's spine. He had heard that voice before.

"What're you talking about?" Rajiv said. He sounded angry.

"Maybe in India," the Spaniard said, a touch of arrogance replacing the former fear in his voice, "science labs are open to the uneducated public, but in Spain—"

"You know what, Andrés?" Rajiv pushed his foot against the door to hold it open. "I'm getting really tired of your arrogance. Your bigotry and your hatred. So just shut up and move out of my way."

"You don't know what the fuck you're talking about, Rajiv!" The voice muffled as Rajiv removed his foot, slamming the door behind him.

"Let's get out of here." Rajiv grabbed Diego by the arm and steered him down the hallway. Almost too quickly, he led Diego to El Cántaro, a small bar across the street from the university.

42

Rajiv

Rajiv popped a Tums and washed it down with tonic. His temples throbbed. The plan was to let the tonic push back his acidity, and then to get the hell away from Reina Mercedes.

"Let's go." He tossed a few bills on the bar beside his drained glass. His chest felt like a furnace, but it was time to leave. He had to put distance between Andrés and Diego.

Now rather than later.

Diego didn't move. He lowered his gaze and focused on the wooden counter of the bar. "Who was that man?"

"What man?" Rajiv slid Diego's half-empty glass to the edge of the counter, indicating to the barman that they were finished, and would soon be moving on.

"In the lab," Diego said. "Who was that man?"

"Forget about him. He's troubled." Rajiv nodded toward the exit. "Come on, let's—"

"What's his name?" Diego traced his finger through a ring of moisture left on the bar by his sweating glass.

"Why? Why do you need to know?"

Diego continued drawing circles on the bar. "What's his name?" he said again.

"Andrés, all right? His name's Andrés. Now can we go?"

"Andrés what?"

"Aragón!" Rajiv shouted. "Andrés Aragón. You happy now?"

The circles stopped. Diego looked up.

"What kind of car does he drive?"

"Couldn't tell you." Rajiv's heart beat wildly. While he had almost spilled Andrés's secret in El Bar Modernista—and even felt slightly good about it—now was not the time to blow it. Andrés was volatile and Diego determined. This conversation ended here.

Blast the both of them for putting him in the middle.

He took a deep breath in a futile attempt to slow down his racing heart. And then quietly he spoke.

"Enough. I don't want to talk about—"

"What kind of car does the man drive?" Diego spoke slowly, over enunciating each repeated word.

Rajiv stared down his friend. Then took the only opportunity he could see to put an end to the questions.

"I have only ever seen him drive a scooter," he said. A half-lie that was also an important half-truth. He had never actually seen Andrés drive the black Mercedes Diego was hoping to identify.

Diego looked away. Nodded. He was satisfied. At least for now.

"Can we please leave?" Rajiv turned toward the door, feeling as equally guilty as relieved. He hated lying to his friend. Almost as much as he hated being the guardian of a secret he had never asked to be entrusted with.

"I need to talk to you," Diego said.

Rajiv sighed as he spun back around. "What's on your mind?" He sat down. He knew he needed to listen to his friend.

"I've made some mistakes," Diego said. "Hurt a lot of people." A dark shadow passed over his eyes. "And I don' know what to do to make things right."

Rajiv played silently with the utensils lying on the counter. Debated whether to push Diego out the door, or to stay seated and hear him out.

The decision soon became clear. If he broke the fragile line Diego had thrown out to him, the help he could potentially offer would be permanently lost. Diego's need to talk was urgent and immediate. And superseded any fear of an encounter with Andrés.

Slowly, Rajiv picked up the knife.

"Mistakes are like knives," he said. "They can either serve us or cut us, depending on whether we grasp them by the handle . . ."

He ran his finger over the wooden handle of the knife. "Or by the blade." He glanced up at Diego. "Which side of the knife are you going to take?"

Before Diego could answer, the door swung open.

Rajiv's heart took a dive. Andrés, followed by his lab mates, sauntered into the bar.

Andrés pulled out a chair and sat next to Maricarmen. "Hey Rajiv," he said, his back turned. "Glad you're here." He dug a pack of cigarettes from his front pocket. The flick of his lighter pierced the heavy silence that had descended upon the room. "I invited the lab for a post-Holy Week drink. Come join us." He took a heavy drag. Then turned to face Rajiv. "And please, invite your friend." His tone was gracious, impeccably charming, setting Diego up for reproach should he choose to refuse the invitation.

Checkmate. Andrés had played well. Game on.

Andrés shifted his gaze to Diego, studied him for a moment, and then said, "Do you study at the university?"

Diego's hand froze in midair, his fingers paralyzed over the cigarette he was about to bring to his mouth.

"No," Diego said. "I do not."

"I didn't think so."

Rajiv stiffened. He didn't like the newly adopted tone of Andrés's voice. Polished but subtly arrogant. He glanced at Diego, carefully monitoring his friend's reaction.

Diego stared at Andrés, as if trying to unlock some mystery from the far corners of his mind. Drawing the cigarette to his mouth, Diego dragged. Then he lowered his gaze and stared at the smoldering tip, watching as its burnt ashes fell slowly to the ground.

"Not too many of your people go on to higher education, do they?" Andrés said.

"*Por favor*, Andrés . . ." Javier protested.

"But then who needs an education when you can make more than a doctor stealing cars and selling drugs?" Andrés reached for the ashtray. "I have to give your people credit, though." He flicked ash into the dirty tray. "It takes a lot of skill to hot-wire a car without being caught."

Diego reached across the table, slid the ashtray closer, and snubbed out his cigarette. "It takes even more skill for *my people* to—"

He stopped. Rajiv had picked a knife off the table and was holding it with the blade tucked under his hand, the handle facing outward. In a slight move barely noticeable, he tapped his finger steadily on the wooden handle.

"Sometimes, the more one studies," Rajiv said, "the less he seems to know."

A shocked silence descended upon the group.

"*Vale, vale,*" said Josemaría with a nervous laugh. "Why don't we change the subject?"

A mad flash passed over Andrés's eyes, and then it was gone—controlled, but not completely extinguished.

"Or the more he thinks he knows," Andrés said, fixing his eyes coolly on Rajiv, "the less he understands." He stared at Rajiv over his cigarette, his eyes narrowing behind a ring of gray-blue smoke that spiraled upward and curled over his head.

Rajiv breathed out, hard, as a waiter came over to the table with several bubbling dishes of melted cheese and a pile of hot tortillas. Had he not appeared at that precise moment, the afternoon might have gone differently.

"Pepe, did you find that cheese I asked you about?" Andrés squashed his cigarette into the ashtray and turned his most charming smile upon the waiter.

"I sure did." Pepe placed several ceramic dishes on the table. "*Queso a la cazuela*, just like you ordered." He added a plate of jalapeño peppers on the side.

Rajiv glanced at the jalapeños, and then at Andrés. A faint smile edged up the corners of his mouth, but as suddenly as it had appeared, it was gone.

"Andrés, try these peppers," Rajiv said. "They're really good." He popped a jalapeño pepper into his mouth and chewed it whole.

"*¿Estás loco?*" Andrés sat back slowly in the chair. "You crazy? Those things are hot."

"Hot is only a matter of perception." Rajiv did not remove his eyes from Andrés as he chewed and then swallowed the jalapeño, showing no reaction to its spicy heat. "And tolerance."

"Go ahead, Andrés, try one." Josemaría reached across the table, grabbed the plate of jalapeños, and offered it to Andrés. His challenge rose, and then lingered on the air.

Maricarmen blew a stifled laugh through her mouth.

Javier sat back in his chair, arms folded. Smiling.

Andrés squinted, directed a curse at Josemaría, and then brought a jalapeño to his mouth. He bit down, and then began to chew. His face turned red. And then his eyes began to water.

"*¡Coño!*" Andrés grabbed his beer and downed it in a single gulp. Then he snatched Javier's half-empty glass and sloshed it down as well.

Rajiv sat back and observed the chaos as his colleagues laughed.

"*¡No llores, hermano!*" Josemaría laughed, and then handed Andrés a handkerchief to wipe his eyes.

Maricarmen let out a tiny giggle, then quickly lifted her hand to her mouth to squelch it.

Andrés mopped at his tears, responding with a forced laugh.

"*¡Hombre, por poco me muero!*" Andrés's smile was strained. "You trying to kill me, Rajiv?"

Diego looked over at Rajiv. A slow smile formed.

Rajiv's mouth twitched in response.

The exchange was not lost on Andrés, who got up abruptly and walked over to the bar to get another beer. He stood with his back turned toward the group. They could not see his face as he reacted to the continued laughter of his peers.

"Rajiv, you're bad!" Maricarmen chuckled.

"I've never seen him drink so fast!" said Josemaría, rocking with laughter.

Rajiv closed his eyes and shook his head, saying nothing at all.

Andrés returned with his beer, slamming another in front of Javier in mock bravado. He lit a cigarette and then sat down. His cool swagger had returned.

"Andrés, you look so sexy with tears in your eyes," Maricarmen said.

"Come home with me, *nena* . . ." Andrés kissed her lips. "And I'll cry for you all night."

"Promise?" She kissed him back, even more sensually than he had kissed her.

Andrés took the opportunity to make sure that everybody at the table knew who was in charge. After a long-drawn-out display of hyped-up passion, he broke away from Maricarmen, lifted his glass, and said, "A toast . . . to all my good friends."

Diego did not raise his glass.

"Aren't you going to join the toast?" Andrés turned his glass toward Diego.

His eyes fixed firmly on Andrés, Diego reached for his wallet and pulled out a few bills. Throwing them in the center of the table, he stood up. "No," he said.

Andrés was silent. The tip of his cigarette ignited into a smoldering orange glow as he dragged on the wasted butt.

Without looking down, Andrés dropped the cigarette to the floor, crushing it under the toe of his fine leather shoe.

He rotated his ankle slowly, grinding the smoldering butt until it was flat against the floor.

One last wisp of smoke escaped, floating upward only to be smothered by a final twist of his neatly polished shoe.

Diego and Andrés locked eyes. The stare Diego returned was as hard and as cold as the one Andrés gave him.

A few moments passed. Diego shifted his gaze. He nodded at the group, a perfunctory goodbye, and then he turned and walked away.

Rajiv jumped up. Sprinted after Diego. God only knew what the man was thinking now. He felt resistance as he reached to open the door. He yanked harder. A woman fell through from the other side.

"I'm so sorry, I . . ." His heart thudded. The woman standing only inches from his face was Crystal Webb. He stared at her. She stared at him. And then she started laughing—a soft, bubbly sound that smoothed over the awkwardness.

"You have a beautiful laugh," he said. Amazingly, he felt neither clumsy nor awkward. Diego's training? Or Crystal's natural ease. It took him less than a millisecond to decide. It was Crystal all the way. "What are you doing here?"

"Meeting Andrés."

"Andrés?" The surprise slipped out. "You're kidding, right?"

"No." She looked at him curiously.

"Oh, right. Sorry then." He bumbled a bit more, until she stopped him with a question.

"Are you leaving?" she said.

Her question posed a dilemma.

What he wanted to do was stay. With her. What he knew he should do was run and catch up with his friend.

He sighed and said, "Unfortunately, I have another commitment. But maybe we could—"

"I'd love to," she said. "I'll give you my number."

She dug a notebook and pen from her bag. Then handed him a slip of paper.

"Call me," she said. Her smile was warm, inviting.

It was going to be hard to walk out that door.

But he did. And then he ran after his friend.

Panting heavily, he fell into step behind Diego.

"Hey, slow down." Rajiv gasped for air. He wanted to say more, but was having enough trouble simply breathing.

Diego stopped abruptly.

"I need answers," he said, turning to face Rajiv.

"Answers to what?" Rajiv spit out.

"You don' want to know."

"Then why am I asking?" Rajiv was now officially annoyed.

Diego kicked away a crumpled can. He was silent for a moment. And then he said, "I need to know who killed my wife."

Rajiv swallowed, hard, wondering what he could possibly say that would have any meaning to his agitated friend.

"Walk with me," Rajiv said. And then he took a decision. Right or wrong, he decided to lie.

"Andrés is not the man you're looking for," he said.

Andrés was many things. Rude. Offensive. Intolerant. But, he was not heartless. He could not have left a dying woman stranded. Whatever answers Diego thought he could find in Andrés were not the ones he needed.

Rajiv's lie seemed to calm his troubled friend. Diego's jaw slackened and the crease between his eyes disappeared. Rajiv hoped to God that his belief in Andrés was justified.

43

Andrés

Andrés cursed Rajiv as he jumped onto his scooter. *"Cabrón."* Rajiv was going to pay for that humiliation. But not now.

Now he had more troubling issues on his mind.

Giving some vague excuse about needing to run home to check on Adela, he walked out on his own party and headed down Reina Mercedes to the other side of town. The poor side. The side he went to when anger—or fear—controlled reason.

His mind was reeling. To have finally come face to face with the man who had made his life a living hell over the last year was like a bad trip. His head pounded and his heart ached. Out of the four thousand people who lived in Las Tres Mil, why did the one man he least wanted to see have to show up at his door?

Had the man recognized him? Andrés didn't think so. Diego Vargas wouldn't have sat with him, sharing a drink. No, he couldn't have recognized him. If he had, Andrés would now be dead.

Or maybe, the man was baiting him. Prolonging his suffering. Maybe a single knife wound to the heart wasn't enough. If that were so, Diego Vargas would be back. Tonight. And by tomorrow morning, Andrés would be joining Catalina Meléndez in the afterlife. Hell, in his case. Not heaven.

"¡Coño!" Andrés slammed on the brakes while swerving to avoid a pothole. The Southside was a sordid, disgusting place. He only came here for one reason.

He didn't do coke often. But whenever he was at an all-time-low, there was no better high than El Tiburón's potent cocaine.

When Diego Vargas first appeared at the lab, the initial shock threw Andrés into asshole defense mode. Subconsciously, he must have wanted to act like the jerk that Gypsy thought he was. He didn't really believe all that crap he had said to Rajiv. But then when Rajiv humiliated him in front of his friends, in defense of Diego Vargas, Andrés meant the insults he offered.

Now he just wanted to forget. Everything. Diego Vargas. His father. Rosa. Even that insolent fool, Rajiv Kumaran.

Andrés cruised the streets he had come to know so well. While most *payo* public servants were afraid to respond to calls in the Southside, his father had been offering medical services to the Gypsies for as long as he could remember, back to the time when he used to believe that his son was still going to be a doctor. Every Saturday morning, he would drag Andrés on his humanitarian mission to Tres Mil Viviendas, teaching him what it meant to be a doctor—someone who heals others while wounding his own.

"How can you expect to study medicine if you faint like a girl at the sight of blood?" So much for forgetting. Andrés cursed at the voice in his head. But his father's words pushed him into the angriest, deepest corners of his mind.

Then he hit a pothole, lost control of his scooter, and crashed against the curb.

Heart racing, he lay still on the pavement. His breathing accelerated, and then slowly stabilized. Hands still shaking, he picked up his scooter and kicked down the stand. Except for a scraped arm that had caught the impact of the fall, he was able to walk away from the crash. Now, even more agitated than before, he entered a dilapidated bar on the corner of the street.

A woman looked up from her mopping.

"Can I help you?" she said.

"Give me a shot of whisky."

She looked at him warily.

"Are you all right?" she said, glancing at his arm.

He set his jaw firm. And then without answering, he pushed his dark glasses up into his hair and scanned the room. Besides the woman and a young boy, the bar was empty.

"All I have is Cutty Sark," the woman said, putting down the mop. The clean smell of Pine-Sol countered the rank odor of the street outside.

"Then give me Cutty Sark." He sat down on a broken chair and lit a cigarette.

The woman disappeared into the kitchen, returning with a lumpy piece of cloth in her hand.

"Here." She handed him the cloth. "Put this on your arm."

Several pieces of ice were wrapped in the clean white rag.

Slowly, he placed the improvised ice pack over the wound on his arm, trying hard to ignore the thudding of his heart. It was the first time anyone had ever offered him ice for an injury.

He watched her pour his drink. She was a dark-skinned beauty. Quite striking, really. Her modest dress accentuated a graceful figure. The apron tied around her waist highlighted the curve of her hips. The gold chain around her neck drew out the rich color of her skin. A small cross hung from the string, falling neatly in the center of her ample cleavage.

"Put that guitar away," she said, addressing the young boy. "It's time to start studying." She walked around the counter and served Andrés his drink.

Andrés removed the ice from his arm, now studying the boy. The kid was so absorbed in his playing that he didn't hear her.

The same thing happened to him when he painted.

"Now, Tito," she said, gently removing the guitar from the boy's hand and placing it in a beat-up vinyl case. "You can practice later."

The boy nodded, picked up a pencil, and opened one of the books lying on the table.

She returned her gaze to him.

"Let me bandage that arm," she said, her voice wary but kind.

"Why would you do that?" Andrés felt the surprise of a child shown an unexpected kindness.

"Why not?" she replied, as if kindness were something she always expected of herself.

And then she headed for the kitchen, returning with a small bowl of water, a washcloth, a gauze bandage, some alcohol wipes, antiseptic cream, and tape. She pulled a chair next to him and took his arm in her hand. Gently, she washed off the blood and cleaned the area with alcohol. After applying a thin layer of cream over the wound, she bandaged his arm.

He watched her intently, and in his obsessive gaze, her face slowly transformed into another—like a painting by Dalí where one reality is superimposed over another.

"¡Madre!" he cried out. Mother.

She looked up, nervously, and then pushed the chair out behind her, hurrying to stand.

He reached for her, holding onto her hand.

She snapped her hand out from under his.

"You're a beautiful woman," he said, taking back her hand, "with gentle, loving hands." He stared at her, and she met his gaze.

"You have soft skin," he murmured, turning her hand over and stroking her fingers until they opened before him.

She caught her breath, and then jerked her hand away.

He sat back in the chair. Picked up his cigarette.

"Are you frightened of me?" he said. His eyes narrowed as he stared at her from the haze of smoke escaping from his mouth.

"Should I be?"

His lips stretched into a thin smile.

He leaned forward and she moved away slightly, but not completely. Andrés observed her reaction. He had never felt so charged. But she must have felt the air turn cool, for she shivered before springing to her feet.

Andrés leaped from the chair and snagged her around the waist.

"Not so fast." He pulled her against him, drawing his face close to hers. He could feel her breath upon his cheek.

Her scent was not what he expected. Instead of garlic and unwashed flesh, she smelled of soap, mint, and pine.

He could feel the soft curves of her body pressing against his. For a moment, he faltered. And then he smiled.

"You didn't give me a chance to thank you," he said.

She pushed him back.

"That's not appropriate," she said, anger in her eyes.

"Forgive me." Andrés found his most gracious smile. "I have taken advantage of your kindness."

She steeled her eyes and braced her stand. "Please, just leave."

He nodded.

"I'm sorry if I offended you," not saying what he thought.

He glanced at the boy, whose eyes had grown large. *Now is not the time to tell you what I really think about Gypsy women.*

Tough words. Andrés pulled a few bills from his wallet and headed for the door. But they were just more of his bullshit talk. He would never intentionally hurt the woman.

She had been kind to him.

* * *

An hour later, Andrés had scored an ounce of cocaine, but he had not inhaled it. For the first time in a long time, he felt something other than self-pity. Drugs weren't going to give him what he needed.

Blankly, he stared into the empty space of the confessional. He could not erase that Gypsy woman from his mind.

It was because of her that he was here.

After leaving the bar, he had felt something he never felt before, something so deep and so painful it was as if a knife had slit open his gut and torn its way up to his throbbing heart. If he had entered that bar after buying, and then using drugs, or if he had not had that accident with the scooter, he might actually have hurt the woman. Like he had hurt Maricarmen. Or, unintentionally, Catalina Meléndez.

He was seized by the memory of that dark night when he had encountered Diego Vargas standing in the middle of the road. What he would not give to do that night over again. To make different choices. If he'd known there was a woman bleeding in a car parked on the side of the road, he never would have left her stranded.

But he didn't know and she didn't get help in time and she died.

Because of him.

Andrés jumped as the window to the confessional scraped open. The mingled scents of beeswax and incense drifted in from the sanctuary. There was a heavy pause, then the priest greeted him and invited him to confession.

"Good afternoon, my son." It was Father Sebastián. His Basque accent was unmistakable.

"Bless me father, for I have sinned." Andrés shifted nervously in the shadows of the dark confessional as he began the rite of confession. "It has been fourteen months since my last confession."

"What would you like to bring before the Lord today for confession?" said Father Sebastián.

Andrés clenched his fist tightly around his silver medallion, the cold metal pressing into his palm. His stomach was churning and his head felt heavy. He had never felt so horrible in his life, and he had had many bad days to compare to this one.

"I . . ." Andrés stared at the shadowy figure of the priest on the other side of the carved wooden grate. His knees ached as he shifted painfully against the hard wooden kneeler.

"Yes, go on."

"I got into a fight with one of my colleagues," Andrés said, starting his confession with what was easy, with what Father Sebastián had heard many times before.

Father Sebastián remained silent, allowing Andrés to continue his confession before saying, "Is there anything else you need to bring before the Lord?"

Andrés took a deep breath. His mouth felt dry, and he could barely speak. A pulse throbbed on the side of his neck. His confession was about to get more difficult.

"I am the Spaniard who left Catalina Meléndez stranded," he said, swallowing hard against the dryness in his throat. It made a hollow sound that cut through the silence of the cramped confessional. "I thought Diego Vargas was trying to steal my car."

Andrés looked away from the grated window of the confessional, his stomach in knots.

"I was sure he had a knife, Father. He had blood on his hands."

"I see." Father Sebastián cleared his throat with a dry, uncomfortable cough. "It is good that you are asking God's gift of forgiveness in the sacrament of confession." Father Sebastián's voice was neutral, but concerned.

Andrés took a deep breath, and then let the air out slowly. The gloominess of the confessional closed in on him. Mixed odors—stale sweat and musty wood mingled with incense—stifled him, suffocating him with the scent of his confession.

He heard movement as the priest's silhouette shifted closer to the grated window.

"Andrés . . ." Father Sebastian's voice was calm, level, that of a gentle pastor guiding his lost sheep away from the raging lion that lurked on the other side. "Now that you have confessed what has long burdened your heart, you must seek God and through him, make amends for the loss and pain you have inflicted on others."

"By doing what, Father?" Andrés was breathing heavily now, his labored gasps echoing along the walls of the dark chamber. "How can I ever make up for the pain I have caused?"

"By going to the two families and telling them what you just told me."

"That is never going to happen. I'll be dead before I walk out the door."

Even though some small part of him wanted to do what was right, a much larger part wanted to survive. Death by an angry Gypsy mob wasn't even his greatest fear. If he went to talk to the Vargas/Meléndez families, his confession would be all over the news. If the Gypsies didn't kill him, his father would.

"It is the only way you will be at peace," Father Sebastián said.

"Then I will live tormented. The way I always have." A heavy sadness pressed down on him, keeping him weighted to the confessional. "Sorry, Father, but I can't do what you ask."

Andrés barely heard the penance that Father Sebastián assigned his sin. He listened only for the priest's prayer of absolution, dismissing him from confession.

"Through the ministry of the Church may God give you pardon and peace." Father Sebastián moved his hand in blessing. "I absolve you from your sins in the name of the Father, and of the Son, and of the Holy Spirit. Amen." The priest made the sign of the cross. "Now go in peace and serve the Lord."

Father Sebastián closed the window of the confessional.

Andrés sucked in a gulp of stale air, then cried through the knuckles that covered his mouth, "How the hell do you expect me to go in peace when there's a man out there determined to hunt me down?"

44

Diego

Diego traced his finger along the crack in the table situated at the far corner of Pablito's bar. He was finding it hard to know whether to trust Rajiv or not. Rajiv had never given him a reason for distrust, but Diego could not let go of his suspicion that Andrés Aragón was the man he was searching for. The face did not look particularly familiar. It had been too dark that night to distinguish the man's features. But the voice. The arrogance. It was hard for him to dismiss the obvious. Andrés Aragón could easily be the man he sought to reorder his world.

Rajiv had encouraged him to go home and then, to make sure he got there, hopped on the bus with him. Diego didn't protest. First, because he wanted to watch Rajiv closely. Look for signs that his friend was lying. And second, because he wanted to make amends with Amara. She had turned her back on him all day yesterday, and avoided him all day today. And now, while half the neighborhood crowded into Pablito's place to meet his new friend from India, she did not show even the slightest interest in the man Diego had talked so much about.

Amara lived her emotions intensely. When she loved, she loved passionately. When she was angry, she held onto her anger completely. He knew he would have to wait for her fury to subside before he could approach her again. But while he waited, he wanted to be near her. He wanted to see her, feel her presence, and if he had to, absorb her anger.

He looked up as Elena approached the table. She held a thick textbook in her hands and was headed directly for Rajiv.

"Do you know algebra?" She spoke tentatively, shifting the heavy book from her right to her left arm.

"I do," Rajiv said, clearing space for her book.

"Can you help me?" Elena set the book down in front of him. "I can't do this. It keeps coming out all wrong."

Diego considered Rajiv's instant popularity with his family and friends. Normally wary of outsiders, they had embraced him with the confidence and warmth they usually extended only to their own.

Rajiv moved the book closer. "Show me what you've got."

Elena pulled up a chair and sat beside him. She opened a lined notebook and showed him a page of mathematical equations.

Rajiv glanced at the notebook and then looked up.

"You don't know your tables, do you?" He shook his head, pretending to be amazed.

"What tables?"

"The multiplication tables. Do you know them?" He tapped the pencil on the table in mock reproach.

"Some. Not the eights and nines, though." Elena's voice was reverent.

"That's your problem." Rajiv slapped the table. "You know the formula, but you're making mistakes on the multiplication." He smiled. "Let me show you a trick."

Elena sat straighter in the chair, her eyes bright.

"I want to see the trick too!" Manolito ran over to the table, knelt, for there were no more chairs, plunked his elbows on the table, and rested his chin between his hands.

Pablito dropped his towel on the counter and came to stand beside his son.

Diego observed his friend, looking for the lie.

"Okay, look." Rajiv appeared slightly flustered. He had told Diego once that he hated attracting attention to himself, but he was certainly the center of attention now. "It's simple," he said. "Nine times two equals eighteen, right? What's nine times three?"

Elena began to count with her lips, but Rajiv stopped her.

"Wait, let me show you something."

Rajiv drew a large number eighteen in Elena's notebook.

"Take the number eighteen, the sum of the last equation, and increase the digit on the left by one."

He wrote a number two. "And then decrease the digit on the right by one." He wrote a number seven. "What do you get? Twenty-seven." He wrote the answer in her book. "Nine times three is twenty-seven." He looked up. "So, what's nine times four?"

"Thirty-six," Elena said, excited.

"And nine times five?"

Elena thought for a moment, lips moving. "Forty-five!"

"Excellent, you've got it!"

"I didn't," Manolito said, puzzled. "I hate math."

"But you like music, don't you?" Rajiv put down the pencil and turned his attention to the boy.

Manolito nodded.

"Well, music is not that different from math. Two notes together form a completely different whole. If you want to be really good at music, go to school and study your math."

"Diego never finished school," Manolito said. "But he's the best guitar player in the whole *barrio*."

Diego flinched, then spoke abruptly.

"I am not a good model, Manolito. Don' do what I did. School is important."

Manolito looked down at the table, his cheeks flushed.

"You're an excellent model." Rajiv caught Diego's eye. "That kind of praise is not earned easily."

Diego glanced over at Amara. He saw the faint trace of a smile on her face. He lowered his eyes, showing no reaction externally but smiling inside. Rajiv certainly seemed trustworthy now.

Pablito looked over his shoulder, glancing at the kitchen door. "Don't let Elena's grandmother catch you teaching the children those tricks," he said. There was a playful sparkle in his eyes.

"But I love working with numbers." Elena's face glowed with excitement.

"You nothing." Abuela's voice boomed from the kitchen. "You fill your head with numbers and rules. Too many rules." Abuela's voice grew closer. "Why you need so many rules?" Abuela's matronly figure filled the small space behind the bar. She held two steaming bowls of *potaje* in her hands, and was slowly making her way over to the table.

"If Elena is going to study medicine," Rajiv said, eyeing Abuela cautiously. "She'll need to know math."

An orange splash of watery liquid sloshed onto the floor.

"No study," Abuela said, leveling the tilted bowl in her hand.

"Make babies," Elena mouthed, rolling her eyes as she turned away from her grandmother.

"Eat." Abuela plunked the two steaming bowls of chickpeas and spinach in front of Rajiv and Diego. "You need more meat on those bones," she said directly to Rajiv.

Rajiv squirmed in his seat.

"Thank you," he said. "But I'm not hun—"

"*A jalar.*" She scooped up a spoonful of liquid and dragged it over to his mouth, spilling a few beans on the table.

Rajiv grabbed the spoon from her hand.

"Thanks, but I'll do it myself."

Pablito grinned at Diego, then watched Abuela as she entered the kitchen, returning with another bowl of *potaje*. Pushing Elena's books aside, she put down the bowl, thrust her chin at Pablito, and said, "Eat."

"Yolanda, to what do I owe this honor?" Pablito said with a smile. "You serving me in my own bar?"

"You good man . . . I serve you."

"It wouldn't have anything to do with Diego's new friend?" Pablito spooned some of the hot broth into his mouth. "A little curiosity perhaps?"

"What curiosity? You no appreciate good service."

"Sorry, my mistake." Pablito's face broke out into a grin.

Elena finished her equations, which Rajiv checked and found correct. All of them. She was ecstatic.

Diego looked back at Amara, then glanced over at Rajiv, who was studying him intently.

"Let's take a walk," Rajiv said. He stole a glance at Amara. "You haven't taken your eyes off her all evening."

Diego lowered his gaze, nodded.

He waited while his family and friends showered well wishes on his friend, and then followed Rajiv out the door and into the neighborhood.

"So, do you want to talk about what's going on between you and Amara?" Rajiv placed a hand on Diego's shoulder. "I know you didn't bring me to Pablito's bar to entertain your friends."

"Now it is you going on the cover of *Entertainment Weekly*." Diego lit a cigarette, then offered it to Rajiv.

Rajiv smiled. "So, what's going on?"

The sincere sound of the question made it hard for Diego to continue to look for inconsistencies.

"She's mad at me," he said.

"I could see that." Rajiv took a drag and handed the cigarette back to Diego. "What did you do to her?"

"Me?" Diego stopped walking. "What did *I* do to *her*?" He took a drag. "She's impossible."

"*Uh-huh*, and you're easy to deal with?" Rajiv took back the cigarette.

Diego sighed.

"All right, maybe she has a reason to be angry with me."

Letting up slightly, Diego led Rajiv into a small bar at the end of the street. And then cautiously, he began to recount his story.

It was hard not to trust Rajiv.

Before he knew it, afternoon had crept into evening and he had talked, and talked, and talked until he felt ill about things he had been too afraid to talk about before. For the first time, he talked about how powerless and entrapped he felt.

"I feel like I'm pushing a heavy stone up a very big hill," Diego said, mixing Spanish with English to get his point across. "At the top of the hill is the Spaniard sitting in his black Mercedes. At the bottom is El Tiburón, holding a gun to my back. Everybody I love is at the bottom of the hill with him. I want to let go of the stone, but I can't. Because if I do, it will roll backwards, crushing me and endangering the people I love. But I can't go forward because I have no strength left. And there is no one who can help me because I took the decision to start pushing the stone."

Rajiv played with the saltshaker on the table.

"By your own strength, it's true, you won't be able to push that stone." Rajiv slid the saltshaker to the middle of the table. "But if someone is standing beside you . . ." He slid the peppershaker next to the salt. "You can let go of the stone, and the person beside you can pull you away before the stone begins to roll."

"Maybe. But what about all those people I love who will be right in the path of that falling stone?"

"If you warn them about what might happen, they will be prepared to move. The man with the gun, however, having had no warning, will not be as quick to react. And the stone, rolling at a velocity faster than his ability to move, will ultimately crush him."

Diego stared at the shakers.

"So what you're saying is that I have to warn Amara about El Tiburón?"

"Amara and everybody else who might be in danger."

Diego shook his head. "I can' do that. Nobody—except Amara and Joaquín—knows that I'm involved with El Tiburón."

"Do you really believe that?"

Diego swallowed. He wanted to believe it, but the truth was, no, he did not.

"All right, say I talk to them, and then what?"

"Then you have to go to El Tiburón and tell him you're out."

Diego shook his head. "He'll never let me go."

"No, he probably won't."

"Then?"

"Then pay him off. Turn him in to the police. Do whatever it takes to remove him as an obstacle."

"Impossible," Diego said. "The police are on his payroll."

"Is there anybody in your community who has something over him? Some kind of power that he'd respect?"

Diego thought for a moment. And then, his heart rate accelerating, he said, "There is one man, Don Antonio Vega."

"Who's that?" Rajiv said.

"The patriarch." Diego's mind raced with possibility. Don Antonio was a "man of respect," an "old Gypsy" revered for his deep knowledge of Gypsy law and considerable understanding of the intricacies of human nature. By having acquired respect—that is, deference and hence obedience—he was the ultimate authority and mediator within the Gypsy community. His counsel was sought with great respect, and his decisions accepted without question or discussion. His word was law, and no one—not even El Tiburón— would challenge that word.

Maybe there was a way out, after all.

45

Andrés

After Andrés's confession he saw no choice. He would go on living. Tormented. And die with his secret.

Better that than letting the world discover who he really was.

A churning sickness rose up his throat. Someone had already discovered the truth. How Rajiv knew about Catalina, he wasn't sure. But the man had made it clear. He knew what Andrés had done. And was capable of using that knowledge against him.

Andrés threw open the door and strode into the apartment.

Tiny heels clattered down the hallway.

"That's it, mister. No more excuses." Adela planted her feet in front of him, her finger raised. "You're taking me to the ranch today."

"Not now, Adela, I'm not in the mood." He brushed past his sister.

She ran after him. "It's not fair." Adela slipped around him. Blocked his path. "You promised me."

"Get out of my way, Adela." He pushed her aside. "I can't deal with this right now."

"You promised!" She grabbed his arm. Then she pinched him. Hard. Her nails dug into his skin as she twisted the chunk of flesh caught between her fingers.

"¡Coño!" He grabbed her and pried her hand away. "You little bitch!" He threw her back.

And then, violently reacting, he slapped her face.

She landed on the floor like a broken marionette, her arms and legs gone limp.

His heart plunged. "I'm so sorry." He rushed to help her up.

A single tear spilled over her right eye.

"What the hell is going on here?" His father stormed into the hallway.

"Andrés hit me!" Adela was sobbing now, both hands cupped over her left cheek.

Quickly, Andrés pulled Adela to her feet. His heart pounded. In less than five seconds, he had become the man he most despised.

"Go wash your face, Adela," his father said. "Andrés is taking you to the ranch."

Abuela appeared, took Adela by the hand.

"*Vente,*" she said. "Come with me."

Her shoulders shaking, Adela followed their grandmother down the hallway.

Too shocked to speak, Andrés stood frozen, his father's words swirling like hornets over his head.

"Don Enrique has arranged to give Adela riding lessons," his father said. "Starting today. Her horse is now broken into saddle." His father spoke in the same businesslike tone he used with his clients. "She's a beauty. Sweet, but spirited. Make sure Adela completes the lesson. And that she rides alone."

"What?" Andrés squeezed his temples. It was like the man was immune to violence.

"Don't let her get off the horse, even if she cries." His father was on a mission. And right now, nothing else mattered.

Except for the fucking horse.

"Are you out of your mind?" Andrés's thoughts were coherent now. "She won't ride that horse alone."

His father's eyes were cold when he turned them on Andrés.

"You will take your sister to the ranch and get her on that horse. Do you have a problem with that?"

Andrés looked away, his heart plunging. Once, a long time ago, his father had spoken almost the exact same words to him. "*You will get back on that horse. And you will not cry. Do you understand me?*"

Andrés had understood. And by force, he had learned to ride.

* * *

Thirty minutes later, he was on the road to the ranch. Adela slept in the back seat, her arm tied in a mock sling she had fabricated from a doll's blanket. There was a pink welt on her wrist.

Clenching his teeth, he pressed down on the accelerator. How could he have hit her? An innocent, powerless girl. She had no chance against him. How could he have used his strength to hurt her?

He knew why. He'd always known that someday, he would become his father.

46

Rajiv

The aroma of melted chocolate and freshly baked pastries stimulated Rajiv's senses as he opened the door to La Campana. He had been with Diego most of the day. But now, by mandate of his love guru, he left the Southside to share a cup of tea with a woman who would definitely upset his father. Crystal Webb.

After much procrastination, he had finally summoned the courage to call her. Or, better said, was pushed into the act by an enthusiastic group of locals at Pablito's bar.

"What can I get you?" the waiter said.

"Un momento." Rajiv pulled out a chair for Crystal. "What would you like to drink?"

"Hot chocolate," she said.

Rajiv turned to the waiter.

"Una infusion y una taza de chocolate."

His Spanish had improved tremendously after only a few weeks of frequenting Pablito's bar.

In fact, his new life in the Gypsy Quarter had been good for him on many levels. He felt relaxed. At ease. Free. Time did not seem to matter as much. Enjoying life did.

He liked the way he was with the Gypsies.

Refreshingly unpredictable.

When he first arrived in Seville, he had worked through coffee breaks and well past lunch—a pattern he had followed every day through six years of graduate school.

While most of his classmates had chosen to experiment with breaking taboos—buying alcohol from seedy representatives of the underground market and meeting with women in secret, forbidden arrangements—he had remained in the lab working, obsessed with finishing the experiments that would get him away from the suffocating structure and oppressive control his father had forced upon his life.

Six years later and thousands of miles away, he had continued to follow the same neurotic pattern. The same rigid routine.

Truth be told, he had started to bore even himself.

Although, he had to admit, life had been anything but boring since he'd arrived in Spain. He had been spat on, laughed at, come on to, hated, admired, and desired. He had never felt so sick, so miserable, so lonely in his life. Nor had he ever felt so alive. He had tasted the pleasure of sin, of wine and women, and those stolen tastes had only left him wanting more. He looked forward to another glass of wine, another woman to share it with. Although in the future, he would be more careful about the women he chose to be with.

Pili had finally lost interest in him and moved onto a more muscular, less intellectual Spaniard. The Olympic trainee was probably better for her, anyway. Rajiv's own awkwardness often left her frustrated. But he was getting more comfortable in his skin. Thanks to Diego and the Gypsies. Who would, right about now, be encouraging him to get on with the evening.

Turning his attention back to Crystal, he noticed she was reading the newspaper that the former patrons had left on the table. Her face had taken on a strange intensity. He was about to ask her what she was reading when the waiter returned with their drinks. He concentrated on dunking the tea bag into the scalding water.

"Anything interesting in the paper?" he said. The headline she was reading had something to do with Holy Week.

She looked up, her eyes blazing blue neons that caught hold of him and made him shiver.

"Have you ever wanted something so much that . . ."

She looked away, tucked a loose curl behind her ear.

"That you were willing to give up everything you knew to find it?"

She looked back, finding his eyes.

He held onto her gaze, not answering for a moment.

"Yes," he finally said. He wanted to say so much more, but waited for her to finish her thought.

"Do you ever feel like you don't belong inside your skin? Like you don't fit in where you came from? Like part of you belongs to some other time and place, but at the same time, it doesn't?"

Rajiv nodded, letting her know that yes, he understood. And then, he finished her thought.

"It's like you can't go back, because you never fit in in the first place," he said. "But at the same time, you don't fit into your new life either."

"Exactly." Her eyes opened wide.

"I know, I feel the same way. My mother wants me to return home over the summer and get married, as if I could just go back to life as I once knew it."

"So what does your girlfriend have to say about that?" The tension in her face relaxed into cautious curiosity.

"No, I don't have a girlfriend. But my parents would like it very much if I had a wife. They've spent the better part of the last two years engaged in the seemingly impossible task of finding a suitable bride for me."

Rajiv tugged out his wallet. He pulled out a crumpled photograph and showed it to her. "Here's their latest selection."

Crystal studied the glossy photograph, then looked up at him. "She's beautiful."

You're beautiful.

"Look at her hair, it's past her waist."

But yours is soft and smells like rose water.

"How do they make these selections for you?"

"Through ads in the newspaper," Rajiv said. "Or family contacts."

"What do you think your ad says?" Crystal said. And then she started the fictitious ad for him. "Handsome twenty-six-year-old male seeks life partner. . . ."

"Must be from the Brahmin class," Rajiv continued, imitating his father. "Lighter skin preferred, but will consider a dark-skinned woman with the proper educational and ethnic background."

"And just what is the proper educational and ethnic background?"

"She must be a Hindu, from an upstanding South Indian family. And she will be required to have at least a masters in science, if not a PhD. Of course . . ." Rajiv's mouth relaxed into a playful smile. "She would also have to come up with at least a herd of sacred cows, a flock of royal peacocks, and one of the rarest animals on God's earth—the blue elephant."

"Wow. That's tough." Crystal sloshed her chocolate around the cup in mock concentration. "Of course you know that the sacred cows would come with a lot of sacred crap, but no problem—you want sacred cows, I'll find you a herd."

"No thanks." Rajiv laughed. "I already have enough crap to last at least five lifetimes."

Crystal smiled. "Tell me, what kind of ad would *you* write if you were looking for a wife?"

"Wanted," Rajiv began, looking at her intently. "Caring, compassionate woman who is not afraid to go against tradition. Skin color unimportant. Sense of excitement and adventure required. Religion unimportant. Caste unimportant."

"Ethnic origin unimportant," Crystal continued. "American women welcome to apply."

"Definitely." Rajiv smiled. "American women *encouraged* to apply."

Crystal laughed. "You know what, Rajiv, you remind me so much of my dad."

"In what way?" he asked, not sure whether to be intrigued or appalled.

"I don't know, he's steady . . . and wise. Philosophical, but on a practical level."

Rajiv sighed. "In other words . . . dependable, but boring."

"Dependable is a good thing," Crystal said. "You should remember to put that in your ad."

"I'll make a note of it," Rajiv said, smiling.

Now feeling more at ease, Rajiv was comfortable with the intimate conversation Crystal began. They talked about their families, their homes, the different paths that had brought them to Spain.

The coffee shop grew darker as afternoon faded into evening. Without either of them being conscious of it, they had created an intimacy, a bond of friendship that only strangers alone in a foreign land could come to understand.

Crystal looked at her watch. "It's late. I should go. But thanks for inviting me. I had a really great time."

"How about another cup of chocolate?" Rajiv said.

"No, thanks. I mean, I'd like to, but I still have to prepare my lessons for tomorrow."

She reached for her book bag and then stood, adjusting the straps of the backpack over her shoulders.

Rajiv stood with her. "No problem. I understand."

He had learned over the course of the evening that she was an English teacher at a private language academy, which paid just about enough to cover room and board, but allowed her the work visa she needed to remain in the country legally. She was doing research, she said, on the celebration of Holy Week in Seville, and spent hours at a chapel devoted to a Virgin she called La Esperanza de Triana. What she hadn't said was why.

Somehow, Rajiv had the distinct impression that her research had more to do with some kind of personal odyssey than with a simple pursuit of knowledge. It was the only subject, of the many they had discussed, that she refused to enter into with more than just perfunctory details.

And the mystery of it left him wanting to know more.

"I'll see you later, okay?" She kissed him on both cheeks, Spanish style, and then headed for the door.

"Wait." He called her back. "One last question before you leave."

"Yes?"

"What sign are you?"

"You mean Zodiac sign?"

He nodded.

"Virgo."

"Oh, wow." Rajiv shook his head, feigning alarm. "Two Virgos together is an explosive combination."

"Why, what are Virgos supposed to be like?" She pulled off her bag and dropped it to the floor.

"Analytical, critical, logical . . ."

"Sounds like a scientist, like you." She pulled out the chair she had vacated only minutes before.

"But also helpful, sensitive, caring, and inquisitive." He smiled and motioned for the waiter. "Which sounds like you."

"So does that mean we're a good match?"

"Couldn't tell you," Rajiv said. "Only the stars would know."

As he ordered another cup of chocolate and one more tea, Rajiv wondered if in that part of his story still left to be written, the next chapter would include a woman. A fun-spirited, American woman with black curls and blue eyes.

And a mystery still yet to be solved . . .

47

Diego

Diego wanted nothing more than to forget the last conversation he had had with Rajiv. He did not want to upset Amara any further by telling her the truth about his involvement with El Tiburón. But Rajiv was right. He had to take that step forward or he would be forever falling back. Not only that, he needed to protect her. He would rather lose her love than risk putting her in harm's way. But before he talked to her, he wanted to speak with her father.

He looked up as Pablito entered the living room with two cups of coffee on a small tray. He had sent Amara and Manolito to visit with their aunt so that the two of them could be alone. Pablito set the tray down on the center table and spooned sugar into the coffee. He handed Diego one of the cups and took the other to the chair opposite him. He sipped on his coffee, and then invited Diego to share what was on his mind.

Diego swallowed. His hand trembled as he set his cup on the table.

"I need to tell you something, Pablito." Diego's voice faltered but he kept his gaze steady.

Pablito nodded and waited for him to continue.

"And what I have to tell you may change your opinion of me." Diego could barely speak over the lump that had formed in his throat. "I should have told you before, but . . ." He lowered his eyes. "I couldn't."

"Go on, son," Pablito said.

"A few months after Catalina died, I became involved with El Tiburón." Diego kept his gaze down so that he would not have to see the shock and anger in Pablito's eyes.

"I started stealing cars for him. Not because I needed the money, but because I thought I could find justice. I was so confused, so angry. I could not get rid of the image of that black Mercedes, that arrogant Spaniard. And I wanted that man to suffer. I wanted him to feel as much pain as I felt. But instead of feeling better for having found some kind of order in my crumbled universe, I became even more frightened."

Pablito finished his coffee, placed the cup on the table, and steepled his hands. His brow folded as he concentrated.

Diego's heart thudded as he awaited Pablito's response.

"It is normal to feel the way you felt," Pablito said. "Everyone who suffers loss will experience anger, and fear, and perhaps even the desire for revenge. When my wife died, I felt the same way. The pain of her loss was so severe because the pleasure of having loved her was so great."

"Yes." Diego edged forward on the sofa. Finally someone understood. It was as if the screaming pain he felt demonstrated the supreme value of what he had lost.

"But," Pablito continued, "Pura's death threw me onto a path I didn't want to travel down. God had given me not only a tremendous burden, but also a terrible challenge. I had two children I needed to live for, even though all I wanted to do in those first weeks after Pura's death was to crumple up and die. I felt so exhausted, so anguished, that I wondered whether I could survive another day, whether I *wanted* to survive."

"That was exactly how I felt." Diego's heart pumped wildly. Pablito's response was not what he had expected, but it encouraged him to say more. "Sometimes I felt like I was walking under this huge, black shadow. Everything was dark, and I felt punished by simply being alive."

"Sudden and tragic loss can lead to terrible darkness," Pablito said. "And that darkness will come, no matter how hard we try to hold it off. But you have come out of the darkness, Diego. And now you have the opportunity to choose the direction your life will head."

"But that's the problem. I already made a choice. A bad one. And now I can't reverse it."

"You just did. You reversed one choice by making another." Pablito stared at Diego for a moment without speaking. And then, quietly, he said, "Why did you choose to tell me this now?"

"Because people I love may be in danger. You, Amara, Manolito. I have put you and your family at risk, and I would rather lose Amara through the truth than see her hurt through a lie. I don't want to bring pain or suffering into your household. I would rather die than cause that to happen. But because of the man I have become, sooner or later, I will bring suffering and destruction into this home."

Pablito nodded. "What you say is true. But not entirely. Because of the man you have become, you will bring not suffering into my home, but honor. You chose to remain static in the darkness, and because of that decision, other decisions followed. But while you were living in that darkness, something interesting happened. As tragedy increased your soul's capacity for darkness, it also increased its capacity for light. The soul is elastic, Diego, like a balloon. Loss can enlarge its capacity for anger, depression, despair, and anguish— all natural and legitimate emotions whenever we experience loss. But once enlarged, the soul is also capable of experiencing greater joy, strength, peace, and love. All of a sudden, we find ourselves more sensitive to the pain of others, more compassionate. That's what happened to you, Diego, when you finally got out of yourself and turned back to the world again."

Diego fell back against the couch, stunned.

"The suffering you have experienced," Pablito continued, "is part of an ongoing story that is still to be written. You will never totally get over Catalina's lost life, but you will absorb that loss into your life, until it becomes part of who you are. But as tragic as your loss was, it was also the beginning of something new. That loss brought you a new love, Diego."

Diego shot back up.

"But what if I'm not capable of giving enough to that love?"

"If you want to grow through loss, Diego, you must eventually decide to love even more deeply than you did before."

Pablito rubbed the tips of his fingers along the arm of the sofa.

"I also had a choice after my wife died. I could have died to my children and allowed them to experience another loss on top of the loss they had already suffered. I could have drowned myself in sorrow and distanced myself from them. But I chose to respond to the loss by embracing love with renewed energy and commitment."

Pablito's fingers fell still.

"I understand that it's frightening to love again. If loss increases our capacity for pain as well as love, then an increased capacity for love will only make us feel greater sorrow when suffering strikes again. Which it will. Life hangs on a delicate balance between sadness and joy. There is no simple solution. Choosing to withdraw from people and to protect the self diminishes the soul's ability to learn to love even more deeply than before. It takes tremendous courage to love when we are broken. Yet I wonder if love becomes even stronger when it grows out of brokenness. I know it did with me. The love that grew between my children and me after my wife's death was not just the love of a man for his offspring. It was the deep, sacrificial love of a father who had learned to cherish his children."

Pablito looked back at Diego, studied him for a moment, and then said, "It took courage to come to me the way you did today. Yes, you made a bad choice when you decided to get involved with organized crime. But there is a way out. We Gypsies are many things. Stubborn. Proud. Vengeful. But we respect our elders and our laws."

Diego leaned forward, hopeful now that the bad choices he had made would no longer define him.

"I'm going to take this matter of your relationship with Tiburón to Don Antonio," Pablito said. "I will take what you told me under counsel and, with his help, determine the appropriate course of action."

A formal counsel with the patriarch was a serious move. But the decision that would come from that counsel, Diego knew, would be both fair and final.

After hearing Diego's case—as presented by Pablito—Don Antonio decided to intervene on Diego's behalf.

Two days after Pablito spoke to him, Don Antonio called a meeting with El Tiburón, at which he requested Diego and Pablito's presence. Don Josemi was also asked to attend.

In that meeting, the patriarch appealed to The Shark's "benevolence" and requested that El Tiburón release Diego.

"The boy has suffered enough," Don Antonio said. "He was young and foolish and had not thought before he acted. A wise man would let him go. A generous man would not only let him go, but wish him no harm."

The Shark moved his jeweled finger up and down over the table. He wasn't conceding anything. Not yet.

"Knowing that Rafa León is not only a generous man, but a benevolent one as well," Don Antonio continued. "I am sure that Mr. León will have no problem doing what is morally right."

The finger stopped, and with it the thumping.

A hushed silence fell over the room.

"Diego is released," The Shark said. He turned to Diego, extended his hand, and ended their association.

Through the iron grip that tightened over his hand, Diego could feel El Tiburón's rage. In his eyes, he could see the fury. But in his voice, Diego heard nothing but a smooth, practiced benevolence.

"I wish you well," El Tiburón said.

Everybody knew he didn't mean it.

But they also knew he would never go against the patriarch.

It was the Gypsy way.

"Mr. León has wished you well," Don Antonio said, "which is also my desire. But rarely in life is wishing ever enough. For you to be well, you need to act well. Your loss does not have to be the defining moment of your life. That moment can, and should be, your response to that loss. I want you to find that moment, Diego. I want you to go back to the forest. Your cousin Lorenzo may accompany you."

Those were difficult words for Diego to hear. But out of respect for Don Antonio, he bowed his head and nodded his consent. Just as The Shark had done before him.

And then in obedience, he prepared himself to return to the forest.

48

Diego

Diego glanced over at Lorenzo, seated beside him in the car. Lorenzo had his head thrown back against the seat, eyes closed.

Diego tightened his grip on the wheel as he stared out over the road to Huelva. Don Antonio was a wise man. He knew that the only person Diego would ever return to the ranch with was Lorenzo, the man who had first introduced him to the horses.

Groves of orange trees stretched for miles along the country road, filling the wind with their traitorous seduction.

"Close your window," he said sharply, rolling up his own.

Lorenzo's eyes opened lethargically and he was slow to respond.

"Why?" he finally said. "It's hot."

"Just do it." Diego heard the sharpness in his tone and looked back at Lorenzo.

His cousin's lips were tight, eyes nailed on the road ahead. Silently, Lorenzo rolled up the window.

For several kilometers, there was nothing more than long stretches of open land, fenced in with barbed wire. The smell of horses and hay drifted in through the small crack at the top of the window and something within him stirred—an unsettling feeling that tightened into a knot at the pit of his stomach.

Diego inhaled sharply. They had arrived at the spot in the road now marked by a wooden cross and faded plastic flowers. His heart pounded and it hurt to breathe.

"I can't do this," he said, gunning the accelerator.

His heart racing, Diego pulled off the road and cut the engine. Throwing his head back against the seat, he cursed into the air.

"Dammit! Why did she have to die?"

"She died," Lorenzo said, "but she would have wanted you to live."

"I died with her that night."

"No, you didn't." Lorenzo leaned over, turned the key in the ignition, and started the engine. "You just chose not to go on for a while."

Diego stared out the windshield, shifted the car into gear, and then turned back onto the road in silence. The blinker clicked as he abandoned the main highway for the exit. After crossing the town of Aznalcázar, he drove along the boundaries of El Rancho del Cielo. When he reached the entrance to the ranch, he braked and shifted the car into neutral. There was no turning back. His former boss was standing at the open gate that secured the property.

"*Adelante.*" Don Enrique pushed a few stones away with his mud-caked boots.

Gravel shot from beneath the car's wheels as Diego drove forward onto the property.

"It's been a long time." Don Enrique greeted Diego with a tight hug and sound slap on the back.

Diego gazed into the distance, hands stuffed into his pockets.

"I'm attending a client," Don Enrique said. "We'll talk later." He squeezed Diego's shoulder and then headed for his office.

"Come on," Lorenzo said. "Lucero will be glad to see you."

Diego hesitated, but then followed his cousin to the paddock where a number of horses were grazing.

"Keno," he murmured, opening the gate and walking toward the brown mare. He rubbed her neck. She whinnied in response.

Then he moved over to Hidalgo, passing a hand over the gelding's broad forehead.

Finally, he looked up, his eyes landing on Lucero.

He gave Hidalgo a final pat, and then made his way across the paddock to his horse on the other side.

"My friend, how I have missed you." He caressed Lucero's face.

A whinny of recognition erupted from Lucero's mouth.

Diego sighed, a deep heavy sigh, and then closed his eyes.

Painful memories flooded back. It had been warm that day, a day much like today. Hot. Humid. The air moist with impending rain.

He opened his eyes and glanced up at the sky. The clouds were grey.

Lucero nudged him gently.

Diego responded mechanically, stroking the horse's neck, but his mind was far away.

Lucero grew impatient. Energy flowed from him as he stepped first forward and then back. He wanted to go, to move, to be out in the open fields. Lucero whinnied loudly and stamped his front foot on the ground, lifting up dust and memories.

"Lorenzo," Diego said, "I want to ride my horse."

Lorenzo nodded. And then walked toward the tack room.

Returning with Diego's saddle, he slung it over Lucero's back while Diego secured the bit.

The supple leather of the reins felt good in his hands. Diego adjusted the stirrups, and then ran his hand over Lucero's neck. He could feel the animal's nervous energy. He took the halter rope and walked Lucero toward the gate. But then he stopped abruptly.

"What's wrong with Fuego?"

Diego stood still, eyes glued on the corral. Fuego's ears were pinned down flat, front legs frantically pawing the ground. A man, his back turned, was mounted on top of her.

"I don't know," Lorenzo said. "The guy seems to be making her nervous. She hasn't been saddled for a while, but . . ."

The man jerked on the reins, yanking Fuego's bit to turn her to the right.

Fuego fought against the bit, mouth open, teeth biting at the air.

"Give the mare her head," Lorenzo shouted. "You're pulling back on the reins and kicking her at the same time. She doesn't know whether to go forward or backward!"

"Fuck off! I know what I'm doing." The man raised his arm, and with a sharp *thwack*, brought his riding crop down on Fuego's neck. Hard leather against the mare's sleek hide.

Fuego's eyes bulged and she threw back her head, tail swishing in agitated circles.

The rider ignored the mare's frustration. Digging his heels into the spot on Fuego's inner girth that would force her to turn, the rider compelled his horse to face the gate.

Diego took in a sharp breath.

The man on the horse was Andrés Aragón.

Diego recoiled as Andrés pushed Fuego toward the gate with a sharp swat of his crop.

"No, don't hit her," Diego cried out, hands clenched at his side. It was as if he had received the blow upon his own back.

"This is going to be a child's horse," Andrés shouted. "I need to know if she's trustworthy." He gouged Fuego with his silver spurs. "Why won't she gait?"

"She doesn't know what you want!" Diego cried. "Your spurs are hurting her."

"*¡Tranquila!*" Andrés shouted at the horse as he began to circle her, loosening the left rein and tightening the right.

"He knows what he's doing," Lorenzo said, watching as Andrés gained control of the horse, moving Fuego in circles until she listened to him.

"But he's nervous," Diego said. "Look how he's leaning forward."

"He's about to come off!" Lorenzo sprinted toward the corral.

Andrés pulled back on both reins, losing his balance as he leaned back in the saddle to correct his position.

Fuego scrabbled in the air with her front hooves, crow-hopped, and then reared up, throwing her rider to the ground.

Diego bolted into the corral and grabbed Fuego by the reins. He whispered in her ear, knowing what she needed. Fuego was the horse he had broken into saddle the day Catalina died.

Though his heart bled with the memory, and he wanted to scream, to cry out in anger, he stood quietly, reassuring the horse, letting her know that she was safe.

The mare's eyes bulged wildly, but after a while, she bowed her head. Then brought it level with her back. Her tail stilled.

Diego rubbed her neck, her face, in between her ears. And then slowly, he led the mare away from Andrés and toward the barn.

From the corner of his eye, he saw Lorenzo offer his hand to help Andrés to his feet.

Andrés shoved Lorenzo away. He did not get up immediately but rose to one knee, his body bent, head bowed. His chest rose and fell rapidly, as if trying to keep pace with an accelerating heart. Slowly, he looked up, his eyes hardening as they locked onto Diego's. Then, in a sudden, violent move, he punched the ground. Then punched it again, pummeling the dirt with an angry fist.

His chest still heaving, Andrés spoke.

"Get that Gypsy away from my horse."

Hate and fury burned in his eyes.

"He's just trying to—" Lorenzo said.

Andrés sprang from the ground and grabbed Lorenzo's arm.

"Get him the fuck away from my horse."

Diego froze in his tracks. There it was again. That voice, that tone of arrogant conceit. His mind refused to cooperate with his memory, but he knew he had heard that voice before. He stared at Andrés, but saw nothing more than a hateful, angry man.

"*Tranquilo, hombre.*" Lorenzo shook Andrés off his arm with a thrust of his shoulder. His tone threatened an unspoken challenge.

Andrés lowered his arm and loosened his tightened fist. He put his open palm to his mouth and wiped his lips. The fury still blazed in his eyes. But he was in control.

Diego saw Lorenzo breathe a heavy sigh when Andrés spun around on his heels and stormed away. Seconds later, Andrés was intercepted by Don Enrique, who was motioning toward the office.

"That guy's a lunatic," Lorenzo said, joining Diego in the barn. "I swear I'll put my fist up his arrogant—"

"What's going on here?" Don Enrique strode into the barn.

"That moron was beating on Fuego," Lorenzo began. "He—"

"That man is the son of one of my best clients." Don Enrique's face flushed red. He grabbed Fuego's reins from Lorenzo, then turned to Diego. "Do me a favor, please go to my office and start filling out the paperwork for his sister's riding lessons. The papers are on my desk. I'll join you in a minute." Then he turned to Lorenzo and said, "I don't want *any* problems, do you hear me?"

"Don Enrique, *por favor.*" Diego's heart thundered in his chest. "It's better if Lorenzo—"

"Please, Diego." Don Enrique's face was hard, his voice stern. "Lorenzo is not acting professionally right now."

"But . . ." A hint of desperation altered Diego's voice as he struggled for something to say.

"I'm attending another client," Don Enrique said. "If Andrés Aragón goes back and tells his father he was treated badly here. . ." He stopped and his eyes flickered. "Please, Diego. As a favor to me."

Diego closed his eyes and let out a heavy sigh. He would do almost anything for this man. For this *payo* who was like a second father to him. But could he control himself enough to walk into that office and face Andrés Aragón without shaming Don Enrique?

He opened his eyes. Yes, he could. He could and he would control himself. For Don Enrique. And for Catalina.

By walking into that office, he would not only honor his boss, but would remember his wife as he searched for the answers he was looking for.

"*Está bien*," he said, successfully hiding the fear that threatened to edge out the strength in his voice. Punching his fist down along his side, he spun around and marched toward the office.

He stood for a moment in front of the door. He could hear his heartbeat in his ears, pounding fast and furious against his head. Finally summoning the strength he knew he had, he yanked open the door and stepped inside.

He could feel the adrenaline pumping as he sat down in the swivel chair behind his boss's desk. Andrés sat directly in front of him. A young girl squirmed beside the man, her arms crossed. She did not look happy. Finding the paperwork Don Enrique had asked him to fill out, he looked up, fixing his eyes on Andrés with a stare as hard and as cold as the one Andrés was returning to him.

"I just need to fill out this paperwork," he said, slowly, in control, "and your sister can start her lessons."

"That horse is *una demonia*." Andrés sneered, his eyes nailed on Diego. "She must have Gypsy blood in her."

A muscle twitched in Diego's face.

"Fuego is actually a gentle horse." Diego's eyes bore into his adversary. "You just have to know how to treat her."

"Ohhhh." Andrés shook his head in mock understanding. "An expert on how to treat— "

The screen door squealed on its hinges. Andrés's eyes flashed over, landing on Chelo—Don Enrique's secretary, Lorenzo's wife.

"—the more delicate sex." A slow smile snaked over Andrés's face as he crossed his foot across his knee and sat back in the chair.

Diego's gaze shifted to Chelo. His mind screamed though his mouth was silent.

"Well, let's see." Andrés rubbed his chin. "She's a stubborn one, but I suppose I could break her." He turned his eyes on Chelo, who mouthed a quick apology and moved over to the file cabinet in the corner. "It's easy when you know how."

Diego clamped his lips together and turned his head to the side, trying hard to contain the words that wanted to explode from his mouth.

"She has a certain fire," Andrés said, still looking at Chelo. "She'd be a great ride—hot and fast."

Diego pushed the chair out from underneath him and stood, leaning forward over the desk. "Do you want to sign these papers, or not?" He enunciated each word with cold precision.

"Am I making you nervous? You seem a little . . . jittery."

Diego remained standing, his eyes drawn to a silver medallion clipped to Andrés's belt loop. He stared at the medallion, jumped when Chelo slammed the drawer to the file cabinet, and then slowly sat back down.

"Stop it, Andrés," the girl said. "You're being mean."

Diego stared at the girl. Her face was crunched into angry creases. She blinked. And then she smiled at him.

"Fill out the papers," Andrés said, calling Diego's attention back. His tone was slightly less arrogant than before.

Carefully, Diego proceeded. "Name," he said.

"Andrés Aragón."

"Address."

"Calle Asunción, 15- B, Los Remedios."

Diego wrote: Calle Azunsión, 15-B, Lo Remedio.

Andrés paused before he spoke. Then he let the words roll out of his mouth with brutal force.

"How sad to see that one of the finest ranches in Andalusia is hiring illiterate help to run their operation." His voice was so steady, his gaze so cruel, that for one suspended moment in time, no one moved.

"Any half-educated ten-year-old would know how to spell such a simple word as Asunción."

Diego threw down the pen, sprang out from behind the desk, and grabbed Andrés by the collar.

Just before he landed the punch Andrés was taunting him to give, Diego was ripped away from Don Enrique's coveted client by Lorenzo.

"Oh, touched a nerve, did I . . . *amigo*?" Andrés sneered.

"Do something smart, *amigo* . . ." Chelo came in between the two men and pushed Andrés back. "Shut your mouth."

"Oh how touching." Andrés scoffed. "A Gypsy bitch defending her wounded dog."

"*¡Cabrón!*" Diego's fist landed with fury on Andrés's face.

Before Diego could land another, Lorenzo grabbed his raised arm and pushed him out the door.

"Get out of here," Lorenzo said, breathing heavily. He turned toward Chelo. "Go!" he said to his wife. "Now!"

Chelo ran out behind Diego, following him into the barn.

"I don't need you to fight for me." Diego's eyes burned with a deep, quiet fury. He snatched a handful of Lucero's mane and swung up onto his horse.

Chelo's curt apology was lost to the air as he pressed his thighs into Lucero's sides and took off in a heated gallop.

Lucero's hooves pounded into the dirt. The muscles in Diego's arms flexed as he tightened up on the reins. His chest constricted, fighting against his thundering heart.

He could feel the anger boiling inside of him. The humiliation. But it wasn't only the shame that altered him so violently. Andrés was beginning to feel more and more familiar to him. That voice. The arrogance.

And that medallion clipped to his belt loop.

Even though he hadn't seen the engraving on the medallion clearly, he knew it belonged to one of the religious fraternities popular in Seville. The members of these fraternities were all devotees of the Virgin Mary. They wore images of the Virgin on chains around their necks, clipped to belt loops, tied around rearview mirrors. And fixed to the dashboard of their cars.

Touching his heels to Lucero's flanks, he took off with his horse, in full gallop, toward the parking lot. Choking for breath, he reined Lucero to a stop.

A black Mercedes was parked in the yard.

Diego's heart snagged in his chest.

On the front dash was the tilted Virgin.

49

Diego

Diego stared at the tilted Virgin for what seemed a lifetime. He could barely breathe. A slow, quiet rage boiled inside of him. Like lava churning in the dark pit of a volcano, ready to explode.

"I finally found you," he whispered to the wind.

Slowly, he turned Lucero around.

"Now you are going to feel what it's like to lose your life."

He kicked Lucero into a run and galloped toward the office.

Andrés Aragón was going to feel what it was like to be left helpless. Diego's thoughts were as wild as the pace he kept. He was going to drag that man to the forest, beat him until he was half dead, and then leave him abandoned.

To die.

He charged on. Clouds of dust kicked up behind him.

But then he reined Lucero to a sudden stop. Andrés Aragón was squatted beside the barn, tucking his sister's hair behind her ear. She was crying.

Panting heavily, Diego edged closer.

"Stop crying, Adela. It's over, okay?" Andrés stuck out his thumb and rubbed away her tears.

"Why were you mean to that man?" The girl brushed Andrés's hand away. "He didn't do anything to you."

"Forget about it," Andrés said.

"You were mean to him!" The girl was sobbing now. "I hate you!"

She started to run off, but Andrés grabbed her arm and held her back.

"Calm down, Adela!"

"I hate you! I hate you! I hate you!" She shouted hysterically.

Andrés pulled her close to his chest and held her tight.

"Shhh," he said. "I'm sorry I upset you."

Heavy sobs shook her body. "Why did you hit me?"

Because he's an animal. Diego squeezed Lucero's sides, about to charge forward, when Andrés answered his sister.

"Because I was a jerk," he said. "I hurt other people because I hurt inside." He rubbed her hair. "But I never, ever wanted to hurt you. Do you forgive me?"

She pulled back. Smiled at him. And then, she nodded.

"Good. Now come on, let's get you up on your horse." He took her hand and started walking toward the barn.

"Will you ride with me?" the girl said.

Andrés's hand clenched, and then unclenched at his side.

"No, you'll be fine."

"Pleeaasse." She stopped in front of him.

"I'll tell you what . . ." He pushed her forward. "After your lesson, we'll take a short ride. There's something I have to do right now."

"What?"

"Nothing." His voice was tight. "Just go, okay? I'll take you for a ride, a little later."

"Into the forest?"

"Wherever you want to go." He grabbed her hand. "But you can't tell Papá."

She let go of his hand, extended her arms, and jumped up on him.

"Of course I won't, silly." She kissed his cheek. "I love you."

"Love you, too." Andrés wrapped her legs around his waist as she clung to his neck. Then walked her to the barn.

Everything Diego had ever felt for this man firecrackered around his head. Loathing. Hatred. All-consuming rage. It was all there. Popping against the words a young girl said. *I love you.*

"Damn you, Andrés Aragón." He turned Lucero around. "For being human."

He squeezed his legs into Lucero's side. And then he rode, and he rode, and he rode. Deep into the meadow. Toward the forest.

50

Andrés

Andrés left his sister in the barn with Don Enrique, and then bolted for his car. Now would be a good time for that cocaine he still had stashed in the glove compartment.

He yanked open the door and fell into his Mercedes. He hadn't used that car since the night Catalina died. But he couldn't exactly take a scooter out to the country.

Had Diego noticed his vehicle? His eyes darted from the door to the dash. There were no signs of vandalism.

But of course, it wasn't his Mercedes that Diego was after.

He jerked open the glove compartment. In less than a few minutes, he had cut and snorted the first line.

A bump shook the car. He sprang forward in the seat, shot a glance out the window. Don Enrique's dog, Negrito, passed to the side of the car, chasing a cat.

Andrés exhaled. And then he cut another line.

He had tried to play it tough in Don Enrique's office but the Gypsy was tougher, fueled by a rage Andrés could easily understand. He knew, probably better than anyone, the power of that anger.

The first drug rush spread through him, more quickly than it usually did. He drummed his fingers on the steering wheel.

Come on, Gypsy boy. I can take you on.

Shit, he was feeling good.

The world outside the window seemed brighter now. The grass that had looked like hay when he drove in now seemed like golden thread. The clouds were smoky grey, as if someone had taken an artist's lead pencil and shadowed over the white.

He bounced his knee, thoughts focused on his sister. She was a good girl, that one. She forgave so easily.

But no, *shit*, that wasn't good. She was too naïve. Too trusting. What if some jerk hit her and she forgave him? What if she married a bully? No, that can't happen. He had to protect her. From all the bad people. Had to protect her. His thoughts were racing.

And then, as if compelled, he fixated on his sister, who had just entered the corral with Don Enrique's Gypsy lackey.

She didn't look unhappy, mounted on Fuego. Why not?

She should be.

Unhappy.

Scared, at least.

Drumming more insistently now on the steering wheel, he sat staring, wondering, fearing, doubting, thinking of things that in a sane man would undoubtedly have seemed crazy.

The Gypsy was on to him, he had to be.

That's why the man had disappeared.

To catch him unaware, unprotected, vulnerable.

But no problem. He was ready.

Clink. Clink. Clink.

Andrés froze in the seat, alert, eyes shifting, looking for the source of the sound of iron against iron, of a hammer against a spur.

Either one could be used to kill him. The hammer or the spur. One blow to the head would do it. One horseshoe accurately thrown into his cerebral cortex.

Or was it the frontal lobe?

Father would laugh at him for not knowing.

"God, it's so fucking hot!"

He ripped at the buttons on his soggy shirt. One button flew against the door.

Clink. Clink. Clink.

There it was again. The requiem to his death.

Fingers shaking, he reached for the bag he had tossed on the dash. One more line.

He'd never done three lines in such a short amount of time. But what harm could it do now?

He was already a dead man.

After Adela had finished her lesson and Andrés his ounce of cocaine, he tried to talk his sister into returning to Seville. He was dead set on taking her away from the maniac that was tracking him. But she was determined to cash in on his promise to go for a ride in the forest.

Damn it. He was trapped.

If he hadn't hit her, she would have no power over him. But now there was nothing he could deny her.

"Are you sure you're okay?" Adela twisted in the saddle to look at him behind her.

Here was his chance. The opportunity to tell her that he had a splitting headache and that his heart was kicking past Olympic speed. But she wouldn't shut up and let him speak.

"Your eyes look like Clarissa's," she said. "Like they're made of glass."

Clarissa was the china doll he had given her for Three Kings' Day.

"Awesome," he said. "Do you think the girls will like me better now? Will they succumb to my charms? Become enchanted with my glass eyes? Will Rosa now return to me? Or maybe—"

"You're acting funny." Adela scrunched up her brow.

"Funny? Now that's funny. I never thought of myself as a funny man. Do you think Rosa finds me funny? How about our father? Do you think he sees any humor in me?" Andrés laughed, a high-pitched noise that came out sounding slightly maniacal. "He doesn't think I'm funny. No, our father doesn't think that. He thinks I'm an idiot."

"Stop it, Andrés." Adela's voice trembled as she spoke. "You're scaring me."

"Oh, I'm so sorry." His apology did not sound sincere, even to him. But then, it wasn't meant to be. He laughed again. Then he made a sharp clicking sound and Fuego accelerated into a fast-paced trot. He was feeling good.

Even though the forest spooked him today.

He looked sharply first to the right, and then to the left. Was that a man lurking in the shadows of the distant eucalyptus grove?

He squinted. But whatever he thought he had seen was gone.

An eagle cried in the distance. He jumped. Wings fluttered as a flock of African flamingos took off in flight. It was eerie. Still. The wind had picked up, stirring the leaves that protected the forest floor.

Someone was out there, waiting for him.

"It's scary today." Adela held on tighter to the pommel. "The forest is all quiet."

Andrés shifted in the saddle. She was right. It was unusually still today. And quiet.

"All the animals are sleeping," he said, swaying slightly. He was feeling hot, almost feverish. His heart pounded and his nose was killing him. He needed water. Desperately. But he had left the pouch back at the ranch.

"They can't be sleeping now," he said, far too aware of his parched throat. "The sun's out."

Intensely, he felt the sun's blistering rays on his back. Lines of sweat trickled down his temple. He swiped his face with the back of his sleeve, now craving water.

"They're taking a *siesta*," he said, forcing his voice not to crack. "Don't you usually sleep in the afternoon?"

"*Sí,*" Adela said with a tiny giggle. "Except when I'm with you."

She leaned back and he felt her body relax against him.

He, however, was more agitated than ever.

51

Diego

Pushing Lucero faster, Diego galloped through the pasture and toward the woods. The steady, insistent thud of Lucero's hooves against the sunbaked earth left billows of dust behind. The wind whipped against his face. He would outrun the pain, the anger and the resentment.

How could God be so cruel as to take from him the one thing that had kept him going over the last twelve months—the possibility of revenge? Now that he had what he had desired for so long, he could not bring himself to act on it. Either God had made him into a coward or a saint. But neither man was the one he wanted to be.

A gusty wind rippled the tall grass, which had turned yellow under the intense heat of late spring. The air was close, uncomfortably humid, and the sun beat down hard, reflecting off tiny pieces of mica that sparkled as brilliantly as cut glass.

But soon, the rains would come.

After a hard, one-hour ride, he slowed Lucero to a walk as he approached the towering eucalyptus grove at the edge of Emerald Lake. His stomach tightened and his hands stiffened on the reins. He pulled back, but Lucero moved forward, headed for the small path that would lead them down into the forest.

"No, Lucero."

He jerked back on the reins but Lucero continued forward. Diego shifted to the right and pressed his legs into Lucero's inside girth to initiate a turn. Lucero resisted.

"No! Lucero, I said *no!*" He struggled to turn the horse back but Lucero continued down the path.

Diego could do nothing to stop Lucero's forward motion. Finally, he dropped the reins, swung his legs over Lucero's back, and jumped to the ground. Lucero stopped and turned his head, nickering softly.

Panting, Diego crouched, lowering his head to his knees. He could feel the strength of his distress coming from him in waves, his chest rising and falling rapidly as he breathed.

After a few moments, his heartbeat slowed and his breathing became more even. He looked up at his horse. Lucero stood still, facing forward.

"You're going down to the lake . . . aren't you?"

Lucero whinnied, a low, sure sound.

"And there's nothing I can do to stop you."

Jaw set, Diego swung back on his horse and allowed Lucero to take him down the path leading into the hidden wooded area that had once been his sanctuary.

The lake was as spectacular as he had always remembered it. The flamingos had returned to their breeding ground. His heart lurched. It was as if they had never left.

Slowly, he dismounted, watching the birds.

There was a loud splash. One of the male birds had jumped on the back of a female. She lowered her head and spread her wings.

He turned away.

And then he broke down.

"Why did you leave me, Catalina?"

He fell to his knees.

"We had so many dreams . . . so many plans."

His heart thrashed against his chest. It was as if all the emotions he had kept locked up inside were beating at the outermost chambers of his heart, crying to be let out.

Do you know how hard it's been for me? Missing you?

His chest heaved. And then a cry of profound grief stabbed the wind as he screamed.

"Are you there, God? Can you hear me? Do you even care? Do you care that a pregnant woman died? Or that a baby did not live to know her mother? Where were you, God, when I lost my family? My sanity? My reason to live? Where are you now?"

"ANSWER ME, DAMMIT!"

A light rain began to fall and then came the tears, like a floodgate finally let open.

He fell prone onto the dry earth. And then he cried and he cried. Until he could cry no longer.

The raindrops were getting thicker, but he did not look for shelter. He heard the heavy padding of Lucero's hooves as his horse approached, and then stood beside him.

For a long time, he could not move. Then a soft blanket of warmth washed over him. It was as if all the love in the universe was concentrated only on him.

For several minutes, he remained immobile. It was as if he were coming out of a deep, much-needed sleep. He didn't want to do anything to disturb the peace.

After a while, he rose to his knees, opened his arms wide, and threw back his head. A cloud burst directly above him and the rain came down like a waterfall from the sky. The warm, heavy rain fell over him. He savored it, allowing it to seep into every pore.

And for the first time since the night Catalina died, he felt free.

52

Andrés

It was pouring now. Andrés cursed the rain. And then he laughed. He should have looked at the weather forecast before caving in to Adela. But damn if the rain wasn't exactly what he needed.

He leaned back his head and opened his mouth. Fresh water hit his throat. He gulped down as much as he could. But it wasn't enough. He opened his mouth again.

"Andrés, watch out!" Adela screamed.

A flock of egrets crashed through the trees. He had gotten off the trail and into their nest.

Grabbing Fuego's reins tighter, Andrés jerked on the bit, forcing Fuego back onto the path. The effort hurt. A muscle cramped in his arm. He stretched out his arm, but instead of easing the knot in his sore muscle, his hand went numb. The tips of his fingers tingled.

What the hell's wrong with me? His chest constricted and his heart went into overdrive.

Fuego whinnied nervously, pawing at the wet earth. She was jittery, hard to handle. Afraid. Andrés pressed Fuego into a steady trot. There was an eerie sense of urgency, of danger in the air.

He used his crop to get Fuego moving. She was skittering from right to left, no longer obeying his commands.

Adela screamed again. "Don't hurt her!"

"*No grites*, Adela." He shouted at his sister to stop her yelling. She was getting on his nerves. He whacked Fuego into a full gallop. The ride was over. They were going back to the ranch.

Fuego's gait was unsteady. She tripped over a branch, throwing Andrés to the side. He was able to maintain his balance. But then, Fuego reared up, bucked, and threw them to the ground.

A searing pain tore through his right leg, and when he tried to lift himself up, his leg buckled and he collapsed.

"Adela!" He called out to his sister, who was sobbing hysterically.

Fuego was running in frantic circles, spooked by something—or someone—in the forest.

Andrés attempted to pull himself to standing, but he had lost all energy. When he finally got to a half-kneeling position, his leg did not support his weight and he crumpled to the ground.

"Go get your horse!" A voice in the distance carried over the pounding of the rain.

Andrés looked up. The silhouette of a man on a horse was outlined against the misty blue-green backdrop of the sky.

He panicked.

"No! It can't be." Diego Vargas had finally found him.

Diego jumped off his horse and ran toward Adela.

"Don't be frightened," he said, taking her in his arms and placing her gently next to a tree, away from Fuego. "Are you all right?" He pushed back her tousled hair. "Does anything hurt?"

She lifted her arm for him to see. Blood beaded off a surface scrape along the length of her right arm.

"I know that hurts," he said, "but right now, I need you to be brave." He ripped off a piece of cloth from the bottom of his shirt and wrapped it around her arm. "Everything's going to be all right." He tied off the material. "But I need you to stay right here, okay?"

She nodded and he sprinted toward Fuego. Grabbing hold of the horse's reins, he whispered in Fuego's ear until the mare stopped her frenzied circling. And then with his back turned, he spoke to Andrés.

"Get back on your horse," he said.

"I can't." Andrés was breathing rapidly. "I hurt my leg."

Diego turned, moved toward Andrés, and went to grab Andrés's arm. But before he could take hold of it, Andrés crawled backward. His heart felt like it was about to explode from his chest.

"Get away from me." Andrés humped back, like a crab, desperate for a hole to hide in. "I didn't mean to leave your wife stranded. It was a mistake. I didn't know she was there. I'm sorry. Don't kill me. I don't want to die. Please, don't kill me."

"I'm not a murderer," Diego said.

"What are you, then?"

"A man, just trying to make it through another day."

I know exactly how that feels. Andrés coughed once, and then began to hyperventilate.

Diego watched Andrés closely. Something was wrong. Andrés had a blank stare on his face and was breathing erratically. His lips were a dark purple-blue.

"Hey, are you all right?" Diego squatted.

No response.

"Answer me."

Andrés murmured something about being sorry. His eyes rolled back. And then, he started shaking uncontrollably.

"Andrés!" Diego grabbed the man's shoulders. "What're you on?"

He'd seen this before. With Joaquín. Andrés had overdosed.

Before Andrés could answer, he fell over, his body seizing.

"What's wrong with him?" Sobbing, Adela ran to Andrés's side.

"Stay back." Diego held her off and then checked Andrés's pulse.

Andrés's heart was racing. His skin was clammy and hot. Diego put his hand over Andrés's mouth and felt for air.

A weak flow hit his hand.

"Andrés, can you hear me?" He shook the man, who was now unconscious. "Andrés, answer me."

When he received no reply, he rolled Andrés to his side. Then turned toward Adela.

"I need you to do something for me." He dug into Andrés's pocket and fished out his mobile phone. White powder dusted the cover. Cocaine. "We have to call for help." He handed her the phone. "Dial 1-1-2."

She stood frozen in front of him.

"Please," he said urgently. "Your brother needs to go to the hospital."

That snapped her out of immobility. Eyes wide, she pressed a number, which must have been on speed dial.

"No, Adela." He grabbed for the phone. "We need to call 1—"

"Papá! Papá!" She kept the phone away from him. "Andrés is sick."

Diego heard a man's voice on the other end of the line.

"Adela! *Tranquilízate.* I can't understand what you're saying."

"It's Andrés, Papá! He's all twisted up. And he's—"

"Adela, listen to me," the man said. "Is there an adult with you?"

Adela nodded. *"Sí,"* she said.

"Put him on the line."

She handed the phone to Diego.

"Your son is unconscious," Diego said. He was on autopilot now. Reacting physically, but mentally far away. This was not the way the plan was supposed to have been carried out.

"Is he breathing?" Andrés's father said.

"Faintly."

"Listen to me carefully. I'm a doctor."

Diego nodded.

"You need to increase oxygen flow to his heart. Put the phone on speaker and do exactly what I tell you."

Diego switched to speakerphone and handed the unit to Adela.

"Stand right beside me," he said, "so I can hear your father."

"If he's not already on his back, turn him over and tilt back his head to open the airway."

Diego did as he was instructed. *"Vale.* Now what?"

"Pinch his nose and blow two slow breaths into his mouth."

Diego breathed into Andrés's mouth.

"Wait for five seconds and then give one more slow breath."

Diego waited. When he breathed into Andrés again, Andrés's chest rose and fell with the breath he gave.

"Keep doing that until his breath is steady. And don't stop until he's breathing on his own." The tension in the man's voice was palpable. "His heart is in a crisis state. He'll have a stroke if you stop the rescue breathing."

Diego absorbed the doctor's tension. He was *not* the one who was going to kill this man.

He heard Dr. Aragón punch in three numbers on another phone.

"Where are you?" the doctor said.

"In the woods, behind El Rancho del Cielo."

Andrés's father repeated the location to someone on the other line, along with instructions to send an ambulance.

"I've notified Emergency Services. An ambulance will be there shortly. Is he breathing on his own yet?"

"No," Diego said. "He's still breathing through me."

There was a short pause and then, "Please, young man, please keep my son alive."

Diego could not bring himself to respond.

"Adela, can you hear me?" Dr. Aragón said.

"*Sí*, Papá."

"Help this man take care of your brother." The man's voice was urgent. "I'll meet the ambulance at the hospital."

She nodded. "I will, Papá."

Andrés's father ended the call.

A loud, choking, sputtering sound emitted from Andrés's mouth. He gasped for air, and then began to breathe on his own. For several seconds, he struggled to regulate his breathing.

"I'm thirsty," Andrés said. His voice was low and weak.

Diego went for the pouch of water he had packed in his saddle bag. When he returned, he helped Andrés to a sitting position, then handed him the water.

Andrés drank. Then rested the pouch on his knee.

"I was wrong about you." Andrés stared at the ground, his thumb moving back and forth over the leather water pouch. "I was wrong about your people." He coughed several times. And then, the hard lines in his face softened.

"Forgive me," he said, breathing steadily now.

Diego leaned back on his heels, his emotions and his energy spent. He did not respond to Andrés. He didn't need to.

Both of them had just made it through one more day.

THE END

A Note To My Readers

Dear Reader:

City of Sorrows is a story inspired by my personal beliefs and experiences. Much of the material was informed by intimate relationships with Spanish Catholics, Spanish Christian Gypsies, and Indian Hindus. Three world views are presented here, three different ways of worshiping God.

It is my personal belief that there is only one God, who has made a great diversity of people. I believe we should accept that diversity, and understand that God reaches his people in as many ways as he created them. That being said, however, not everything you have read in this book comes from a spiritual point of view. I take full responsibility for that. My characters smoke, drink, and use bad language. They look for love through sex, hurting others in the process. Why? Because God's people are flawed. We're imperfect beings. I neither mean to offend nor sensationalize, but hope to inspire compassion for people, whatever their religion, ethnicity, moral choices, or struggles may be. I invite you to leave comments, or to read about my experiences with the group of Christian Gypsies in Seville that authenticated this book by visiting my website: www.susannadathur.com.

I would also like to make a special note that while this story grew out of my beliefs and experiences, not all of the experiences are mine, nor are they representative of the Christian Gypsies I lived with in Seville. Descriptions of car-theft rings, extortion, and the darker side of Gypsy life were not witnessed by me personally, but by author Jason Webster as he related in his memoir, *Duende: A Journey in Search of Flamenco*. Jason graciously allowed me to retell some of his experiences in this book. For a good read, and detailed insight into the Gypsy flamenco world, pick up a copy of *Duende*. You will be amazed at what you will learn about Gypsies, flamenco, and the underside of life.

And just a quick note on the word "Gypsy." I struggled with the use of this word in the book, because to some members of this group, it is considered an ethnic slur. They prefer the word "Roma," "Rom," or "Romani." Others do not mind being called Gypsies. However, as the story is about Spanish Gypsies, and the direct translation from the Spanish *gitano* is Gypsy, I chose to stay with this usage throughout the book. I apologize in advance to any who may take offense at the term.

I would also like to note that much of the grief theology voiced by several characters in this book is attributed to—and used with permission by—Jerry Sittser, an astounding Christian writer and theologian. Jerry suffered the staggering loss of his wife, mother and daughter in a fatal car crash caused by a drunken driver. But as Jerry wrote in his book, *A Grace Disguised*, the experience of loss was not the defining moment of his life. It was Jerry's response to the loss that eventually defined him.

What followed was a story inspired by the beauty and the tragedy of life. The hero may be debated, but the story belongs to three very different men, from three different cultures, three different realities, who were forced to survive in one common land.

If you liked the story, I invite you to write a short review on Amazon.com and/or on Goodreads.com. You will find links to my books on these sites on my website: www.susannadathur.com

Thanks for sharing the journey with me. God bless.

Susan Nadathur

Do not oppress the foreigner, for you yourselves know how it feels to be excluded.

Exodus 23:9

Discussion Questions

1) Before reading *City of Sorrows*, what impressions came to mind when you heard the words, "Spanish Gypsies?" Have those impressions changed after reading the book?

2) *City of Sorrows* is a story of outsiders. How are the three men's stories of exclusion different? How are they the same?

3) Have you ever felt like an outsider in your society? Or, have you ever been labeled something negative because you were different from the majority of the people around you?

4) Do you believe that Andrés was justified in his fear of Diego that first night when they met on the road outside of Seville?

5) Rajiv has his challenges as a Hindu immigrant to Catholic Spain. Have you ever lived in a country where you were the religious minority? What challenges did you face?

6) In chapter eight, Rajiv is hungry and wants only to get something to eat. But, his lab mates want a drink first. Rajiv says, "What choice did he have but to follow along? It wasn't his car. It wasn't his country." Have you ever felt like Rajiv?

7) How did Catalina's death affect and change the city? Do you think people changed what they thought about the Gypsies?

8) Discuss death and loss as a theme that runs through the novel. How does each of the three main characters grow in their acceptance and understanding of loss in their lives?

9) Beyond his anger, what emotions do you think really control Andrés?

10) How are Diego and Andrés different? How are they the same? Discuss these two characters, each as both a culprit and as a victim.

11) The scent that both seduces and torments Diego in *City of Sorrows* is the orange blossom. What scents trigger strong memories for you?

12) In Chapter 33, Pablito says to his daughter, Amara, "Death ends a life. It does not end a relationship." Do you think this is true for Diego?"

13) Do you agree with Pablito that in order for Diego to heal, he had to return to the country and see what he once saw there?

14) In Chapter 34, Rajiv used Abuela's Tarot cards to help reach Diego. He says, "The death imagery sometimes serves to remind us that the more we hate something, the more we are bound to it." Do you agree with Rajiv?

15) In Chapter 36, Diego talks about different kinds of love. How is Diego's new love with Amara different from the love he had for Catalina? Do you think he will ever develop the capacity to love Amara as deeply as he once loved his wife?

16) Discuss the ways hope, redemption, and healing are manifest in this story. Explore how these experiences might affect each of the main characters lives moving into the future.

Acknowledgments

There are so many people I have to thank for helping me not only complete this book, but see me through what was a long, arduous road toward publication.

I couldn't have done it without you.

To all those friends and fellow writers who read and commented on early versions of the manuscript, Angie, John, Judy, María Luisa, Lorin, Jason, Brenda, fellow members of the Squaw Valley Community of Writers, I thank you for your time and constructive criticism.

To my dear friend, Alison, thanks for the laughter, the tears, the years we've had together. And for the numerous edits and rewrites we both laughed and struggled through.

To Pastor Piquera, thanks for opening the door to the chaotic but fascinating world of Gypsy Spain. All you knew about me when you answered my first e-mail was that we served the same God. And that was enough. I will be forever grateful for your hospitality, and for the link you made possible to another world.

To Pastor Pepe, Pura, Mara, Enemías, Antonia, Magdalena, Lolo, Juan, Samuel, Victoria, Sulamita, Pastor José, Juana, Tulia, José "El Torero," Manuela, Blanca, and all my wonderful Gypsy brothers and sisters from La Iglesia Dios Con Nosotros in Seville, thanks for opening the doors of your hearts and homes to me. I will never forget your generosity and loving spirits. Thanks for sharing your lives, your culture, your joys and your pains with me. And for giving me a home away from home. God bless. I love you from the heart.

Now in Spanish for my dear friends, who don't know English:

Al Pastor Pepe, Pura, Mara, Enemías, Antonia, Magdalena, Lolo, Juan, Samuel, Victoria, Sulamita, Pastor José, Juana, Tulia, José "el Torero," Manuela, Blanca, y todos mis hermanos queridos de La Iglesia Dios Con Nosotros en Sevilla, un millón de gracias por haber abierto las puertas de sus casas a esta humilde servidora. Nunca me olvidaré de su generosidad y bondad. Gracias por compartir sus vidas, su cultura, sus gozos y sus dolores conmigo. Y por haberme regalado un hogar, y una familia, cuando estaba lejos de la mía. Dios os bendiga mucho. Os quiero con todo el corazón.

To Heidi and Oscar, thanks for being my family away from home. Who ever thought I'd find two fellow "Boricuas" in Seville? Thanks for all the moments we shared. For the camaraderie, the exchange of cultures, and the special moments we spent together. Our trip to bring God's Word to the Gypsy families in Torreblanca will be forever etched on my memory.

To Silvia and Juan Manuel, thanks for being my "cultural consultants." Your ability to see your own culture objectively, without losing the love and passion inherent in your people, is incredibly insightful. I hope that we can work together to make our two different worlds a little better by taking the best of each and making a new and even more fantastic one.

To Jason and Jerry, thanks for allowing me to use the benefit of your experiences. I wouldn't want to have lived through what either of you did, but I appreciate the permission to use parts of your story in the pages of this book.

To my pastors, Juan and Migdalia, I owe a special thanks for your prayers, council, and patience. I'm the wandering sheep, you my faithful pastors—who search for me when I get lost, and carry me back to the fold.

To Lisa Amowitz, thanks for working with me, over many drafts, on what became a beautiful cover. Your patience and professionalism were much appreciated!

To my daughter Sita, I owe a very special thanks for all the times I ignored you when I was lost in my fictional world, for all the times I closed you out on the other side of the office door. For all the times I "became" one of my characters. Thanks for holding down the fort when I was in Spain, for taking over my chores, and for not complaining when my trip got extended. Thanks for sharing my life, and allowing me into yours. You are one of my greatest blessings.

And finally, to my husband, Govind, I owe the most profound thanks. Without you, this book would never have been written. You believed in me when nobody else even knew I loved to write. Thanks for all your sacrifices, for all the nights when there was no dinner on the table, or the house got messy. Thanks for the trips to Spain and the writers' conferences that you encouraged and sponsored. But most of all, thanks for your undying belief in me, and for the endless pep talks. I am who I am because of you. Thanks for believing in me, for loving me even when I was difficult to love, and for being with me in spirit even when I was miles away.

SUSAN NADATHUR is a widely-traveled writer, teacher, and self-proclaimed "outsider" from Connecticut who lives on-and-off in Spain with an extended family of Gypsies in Seville. A registered nurse with a master's degree in Spanish, Susan teaches language and cultural diversity workshops to childbirth and healthcare professionals, and has authored several books on Spanish language acquisition and cross-cultural communication. She lives with her husband, a philosophical scientist from India, and their multicultural daughter in Lajas, Puerto Rico. *City of Sorrows* is her debut novel. Visit the author online at **www.susannadathur.com**.

Made in the USA
Lexington, KY
12 September 2013